hail mary catch

A NOVEL

CAMELLIA BOOK THREE

MARIE VEILLON

HOMEGROWN PUBLISHING LLC

First Edition March 2025

ISBN 978-1-967217-00-7 (ebook)

ISBN 978-1-967217-01-4 (paperback)

ISBN 978-1-967217-32-8 (hardcover)

Cover design by @cindyras_draws

marievwrites.com

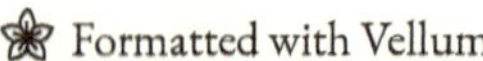 Formatted with Vellum

author's note

This novel could be categorized as a "minty rom-com" or a closed-door romance with the door cracked open. It incorporates Christian themes and specifically Catholic views on prayer, marriage and family, and chastity.

This book also includes heavy innuendo and discussions of sex, chastity, fertility awareness, and natural family planning, as well as semi-steamy scenes, implied nudity, crude humor, and mild language; however, there are no sexually explicit scenes or detailed descriptions of "spice." If it were a movie, it would probably be rated PG-13.

Additionally, please be aware of the following content and depictions, which some readers may find triggering: epilepsy and seizures; ADHD, autism, and neurodivergence; mental health, anxiety, and depression; childhood sickness and diseases; women's health, high-risk pregnancy, and premature childbirth; addiction, alcoholism, and substance abuse; and parental neglect. It is my intent to treat these topics with the sensitivity they deserve, and I promise to deliver a HEA in the end.

On a lighter note, the writing style of this book purposefully reflects grammatical and syntactical quirks more common to those who speak and think in a Cajun accent. In other words, it sounds weird on purpose.

hail mary catch

— **See also, *Hail Mary Pass*;** in football, a last resort play with an extremely low rate of success, usually called with only seconds remaining on the clock or once a team runs out of downs; when the quarterback throws the football as close to the end zone as possible, then the receivers and defenders from both teams vie for the ball; a team's last chance to score a touchdown; a play in which the quarterback is desperate enough to take a shot down the field and pray one of his teammates catches the ball and makes it into the end zone; a miracle

for Evie and Cindy R

and for everyone whose brain
works a little differently

hail mary catch

prologue

EIGHTEEN YEARS AGO

LANDRY

"It's your job as an older brother to look after your sister, Landry," my dad says sternly. "Especially now that Loren is ..."

"Thirteen?" I offer.

He grunts and nods.

I add a "Yes, sir" to make sure he doesn't think I'm telling him something he should already know.

He's right, though. As soon as our older sister, Lilley, moved away for college and left Loren with a bedroom all to herself, Lo wasted no time in plastering the walls with posters of her favorite male actors. I'm afraid my baby sister has officially become boy crazy, and I don't imagine it'll get any better after her first coed party tonight.

Although I'm only one grade ahead of Loren, I've been tasked with chaperoning her and her best friend, Tenley, and I've got my work cut out for me. Every thirteen-year-old boy at that party will be vying for Tenley's attention since she's more stacked than any of the girls at my high school, and I can totally see my sister jumping on the first wingman offer she gets. The thing is, Tenley's always had a crush on me. I mean, I'm decent-looking and pretty good at sports, and

1

having a high school football coach for a dad makes me relatively popular, even though I tend to put my foot in my mouth. But I figure this is one of those "best friend's older brother" things.

Which brings me to the next problem—I can't make a move on Tenley without upsetting Loren, since it's not like my sister has any other close friends. So, despite the fact that Tenley Robin is hot as hell and more than willing to get with me, I've been acting like I haven't noticed the way she follows me around like a lost puppy, mostly because I can't risk distracting Tenley from her job of keeping Loren occupied.

"She's young and gullible. But her reputation is as much your responsibility as anyone else's," my father continues after a while. It's probably one of the longest non-football related conversations we've ever had, so I know he's serious. And I need to take advantage of every opportunity I get to show my dad he can depend on me. He's not easy to impress.

My mom, however, thinks I walk on water. Now that my dad's named me the starting quarterback, at least for practices, she's become my biggest fan. I've also inherited Lilley's job of taking care of her when she's had too much to drink after she brags about me to every person she crosses in town.

Which reminds me—I'll have to get home at a decent time tonight, or else Mom will be trashed when I return, and it'll be harder to drag her to bed. At least she can stumble there with my help when she hasn't completely passed out.

"Yeah, I'll make sure she's good, Dad," I say after a while.

My dad furrows his brow. "Yeah?"

"Oh, sorry. Yes, *sir*."

He nods once before he gestures to the door, signaling for me to get out of his truck.

"Thanks for the ride," I add quietly, but he only glares impatiently, waiting for me to shut the passenger door behind me.

I search the host's backyard as I walk into the party, scanning the crowd for Loren. She's supposed to have gotten a lift from Tenley's older sister, which is concerning in and of itself. I spot her and Tenley beside the pool, a small crowd of eighth-grade boys surrounding them. I roll my eyes when I see the way Loren's eating up the attention, even though it's not directed at her.

"Hey, Lo-Lo," I call out loudly as I approach, causing most of the guys to scatter.

Loren frowns and crosses her arms when I make my way over. "Seriously? Did you have to do that?"

"Uh, yeah, actually, I did. Those kids are all creeps, and I'd have to beat the crap out of any of them if they so much as tried to lay a hand on you." I glance at Tenley, who's already giving me *the look*, and I shoot her a flirty smirk.

Loren lets out an exasperated groan. "Gah, Landry. No one's even asked me to dance yet," she protests. "And now they never will."

"Then I guess I'm doing my job," I retort, pursing my lips and shrugging. My eyes dart to Tenley again, measuring her reaction. She's still staring hopefully. "How about you, Ten?"

She bites her lip and shakes her head.

"She's lying," Loren says dryly. "She's just been waiting for you to ask." Tenley's eyes widen in embarrassment as she elbows Loren in the arm. Loren yelps, and I can't help but laugh.

Tenley *is* pretty cute ... and she's definitely into me.

She licks her lips this time and looks down shyly, making her eyelashes flutter. And for a second, my stomach mimics the action.

I allow my gaze to travel over her. I'd be lying if I said I wasn't interested in being the first guy to claim that territory. Not to mention, the idea of someone actually liking me for *me* and not just because I'm Coach Reed's son feels nice.

But what if Tenley's been using Loren to get to me? Or she's only showing an interest because she thinks it'll make her more popular?

I furrow my brow as I regard her again, and her eyes finally meet mine. I think back to our interactions over the past few years, the way she's always seemed flattered by my attention but disliked the recognition from the others. Tenley's too innocent to use me for that, and she's been Loren's friend for too long to risk hurting her now.

I turn back to my sister. "Think you can stay out of trouble for five minutes?"

"What do you mean?" Loren asks.

"Your friend needs rescuing," I say, offering a hand to Tenley.

Her shoulders rise, and her eyes flutter again, but she immediately turns to survey Loren's reaction. "Oh, thanks, but I'm fine—"

Loren groans in disgust again, reaching out to shove Tenley forward. "Good *grief*, Ten. Please, dance with my idiotic brother. Just try not to get too gross."

I glare at her as Tenley takes my hand, but Loren just smirks and crosses her arms as if she's satisfied with her work as a matchmaker. Then I pull Tenley onto the makeshift dance floor just as another slow song begins.

"So, how many guys have you actually turned down so far tonight?" I ask, tentatively slipping my hands around Tenley's waist while she carefully places hers on my shoulders. It's not that I'm nervous, since I've dated a couple of girls by now, but I'm suddenly aware of all the ways I could screw this up.

"A few," Tenley replies coyly, inching closer. "But I'm only interested in one guy."

I raise my brow, her forwardness catching me off guard for a second. "And who might that be?" I ask, lowering my hand.

A smile creeps across her face before she answers, "I think you know."

I feel the corners of my mouth curling up to match hers, and I almost blurt out some cocky offer to take her out back to the pool house. Instead, I remind myself that, despite the way she's totally coming on to me and the fact that I am totally into it, I need Tenley to be Loren's friend more than I need her to be my girlfriend.

But it's hard to keep those thoughts in the forefront of my mind while Tenley's biting her lip and staring at me longingly like this, like she wants me to kiss her. And all it takes is for her to press her ample chest to mine and fist the back of my shirt in her right hand for me to lose the ability to think at all and begin running purely on instinct.

I'm not the kind of guy who would pressure a girl into something she wasn't ready for. But I've unfortunately never been very good at that impulse-control thing, as my school counselor and my doctor consistently remind me. And since the effects of my ADHD medication have worn off by now, my mind goes straight to *I need to know what that feels like.*

I lean down to press my lips to hers, immediately urging her mouth open and pushing my tongue inside. She seems a little more hesitant to reciprocate the kiss than I expected after all that flirting, but I'm too far gone to pull back now.

Consequences? What consequences?

She loosens up after a minute, stepping forward and allowing her body to melt into mine, and I figure she was just feeling awkward or nervous before. After all, this is probably her first kiss. But when she sighs and tilts her head to the side as she drags her hands over my shoulders to my chest, I forget she's supposed to be the inexperienced one. Her fingertips dig in gently, and I wonder if she's not hinting around about what move she wants me to make next.

Aaand, there's that irrepressible urge again.

It's not like I'm *that* hard up to cop a feel in the middle of this party. Seriously, I've gotten to second base before, and it's great and all, but that's not even what this is about anymore.

The idea has been planted in my brain, and I have no choice but to follow through this time.

Must. Touch. Boob.

It's like a compulsive need now. And there I go, just as the song ends, sliding my palm up her side and cupping it around her chest. I get a full second of satisfaction before Tenley pushes away from me roughly.

"Seriously, dude? What the hell is wrong with you?" she cries out incredulously.

My heart begins racing, and I feel my face heat up in embarrassment. Because she's right—there is something very, *very* wrong with me.

I should apologize.

But when I open my mouth, an overly defensive "Gah, Tenley, I thought it's what you wanted" tumbles out instead.

"Well, it wasn't," she continues, glaring at me with disgust before she turns and locks eyes with one of the other kids observing our interaction. Her expression softens as they continue staring at one another, and I scoff aloud, but it doesn't seem to faze either of them.

And now I'm even more confused, because I thought I was the jerk in this scenario. But Tenley's already making eyes at another guy —JD Bourgeois, the younger brother of her and Loren's classmate, Blake. I know the kid plays up in sports because he's huge for his age, but come on.

"Look, I need to go and check on my sister," I blurt out, hoping to break the spell between them, but the girl JD was dancing with before has already pulled him away.

"Yeah, same," Tenley says, cringing and wiping her mouth with the back of her hand. Apparently, I really *am* that disgusting. I can feel the self-pity coursing through me as I turn and scan the crowd for Loren's tiny form.

I'm still calling out for her a few minutes later when we run into JD again, who's also hunting for his brother. Before I can question him, though, Loren and the other Bourgeois emerge from the pool house together. Her face is unmistakably flustered, and she presses her lips together guiltily when she sees me. Meanwhile, Blake looks entirely too smug for my liking.

"Oh great, *you* found her ..." I mutter under my breath, and Tenley glares at me again. "Lo, I've been looking for you everywhere," I add in a softer tone.

"You have?" Loren asks innocently.

I clear my throat. "Yeah, I hadn't noticed you disappeared at first."

Tenley snorts and rolls her eyes, and Loren mumbles something about being invisible. It makes my chest ache to hear the way I've made Loren feel so insignificant, especially since I know the feeling all too well. I open my mouth to say more, but I'm interrupted.

"I noticed her," Blake declares, his chin lifted in a dare. "In fact, she's been here with me the whole time."

Oh ... oh no.

One job. I had *one*. Freaking. Job.

Protect my baby sister and her reputation—that was my mission. But I let her out of my sight for ten, fifteen minutes, tops, and the first thing she did was make a hot dash for the pool house with the preppiest guy in her class—the kid who also happens to be gunning for my QB1 position, and he's not even technically in high school yet.

I don't know if I'm angrier with Blake, Loren, or myself at this point. And most of what I'm saying out loud isn't even registering with me, because all I can think about is the way I've failed my father. I can only imagine the look on his face when he hears about this.

"Landry, don't. Nothing happened, all right?" Loren pleads, bringing me back for a second, but it's too late. I've already let myself get swallowed up by my anger, and before I know it, I'm standing face to face with Blake, daring him to admit that he's been defiling my sister in front of a crowd.

I'm not sure what I'll accomplish with this tactic, since I'm certainly not saving her reputation—unless he were to confess that he forced himself on her, which obviously isn't the case. I can see the way his eyes keep darting to Loren, which I think means he must really care. But I'm also famous for misreading people and situations, as evidenced by my epic failure with Tenley earlier, so maybe he's just really guilty.

"I would never ..." Blake begins, cringing as soon as he says it.

"Right, because who would?" Loren fires back before she begins crying, then Tenley pulls her away as Blake stutters and struggles to save face. Meanwhile, his punk-ass little brother rejoins us, bumping my shoulder as he walks by and making me see red.

"Come on, Tessa's on her way," Tenley tells Loren. She shoots one last disdainful look my way and ushers my sister into the front yard, and Blake has the balls to move as if he's going after them. I plant myself in front of him, daring him to take another step, but JD shoves me out of the way.

I barely get the chance to recover before a hard right hook slams into my jaw, courtesy of Blake, and I stumble backward in shock. I can't believe the kid actually hit me.

Maybe he does care about Loren ... or maybe he's jealous and trying to make me look bad while he swoops in to steal my starting quarterback spot. Either way, I'm still rubbing my jaw and wondering exactly how this all went wrong as I watch the Bourgeois brothers saunter away.

daisy

Plop.

The pat of butter I didn't have time to spread slides over the edge of my toast and down the front of my lavender linen dress, leaving a greasy streak down the bodice.

"*Mais la*," I groan and shove down the last couple bites before I attempt to peel my dress up and over my head. I've almost gotten it off safely when one of the tiny buttons I love so much snags in my hair. I yank harder and yelp as soon as I realize that tactic's not going to work if I want to keep my long locks intact.

I barely hear the doorknob jiggling before the front door flies open to reveal a ruggedly handsome man carrying a stack of plastic totes. He freezes in place as soon as he crosses the threshold. A jolt of panic induces me to reach for the nearest weapon, which happens to be the cast iron skillet sitting on the stove, but my arms are still tangled up in my dress. Luckily, I recognize the intruder's dark hair and lovely cheekbones, and I sigh with relief.

And then I'm back to despairing as soon as I remember that my dress is currently hovering above my head. My visitor's brow shoots up as his eyes skirt over my body, and I can already feel the blush creeping up my neck.

I hunch over and attempt to cover my bits with my elbows. "Um, hi?"

My older brother's best friend blinks a few times, his chin resting atop the boxes he's carrying. "Daisy?" he asks incredulously.

"Who else did you expect to find when you barged into my house without knocking?"

He clears his throat and finally turns his gaze away. "Last I checked, this is my sister's house. What are *you* doing here?"

"I just told you. I live here."

"But ..." He sets the totes on the ground and holds up one hand, making the light glint off a metallic surface. "Blake said I could move in. And I already have a key."

"A key doesn't give you the right to impose on paying tenants, Landry Reed, especially when you walk in unannounced," I retort. "Neither does being my landlord's brother."

"No one told me you were staying here. And I've already made a deal with Blake," he repeats, his eyes moving up to my face again.

I sigh. "Yeah. I heard you the first time. But it doesn't change the fact that I already moved in. Also, do you mind looking anywhere else but at me for now?"

"Sorry," he says, ducking his head. "When did this happen?"

"About a week ago." I grunt as I struggle to untangle the stubborn strand of hair twisted around that button again.

"*How* did this happen?"

"Loren mentioned to Rowan that she still needed someone to take her place while she was on maternity leave, and he recommended me. Then she helped me get set up at Camellia High."

"Yeah, I'd heard about that part from your brother, too. I meant how did you end up living *here*."

"She offered to rent her house out to me since she's apparently going to be staying with Blake for the indefinite future," I explain. But I still can't untangle my hair. "Fudge sticks up a fudge tree!" I growl, and Landry snorts.

"What kind of curse is that?"

"The LaFleur kind," I grumble before letting out a defeated sigh.

"I think you should be used to them by now. I hate to ask, but since you're here, think you could help me out?"

He swallows hard, his eyes still locked on his feet. "With what?"

"I spilled on my dress, and when I went to take it off to clean it, the buttons got caught in my hair. Then your surprise intrusion caused me to panic and make things worse, I'm afraid."

He coughs uncomfortably. "I can't help you without looking at you."

"Well, you've already witnessed me in all my glory." I glance down at my bra and panties. Thankfully, they're decent looking, even if they don't match. "And you're a doctor. I'm sure you've seen plenty of humans in their underwear before today."

"It's not quite the same, since the majority of my patients wear diapers or Bluey undies, but I can be a mature adult, despite what Rowan might say about me," he replies with a smirk before his head pops up. He casually strides through the small living area to meet me in the kitchen. "Besides, I'm pretty sure I've seen most of the LaFleurs in their drawers at some point," he adds with a light laugh. "You guys might be modest, but you aren't exactly shy."

I frown as he comes to stand in front of me. "I'd like to think I've been keeping myself fully clothed in front of visitors since the age of twelve or thirteen."

"Were you even that old when I first started coming around the homestead?" he asks, slipping his large hands into the fabric and digging around.

"Mm-hmm," I say quietly. Then I hook my pinky around his finger and guide him to the hair-covered button, and his brow furrows as he tries unsuccessfully to free it. He growls in frustration, his eyes never venturing away from my face. And it's not that I'd believe Dr. Landry Reed might ever be interested in me, but I can't help but feel a little disappointed when he doesn't even bother to check me out. I may not be unusually curvy, but I am a mostly naked, fully grown woman standing right in front of him, after all, and Landry's certainly a red-blooded male. There's no questioning his masculinity, not with that sharply chiseled and five-o'clock-shadow-covered jawline hovering mere inches away from me.

I sigh, then I force myself to hold my breath once I accidentally catch a whiff of him. He's wearing a dark green button down and slacks in addition to that delicious cologne, and his thick, black hair falls into his face as he works. I lower my eyes after a while, trying not to seem so obvious in my ogling of him.

I don't get out much, okay?

"I, um, I'm sorry about the house thing. If I'd have known you were planning to move in, I wouldn't have taken Loren up on the offer," I say softly. I also have a habit of filling awkward silences with awkward words.

He shrugs again, but he still looks angry. "I guess it's not your fault. I should have known better than to trust Blake. And Loren should have said something, especially when I mentioned I was moving in this morning. In fact, she was so quick to get off the phone with me earlier that she didn't even listen to my advice about not having a big baby shower in the first place. She just cut me off and told me—" He stops abruptly and shakes his head. "Never mind."

I bite my lip at the way his face falls. "I'm sure she's just tense with everything on her plate right now," I offer quietly. But he doesn't take it as a consolation, if his broody expression is any indication.

After a while, he removes his hands and takes a step back. "I'm sorry, but I don't think I can get it without ruining either the dress or your hair."

I stick out my bottom lip in a pout. "That grease stain has probably set by now, anyway."

He nods and reaches in, this time grasping the bodice of the dress in both hands and yanking roughly. I flinch when I hear the delicate linen ripping as the dress splits into two, but my arms are finally free. He continues tearing until only a small square of material hangs from my hair. Then he places the remnants on the counter before he averts his eyes again.

"Thanks," I tell him, his manly scent still hanging in the air between us.

"No worries. Sorry again about barging in. I've never been good at sensing when I'm not wanted," he returns sarcastically.

I cringe. "So, where are you going to stay?"

"I'll crash at my dad's for now, I guess. Until I find something else or he gets sick of me, whichever comes first."

"Oh, okay. Um, would you like some toast before you go? Coffee?"

He clears his throat and looks up at the ceiling. "I'm good. Don't you need to get dressed?"

"Well, yes, but I was trying to be polite. The least I could do is offer you some breakfast since I'm sort of the reason you're homeless now."

His head barely moves in a nod, and his eyes run over me one more time before he turns around to face the front door. "Daisy, don't take this the wrong way, but, uh ... could you please put some clothes on?"

"Yeah, of course, be right back," I chirp as a satisfied smile creeps across my face. Maybe my bare body *did* manage to bother him, after all.

I practically skip into my room where I pick out another dress of a similar style, this time in mint green. Then I remember I still have a small scrap of the old dress stuck to my head, but it only takes a second in front of the mirror to successfully free my hair. I pull on my clothes, run my fingers through my wavy, blonde locks, and dart back into the kitchen, hoping Landry's still there.

"Thanks again for your help," I venture, pleased to find him in the same place I left him. "Oh, you can turn around now."

He obliges and rotates to face me. "Hey, can I ask you something?"

I shrug as a few flutters overtake my stomach. *Gah-lee*, he's attractive. I guess I've always thought Landry was good looking, but I'm having a hard time not letting my imagination run away from me right now, especially when he's posing open-ended questions and stepping in so close to me ...

"Have you always had that freckle on your neck?" He reaches out to touch my left shoulder.

I hold my breath again as I tilt my head to the side so he can inspect it. "I have a lot of freckles," I manage to squeak out.

"I'm talking about this one here. Has it changed lately? You know, shape, color, size?"

I swallow hard when he leans in. Somehow this feels more intimate than before when I was literally standing in my underwear. "Not that I've noticed."

"Hmm," he hums thoughtfully, and I try to hide the way it makes me shiver. "Keep an eye on it, would you? I'm not sure I like the look of it."

"Yes, doctor. Anything else?"

He rolls his eyes as he backs away. Then he crosses his arms and adopts a more serious expression again. "How have you been doing? You know ..."

I cringe and look away, the mood changing in an instant. "I'm fine."

"Day-*sie*," he drags my name out, disappointment in his tone. "When was your last seizure?"

I heave out a heavy sigh. "Last Thursday."

"What?" he nearly yells. "Does your family know?"

"I'm fine," I repeat, holding my hands out to placate him. "Really. It was a very minor episode. And no, they don't know, but it's going to stay that way."

He shakes his head. "You shouldn't be driving."

"I know I shouldn't. But it's not like I can call an Uber in Camellia, and I can't keep bothering Blake every time I need to leave the house, especially when Loren's not really supposed to be driving either," I mumble, crossing my arms to mirror Landry. "I'm sure I'll find someone at school to carpool with eventually. Blake's brother is our assistant principal, so I was thinking of asking him for a ride in the mornings."

He straightens up. "You're going to get a lift from JD Bourgeois? Every morning?" I smile and nod, but he clenches his jaw.

"He's very nice, and everyone seems to love him. Besides, all he ever talks about is his wife and their kids. I think he's more than trustworthy."

"Come on, I'll drive you to the baby shower," Landry says through his teeth.

"You don't have to do that," I reply, blinking awkwardly. "It's not that far. And I feel great today."

"Let's not take chances when we don't have to, *hmm*?" His expression softens as he lowers his chin and peers down at me like an adult reprimanding a child, making my stomach turn in a less pleasant way than before. But I'd rather get scolded than pitied, and I know Landry just well enough to understand that he's not going to budge. More importantly, I'm officially under his care now, which also means I'm at his mercy if I want him to keep my secret from my parents and my brother.

And I can't let any of them find out that my anti-seizure meds have been slacking off or they'll force me to move back home. This is my one chance to prove that I can take care of myself, epilepsy be damned.

I'd been feeling better for the past year and had finally convinced my mom that I should get my own place when Rowan found out about this opportunity from Loren. Ironically, Landry's sister ended up becoming one of my brother's high-risk pregnancy patients shortly after Landry had tried setting the two of them up. Obviously, they were better off as friends.

And I like Loren. She and her boyfriend, Blake, have been helping me get settled, despite her being on bed rest. They even invited me over for dinner a few days ago, along with Blake's brother and his family. It's too bad I don't remember most of that evening, though, since I woke up on my couch later that night without a clue as to how I made it there. And I didn't say anything because my family would be all over me if they so much as suspect I'm having seizures again.

I know it's because they love me. They just don't realize that they're slowly suffocating me by not letting me live my own life. But I'm twenty-five-years old. It's past time I learned how to live alone. So

I've been really careful with my daily habits since then, staying hydrated and resting, taking my medicine on time, and eliminating processed sugar and junk food, all in the hope that my body will better regulate itself under the ideal conditions. It's a lot of work, but I'm willing to do anything to prove to my family—and to myself— that I can be self-sufficient.

Landry's still right, though. I shouldn't be driving and putting the rest of the residents of Camellia at risk. And as determined as I am to do this without relying on anyone's help, I'm also mature enough to recognize when it's time to prioritize my health and safety over my pride. I sigh again, dropping my arms in defeat.

"Okay, thanks," I tell Landry. "Just let me grab my shoes." He nods and moves to pick up the totes he set down earlier, but I stop him when a silly idea crosses my mind. "Why don't you leave those for now? You can always get your things later after you bring me home from the baby shower. That way it won't melt in the heat."

"Yeah," he agrees thoughtfully. "I forgot my Jeep's packed down, so I guess I'd have to unload some stuff to make room for you, anyway."

I nod cheerfully. "Let me help you with that. It may not look like it, but I'm stronger than you think."

He smirks when I flex my arms for him. "Nice try, but I can carry my own baggage."

"And I'm not riding with you unless you accept my help too," I say matter-of-factly while I slip on a pair of sandals.

He sighs and turns to the door, but I follow him. "It's going to be too heavy for you, Daisy."

"You're just saying that because you'd rather stay mad about this house stuff than let me do something nice for you."

He stops abruptly. "That's not what I'm doing."

"Then hand me a box. And don't forget to thank me."

He glares at me before shaking his head and walking to the car. "Suit yourself."

I trail at his heels until he dives into the front seat, then he stares me down as he loops a strap around my neck and drops a duffle bag into my waiting arms.

"Oof," I accidentally grunt when the bag's weight knocks me off my center of gravity, and I sway forward until Landry snorts and moves to support my arms. "You could have given me one of the lighter boxes or something," I mumble.

His lips twitch as he bites back a smile. "And deny you the pleasure of proving me wrong? I would never." I feel myself grinning back at him as he slowly lowers his hands, allowing me to adjust to the bag's weight this time. "Oh, and thank you, Daisy," he adds, just before he lets go completely.

I whimper quietly as I turn and stagger toward the house, and he snickers to himself when he passes me up carrying another stack of totes. By the time I make it up the front porch steps, he's already back and pulling the strap up over my head.

"Ouch," I whisper when my hair gets tangled, and he cringes but doesn't let go of the bag. He lifts it as though it doesn't weigh a thing and turns to bring it inside without another word. I follow him into the house to grab my baby shower gifts, and he waits for me at the door.

"You're welcome, Landry," I tell him as I pass, making him smile again.

landry

I UNSUCCESSFULLY ATTEMPT to keep my face emotionless as I watch my sister's boyfriend wrap his arm around her and pull her in to pose at his side for a group picture. Loren and her best friend giggle when they bump baby bellies. But all I'm thinking is that it was supposed to be me up there beside Tenley Robin, smiling and patting Loren's stomach.

Okay, not like *that*. Despite what everyone might think about me, I *am* above lusting after another man's wife, even a woman as impressive as Tenley. The fact that she and the Golden Boy seem nauseatingly blissful together actually knocks her down a few pegs in my book, anyway.

I should have been the twins' godfather, though. I'd never want anything to happen to Loren and Blake. (Well, at least not to Loren.) But if the girls ever need a wise and responsible backup caregiver, I'm obviously the best man for the job. Instead, I'm stuck playing third string to the freaking Bourgeois brothers *again*.

I grind my teeth and continue watching JD as he pulls Loren in for a hug and stoops to squish his cheek against her belly, making her laugh again. I suppose he's just as much her babies' uncle as I am, but I'm sure I'm more capable. And since he's apparently been busy with coaching, managing a high school, and making his own brood of kids, he's already got his hands full.

Besides, it's bad enough that I'm being forced to stand by and support my sister's decision to reproduce with freaking *Blake the Snake*. It wouldn't have cost Loren anything to let me have this, especially since I'm already moving here to help them.

"Landry? Are you all right?" I hear Daisy whispering beside me, and it takes me a second to realize she's questioning my resting grump face.

"Yeah," I say, clearing my throat. "I'm just worried. She's been spending too much time on her feet. Rowan said she shouldn't be standing for long with her placenta previa, and Blake isn't taking care of her the way he should."

She huffs out a laugh. "Oh, Blake's been very diligent about making her rest, stubborn as she is. I'm sure he just wants her to have this time to socialize after she's been stuck in bed for the past few weeks."

I frown when Blake brings a chair over and coaxes Loren into sitting. My sister never told me she was craving company. I'd have been happy to visit her if she had. And I'm not sure I like the way Daisy's trying to offer me all this reassurance, as if she knows my own family better than I do. I'm falling further down the list by the minute around here.

"Don't worry, I'm sure they'll have more. You'll probably get to be the *Parrain* next time, right?" she leans in and says softly enough that only I can hear her, and I realize I've reached a whole new low.

"You don't know a thing about me or my family," I retort angrily.

Her face falls, and she looks hurt for a second. I groan inwardly, because now I'll have to fix it. I can't just be this much of a dick to my best friend's younger sister, especially someone as sweet and innocent as Daisy LaFleur.

My buddy Rowan and the rest of his huge family are all enigmas. Their parents were trad-Catholic hippies before it was cool, with their small-scale country farm and homeschooled breed of intelligent and attractive yet abnormally good-natured kids. But whatever the

LaFleur offspring lack in social awareness, they make up for with their refreshingly wholesome dispositions. They're all talented, too, all nine of them managing to master some musical instrument, sport, or medical specialty, and most of them are also married to someone exceptional. It's equally as difficult to hate them as it is not to hate them because they're all just so damned ... *nice.*

And although she's probably the bubbliest of the bunch, Daisy is also the least accomplished, to the best of my knowledge. I imagine it's only because of her health issues, though. She's also the baby of the family, which means her parents and older siblings have always fawned over her. In fact, their coddling and sheltering of Daisy is the only legitimate fault I've found in their family dynamic since my first trip out to the LaFleur homestead during my sophomore year of college.

I doubt she's ever been fussed at or denied anything in life, so I seriously doubt Daisy's prepared to handle a real conversation with a grump like me. In that same line, there's also an unspoken obligation for me to take care of her on Rowan's behalf.

"I'm sorry," I mumble after a while. "It's not your fault my sister got knocked up by the one guy I despise most and chose his equally annoying brother to be her kids' godfather over me." I don't mean to divulge that much, but I've never had much of a filter.

Apparently my oversharing makes for a more sincere apology, though, because Daisy nods and gives me a sad smile. "Okay, but *despise* is a pretty strong word. They're both genuinely nice guys, and Blake can't be all that bad if he makes your sister so happy, can he?"

I snort. "You only think that because your parents sheltered you from men like Blake, but you'd feel differently if you knew about his exploits at LSU. And I know for a fact that he earned every bit of his reputation. My nieces can't possibly be the only kids he's ever fathered."

"And you're guilty of spreading gossip—none of which I believe for a second. Blake is a good man, and he's going to be a great dad. Just look at the way he adores her," Daisy argues, gesturing toward them. I glance over to find Blake staring reverently at Loren while she opens a gift. "How could you hate him when he loves your sister so well?"

"I don't *hate* him," I mutter after a while. "But I can't help wondering when the other shoe will drop, because it will. It always does. And it's my job to be there for my sister when things don't work out."

"What a terrible thing to say!" She swats at me with the back of her hand, surprising me. "How can you be so cynical?"

"I'm a Reed, not a LaFleur. My parents didn't crap rainbows and butterflies when I was a kid. They were too busy drinking and resenting one another to teach their kids anything besides preparing to be let down." I don't mean to say it aloud, but it's another of those blurted-out harsh truths that I can never seem to keep inside my head.

"You're obviously wrong," she continues, nodding in the direction of my older sister and her happy, little family behind us. "This sounds more like a *Landry* problem than a *Reed* problem."

And I'm starting to regret being nice to her.

"Yeah, well. You're on my shit list, too, you know," I grumble.

"You have the worst language," she whispers harshly and backhands my chest again.

I roll my eyes. "Fine. You're on my *Bougie-bro* list."

"What have I ever—oh, right, the house." She cringes and shoots me an apologetic smile. "To be fair, neither Loren nor I knew you were planning to stay there when she offered it to me."

"Yet another example of why I can't trust my brother-in-law-to-be," I say under my breath.

I was furious when I arrived in Camellia this morning with all of my things packed in the back of my Jeep, only to discover that my sister was renting out her house to someone else, even though Blake had already promised it to me a couple of months ago. Loren had moved in with Blake after she'd started experiencing complications with her pregnancy, and he was hoping to keep her there. So he and I worked out a deal in which he was supposed to convince her to rent her place to me in exchange for my blessing and support when he eventually proposes. But even if I were willing to remind that snake of a lawyer about the bargain he apparently never intended to keep, I can't imagine Loren wouldn't feel obliged to Daisy, and Blake will undoubtedly side with Loren.

It's not like I'd let them put Daisy out just to prove a point, anyway. Despite what everyone seems to think, I'm capable of being flexible—I just need a moment to adjust to the idea of not getting my way before I bend. Had I not been so stunned by walking in to find my college roommate's baby sister standing in her underwear this morning, I probably wouldn't have been so civil to her. But once I'd gotten over the shock of seeing Daisy half-naked and all grown up, I reminded myself that Rowan would want me to look after her just as I expected him to care for Loren. It's not exactly the same, since I'd technically tried to set the two of them up before, and Daisy's practically still a kid.

Regardless, I'm not thrilled about the prospect of sleeping in my childhood bedroom and playing second fiddle to the Bourgeois brothers all over again while Daisy has my sister's cozy little house all to herself, even though she probably shouldn't be living alone in the first place.

"Do you think it'll be hard for you to find another place to rent?" Daisy asks, reading my mind.

"Probably. The rental market in Camellia seems pretty scarce, and it's not like we have apartment complexes around here. I'll just have to take what I can get, though. I want to be close enough to help Lo after the twins are born, and I'm sure I'll wear out my welcome with my dad before long."

"Oh, well, I really am sorry, then."

I sigh, feeling guilty again. "Don't worry about it. I'll figure something out."

"Well, what if you ... I mean, we could always ..." she starts and stops, then squares her shoulders before she goes on. "There *is* a second bedroom. It's tiny, only big enough for a twin-sized bed, and we'd have to share a bathroom, but ..."

I lift my brow. "Are you making me a pity offer?" I ask incredulously. "Daisy, I'm a thirty-three-year-old man. I can't be your room—"

"I mean, most of your stuff is already in the house, right?

"Daisy—"

"It would actually be kind of perfect," she continues, ignoring my protests. "You need a place to crash, and I need a built-in designated driver and a standby shower-spider catcher. You wouldn't even have to pay rent. I can cover it myself."

"Daisy," I begin, more sternly this time. "It's not about that. I can afford the rent. But we can't live together. It would be totally inappropriate."

"Says who?" she replies, lifting her chin haughtily. "You lived with Rowan for years, so I already know you're not a murderer or a rapist or even a creep. You're a gentleman ... with a few jerk-like tendencies."

I can't help it when one side of my mouth turns up. "Did you just call me a jerk? What happened to *cynic*?"

"I said you had jerkish *tendencies*. And your pessimistic take on love is exactly why you'd make the perfect roommate, since there won't be any danger of something improper happening between us."

My smile widens. "You do realize adults can still do 'improper things' if they aren't in love or married, right? In fact, that's actually what makes them improper, at least by your family's standards."

Her eyelashes flutter, and she crosses her arms as she blushes adorably. "I take that last part back. Maybe you are a jerk."

"Told you so," I say, still grinning at her. "Wanna rescind that offer yet?"

Her chin rises again, and she glares at me. "I think I'll be fine. After all, we've already proven you're not attracted to me."

"What?" I ask abruptly. When was that test? And how did I manage to pass it?

"You seemed relatively unbothered when you walked in on me in my underwear earlier," she explains, shrugging. "Especially for someone who seems so easily bothered. I assume you'd have tried to take advantage of the situation or at least attempted to get a better look if you were interested in what you saw."

Wait, she only sounds so defensive right now because I teased her about being naive, right? And not because I managed to ignore the impulse to check her out this morning? Now I'm the one blinking away my confusion and embarrassment.

"Sure," I affirm, somewhat awkwardly. Thankfully, she rolls right into her next point.

"And this way you'd be able to keep an eye on me on my brother's behalf and convince my family that I'm doing well on my own." Her smile grows wider again as she dangles the bait in front of me, knowing I won't be able to refuse her now. "Pleeeease?"

"Okay, fine," I groan, and she lets out a tiny squeal. "But this isn't going to go the way you think it is, the two of us having slumber parties every night and becoming best friends. I really *am* an asshole. Are you sure you can handle that?"

"I can handle more than you think," she fires back. "And we'll see about the slumber parties. I bet I'll have you braiding hair and painting toenails in no time."

I growl, secretly biting back another smile. "You might change your tune once you have to interact with me before my morning coffee. If you think I'm moody now ..."

"I'll make your morning coffee, Landry." Then she stares me down with a smug look on her face. "In fact, I'll make it so good I'll turn you into a morning person, just you wait."

I swallow hard, surprised by the ungentlemanly ideas that materialize as soon as she issues her challenge. Now, *that's* something I'll have to get a handle on, though it shouldn't be difficult. I'm not the kind of guy who objectifies women, even if I don't want anything more than occasional physical companionship from them. More importantly, Rowan is like family, which makes Daisy as good as a little sister to me. I could never think of her in *that way*.

Although she's certainly developed the body of an adult woman if what I saw this morning was any indication.

Not that I was *really* looking.

CHAPTER 3

landry

"WE'LL NEED some house rules if we're going to make this work," I tell Daisy once I clear my head again. "Like being fully clothed at all times."

She's still glaring at me, though I see her lips twitch this time. "Fine. I'll try not to get my dress stuck in my hair again, as long as you learn to knock before you enter a room."

I chuckle under my breath. She's definitely feistier than I remember. "Let me guess, rule number three has to do with leaving the toilet seat down?"

"That's rule number four. Three is 'What happens in Camellia stays in Camellia.'"

There she goes again.

"You can't say anything to my family about the seizures I've been having, no matter how worried you get. It's my secret to tell," she continues.

I furrow my brow. "I don't like that rule."

"Then think about it as doctor-patient confidentiality. You wouldn't violate my rights if I were one of your patients, would you?"

"I guess not." I sigh, although thinking about her as a patient isn't a bad idea.

"Dr. Reed." We're interrupted by Dr. Broussard, one of the partners in the pediatrics clinic. He comes over to greet me with a smile and offers his hand. I shake it and nod politely before he introduces his wife.

"And this must be your ..." he trails off as they all stare at me, waiting for me to speak. I open my mouth, but I freeze, unsure of how to introduce my unofficial new roommate.

"I'm Daisy," she answers for me without missing a beat. I shoot her a look as she sidles up to me and ducks under my arm. "You must be one of the amazing pediatricians Landry's hoping to work with?"

"Guilty as charged," Dr. Broussard replies, already charmed by her. Meanwhile, I'm still squinting and trying to figure out what in the hell is going on.

"Camellia has the best doctors and nurses around. You're all so nice. And I would know, since I've got a few of them in my family," she rambles, scrunching up her nose and adding an appealing laugh.

"Well, you know, some of us doctors can be a bit quirky," Dr. Broussard replies, and they all chuckle together. I stand there quietly, unsure whether it's a dig at me or not.

"How did you get invited to this, anyway?" I blurt out, proving his point. Daisy nudges me in the side, and I clear my throat. "I mean, I didn't know you were acquainted with my sister and her boyfriend."

"We're here for Nurse Tenley," he says with a knowing smirk. "But Drake and Monica Bourgeois were good friends of ours, so we've known Blake and JD since they were ... well, I guess I was their pediatrician when they were born," he adds with a chuckle. "As well as yours. Heck, I've probably circumcised half of the men around here back when they were infants."

His wife pats his arm gently. "Yet another reminder that it's past time for you to retire, Steve."

"Right," I say shortly, trying to process while everyone laughs again.

"But I imagine that's one of the reasons you're thinking about joining us at the clinic?" he poses, referring to my recent job application. "You must be looking forward to working with Nurse Tenley, since she's practically family."

My nostrils flare at the reminder that one of my job duties would include checking out the newborn babies Tenley helps deliver as the town's resident midwife—not that it would be so bad seeing Tenley every day. But it means I'll undoubtedly see more of JD, too.

Daisy interrupts my thoughts when she jabs her elbow into my side, and I stifle a protest before I respond. "I'm really here for my sister, to help her with the twins."

"That's right. Congratulations on becoming an uncle," the doctor replies.

I swallow hard. I am excited about gaining two new nieces, even if I'm not thrilled about the circumstances.

Daisy smiles genially when I hesitate to thank him. "Those baby girls will have him wrapped around their little fingers in no time, right?" She glances over at me, encouraging me to play along. "And Landry just couldn't resist the opportunity to work alongside his old friends and family. There's nothing like living in a small town, and Camellia really is the best community. I know I'm loving it here so far."

"You've recently moved to town?" Dr. Broussard asks, raising his brow at me approvingly.

"We're moving in together," I blurt out a little too loudly. "In a house. You know, just the two of us."

They smile at Daisy and me. "Congratulations, then," Dr. Broussard says awkwardly. "We look forward to seeing you around, especially if we're able to convince Dr. Reed to join our staff."

"I sure hope so," Daisy drawls, and Dr. Broussard bids me goodbye until our interview. She cringes as soon as they walk away. "I know we technically didn't say anything untrue, but that definitely felt like lying. Do you think he assumed ..."

"Yeah, thanks to you," I say, taking my arm back.

"You're the one who volunteered the information about us moving in together. In a house, you know, *just the two of us*," she retorts, lowering her voice to mock me.

"I'm not the best liar, okay?"

"You don't say," she replies sarcastically.

"I guess it doesn't matter, anyway, since no one would believe we were an actual couple once they got to know us," I mumble. "You're so nice. And I'm so ... old."

She laughs softly. "Oh, come on. We're only, what, eight years apart? Besides, don't all you doctors have a thing for younger women?"

I shake my head and hold back another smile. She keeps surprising me. "I'm not like all the other doctors."

"Right," she says, biting her lip. "Because they're all so quirky and awkward."

"Geniuses usually are," I declare, and she smirks. I stare at her until I notice the crowd gathering over near my sister and Blake, and I pull Daisy forward to get a better look.

"Well, shit," I curse under my breath when I realize Blake is down on one knee. I guess I didn't think he'd really go through with it, certainly not this soon.

"So ... ah, will you? Marry me?" he asks tentatively, holding up a ring in front of her. He isn't wearing his trademark cocky, arrogant expression either. He looks ... well, terrified.

Hell, is he *crying*?

"Oh, uh, yeah, sure," Loren answers after a while, her tone uncertain, and I almost feel sorry for him.

"Sure?" he repeats.

"I mean, of course I will," she says a little more convincingly before everyone applauds. But I can't tell whether she's cringing or smiling as he slips the ring onto her finger and wraps her up in a hug.

That son of a ...

He's guilting her into marrying him because of the babies. There's no way Loren wants this, if her expression is any indication. He's probably using her to fix his reputation so he can get ahead politically. I'm sure that's why he's proposing now, while the assistant district attorney and his wife are here. I'm barely holding back a growl when I feel Daisy's hand on my arm.

"Landry?" she whispers.

I watch helplessly as Blake ushers Loren into the house. "I have to—"

"No, you don't," she tells me, tugging me back when I instinctively move to follow them inside.

"Lo needs me to—"

"Nope," she cuts me off again. "She doesn't need anything from you except your love and support, right?"

I pout. "But she clearly didn't want to say yes," I point out.

Daisy sighs, her eyes darting around nervously when I say it loudly enough for someone to overhear. "Look, I don't know enough about your relationship with Loren to make a whole lot of assumptions, but I'm pretty sure your skepticism is the last thing she wants to hear right now," she explains quietly. "Not to mention, she doesn't seem to be the one who just got her heart broken in front of everyone."

I take a step back and blink at her. "What's that supposed to mean?"

She tilts her head to the side in a gesture, and I follow her to the edge of the lawn. "Landry, I know you're worried about Loren, but Blake is obviously head over heels for her while she's, well ..." She pauses to sigh before she continues. "I get the impression she's been testing his loyalty."

"She's having his babies. I think that's fair."

"You're right, and she shouldn't be forced to marry him if she doesn't want to. But I don't think he's proposing just because she's pregnant, which means he's going to be devastated if she tells him she doesn't feel the same."

I purse my lips as I reconcile Daisy's take on their relationship with my own observations over the years. "Are you saying my sister's the asshole here?"

She stifles a smile. "I'm saying she's capable of looking out for herself. And she and Blake probably need to talk this out ... without your help."

I think back on the last serious conversation I had with Blake when he asked me to be more supportive of their relationship because

Loren couldn't seem to get over our parents' failed marriage. And the way he's repeatedly stood up to me on her behalf does sort of track with the idea of him having been in love with her all this time.

But then again, there's no way Loren or anyone else could possibly believe the Blake Bourgeois I knew throughout college could ever be trustworthy, not after all the women I've seen him go through.

I'm still mulling it over when I catch JD and Tenley walking into the house. "Wait a minute, why do they get to go inside?" I demand, gesturing in their direction.

"Because she's Loren's best friend. And he's Blake's," Daisy says plainly. She looks me in the eyes again. "Get over it, Landry. If you really love your sister, you'll back off and let her make up her own mind. All she needs is your love and support, remember?"

I growl under my breath. "Fine. But don't blame me for saying 'I told you so' when this blows up later."

She pats my arm. "You know, *if* this does indeed blow up, we're both out of a home. Maybe you should think twice about your allegiance here."

I smirk, impressed again with her ability to read the situation. Even for a homeschooled kid who's spent half her life in and out of the hospital, she's already way better than I am at this. Though that's not saying much. "You're not as naive as you look, are you?"

She grins in return. "Oh, I'm practically clueless. But I'm also a fast learner."

Eventually, my sister and her alleged fiancé return to the party, looking a little worse for the wear. Loren's obviously been crying, and Blake's clothes look suspiciously wrinkled. But I can't tell whether they've been fighting or celebrating.

Scratch that. Blake wouldn't be frowning like that if it were the second option.

I narrow my eyes and stare at Loren carefully. Her color is off, and she's moving slowly, cautiously, like she might just faint from exhaustion at any second. She's also in pain, judging from the way she keeps alternating rubbing her belly and her lower back as the sunlight glints off the huge rock on her left ring finger.

I don't like any of this.

"You're doing it again," Daisy whispers beside me.

"What? Oh." I relax my face when I realize what she means. "But don't you think Loren looks—"

"Let it go, Landry," she begins again. "Loving and supportive."

I heave out a deep sigh as Blake speaks. "I'll try."

He says something about Loren needing to rest now, which somewhat appeases me, and the other guests begin filing out of their backyard. Daisy and I both join the cleanup efforts, and before long, only our family and Tenley's remains.

"I'm going to go wait in the Jeep," Daisy tells me once most of the work is done. "I'm sure you want to congratulate her." She gestures to my sister across the kitchen, and I nod appreciatively.

"You should be resting," I tell Loren sternly as soon as I approach her. "You're looking pale."

She rolls her eyes, but even that small effort seems to tire her. "I'm fine," she murmurs.

I open my mouth to argue, but Daisy's words echo in my mind. *Loving and supportive.*

Loren is a grown woman, as much as it pains me to admit it. And I'll have to start letting her make her own mistakes at some point, right?

I soften my expression. "If you say so." Then I reach out to wrap her up in my arms before I lose the nerve. She hesitates before she returns the embrace, which honestly stings a little, but she melts into the hug after a second.

"And congratulations. I love you, Lo," I add after a while. "Be safe and call me if anything changes. I want to be here when my girls arrive and check them out myself."

There. That was loving and supportive, right?

She pulls away, rolling her eyes again and looking more like herself. "Yeah, yeah, we get it. You're a doctor," she quips, making me laugh.

I want to say more, to demand that she put her feet up, but my gaze meets Blake's from across the room, and I can see the same concern in his eyes. I make my way over to him as the rest of my family crowds Loren.

"Congrats," I say dryly. It takes all I have not to remind him that I'm holding up my end of our deal even though he failed to do his part.

Hey, I'm trying.

"Thanks, man." He smiles softly, extending an open hand. I return the handshake, but I don't miss the way his eyes dart to Loren again when my mom goes in for a hug. Blake might be just as worried about her as I am.

"Can you make her—"

"Yeah, I'm on it," he cuts me off, patting my arm before he strides over to her, and I nod to myself before I go, feeling slightly more confident in his abilities to take care of my baby sister.

I watch as my dad takes Blake's hand and embraces Loren next. I don't know if I've ever seen him looking so pleased with anything his own kids have ever done, but I suppose it's different now that a Bourgeois is involved.

I guess some things never do change.

No one seems to notice when I walk out of the house and join Daisy in the car, with the exception of Tenley's nephew. He gives me a short nod when we make eye contact before I pull out of the driveway, and the drive home is silent.

"You did good today, Landry," Daisy tells me as we reach the house.

I huff. "I didn't know I was being graded."

She cringes. "Sorry, I need to do a better job of thinking about what I say before I say it. You know my family's very ... open with their thoughts and feelings."

"Yeah," I retort.

"And they're sort of all I've ever had, so that doesn't leave me with a lot of experience in socialization."

"Right." I already hate having to feel this guilty all the time. "Daisy, no offense, but I'm not sure this roommate arrangement is going to work out."

Her shoulders droop as soon as the words leave my mouth. "I didn't mean to upset you. I was just trying to be helpful."

I groan and run my fingers through my hair. "I know. And that's why we can't live together. Neither of us understands how to read a room. And if you're going to keep saying stuff that annoys me, I'm going to keep hurting your feelings."

"But I'm a fast learner, remember? I'm sure I'll pick up on what not to say after a while. And I can develop thicker skin. We can make it work." Then she turns her doe eyes to mine. "I promise."

"You can't really think putting up with me is going to be worth the taxi service," I grind out, trying desperately to resist her pleading.

"This is my one and only chance to make it on my own. I'll never prove to my parents that I don't need them smothering me to survive if I have to go crawling back before the first month is up."

She's added a trembling lip now, and fluttery eyelashes. *Dammit.*

"You're not technically doing it on your own if you need me around," I grumble, holding on to my resolve.

"You'll just be my safety net, right? I won't bother you unless I really have to, besides getting a ride now and then."

I turn away. I don't believe that for a second.

She sighs wearily. "I understand if you don't want to live with me, though. And I'll manage alone."

"Oh, will you?" I pose.

Her expression shifts. "I spoke to JD earlier. He said he'd be more than happy to pick me up in the mornings on his way to school," she declares with a smug smile.

My own face hardens. "You're bluffing."

"Am I?" she chirps, batting her eyelashes again.

I growl.

"What exactly do you have against JD anyway?" she asks, narrowing her eyes at me.

"Long story," I grunt.

"We'd have plenty of time for long stories if we were having slumber parties every night. Or you could tell me about it over your morning coffee." She's grinning now, confident in her victory.

"If I talk more, will you talk less?" I don't deliver the line with as much sarcasm as usual though, probably because of the effort it's taking me not to smile.

"Probably not," she replies. "But I'll do my best to wait until the caffeine kicks in before I start."

I can't help it when a laugh escapes. "Fine."

"Thank you, Landry," she drawls sweetly and surprises me by climbing onto her knees and leaning over to press a kiss to my cheek. I turn in time to see the way she rolls her lips in as she sits back, almost looking embarrassed. "Sorry. That's probably—"

"I don't like being touched."

She nods quickly. "Got it."

Then I furrow my brow. "Well, I guess I do, but not, you know ..."

"By me?" she offers.

I'm not sure how to save myself on that one, but luckily, I'm interrupted by my phone ringing. I'm so concerned when I see Loren's name on the caller ID that I don't even apologize to Daisy before I answer the call.

"Lo? What's wrong?"

"Landry," says a familiar voice on the other side, though it's not my sister's. "It's JD. I'm calling you from Loren's phone because we're on the way to the hospital. I thought you'd want to know."

"What?" I ask dumbly. "Is she ... are the babies ..."

"Tenley thinks she's having a placental abruption."

"I'm on my way." My breathing quickens, and I turn to Daisy. "Get inside. Now."

Her eyes widen. "What's going on?"

"It's Loren. I've gotta go," I practically yell.

Daisy nods and scrambles out of the passenger seat. "Will you let me know if they're okay?"

I nod shortly to get her out of the way before I throw my Jeep into reverse and peel out of the driveway, leaving Daisy at the edge of the front porch with her arms wrapped around her middle.

CHAPTER 4

landry

I DON'T MAKE it back to the house until after ten that evening, and I only leave the hospital once my older sister Lilley tells me I've overstayed my welcome. Loren and the twins are all stable, even though she'll need a few days to recover from the surgery and the babies will be spending some time in the NICU.

I sigh and run my fingers through my hair after I pull into the driveway and park beside Daisy's green Volkswagen Beetle. I guess I was so distracted with unpacking that I missed it this morning.

This morning seems like a lifetime ago. And the problems that seemed so big earlier today feel so petty now.

My eyes sting as I let the events of the last few hours sink in, and my hand flies to my chest as it heaves against my will. It still feels like I'm due to wake up from a horrible dream any second now. Loren was so close to losing her babies, and we were so close to losing her. My sister and I might have our differences, but she's still one of the most important people in my world. And the worst part about all of this is that I have no control over the situation. I'm a doctor, yet I couldn't stop it from happening. Hell, having a maternal-fetal specialist on speed dial couldn't even help this time. And it gets even harder to breathe as I recall the way I tried so hard to prevent all of this in the first place.

Aside from the irony of Loren getting pregnant with a guy like Blake, what are the chances that she'd conceive twins and develop a condition like placenta previa? And after months of begging both of them to take her health more seriously and getting repeatedly told to butt out, my worst fears were all playing out right in front of me. Thankfully, Tenley was around to diagnose Loren's placental abruption and get Dr. Simms to perform an emergency C-section in time. Still, this could have all been avoided had they just listened to me.

I don't know that I've ever felt more scared or angry in my life.

And that's why I couldn't stop myself from marching into the hospital waiting room and calling Blake Bourgeois a selfish bastard. The man was sitting on the floor with his head in his hands and his back against the wall, blood staining his arms and clothes. I knew he was gutted. I knew he'd have done anything to take Loren's place or to go back in time and do things differently. He must have been at a loss as to who or what to hope for as he waited for someone to come out and announce he'd lost one or both of his daughters or their mother.

While I love my sister and have always made it my priority to keep her safe, I can't claim the same level of devotion a father is supposed to experience with his children. I imagine that must be a different kind of love, something compulsive, involuntary, and biologically ingrained. Then again, I've seen too many cases of child abuse and neglect to believe that's true for all parents. And if Blake's attachment is anything like what my father apparently felt for his wife and kids, then my loyalty to Loren is still unrivaled.

And now I'm letting myself get bogged down in all of the negatives again.

I try to shift my thoughts to something else, but I can't get past the miserable look on Blake's face when I gave in to the impulse to lash out at him. He kept his eyes down, silently nodding in agreement as another sob wracked his body. I pinned him with the blame, knowing he'd feel too guilty to defend himself, and he simply accepted it. It was his brother who cut a dangerous glare my way and ordered me to either keep my mouth shut or go home. At the time, I couldn't believe JD had the audacity to threaten me—I mean, Loren is *my* sister, not his. He may be her friend now, but I've been taking care of her for years. I was the one consoling her each time our parents let her down, while the Bourgeois brothers were busy contributing to the problem by stealing our dad's attention.

But now that I'm taking the time to process all this, I can't help thinking JD was only trying to defend his sibling as fiercely as I was trying to protect my own. And it turns out that "I told you so" wasn't as satisfying as my anger promised it would be, and it certainly hadn't helped Loren or the babies.

In the end, I managed to keep the rest of my uglier remarks to myself in exchange for Blake's consent to check on the babies in the NICU, and I at least got to look in on my sister in recovery. But my presence only served to make myself feel better, if I'm being honest.

"Shit, Landry," I mutter to myself and pound my fist against the steering wheel. It takes a few more deliberate inhales and exhales, as well as a reminder that Loren and the twins are, in fact, going to be okay for me to shake the worst of those overwhelming feelings of dread.

I lift my head and glance up at the small shotgun house in front of me. It's such a strange contradiction to my current mood: quaint, cheerful, cozy. There's a fresh coat of mint green paint on the front door. The plethora of new plants scattered throughout the flower beds and the pots lining the porch must also be of Daisy's doing, since I've never known Loren to have much of a green thumb. And Daisy would certainly know a thing or two about gardening.

She also seems to understand how to get along with everyone in Camellia better than I expected, given her negligible opportunities for socialization before now. Not to mention she's only been here a short amount of time. While my last roommate shared the same last name and generically likable traits as Daisy, his people skills hadn't really rubbed off on me. But Rowan isn't as talkative or extraverted as his baby sister, so I guess there's a chance I could benefit from observing her interactions.

Maybe I could learn a little something about focusing on the positives from my new roommate. That is, if her sunshine doesn't give me a sunburn first.

I grab the rest of my bags and walk up to the door, hesitating with the key. Am I supposed to knock now? We might have formed an informal verbal roommate agreement, but Daisy had also made it clear she didn't appreciate the way I'd surprised her this morning.

I swap my keys out for my phone, intending to text Rowan for Daisy's contact, when I see a string of messages from an unknown number.

UNKNOWN

Hey Landry, it's Daisy. Hope you don't mind that I got your number from my brother. I just wanted to see if there were any updates on Loren and the babies.

I'll keep praying until I hear back from you.

Any news?

Hi. I hate to bother you rn but i ve started feelingg off and worried abt having an eppisode

landry im sry but im going to hav a seizur

The last message came through about twenty minutes ago. I curse under my breath before I drop my bags and scramble to get the key into the lock. I push my way into the house to find Daisy lying on her side on the couch, her long hair curtaining her face.

"Daisy? Are you okay?" I call out as I dart over to her, immediately brushing her hair aside to check her breathing and pulse.

She doesn't respond, but she does seem to be okay, to my relief. Judging from her current position, she managed to avoid a fall and keep her airway clear, though I can't tell the extent of her episode. And since I've never seen Daisy have an episode before, I don't know what to expect.

I settle on the floor beside her as I continue my inspection. Her muscles still seem tensed, and I observe a few residual spasms in her legs. I spend the next few minutes softly stroking her hair and reminding her that I'm here, mostly because I don't want her to panic when she regains consciousness to find a stranger in the house. Eventually she whimpers and cracks her eyes open slightly.

She takes a deep inhale when she recognizes me. "Hi," she rasps. "Sorry about this."

"No, *I'm* sorry," I correct her and swallow down the lump of guilt lodged in my throat. "I should have checked my phone sooner."

"How's Lo?" she asks, slowly stretching her limbs.

"She's doing well, considering."

"The babies?"

I shouldn't be surprised that she's more concerned with them than herself.

"They're good. Tiny but strong, like their mama." I smile, even though it's hard to get the words out. "They'll be in the NICU for a while."

"Thank God," she whispers, relief washing over her face.

I realize I'm still running a hand over her hair, and I clear my throat as I put some space between us. She pushes herself up to a seated position, a string of rosary beads still clutched in her palm. It reminds me of the rosary I saw dangling from JD's hands at the hospital earlier.

"Thank you for praying for them," I say, surprising myself.

"Of course," she replies, rising to a seated position. "I'm so glad they're okay. How are you?"

I let out an incredulous laugh. "I'm more worried about you. Did you fall or hurt anything before you made it to the couch?"

She shakes her head slowly. "I'm fine. Just feeling a little groggy, but it's nothing I'm not used to."

I frown. "Can I get you anything? Something to drink?"

"Water would be nice. Thanks."

I nod and go into the kitchen, relieved to open a cabinet and find most of Loren's old furnishings. I bring her a glass of water before I retrieve the backpack and duffel bag I'd left on the porch, which are now covered with bugs. Because we're in Louisiana.

"You never answered me," Daisy points out after a while.

"Because I'm not the patient," I say as I return to the living room and sit beside her, our shoulders bumping. I make a mental note to get another chair, since we only have the one small sofa right now.

"But I imagine you've had a rough afternoon. How are you feeling about everything?"

"I'm fine," I spit out automatically.

She takes a sip of water and eyes me skeptically. "Landry, it's okay to admit you were scared. I was scared for you."

"Is that why you had a seizure?" I ask quickly.

"I doubt it," she replies. "More likely the stress of the move in general. And I don't think this was a particularly bad episode, since I'm not feeling as terrible as I could right now."

I nod. "That's good."

"Did you see it at all?" she ventures.

"Not really. I only made it back a few minutes before you woke up."

She smiles ruefully. "Thank you for coming to take care of me. I'm sorry this happened within hours of you agreeing to move in, especially when you were busy with your family—"

"Daisy, please stop apologizing for something you have no control over. If anything, I'm impressed by the way you alerted me when you felt it coming on. And I'm glad you were able to get to a safe position."

"So I haven't scared you off already?" she poses, batting her lashes over her big, green eyes.

I laugh shortly. "Takes a lot more than that to scare me off."

"You mean you'd rather live with an epileptic than an optimistic extrovert?"

"You're not an epileptic. You're a person who just happens to have epilepsy," I correct her.

She smirks at me and lifts her chin proudly. "I am."

"And you also talk a *lot*," I add, smiling.

"Yeah, well, you cuss too much," she retorts.

"Damn, you're right."

She nudges me, and I laugh again. But then her smile falters when her gaze lands on the pile of crates in the middle of the room. "I guess we should start unpacking. You'll probably want the bigger bedroom."

"I'm not kicking you out. I'll be fine in the smaller room."

She bites her lip. "There isn't even a bed in there yet. I bought an air mattress in case Rowan or anyone else came to visit me, but that's all I have for now."

I groan inwardly. At my age, one night on an air mattress is enough to trigger at least a week's worth of back pain. I could go to my dad's place tonight, but it's late. It's been a long-ass day, and I can't just leave Daisy here alone after that episode.

"I'll take the air mattress tonight," I tell her after giving the couch a good once over and deciding it's too small. "I have a storage unit in Baton Rouge with a bed. Tomorrow I'll borrow my dad's truck and swap out some of this other stuff for the mattress, at least."

She furrows her brow. "You're not getting a very big mattress in there. Not if you want a dresser, anyway."

"Okay then," I say on a sigh. "Looks like I'm going shopping in the morning."

"Oh, mind if I come along?" she asks cheerfully.

"Why the hell not?" I mutter, and she grins.

"Great. Let's get you to bed, roomie." She bounces up onto her feet and practically skips out of the room. I have a sinking feeling that things will never be the same after today, in more ways than one.

daisy

You're not on the homestead anymore, Daisy.

"Homework? Man, she's trippin' if she thinks I'm reading this shit when I get back from practice," grumbles the boy sitting closest to the door. "I don't care how hot she is."

"Watch it, Damien," Tenley Robin's nephew, Ethan, growls back at him.

"Why, she another one of your aunties?" Damien laughs and nudges the kid in front of him, and I pretend not to notice as I straighten the papers on my desk.

"Maybe she is. Either way, if I were you, I'd be more worried about catching a pass every once in a while," Ethan replies and shoots him a dangerous glare just as the bell rings. Thankfully, everyone scatters before things get too heated.

"See you all tomorrow. Have a great afternoon," I call out, but my voice is drowned out by the herd of juniors scrambling to vacate my classroom.

"Ugh. She doesn't even wear makeup," says one of the girls walking out of my last period class. I force a smile when she turns her nose up in disgust.

"That's because she doesn't need to," replies another girl bitterly.

This one turns to shoot me an apologetic look before she locks hands with Ethan, and he leads her out to the hallway.

I exhale loudly and return to my desk to stare blankly at the walls. It's not that I expected teaching to be easy. But I hadn't imagined it would be this hard. I'm barely a week into the school year, and there's so much to do that I don't even know where to start. I can't imagine doing this without all of the lesson plans and activities that Loren had prepared for me.

My chin trembles and my eyes sting, but I sniff hard, refusing to give in to those feelings of hopelessness. Because I *can* do this. I *have* to do this. I've survived much worse, and I'm not giving up on this job, at least not until I get the hang of being self-sufficient. Then I'll worry about finding my way and figuring out whether this is what I'm really meant to do. I blink back the tears and take a few deep breaths, reminding myself to trust in God's plan for my life. I'm sure I'm meant to be where I am now for a reason, even if it's not for a long time or for reasons I understand.

I'm reciting one of my favorite prayers when I hear JD's voice at the open door.

"Knock, knock," he calls out before he appears. "How's it going, Miss Daisy?"

His expression falls as soon as he sees my face, so I paste on a smile. "Oh, it's great. So far, so good, you know!"

"So that's why you're sitting here contemplating all of your life choices and wondering how you got to this point, right?" He laughs softly, and another teacher walks in behind him.

"Yeah, pretty much," I reply, my smile feeling more genuine now.

"Daisy, I'm not sure if you've gotten the chance to meet Mrs. LeBlanc, our amazing Ag teacher," he continues, gesturing to the woman who comes to stand beside him.

She's wearing thick, navy cargo pants and a matching Carhartt button down with steel-toed work boots, and her brown hair is pulled back into a tight French braid. It's all a stark contrast to my purple linen sundress and light green ballet flats, as well as the flower pinning back my long blonde waves.

"No, I can't say I've had the pleasure. But it's great to meet you," I offer cheerfully, moving to extend a hand. She only lifts her chin in a silent nod and crosses her arms, so I pull my hand back quickly.

JD clears his throat. "Claire is also the head of our CTE department, so I was thinking the two of you could get acquainted now. Mr. Soileau already talked to you about Mrs. Joanie retiring at the end of the semester, leaving us with a permanent opening for a home ec teacher. And home ec falls under the career and technical education umbrella. If we're lucky enough to get you to take Mrs. Joanie's place, Claire would become your mentor teacher."

"Oh, well, that's … that sounds great," I say, nodding too quickly.

"Except no one will ever replace Mrs. Joanie." Claire presses her lips together in a flat line as she looks me up and down. "She's a Camellia High institution. She's been here longer than some of us have been alive."

"Absolutely," JD confirms. "All the more reason she deserves to retire."

"Hmpf," Claire grunts. "You certified yet?"

"Who, me?" I squeak.

"No, the other flower-child Barbie. Of course I mean you."

JD glares at Claire and clears his throat, and she rolls her eyes. "Sorry. It's been a long day," she mutters after a second.

I nod. "I graduated with a minor in elementary education, but I still have to take the certification exams for high school. I hadn't planned on teaching older kids."

"No kidding," she deadpans.

"Hey, we all know alt-cert teachers are the best because they're forged by fire. If you can survive your first few weeks in a high school classroom with little to no prep, the next thirty years will be a breeze, right?" JD says, his eyes roaming my desk. "You don't have any snacks in here, do you? Didn't Lo—I mean, Ms. Reed—leave some peanut butter cookies behind or something?"

I stifle a laugh. "Sorry. All out of snacks."

He lets out a disappointed hum, and I know it doesn't matter, but I still feel guilty for letting him down. I make a mental note to bake something tonight and keep it on my desk for later. Truthfully, JD's been nothing but nice to me, and I need all the help I can get.

I glance over to Claire, secretly wondering what I could do to impress her. She's wearing the same look of disapproval as the catty girl with the contoured cheekbones and the unnaturally thick eyelashes from last hour. I'd be lucky to get her to not hate me at this point.

"So, I guess this means I need to get to work studying for that high school pedagogy exam?" I say after a while.

"Exactly. The sooner you pass that test, the sooner we can get you a full teacher's salary and benefits," JD remarks, making my stomach dip, and not in a good way. "Claire, think you can help her with the test prep?"

"Wait, I'm sorry, but did you just say I won't get benefits?" I ask carefully. "As in, no health insurance?"

"Subs don't qualify for health insurance in our district. But pass that test in the next few months, and you'll get a bump in pay as soon as the board approves your hire for that full-time position," he explains.

I swallow hard, ignoring the panic rising inside. "Oh right, of course," I reply, my voice cracking. "Thanks for clearing all that up for me."

They both frown, apparently sensing my distress. "I still have a test prep book in my classroom. You can use it to study," Claire offers, to my surprise. Her posture softens a little when I thank her.

"Let me know if you need anything, Miss Daisy," JD says. "Hang in there. It'll get better. And let me know if my boy ever causes you any trouble."

"Ethan's been great," I tell him, and he grins proudly.

"He'd better be. And the same goes for the rest of the football team," he adds, making me cringe. Claire huffs out a laugh when his tone shifts. "Text me a list of names before practice this afternoon," he adds, his voice almost a growl.

I assure him that everything's fine before ushering them out, mostly because I'm afraid the kids will only get worse if they suspect I ratted them out to their football coach. At least Claire seems to have warmed up to me a little.

After that, I go down to the teachers' lounge to heat up my lunch. Unfortunately, I don't get in before the rush to the microwave, and I'm stuck waiting in line as precious seconds tick away before the impending bell.

I try to start up a friendly conversation with a few of the other teachers, and although most of them are generically nice, they're also too busy to socialize. And the ones who have time to chat also seem a little cliquish.

"Well, well, well, Jaz," croons the French teacher, Madame Beth. "If it ain't our favorite coach."

Jasmine, the pep squad sponsor, rolls her eyes when one of the baseball assistants passes by in a rush. "A grown man walking around with a backpack at work, let that sink in."

"*Mais, gardez donc,*" Beth continues, clicking her tongue. "He must be using it to store his boudin stash, because he's sure not using it to carry the test papers he grades at home."

"Ah, that's what that smell is." Jasmine smirks.

"All I know is Dora needs to get his ass to school on time so the rest of us ain't stuck babysitting his classes," Mrs. Rachel chimes in as she passes by.

Teachers don't like having to pick up one another's slack. Noted.

"Oh, speaking of, I've gotta leave about thirty minutes early for tomorrow's meet. Can you take my last period?" Jasmine asks Beth, who happily agrees.

"You still covering my parking lot duty Friday morning?" Beth goes next.

"Yep. I got you," Jasmine returns.

"*Merci beaucoup,*" Beth says, grinning.

Hmm. Okay. Correction to that last observation—*teachers like feeling appreciated when they have to pick up one another's slack.*

The bell rings again, and I'm left with my cold leftovers in hand. I shovel it in on my way back to class, and the last few periods of the day go even worse than the first. I rush down to the copy room as soon as the dismissal bell rings, only to find the machine already back-logged with jobs. I feel my stress levels rising as I watch each sheet come off the copier, one at a time, hoping it'll clear up by the time Landry gets here to pick me up. Then my phone chimes at the same time a paper jam ensues, and I'm doing my best to multitask between the copy machine and the group chat my sisters have started. My mom and dad have been leaving me in peace for the most part, settling for a daily text or a phone call every other day, but I know my sisters will only pester me more or alert my parents if I don't reply right away.

MARIGOLD

How's it going, Daisy?

IRIS

Are you teacher of the year yet?

MAGNOLIA

Did you snag a man yet?

ROSEMARY

How have you been feeling?

VIOLET

Are you coming home this weekend? I need your help with a sewing project.

IRIS

Why aren't you answering us?

MAGNOLIA

Are you still at work?

I groan and use the speech-to-text feature on my phone to send them a reply.

DAISY

> I'm fine but I'm still at work and the copy machine's broken so I can't answer now but don't worry because oof oh you son of a mother trucker oh I'm sorry Madame I didn't mean to stop your copies but it was jammed yes okay I'll just come in early tomorrow okay thanks have a great afternoon.

I glance down at my message and growl again in frustration. My sisters are going to jump all over that. My phone buzzes again, but I switch to *Do Not Disturb* mode and tuck it away before I run upstairs to grab the rest of my things. Then I head outside to find Landry's Jeep parked at the gate with him looking practically irate from his place in the driver's seat.

"Hi," I say cheerfully. "Thanks for coming."

"Where the hell were you? I've been waiting almost twenty minutes," he spits out.

I flinch. "I'm sorry. The copy machine jammed, and I couldn't just leave it that way."

"Then why didn't you answer me?" he grumbles as he turns onto the main road.

"You texted me?" I pull out my phone.

LANDRY

> Hey, I'm here.

> Everything okay?

> Do I need to come inside to help you?

> Daisy, if you don't answer me soon, I'm calling the school.

Shitake mushroom salad.

There's also a missed call from him, along with another dozen texts from my sisters.

"I'm so sorry. My sisters put me in a group text and I—"

"Look, I don't mind helping you. But I have enough on my plate without needing to worry about whether you're in there having a freaking seizure on the stairs or getting accosted by a student, so the least you could do is answer the damned phone when I call."

He's not yelling, but his stern tone is enough to push me over the edge. I'm powerless to stop the tears from flowing this time, as much as I wish I could hold it together for a few more minutes until I make it to the sanctuary of my own bedroom.

"I'm sorry, Landry," I choke out.

He glances over and groans. "Of course you're crying."

"I've been having a rough day, all right?" I reply quietly, trying not to break out into full-on sobs.

"Yeah, well, spending the day in the NICU with my sister and my nieces wasn't exactly a walk in the park for me."

"Is everything okay? Did something happen today?" I ask quickly.

"Nothing's changed," he says flatly.

"Oh. Okay," I reply, sniffling and wiping my cheeks.

We're both silent from then on, and Landry slams the front door angrily behind us once we're back in the house. I've made it a point to stay out of his way each time he gets like this, which seems to be every time he returns from a visit with his family. And he's been checking in on Loren and the twins nearly every day since we moved in together a couple of weeks ago.

Although I intended to hide away in my bedroom for a while, I stop by the kitchen first once I remember how hungry I am.

"Landry?" I call out reluctantly. I hear him shuffling around near the laundry nook. "I'm making myself something to eat. Would you like anything?"

"Is it more eggs?" he retorts sarcastically.

I frown at the carton in my hands. "Maybe."

I think I hear him snort before yelling, "No thanks." But before I can finish heating the frying pan, he stomps into the kitchen and tosses a small bundle of clothes onto the counter.

"Um, can I help you?" I ask curiously.

"Is there anything left sacred here?" he rants, snatching something from the pile and waving it in front of me.

My lips twitch, but I bite back a smile. "Whatever do you mean?"

"You leave me no space! Everywhere I go, the shower, my Jeep, the couch—all I find is blonde hair. I can't make a trip to the grocery store without you. You drank the last of my milk this morning. And God forbid I wash a load of laundry without something of yours ending up in it!"

I should be upset. Usually, this is the part when I'd start crying again. But whether it's a culmination of this lousy day or the fact that he's using my underwear to prove his point, I can't find it in me to do anything but laugh. I cover my mouth and choke back a giggle, which only serves to further annoy him.

"What the hell is so funny?" he grumbles.

"I'm sorry. I don't know what I'm supposed to do about the hair," I barely get out. "But I promise to be more deliberate about keeping our laundry separate if you're really all that threatened by my panties."

His dark brows draw together before he glances down at the fabric in his hands. Then he picks them up and inspects them for a second. "You were wearing these when I walked in on you the other day," he mumbles absently, and my laughter subsides.

I swallow hard and reach out, but he quickly snaps back into Irate Landry mode and tosses the underwear at my chest as if it were a ticking bomb.

"I'm sorry," I repeat, shaking my head. "I didn't realize mixing our laundry would bother you so much."

"Yeah, well ..." He crosses his arms and looks away.

"Is it the washing or the sorting that makes you uncomfortable?" I ask carefully.

"What?"

I sigh. "If you have something against washing our clothes together, we can get separate laundry hampers and set a schedule for using the washer. But if you just don't like finding my clothes when you go to fold yours, I don't mind taking over that chore for both of us."

"You want to do my laundry?"

I shrug. "Sure. It's not a big deal. And I know you won't have as much time to do it yourself when you start working full time at the clinic."

He presses his lips together in a hard line. "Okay. Fine. You can handle laundry. I'll supply the detergent."

"Deal." I smile cheerfully. "And while we're at it, would you mind terribly if we made a trip to the grocery store? I need to get more eggs ... and some baking supplies."

"Baking supplies?"

"I want to make peanut butter cookies for ... some friends."

"What friends?" he asks, raising an eyebrow.

"Loren ... and JD. He mentioned that your sister used to keep peanut butter cookies on her desk, so I thought it would be nice if I made a batch to share with him at school since he's been so kind to me, and we could bring some to Loren to cheer her up, you know?"

"You want me to bring you grocery shopping so you can bake cookies for JD mother-freaking Bourgeois?" He enunciates the words so carefully that I know he means to show me he's censoring himself.

"Maybe?"

"Do you even know how to bake peanut butter cookies?" he asks through his teeth.

I lick my lips nervously. "Not exactly. I mean, we never made anything with peanut butter back home because of Rowan's peanut allergy, but I've seen my mom make other cookies before. How hard can it be?"

He growls.

"Oh." I cringe. "And I almost forgot. Tomorrow is the Feast of the Assumption of the Blessed Mother, so it's a holy day of obligation. Would you be able to bring me to Mass at six in the morning?"

Another loud rumble resonates from deep within his chest, and he stomps off without giving me an answer. I should have known that would push him over the edge, since he's apparently more of a night owl and prefers to sleep in, while I'm an early-to-bed, early-to-rise kind of girl.

I sigh and return to my eggs, wincing when I hear him slam the bathroom door a few seconds later. He marches back into the kitchen, this time wielding a small silicone cup and an expression that makes me warm all over.

"Daisy." He pauses to inhale deeply. "Do I even want to know what the hell this is?"

"Nuh-uh," I squeak and shake my head.

"Daisy."

I shiver at the sound of my name in his deep, authoritative tone. Maybe I should be worried by the way he's staring at me with his jaw clenched and his eyes blazing. But I know Landry would never physically harm me, no matter how much I annoy him. He might say something hurtful, but he wouldn't mean it. And the truth is that he's ... well, he's kind of sexy when he's angry.

I clear my throat and move forward to carefully pluck the item in question from his hands. "It's my menstrual cup."

"Your ... *what?*"

"My menstrual cup. It's what I use in the place of ... you know, tampons."

He blinks at me. "And you thought it'd be cool if you left your period cup on the sink ... next to my toothbrush?"

I bite my lip. "Sorry?"

His nostrils flare, and I know I shouldn't be thinking it, but *gah*, he's hot.

"I can't ..." He pauses, swallows hard, and breathes through his nose before he begins again. "Look, Daisy, I wanted to help you. But I didn't sign up for PMS and panties and period cups and ... baking cookies for your work crush. So you can either grow the hell up or find another damned roommate."

This time he stomps out of the front door, slamming it behind him.

daisy

"Hey, Daisy, hang on!"

I try to keep my expression somewhat neutral when I turn to face Claire LeBlanc, but the truth is that I'm nearly giddy with excitement at the sound of her calling out for me. I don't even know what she wants yet, but I'm hoping she's chasing me down to tell me she thinks we should be work besties. Then again, judging by the book she's waving in her hand and the uninterested look on her face, I could be reading this all wrong.

"Um, hi, Claire," I say hopefully, shifting my weight under the heavy bags I'm carrying.

"Hey," she returns when she reaches me. "I found that study guide for you."

"Oh, thanks." I force a smile and take the book she offers. "Can't wait to get started."

She lets out a short laugh. It sounds genuine though, despite her stoic look. "Listen, I wanted to say I'm sorry for my shitty attitude yesterday. You and JD caught me at a bad time. But it's not your fault I was having a horrible day."

I feel my shoulders relax when I realize she's saying she doesn't actually hate me. "Thanks, but no apology necessary. I was having a pretty yucky day myself, so I'm sure I wasn't—"

But she cuts me off by throwing her head back and cackling loudly this time. "Oh, stop it. I was a bitch to you, and you know it. But it's cute that you want to make excuses for me."

My jaw hangs open, and I blink a few times before I find my voice. "No—no worries. This was really nice of you," I tell her, holding up the test prep guide. My phone vibrates in my pocket, and although I'd normally ignore it, I figure I'd better not risk upsetting Landry any more than I already have.

"I'm sorry, this is probably my ride home," I say to Claire before I check the message.

LANDRY

I'm here.

I glance to the right and see his black Jeep parked against the fence. Then I roll my eyes before punching in an answer.

DAISY

Be there in a second.

I'm still not happy about the way he yelled and stormed out last night in addition to the silent treatment he gave me when he dropped me off at church early this morning. But my options are still limited for now.

"You don't drive?" she asks as I struggle to put my phone away. Then she sighs and plucks it from my hands, turns it and uses my face to unlock it, punches in her contact information, and send herself a text, all before she slips it into my cardigan pocket.

"Oh, thanks. Um, no, not right now. It's a long story. But my roommate's helping me out for a while."

"Don't you live in Loren's old house?"

I nod.

"I pass right by your place every day. I can give you a ride whenever you need. Just call me." She frowns harder, despite the kind offer she's extending.

"Wow, that's really nice of you. Thanks," I say, trying to hide my surprise.

"It's nothing," she replies with a shrug. "That your roommate?" she asks when she sees my eyes darting nervously to Landry's car.

"Yeah. I'm sorry if I seem distracted. He can be a little impatient—"

"Isn't that Loren's brother?" She squints at the Jeep and shields her eyes from the sun to get a better look. "Damn. Nice job, sis. He's pretty hot."

I snort out a laugh. "He's definitely both of those things, and he's a doctor. But we're just friends."

"You're friends ... with that guy? Isn't he, like, a total dick?"

"Not *totally*." She shoots me a skeptical glare. "He and my brother were college roommates, so he's actually been really nice to me," I say with a shrug.

"I'd probably find an excuse to accidentally walk in on him in the shower. Just sayin'. If you have to put up with his douchey ass, might as well make it worth your while."

I chuckle. "Not a bad idea." My phone chimes again, and I groan.

"Good luck with that, then," she offers, patting me on the shoulder. "See ya 'round, Daisy."

"Thanks. See you around, Claire." I grin as I make my way to Landry, my smile fading when I see the disgruntled frown he's sporting.

"Thanks for waiting," I mumble as I buckle my seatbelt. All he offers is a grunt in response, so I guess he's picking up where we left off this morning.

We drive home in silence, and he has the audacity to come around and grab one of the bags from my shoulder when I step out of the car. I shoot him the angriest glare I can muster, but I can see the remorse in his eyes before he turns and leads me into the house. I drop my things in the living room before marching out the front door to pick up my watering can.

A few minutes pass before I hear the door creaking open and his heavy footsteps on the wooden porch.

"Hey," Landry says when he approaches, his head bowed. "Mind if I join you?"

I study him for a second as I continue watering my plants. "Only if you've come to apologize."

"I have," he replies, holding back a smile.

"Let's hear it, then." I move to sit on the front porch steps and pat the space beside me.

"I'm sorry," he mumbles, groaning softly as he lowers himself to sit.

"That's it? Really?"

He sighs. "Fine. I'm sorry for taking my stress out on you yesterday. You didn't deserve most of that. But this is exactly why I hesitated to move in together. So if you can't handle—"

I click my tongue in disappointment. "You're crummy at apologies, Landry."

"Yeah, well, you're shit at cussing," he says with an eye roll.

"Look, I can't begin to understand what you've been going through. I'm sure it's killing you, having to stand by and not being able to help. But it doesn't exempt you from being kind to everyone else. You're still responsible for working on yourself, even in hard times. Just think of it as an opportunity to grow as a person."

He rears back in surprise. "What's that supposed to mean?"

"How we handle tragedy and setbacks says a lot about us, and offering up one's suffering for the betterment of others is more rewarding than you'd think."

"And I've told you before that I don't need your help *to grow as a person*," he retorts indignantly.

I shrug. "Sure seems like you do."

I know I'm pushing my luck, but he needs to hear this, so it might as well come from me. And after the hissy fit he threw last night, I think I'm entitled to call him out on his bad attitude.

"What would you know about adversity, anyway?" he blurts out, but he looks regretful as soon as he says the words. "I'm sorry," he adds softly. "Forget I said that last part."

"Like I told *you* before, I can handle more than you think. You're not the only one who's had a rough childhood, you know, even if my problems looked different than yours," I tell him, reaching out to pick one of my flowers.

"Yeah, I'm sorry," he repeats after a while. "I'm just not fond of getting lectures from a kid."

"I'm twenty-five, you know, old enough to need a period cup," I say dryly as I roll the pink camellia's stem between my fingers. "And despite the way it looks, I've lived through more than most people my age."

"Maybe you have endured a lot, but you still haven't learned that most people aren't as inherently good as you and the rest of your family. The majority of us aren't looking to grow or better ourselves. We're trying to survive and take care of the people we love, and we don't have the time or energy to bother with the rest."

"I refuse to believe people aren't inherently good," I reply. "Especially you, Landry."

He clears his throat and looks away. "Good luck holding onto that philosophy as a high school teacher."

"Yeah," I admit. "I know they're all good kids, but some of them just act like downright ... twerps."

He snorts. "*Twerps?* No wonder they're having a field day with you."

I shove him playfully. "I don't know what you're talking about."

"Come on, Daisy," he says, glaring at me incredulously. "You're young and beautiful, and you flinch every time you hear a bad word. You're practically begging them to give you a hard time."

My jaw lowers. "That's not true at all."

"If you don't think you're locker room fodder yet, then you're even more naive than I thought."

I frown and bring my knees up to my chest. "I'm sure those kids don't care enough to give me a second thought once they leave my classroom."

"And I can't imagine the male population of Camellia High isn't infatuated with you by now," he says with a smirk, but his expression shifts. "You're not wearing anything too sexy or revealing, are you?"

I blink. "I don't think so. I mean, I'm pretty sure everything I own is relatively modest."

He leans back as his gaze runs over me, making it harder for me to breathe. I'm wearing a sleeveless dress today, but I'm pretty well-covered.

"You could add an extra layer, like a sweater or something, just to be safe," he says, his voice thick. But his eyes are still locked onto my shoulders. I bring my attention back to the flower in my hands when I feel my cheeks flushing.

He clears his throat and adds, "Not that you're doing anything wrong. It's just ... teenage boys are pretty disgusting."

I nod, but I can't bring myself to look up at him. For some reason, I feel more vulnerable right now than I did when I was standing in front of him in my underwear the other day.

"Daisy, have any of them said something to make you uncomfortable?" he ventures after a while.

I shrug. "Nothing all that bad. I just pretend not to hear them."

"They haven't threatened you or anything, have they?"

"No, of course not," I say, shaking my head. "They're immature, but I don't let any of it bother me, I promise."

He grunts. "You ought to tell them you're JD's cousin or something, call him to your classroom the next time they start talking shit. I mean, isn't that his job?"

My brow rises. Last I checked, asking JD for help equated to pushing one of Landry's buttons. "I can't call the assistant principal for every little thing. They'll think I'm a pushover and spread the word that I can't handle them myself." I lift my chin as I say it, hoping it makes me look more confident than I feel.

"Hmm. You may be right," he admits.

"I'm not as dumb as you think," I murmur.

He frowns. "I don't think you're dumb. I just hate the idea of you getting bullied or objectified by a bunch of punk-ass teenagers."

"That's why I wanted to bake those cookies, you know, to give JD an excuse to stop by my classroom throughout the day. I figured it couldn't hurt to make the kids think he might pop in unannounced,"

I say, hesitating before I add the next part. "And I'd never crush on a married man, for the record."

"I'm sorry. I shouldn't have said that, either." He pauses and lets out a breath. "The truth is, I got really scared when you didn't answer me yesterday afternoon. All of these horrible scenarios started running through my mind, like you'd had a seizure and hurt yourself and the students were making fun of you instead of helping ..." He shakes his head when he trails off, and my chest tightens when I imagine him sitting in his car stressing over my safety while I was wrestling with the copy machine. "I debated going inside to check on you, but I didn't want to embarrass you. Then I felt so stupid when you came out, even though I was relieved to see you were fine, and I let my frustration get the best of me ... just like I always do."

I instinctively reach out to place my free hand over his, and I'm surprised when he doesn't flinch or pull away from the contact. "I'm sorry, too. It was careless of me to leave you hanging like that, especially when you're already worrying about your sister. I should have known you'd be easily agitated."

His mouth turns up on one side. "I'm always easily agitated. In case you haven't noticed, that's kind of my thing."

I let out a soft laugh. "You know, you're not always the grouchy, old grump you promised you'd be. I think you just let yourself get worked up because you carry so much weight on your shoulders."

"Maybe," he chokes out after a while.

"Then you shouldn't waste your energy worrying about me so much," I say, glancing down at our hands.

"I can't help it." He shrugs and looks up at me. "Rowan's always treated me like a brother. That makes us as good as family, right?"

"Right," I reply, tugging my hand back and forcing a smile.

"I'll try to be better about not letting my anxiety get the best of me and not snapping at you every time I get overwhelmed."

I swallow hard. This apology is getting much heavier than I expected. "And I'll try to be more considerate, especially about giving you your space when you need it."

He nods. "Thank you."

"What if we tried to split more of the chores? It might make things easier if we weren't doubling up on some things and trying to work in the same space."

"Like when you offered to take over laundry duties?" he asks.

"Sure." I shrug. "I don't mind doing dishes, either, or cleaning the bathroom, since my hair's always clogging the drain. And I'll take care of the gardening, obviously."

He smiles. "I suppose that leaves me with transportation and logistics?"

"Naturally."

"I'll handle all the grocery shopping and keep all of our supplies in stock, as long as you let me know what we need. Maybe we could start a shared list?"

"Yeah, that works," I agree.

"What else do you want me to take care of? This feels a little one-sided."

I laugh. "I don't mind. But if you really want another job, you could take over culinary duties. I'm not a very good cook."

"Neither am I," he admits regretfully. "But I do make a mean peanut butter and jelly sandwich, or so I'm told."

"Perfect. I've never had one," I say with a grin.

He stares at me in shock. "You've seriously never had a PB&J? I know you grew up in a peanut-free household, but that's just un-American."

"Then I guess that also makes you the director of first-time experiences," I say, giggling before I realize how awkward that sounds.

He clears his throat and stands, and I curse myself for ruining the moment. But then I see the hand he's offering me, and I smile before I clasp it and let him pull me to my feet.

"Why don't we start by taking that trip to the grocery store? You can look up cookie recipes on the way. There's gotta be a TikTok or YouTube video for that, right?" He smirks at me, and my heart literally skips a beat. "And maybe you could bring some of your flowers to Lo when we drop off her cookies later?" he adds, gesturing to the one in my hand.

"That would be great," I say softly, hoping I'm not wearing my adoration as plainly on my face as it feels.

landry

"Hey," I greet Daisy as I walk into the house. She's sitting on the couch, attempting to thread a needle.

"Oh, hey," she returns when I get closer, but she sounds more anxious than usual. "Sorry, I didn't hear you come in. Um, how was your interview?"

"Good. I guess I'm officially hired now." I hold up a stack of onboarding paperwork.

"Congratulations, Doc." She offers me a forced smile as she pulls the needle through a button, but I can tell there's something bothering her.

"How was school?"

"Fine," she says on a sigh and shifts to tuck her feet beneath her. She's wearing another one of her linen sundresses, this one with skinny shoulder straps. But I spot a cardigan sweater draped over a chair back at the counter.

"Did you have any trouble finding a ride home this afternoon?"

"Not at all. My mentor teacher Claire gave me a lift. How were the girls?"

She's deflecting, but I can't help smiling when I talk about my nieces. "Great. Loren got Penny to nurse for the first time today."

She looks up from her sewing, and her face lights up more

genuinely. "Oh, that's awesome! They're already making so much progress. I bet they'll be home before we know it."

"Yeah," I agree, moving to sit beside her on the couch. I drop the folder full of work forms on the coffee table, and she scoots over to accommodate me. "Everything okay?" I ask cautiously.

"Mm-hmm," she squeaks, obviously lying. Then she winces and shakes her finger out when she pokes herself with the needle.

I grunt quietly but let it go. "Any plans for dinner?"

She rolls her eyes. "Not for the foreseeable future."

I fidget uncomfortably before I reach for the remote. "Kinda figured you'd have made a few friends by now. You're good at that."

"I've made friends. It's just that most of them are busy with their own families or have coaching obligations."

I raise an eyebrow. "Coaching?"

Daisy shrugs. "Beth's busy with pep squad, Jasmine's coaching cross country, and Claire hasn't invited me to hang out outside of school yet. And I guess I'm too afraid to ask."

I'm admittedly a little relieved we're talking about a *she*.

"Since when do you get shy around strangers?" I pose jokingly as I turn on the TV.

"I don't know. I guess I've been feeling a little overwhelmed. Maybe it's put a damper on my confidence," she admits quietly, pulling the thread taught again. "Or maybe I'm not as good at all this adulting as I thought I'd be."

I frown. "What do you mean?"

"I guess I thought I'd be better at most of this ... teaching, cooking, making friends, dating, being a self-sufficient twenty-something-year-old in general ..."

"You're not supposed to have it all figured out yet. Most people do a lot of living in their mid-twenties," I grumble, because I refuse to see Daisy as an adult. But then my eyes dart over to the side, running over her mostly bare shoulders and the sexy scattering of freckles down the back of her neck, and I gulp.

No—I'm not going there. It's wrong on so many levels.

I look away quickly, forcing my gaze back to the TV. Daisy sighs wistfully, and I struggle to keep my eyes off her.

"Is this living?" she poses thoughtfully.

"Work and responsibility are just about all I've ever known," I reply.

"I'm sure you had *some* form of fun at my age, right?"

Memories of balancing part-time jobs, helping my alcoholic mom get back on her feet after another round of rehab, and laboring through medical school flood my brain.

"Less than you might think," I turn to tell her, and she gives me a sad smile.

"More fun than having to rely on your brother's best friend for everything and stressing over your lack of health insurance?" she asks sardonically.

I furrow my brow. "What do you mean by a lack of health insurance?"

She cringes. "Did I not mention I won't actually qualify for benefits as a long-term sub?"

"What? Are you sure?"

"Yeah. I double checked in my employee portal. Apparently, I'd have to get a regular teaching position for all that to kick in."

"Shit, Daisy, how could you miss something so important?" I realize a second too late that it sounds like I'm scolding her.

"I guess I misunderstood that part when I took the job," she replies meekly.

I sigh. "Have you told your parents? Aren't you still on their insurance?"

She shakes her head. "I'm covered until the end of this month, but I made such a big deal of them taking me off their policy that I *have* to figure this out myself."

"Wouldn't you qualify for Medicaid if you filed for disability, you know, because of the epilepsy?"

"I'm not filing for disability. The whole point of coming out here was to work and become more self-sufficient," she says resolutely.

"Then what the hell are you going to do? You can't go without your anti-seizure meds, right?"

"I guess I'll be saving every spare penny and using it to pay for my prescriptions out of pocket. I should get a permanent position after the holidays, once the home ec teacher retires, which means I should be eligible for coverage after the first of the year."

"And what if you have another episode before then? What if you need to go to the hospital or see your doctor?"

She shrugs shyly. "I suppose all I can do is pray for a nice, seizure-free spell. And in the meantime, I'll luckily be living with an actual doctor—a really good one. Right?"

She sounds like she might be looking for my reassurance, but my mind is already reeling, sorting through the details of her situation in search of a practical solution. "There's gotta be something we can do. I'll call the pharmaceutical company tomorrow to see if I can get you a rebate or some samples of your medication."

"That would actually help a lot, thank you." She reaches out to squeeze my forearm, and I barely resist flinching at the contact. "I don't know how I'd get through all this without you, Landry. You're practically my guardian angel at this point," she continues anyway.

"I'm no angel," I blurt out harshly. She turns her big, round eyes back to me, and I clear my throat in an attempt to soften my tone. "I owe it to Rowan to look after you, don't I?"

"You don't owe my brother anything," she says, shaking her head.

I swallow hard. "He's been good to me over the years. Better than my real family most of the time. The least I can do is treat you like family, too."

"Are you sure you're not just being nice because you're a good person?"

"It's probably because I can't help thinking of you as another little sister since you're just as persistent and stubborn as the one I grew up with."

She bites her lip and looks down at her sewing again. "Well, regardless of your motives, I'm grateful. And I'm not going to stop reminding you of it until you learn to accept a compliment."

My chest warms a bit, and I laugh softly as I reach up to rub it without thinking. "I can see that."

I notice the way her cheeks flush, and they grow even darker when she catches me staring. She tucks her long hair behind her ears, exposing her neck and shoulders again, then her eyelashes flutter and her lips turn up into a demure smile.

Is she ... trying to flirt with me?

No, of course not.

Maybe she's embarrassed? I suppose referring to her as my baby sister might have made her feel worse, especially given the fact that she's not adulting so well.

Either way, I can't acknowledge it without opening up an inconvenient and inappropriate can of worms.

"Don't worry about the insurance stuff. We'll figure this out," I tell her brusquely, then I get up and walk into the kitchen without waiting for her response.

I realize I'm actually hungry once I get there, and I dig around in the pantry before settling on a snack. "So what are we attempting to make for dinner tonight?" I call out after a while.

"I found a new TikTok recipe for scrambled eggs," she jokes from the living room.

I return with a bowl of popcorn and sit beside her again. "Is that really the only thing we can make between the two of us?"

"After the great peanut butter cookie debacle earlier this week, I'm afraid we're limited to omelets and sandwiches, at least for now," she says longingly.

"Maybe we should find a cooking show to record or something." I grab the remote again and pull up the guide.

"I was also thinking we could look into one of those meal delivery kits," she adds, going to trade her sewing project for her phone and inadvertently bumping the new hire forms I left on the coffee table earlier. "Crap on a cracker," she protests as we both reach for the papers scattered on the floor. Our fingers brush, and a spark zaps through me from our point of contact. I yank my hand back and mumble an apology before returning to the couch, chalking it up to static electricity.

She finishes cleaning up and gestures to the forms with a sigh. "It's too bad you can't add me to your insurance policy, right? I could have paid you back for my half of the premium."

I laugh shortly as she joins me on the couch and dips her hand into the bowl of popcorn. "No kidding."

"With the way so many people avoid commitment and refuse to get married these days, you'd think they'd make living together the only prerequisite for coverage," she continues, almost sounding sad about it.

"No—you're right. Maybe there's some kind of loophole," I say thoughtfully before handing her the bowl and picking up the paperwork. She crunches on the popcorn and watches as I skim through the health insurance portion with a renewed purpose.

"Dammit," I curse under my breath after a minute. "It says here that adult partners can only qualify for coverage with documentation of at least one of the following: legal marriage, civil union, current pregnancy, shared children or minor dependents, or domestic partnership of six months or longer."

"Hmm. I don't suppose it would be worth trying to forge the last part."

I drop the papers onto the table again and sigh. "It'd be tough, but possible. We'd have to find a way to make it look like we lived together in Baton Rouge."

"I doubt we could pull it off without my family's help. And I don't like the idea of flat-out lying to them or anyone else," she says, sounding firm.

"Even if it's your only option?"

She shakes her head again. "I'm not willing to sell my soul to save my flesh."

I laugh shortly. "You would say that, little Rowan."

She sticks out her tongue playfully, but I can tell she accepts it as the compliment I intend it to be. The truth is that I've always admired Rowan's moral compass, stringent as it is. I may have given him a hard time over the years about not bringing women home, but besides our views on love and relationships, we shared most of the same values. We'd always agreed that family, school, and work come first, and neither of us cared much for drinking and partying. And while I know I'll never reach the level of genuine goodness or wholesome likability of Rowan or any of the other LaFleurs, I'd be lying if I said I never tried to emulate him or at least consider what he'd say in certain situations. My lack of success with following through with those good intentions is a whole other story, though.

Now I find myself wondering what I'd want Rowan to do if it were Loren facing this same predicament, and the answer is clear—whatever it takes to keep Daisy safe and healthy. Securing her happiness is secondary to her well-being.

"Then that leaves us with no other choice," I begin, only partly conscious of the impulsive move I'm about to make. "We'll have to get married."

Daisy laughs through a mouthful of popcorn. "Yeah, right." But she goes quiet when her eyes meet mine. "Wait, you're not actually serious?"

I shrug. "I'm always serious."

She knocks over the bowl, spilling popcorn everywhere. But she ignores the mess and looks up at me with widened eyes. "You'd really marry me just so I can have health insurance?"

"I can't just let you go the next four or five months without coverage. And I don't really buy into marriage and all that, anyway, so what's the harm?"

Her jaw opens and closes a few times as she tries to find the words. "I don't know what to say. I can't believe you're willing to do this."

"Why not?" I shrug. "It's only temporary. We'll get an annulment after your insurance goes into effect, and it'll be like it never happened. No one else needs to know."

She stares at me a second longer. "And you really think we can pull it off? What happens if either of our families get wind of it?"

"I don't see how they'd find out, but we can tell them whatever you want if they do," I hear myself saying. A tiny voice in the back of my mind objects to the idea of Rowan hearing about this, but my intentions are good, so I don't have anything to hide.

Except I'd probably be tempted to murder any man who married my sister without telling me, regardless of his reasons. Hell, Blake had the courtesy to warn me before he asked my sister to marry him for all the right reasons, and I still wanted to wrap my hands around his throat when I saw him get down on one knee.

"For the record, I think it's better if we keep it quiet," I add after a while, and Daisy nods in agreement.

"What about insurance fraud? Haven't they made movies about this exact scenario?" she asks.

"We're already living together. I doubt anyone would bother investigating us."

She purses her lips and furrows her brow in deep thought. "I guess we can always dress up and look the part when we do get married, just in case. And since we'd only be having a civil ceremony, it wouldn't technically be a *real* wedding, right?"

"None of them are valid to me, so yeah, sure," I reply with a smirk.

She smiles back at me before her eyes grow wide again and her cheeks flush. "We wouldn't have to, you know, consummate anything, would we?"

I force out a laugh, deliberately ignoring the thoughts she conjures up. "Absolutely not."

"Then I don't get it," she mumbles after a while, biting her lip. "What's in it for you?"

Her question catches me off guard, and I lean back as I think about my answer.

"And don't give me any more of that 'I owe it to Rowan' or 'you're like a little sister' baloney," she adds.

"I guess ..." I reach up and run my fingers through my hair. "Maybe I like helping people. Maybe I feel guilty about being a jerk most of the time, and I'm always looking for ways to make up for that."

Her mouth curls up on one side. "Because you're actually a good person with a grumpy exterior?"

I'm already regretting my confession. "Maybe."

"Or am I so pathetic that you think you have to keep stepping in and saving me?" Her chin wobbles as she strains to hold her expression.

I shake my head slowly. "I don't think you're pathetic, Daisy. If anything, I admire your determination, especially since you're not willing to compromise your morals and take the easy way out. But I don't think you've ever really gotten a fair chance. So even though I know you're capable of figuring this out on your own, I want to help you in whatever way I can."

That makes her smile look more genuine again.

"So, just to be clear, you're offering to marry me because you want to make my life easier ... and because you simply care about me as a person—as *your* friend—and not only because I'm Rowan's sister?"

My eyes travel to hers, and I sigh in defeat. "Sure, let's go with that."

Her smile transforms into a full-on grin as she bounces up to tuck her feet beneath her. "Okay, then. I'll consider it."

"You'll consider it?" I retort.

"Well, yeah. Don't you think we should sleep on something this big? Pray about it?"

I grunt, annoyed because she tricked me into admitting all that just to leave me hanging. "You do that, then."

"Landry," she says, her expression almost patronizing. "I want you to have the option to change your mind. If I say yes now, you'll feel obligated to go through with it, even if you find a reason to back out."

The irony of her being the mature adult in this situation and insisting on considering the consequences of our actions isn't lost on me. And it's not very flattering.

"Okay, but you don't have long to make up your mind. There's no point in getting married if we don't get it done before you fall off your parents' policy," I tell her, as if she doesn't know that already. "And I've gotta turn in this paperwork next week."

"I'll have an answer for you by then, I promise," she replies with a smile.

It suddenly feels stifling in the room, so I give her a short nod before I stand abruptly, hoping to put some space between us.

"Landry?"

"Yeah?"

"Thank you. For caring." She lifts one of her nearly bare shoulders and lets it fall, and my attention is temporarily distracted again.

"Yeah—I mean, you're welcome, I guess." I stoop to pick up the spilled popcorn while I cringe at my awkward response. But something catches my eye, and I finally recognize the pile of fabric she set down on the coffee table earlier. It's one of my shirts, but it's no longer missing a button.

"Sorry I couldn't find an exact match," she says from the couch. "But this one's close enough, right?"

I blink down at the formerly empty spot where the new hardware resides, the needle still stuck through one of the button's four holes. No one's ever sewn anything for me before—not even my mom.

My thumb brushes the side of the button, testing it out. But she's secured it well, and she's even managed to cover the holes the old button left behind.

"Uh, yeah. Thanks," I choke out before I let the shirt fall onto the coffee table and retreat into the kitchen.

CHAPTER 8

daisy

My hands tremble as I pour coffee into a pair of mugs. Then I add a bit of cream to each before looping my fingers through the handles and leaving my right hand free to knock on my roommate's bedroom door.

Unless he's my fiancé now?

I'm still in disbelief of Landry's offer to marry me last night. I know he's only acting on some kind of protective instinct, whether it's because I'm Rowan's sister or because of my epilepsy. And he obviously sees this as nothing more than a short-term legal contract. But still ... this is *marriage*. Maybe he doesn't think he'll be interested in getting remarried later, but what if the sacrifice he's making for me now ends up costing him the chance for a real relationship in the future?

I may have been up all night considering the repercussions of this plan, such as the bleak prospect of being a divorced virgin in six months from now, but I can't help but wonder if he's thought any of this through. He made the offer so quickly that he couldn't have realized the gravity of what we'll be doing. Then again, he's already said that he doesn't buy into marriage, so maybe this really isn't such a big deal for him. And he doesn't seem the least bit concerned about any complications, like my brother finding out about our fake marriage or either of us developing romantic feelings for one another.

Ultimately, I'm going to do my best to look on the bright side. I can let all this doubt and stress get the best of me, or I can put my trust in Landry and choose to be grateful that he seems so confident in our plan.

I knock on the door again when he doesn't answer. "Landry, are you up?"

"No," he returns, his voice deep and muffled.

"It sounds like you're up."

"I'm not."

"Can I come in? I have *cof-fee*," I intone.

His groan is loud enough for me to hear. "Fine. Just let me—"

But it's too late. I've already swung the door open to expose him standing there in nothing but his underwear. He coughs and spins around. "Damn, Daisy. Give me enough time to get some pants on."

"Oh, sorry," I squeak, taking the opportunity to admire his butt and the outline of his muscular thighs in those tight boxer briefs while he can't see me checking him out. "I'll turn around until you're ready."

He glances over his shoulder and scoffs when he catches me biting my lip and still staring him down. "Are you going to look away or what?"

"Yep!" I wince and move to cover my face with my free hand, accidentally sloshing hot coffee over the sides of the mugs. "Oh, son of a biscuit eater! That's hot!"

"Shit, Daze," I hear him mutter as he rushes over to take the coffee from me.

"Thanks, and sorry," I say as I lift the hem of my dress to dry my burning hand.

"Are you okay?"

"Mm-hmm. All good."

Just, you know, mortified beyond belief. The usual.

I shake my hand out, hoping the air will cool it off, and try my best not to let my eyes wander over to the frontal view of the very well-endowed man standing just—welp, I tried.

He narrows his eyes at me, obviously annoyed with my lack of propriety, then sets the mugs down on his dresser, and I'm reminded of how small his bedroom really is. He takes my arm and leads me to the kitchen sink, where he gently tends to my burns by running them under cool water.

"Better?" he asks.

"Yes, thank you," I breathe and struggle to keep my eyes on his. Being unable to stop myself from ogling him like a hormonal teenager isn't helping my case for getting him to see me as a capable adult. I should be able to treat the man with respect and dignity, regardless of the fact that seeing him in his underwear makes me *feel* like a hormonal teenager ... or an inexperienced virgin ... even if I technically *am* the latter.

"Are you sure?" he asks, his mouth turning up into a smirk. "You still seem ... off."

I blink and pull my hand back. "I ... I just ... you're making me kind of nervous," I blurt out and cringe.

"Why would I make you nervous?" His eyes search mine earnestly, and I know he's not just flirting. He wants an actual answer.

I shrug shyly. "Well, for starters, I came to your room to tell you that I'm thinking of accepting your proposal."

"Oh," he says, his brow rising.

"Yeah." I pull my hand in and inspect it. An angry, red splotch covers my thumb and part of my wrist. But the burning sensation pales in comparison to the heat radiating from my cheeks. "Although I have a couple of stipulations. Also, I ... um, wanted to ask you for another favor."

"What's that?"

I swallow hard. "I've been feeling a little homesick, and I was really hoping to visit my family this weekend. I know it's a lot to ask, but if you don't already have plans, do you think you might be able to bring me home, just for a few hours?"

His expression softens. "Yeah. Of course. I'll just call my mom and see if she's up for a visit. I doubt she'll mind if I stop by."

"Are you sure?"

"It's nothing," he reassures me with a smile.

"Okay, good, because I was also thinking that if we're really going to do this, we should probably get to know one another a little better, right? I realize we're not going to be acting like husband and wife, but I'd rather not wait until our wedding to hear your full name for the first time," I ramble. "I mean, sure, we've known each other for years and have been living together for the past few weeks, but we haven't really gotten past the surface. So I figured the car ride might give us a chance to fix that."

"Yeah, I guess," he agrees more hesitantly.

"And I know you said I should talk less before, but this stuff seems pretty important," I continue.

He steps in closer, fixing his gaze on my face. "Daisy, are you nervous because you find me attractive?" he asks carefully.

My knees threaten to give out beneath me, and I gulp hard before I manage to form a reply. "I—it shouldn't matter, right? I assumed you didn't intend to leave room for those kinds of feelings in our arrangement."

"No, I didn't," he confirms, his voice deep.

"Then I'm afraid my answer would only keep us from going through with your plan."

"And I thought you just said you wanted to hash all this out now." He crosses his arms and leans back against the counter, and I'm proud of myself when I manage to keep my eyes on his face this time.

"So you'd rather know the truth, even if it's not what you want to hear?"

He shrugs. "Yeah. If we're going to make this plan work, then you can't expect me to spend every second decoding our interactions and worrying about forming an appropriate reply. Socializing is exhausting for me, and I don't want to keep lashing out at you every time I get overwhelmed."

I nod. "That's fair. So how can I make it easier for you?"

"Just tell me what you're thinking, and don't worry about hurting my feelings."

"Should we make it a thing that we're always completely honest with one another, even when it's embarrassing and awkward?" I offer.

He exhales, his posture immediately looking more relaxed. "Yes, please."

"Okay, then. We'll start now." I lift my chin to look him in the eyes. "Since you asked, I think you're a very handsome man, Landry, but I'm going to disregard that because we've both agreed to a platonic relationship. The last thing I want is to risk making you uncomfortable, especially since you don't find me attractive."

He blinks at me, looking surprised by my candidness. "I never said I didn't find you attractive."

And now I'm wondering whether I didn't splash hot coffee on my face at some point.

"You ... you have, though. Just not in so many words," I choke out.

"I haven't been allowing myself to think of you that way at all, since nothing good could possibly come of it," he explains, staring at me with a solemn expression. "I can't be tempted to take you up on any offers later if there's a chance you end up feeling like you owe me something. It'd be like I was taking advantage of you."

I bite my lip. "I see. I don't think we're in danger of anything like that happening, though." We're both quiet for a minute before I go on. "This probably won't come as a surprise to you, but between my disability and the way my parents sheltered me for so long, I've missed out on a lot of life experience, particularly when it comes to dating and relationships."

"So, you're also nervous because you haven't been around a lot of men in their underwear before now?" he asks, narrowing his eyes.

"At least none that aren't related to me," I say with a shrug.

He furrows his brow. "Then by a lack of *experience*, you mean—"

"I'm a virgin, Landry. But I'm thinking you should have guessed that by now," I retort dryly.

"Oh." His eyes grow wider before he seemingly catches himself and tries to look aloof again.

"That's why I'm sure I'm not going to end up throwing myself at you. Because that's not an offer I extend to anyone outside of marriage—I mean, a real marriage," I add the last part quietly.

He nods and clears his throat. "I assume this is some of the stuff you wanted to discuss on the ride to Baton Rouge?"

"Exactly," I confirm.

"Right. Well, um, not that you're asking, but I guess you'd want to know that I'm ... not ... inexperienced."

I bite back a smile at the way he fidgets, as if he's just remembered he's in his underwear. "I didn't expect you were."

"I'm obviously not like, as bad as Blake used to be or anything. I'm just ... I mean, I've had ..." He shrugs and reaches up to scratch the back of his head.

"Somewhere in between, then?" I ask, unable to contain my grin this time.

He purses his lips. "Yeah. Let's go with that."

"And you've never been married before? Or had any kids?"

"No." He shakes his head quickly. "No crazy exes or anything, either."

"Good. I mean, that simplifies things."

"Yeah."

We nod in agreement as the silence stretches. "Should I make us some more coffee for the road?"

"Sure, that'd be great. I'm just gonna," he pauses to tilt his head in the direction of his bedroom, "get less naked. I mean, I should probably be wearing clothes when we tell your brother we're living together. We don't want Rowan to get the wrong idea, right?"

"Mm-hmm," I squeak, unable to stop myself from taking him in one more time.

"Meet you in the Jeep in a few minutes?"

I shoot him a thumbs up before I remember my burns, then I cringe and hide my hand behind my back. He smirks before he moves to go around me, looking amused. But then we accidentally do one of those painfully awkward shuffles in which we both step to the same side and block one another's passage through the tiny kitchen. It takes three tries before we manage to escape, including one full-on body bump that's certain to haunt me for the rest of my life.

daisy

THIRTY MINUTES LATER, we're merging onto the interstate, each of us sipping from the travel mugs I fixed. I'd offered for him to join me in a rosary earlier, since it's a LaFleur tradition to start a longer drive that way, but he politely passed.

"So, uh, I was thinking we could just take turns asking one another questions, but that we could answer our own questions, too," I begin once I put my rosary away.

"Okay," he agrees hesitantly. "Are we doing the full transparency thing now, or are we allowed to pass on some of these?"

"We might as well base this fake marriage on honesty, right?" I offer, and he huffs out a laugh.

"Might as well," he agrees, and I adjust my position in the passenger seat to face him.

"First question, what's your middle name?"

"That's an easy one," he mumbles. "It's Nicholas."

I smirk. "We have the same name."

"What?"

"I'm Daisy Colette, named after St. Colette, who was named after St. Nicholas."

He hums. "How 'bout that."

"Yeah." We're both quiet for a second, and I whisper a prayer for the intercession of our patron saints. "Your turn to ask a question," I say once I'm done.

"I'm not sure I'm …" He frowns and coughs lightly. "Why don't you handle the questions for now?"

"Isn't there something you'd like to know about me before giving me your last name?"

He shrugs. "I don't really do relationships, so I don't bother asking about this stuff most of the time. And the only questions that come to mind now are related to your medical history."

"Oh," I reply thoughtfully. "Well, ask away. I don't mind. You have a right to know exactly what you're getting yourself into."

"It's not that. I just … I'm not sure I know how to care about anything else."

I turn to regard his expression again. His eyes are on the road ahead of him, but I can see the wheels turning in his head.

"Landry, have you ever been in love?"

He flinches and glares at me. "What?"

"Have you ever been in love?" I repeat. "It's my next question."

"I thought we were asking about favorite colors or candy preferences," he mutters.

"Mint green, obviously, and candy corn, specifically the pumpkins. But you know I don't eat candy often because processed sugar makes me more susceptible to seizures. You?"

"Uh," he flounders for a second, apparently caught off guard again. "Dark green, I guess. And I don't eat much candy, either. But I used to like those little caramel jellybean things. Sugar Babies?" I nod, and he glances my way before he goes on, "Not the ones on the stick, though. I'm not a fan of eating anything on a stick."

I smile at the way his lip curls up in disgust. "Why not?"

"I don't know. Apart from it being slightly emasculating, there's something about the idea of waving my food in the air as I eat it that just …" He pauses to shiver. "I also hate reusable straws. No way those things get completely clean."

"Are you a germaphobe?"

"No, I just have a few specific sensory things, especially when it comes to food."

"Is that why you don't like your toothbrush being near a menstrual cup?"

"Yeah, I guess," he replies with a soft laugh. "I'm not afraid of bodily fluids or anything natural, but I am weird about my toothbrush."

I hum in affirmation, thinking about whether I want to ask about his aversion to physical affection. But I decide not to push my luck, since I haven't even gotten him to answer the first personal question.

"My mom was always in favor of developing natural immunities, so I imagine I'm a 'rub some essential oils on it' kind of girl," I say instead, and he nods appreciatively. "Okay, your turn again."

He narrows his eyes at me. "Did you really give me a free pass on that other question, or are you just trying to distract me long enough to bring it up again later, while my guard is down?"

I bite my lip and stifle a smile. "I don't know what you're talking about."

He shakes his head, but he looks more impressed than upset. "I meant what I said the other day about not buying into that crap. Love, marriage, soulmates ... none of it is legit. You can't convince me it's nothing more than a combination of lust and codependency."

"Wow," I say on a sigh. "The cynicism runs deep."

"Yeah. I earned it."

I pull my hair over my shoulder and idly begin braiding it, trying to resist the urge to push him too far. "Can I ask about that?" I venture after a while.

He runs his tongue over his teeth and stares at the road again. "My parents got pregnant and married young. My dad realized a little later that he wasn't interested in following through with most of his vows, but my mom never stopped trying to win him over. Her disappointment led to depression, which led to alcoholism and some light drug abuse, which led to me and my siblings basically raising ourselves while my dad kept his head in the sand. It wasn't until after my mom went through a few rounds of rehab and we'd all moved out on our own that she finally gave up and asked for a divorce."

I reach over and squeeze his forearm, and his jaw muscles tick, but he waits a full second before he tugs his arm away.

"Is that why you're so protective of Loren?" I ask softly.

"Mostly."

"I'm sorry."

"Don't be. I don't need your pity," he retorts.

"It's not pity," I reply, frowning. "I'm genuinely sad to hear you never got to experience the kind of love I've always known in my family. Just like you're sorry I've missed out on stuff because I was a sickly kid, right?"

He clenches his jaw tightly again. "Yeah. I guess."

"Unless you think I'm pathetic because I never went to prom or a high school football game or any of the other things you probably enjoyed doing as a normal teenager," I go on.

"I don't think you're pathetic because you never went to prom," he grinds out after a while. "But there's no excuse for never having gone to a high school football game."

I can't help it when a laugh bubbles up, and I notice the way his lips twitch, as if he's fighting a smile of his own.

"Did you play football?"

"Yes. And my dad coached."

"Oh, right. I knew that. What position did you play?"

He turns and smirks at me. "Would you know the difference?"

"Not really," I reply, making him chuckle.

"I was the backup quarterback, and I alternated at wide receiver and linebacker."

I frown. "Your dad didn't make you the starting quarterback?"

He clicks his tongue. "He let me start for one year, until this other guy who was just a little better got to high school."

The realization hits me, and I cringe. "Let me guess, he had a younger brother who was also good at football?"

"Bingo."

I stare at his profile as I continue. "Did you love it? Playing ball?"

"Yeah, I did," he says thoughtfully. "Despite my dad and the Bourgeois brothers nearly ruining it for me, I still loved the game. And I was good at it, even if I wasn't as good as Blake or JD."

"I bet you were better. I imagine it was hard being the coach's son and getting held to a higher standard," I tell him.

But he shakes his head and smiles wistfully. "Having something to prove only made me work harder. In the end, the competition was good for me. I enjoyed being a part of the team. And as much as it hurts to admit it, I still claim some of the bragging rights I earned from playing alongside a kid who ended up in the pros."

We laugh together before I start again. "Landry?"

"Hmm?"

He turns to look at me for a second, and my stomach flutters. He really is a handsome man, and I'd be lying if I said he doesn't make me feel things I've never felt before. But I'm not here to throw myself at him, especially when he's so far out of my league. Not to mention, I'll never become self-sufficient without his help, as ironic as that seems.

I swallow hard. "Will you take me to a game? You know, at school, and teach me how it all works?"

His smile grows wider. "Yeah, sure."

"Thanks," I breathe, looking away when I feel my cheeks flush.

"All right, enough about me," he says after a second. "Why don't you just do me a favor and tell me all the rest of the stuff you think I need to know?"

I perk up. Not for the chance to talk about myself, but because I get to coerce Landry into spilling the same details later. "Okay, let's see ... I love plants and gardening. I can't cook or bake all that well because my mom and sisters thought it wouldn't be safe to let me near the stove with my epilepsy, so they assigned other chores to me instead, like tending to the animals and some of the smaller gardens, washing the dishes, and folding the laundry. I prefer homemade to store-bought gifts. I enjoy reading, but I'd rather do it outside. My dad always played John Denver around the farm, so his music makes me happy. My faith is very important to me, although you knew that already. And my sisters are great, but Rowan has always been my favorite sibling."

He hums. "If you enjoy that whole homesteading-Jesus-hippie lifestyle so much, then why are you out here in Camellia all by yourself?"

I try not to let him see how much his question deflates me. "Because it's a good opportunity."

"Opportunity for what?"

"To prove I can make it on my own, like I said before," I tell him, but I can't bring my eyes up from my lap. "And even though I miss my family, I guess I was tired of being the only one left at home."

"Do you even want to be a teacher?"

"What?"

He clears his throat. "I like baseball and football, but golf is my favorite sport. It's relaxing, and I'm good at it. And since I'm not a big drinker, I usually beat the pants off everyone when I play in a group, because I'm the only sober one left by the back nine."

I turn to stare at him with wide eyes, and he gives me a sad smile. "Even though Lo and I mostly fended for ourselves as kids, I never really learned to cook, either. We ate a lot of sandwiches. I love my Jeep." He pauses to stroke the dash before he continues, "but besides that, I don't really care much about material possessions, because efficiency and utility are more important than beauty. Country music annoys me because it's too sappy; I listen to medical podcasts instead. Your brother is the only real friend I've ever had."

He stops again and sighs, as if this next part requires more courage to say. "I was diagnosed with ADHD when I was a kid, and I've always struggled to balance the anxious overthinking with actually thinking before I act. You already know I get mean when I'm over-stimulated or stressed. I wanted to join the military, but I was afraid of failing the psychological eval, and I couldn't bring myself to leave my family. It ended up being for the best, though, since I enjoy being a pediatrician. I'm horrible in most social situations, except for when I get to work with kids. They're honest and blunt, and they accept my help. And helping people is the only thing that makes me feel good."

My heart swells when I realize what he's doing, and it takes all I have to keep my eyes from watering as I pick up where he left off. "I don't mind teaching, but I don't love it, either. I'm only doing it because no one believes I can handle anything else. My family never supported my plans to move out or start a career, but when Rowan suggested I come to Camellia to take Loren's place for a while, my parents actually encouraged me to give it a try. They said this would be a perfect fit, since teachers get such great health benefits and all that time off. But I think they only backed me this time because it's a temporary setup. All they saw was the chance for me to get this out of my system without leaving as big of a mess behind when I fail."

He frowns. "What do you really want to do with your life?"

I lift a shoulder. "I guess I haven't thought that far ahead. I just want to be self-sufficient for now." It's only a half-truth, but I'm not confident in any other answers.

"Okay, then. That's what we'll work on until I move out," he says, his voice firm but gentle.

Warmth spreads throughout my chest, and a smile overtakes my face. "Only if you let me help you, too."

He sighs as if he's unsure whether to acknowledge my offer. "How could you possibly help me?"

"I'm not sure yet," I answer honestly. "But don't worry. I won't force you to accept a payment toward my marital debt." I feel myself blushing again as I deliver the last part, especially when he doesn't laugh. I glance over and see him looking confused as he pulls into a gas station parking lot.

"Need anything inside?" he asks gruffly, and I shake my head, still embarrassed because my suggestive joke fell flat. He returns a few minutes later, empty handed.

"You didn't get any snacks at all?" I ask, my voice laced with disappointment.

"No. Because you said you didn't want anything. And I didn't want anything. Hence, nothing."

I pout. "You really don't know how this works, do you?"

"Not a clue," he replies, smiling.

"When a woman says she doesn't want a snack, it's because she's too shy to ask for one, or she's so hangry that she doesn't know what she wants to eat," I explain.

"And how would you know this stuff if you haven't been in relationships either?"

"I've lived with a lot of women over the years, Landry," I retort mockingly. "And it's not like I've never dated at all. It's just hard to progress with either my epilepsy or my virginity getting in the way."

He frowns. "There are guys out there who refused to date you because of something you can't control?"

I notice he only addresses the epilepsy part of my confession. "Yes, but most of the time my health has been the problem. I can't saddle someone I barely know with this kind of life, not when they don't understand."

"They're idiots if they can't see what they're missing out on," he says. "And if any man ever pressures you into sleeping with him, even if he says he's willing to marry you, I want to know his name."

I roll my eyes, unable to stifle a smile. "Don't worry. Some guy is offering to take me off the market for the next few months, and I'm thinking I'm going to accept him."

He grunts. "I heard he's an asshole, though."

"Nope. But he does have some of those *tendencies*."

landry

"So, how is it being back home?" Rowan poses as we sit on the front porch of his parents' house together. I'd gone for a short visit at my mom's before returning to pick up Daisy and found him waiting out here when I drove up.

I heave out an exhale. "It's been ... well, it hasn't been easy after everything that's happened with Loren and the babies."

He nods knowingly. "I'm glad they're all okay, but that's not what I meant. How have you been getting along with your family?"

I frown, slightly offended. "Good enough."

"And you're fine with the engagement?"

My stomach and my jaw both drop, and it takes a full three seconds for me to realize he's referring to Blake's proposal to my sister and not my proposal to his. Although Rowan and I had spoken about Loren's emergency delivery a few times, I hadn't mentioned her engagement. But Daisy must be keeping him posted on the latest developments.

"I'm not thrilled about it," I say. "But Lo seems bound and determined to learn the hard way."

"You do know they were already a thing by the time we went out, right?" he asks with a smirk.

"Yeah, unless you're trying to tell me the twins are yours," I reply sarcastically. But we've both seen Loren's conception date in her chart before, and as far as I know, Rowan's chances of biologically fathering a baby are impossible.

He rolls his eyes. "I mean he actually crashed our date. I don't know whether it was planned, but Blake was at the restaurant where we were having dinner."

I huff. "Of course he was."

"He came over to our table to stake his claim, and Loren's whole demeanor changed the second she saw him, even though she tried to pretend like she was upset about it. But they couldn't take their eyes off one another for the rest of the night. It wasn't surprising when she ended the evening with an awkward hug and an apology for realizing too late that a two-hour commute 'just wouldn't be fair to either of us.' Then I drove home assuming she'd turned right around and went back into that restaurant to meet him," he explains, smiling wistfully.

"Is this supposed to make me feel better about you not giving me a head's up when you caught my baby sister screwing around with the same condescending asshole who once slept his way through an entire sorority?"

"Your sister is a thirty-one-year-old woman, Landry," he reminds me. "And, yeah, I realized he was *that* Blake Bourgeois after he introduced himself, but it wasn't my business to tell Loren who she should date. And it was never your right or responsibility, either."

"That's not how I've always seen it," I mutter under my breath.

"Is that why you tried to set us up for so many years?" he asks after a while. "You figured you were better off with the evil you knew?"

"You're both nerdy. I honestly thought you'd be a perfect match. And yeah, if she's dead set on getting married and having babies, I'd rather see her end up with someone more like you." I sigh again and add the last part quietly. "I also know how much you want to get married and have a family."

He leans over and shoves my shoulder playfully. "There he is, there's Doctor Reed." I furrow my brow. "Sometimes Landry can be abrasive, even though he means well. But Doc Reed is just a big teddy bear, and you know it."

My lips twitch as I fight the smile threatening to overtake my face. "I take back all that mushy shit I just said. No wonder my sister wasn't into you."

He laughs again. "So, speaking of bro codes and all, when were you going to tell me?"

Panic hits me again before I remember he's only talking about Daisy and me moving in together, and I force an apologetic smile. "I'm sorry, man. There was a mix up with Loren's house, and Daisy insisted I take the spare bedroom—just until I find something else," I fib. That's technically how it started, anyway.

"Really? And you listened?" His eyebrows shoot up in surprise.

"Only as a favor to you," I add quickly. "I mean, I know the two of you have always been close and figured you'd appreciate someone looking after Daisy on your behalf."

"Hmm," he hums. "I guess that means *my* baby sister's living with Dr. Reed and not Lando?"

I nod, but I can't tell whether he's really buying my story. "I'm trying my best to be nice. And you have my word—nothing's going to happen."

Nothing that can't be undone with an annulment, anyway.

"Oh, I don't doubt that," he says, looking more amused than anything. Frankly, I'm a little offended by the implication that he doesn't seem to think I'm as worthy of his little sister as I thought he was of mine. "I assumed she'd wrangled you into this from the start and that you'd only said yes so you could have someone to take care of. You know, now that your mom's doing well on her own and Loren doesn't need you as much."

I scoff. "Tell me how you really feel, bruh."

"Why not? You never spare the rest of us," he retorts, and it's one of the only times he's ever been this short with me.

"Sorry," I say quietly. "No one hates the garbage that comes out of my mouth more than I do."

"I know, man." His expression softens again. "But you can't

blame me for worrying about how your disposition might affect Daisy, even if I know you have the best intentions most of the time."

I nod again. "I'm working on it." *But I'm failing miserably.*

"Let her help you," he says plainly.

"What?" I rear my head.

"It's like when you tried to set me up with Loren. You just wanted to see me happy, right? I know you care about me, even if you can't bring yourself to say it out loud. And this is me telling you that I care about you, too, and that you deserve to be happy."

I cock an eyebrow. "I don't understand what this has to do with Daisy and me living together."

"Daisy's good at seeing the positive in everything."

"So what? How is that going to turn me into an optimist?"

"Why don't you try letting her rub off on you?" he suggests with a shrug.

"You really think all it's going to take for me to get over the shit I've been struggling with for the better part of my life is to try sticking a freaking flower in my hair and going around acting like everything's great even when it's not?"

He sighs. "I was actually referring to her willingness to offer up her suffering for others. It's not that far off from the way you've always been willing to make sacrifices for the people around you, only she does it with a smile and a prayer intention."

I look away. "I should have known you'd try to make this religious."

"Look, Landry, I've never tried to force my beliefs on you because I always figured it'd be more effective if I let you come around to it on your own," he says, his expression more serious than usual. "The truth is the truth, regardless of our ability to stomach it. And you may be stubborn, but you're too smart not to recognize the truth for what it is, even if it takes you a while."

"But Daisy's not as patient as you are, is she?" I venture after a second.

He nods. "And if you can't deal with that, then you'd better back out now. Because I'm not letting you break her spirit, man."

I clench my jaw and stare him down, and thankfully Daisy and her mom walk outside to meet us before I have to give him a verbal answer.

I acknowledge his terms with a short nod of my own, and he turns to embrace Daisy while Mrs. LaFleur hugs me and offers her gratitude.

"Thank you again for this," Daisy says as we pull onto the road.

"No worries."

She takes in a breath. "Landry, can I ask you for one more thing?"

I glance over at her and nod.

"I can't put you in a position that would force you to sin. So before we go through with this, you have to promise me you won't lie about it."

"You mean, you don't want us to keep it a secret?" I ask, furrowing my brow.

"No, I definitely think we should keep it to ourselves. But if anyone finds out, including Rowan, you have to tell the truth."

"Okay."

"And we'll probably need to write our own vows. We can't go in front of a judge and make promises we don't intend to keep."

"All right," I say, biting back a smile. "I'm sure that's doable."

"Thank you." She exhales, sounding relieved.

"Is that how you plan to help me?" I ask after a while. "By protecting my integrity?"

"Nah, you're already a good person. But you could probably use some help letting everyone else see how good you are."

daisy

Landry and I both make it into the kitchen at the same time. His expression softens when he sees me in a white sundress.

"You look really nice," he says quietly, shoving one of his hands into his pocket and fiddling with his car keys in the other.

"Thanks, so do you." He's wearing a fitted, white button down and dark slacks with a mint green tie. "My favorite color," I add, pointing to the tie.

He shrugs shyly and reaches up to adjust it. "I didn't have anything light green, but Lo let me raid Blake's closet. And don't worry, I didn't tell her why I needed it."

My stomach flutters when I think about the implications of him going out of his way for something so small. "That was really thoughtful of you."

He shrugs again. "It was nothing. Grabbed these, too." He pulls a hand from his pocket and opens his palm to reveal a couple of simple gold bands. "Were you able to get your flowers?"

"Right here." I gesture to the kitchen counter where a small bouquet of pink and white camellias, roses, and daisies sits. "I made the arrangement myself."

"You did a great job," he replies awkwardly, shoving his hand back into his pocket.

I smile and blush at his compliment, then I step forward to straighten his tie. "Sorry, it's still a little crooked," I say, trying not to dwell on the feeling of his firm chest beneath my fingers or how good he smells.

"All done." I take a step back. "Ready to go?"

He exhales. "I guess it's now or never."

It's not the most romantic thing I've ever heard, but this isn't exactly a romantic proposition, so I'll take what I can get.

He takes me out to his Jeep and opens the door for me to climb inside, and he's quiet on the way to the courthouse. In fact, he's frowning at the road as he drives.

"So, um, you mentioned making an appointment with the judge?" I ask, breaking the silence.

"Yes. I called ahead so we could go right in. I'm hoping it'll give us more privacy."

"Good thinking," I tell him with a forced smile as he pulls into the parking lot.

"I don't see Blake's truck here, so I guess that's a good sign. I was worried he'd have court today," he says to himself, then he lets out a shaky exhale.

"Landry, wait." I reach out and stop him as he goes for the door. "Are you sure you want to go through with this? I mean, I completely understand if you need to back out."

He furrows his brow as he turns to face me. "Have you changed your mind?"

"No," I say quickly. "But I don't want you to have any regrets."

"It's strange," he says absently, "but I can't shake this feeling ..."

"Hey, if your heart is telling you something isn't right, then you should listen to it. It could be the Holy Spirit, you know?" I offer with a sad smile.

"No, it's not like that. I think I've been waiting for something to come up, like a sign that we shouldn't do this. But the only thing bothering me is that I don't feel bad about it."

I blink away my surprise. "Oh."

"Maybe it's because I'm sort of apathetic about marriage in

general, but I can't think of a good reason not to move forward with our plan. How do you feel?" he asks me.

I close my eyes and take a deep breath before I answer, searching for a trace of that doubt he mentioned. But it's not there. "I feel ... safe." I grasp his hand and squeeze it. "Nervous, but safe. Strangely confident in our decision, but also anxious and excited because ... well, because it's my wedding day, I guess."

He smiles and nods. "Yeah. Same."

I don't tell him that last part feels more like butterflies or that I suspect he's the reason those butterflies have taken up permanent residence in my stomach. But they must be here because of Landry, since I'm pretty sure they arrived the moment he agreed to shack up with me.

I glance down at the bundle of flowers in my lap as the silver crucifix from my favorite rosary glints in the sunlight. I'd tucked the string of mint green beads into my bouquet earlier. It might seem silly or even superstitious to anyone else, especially when this isn't a sacramental wedding, but I've always loved this tradition. I usually carry some form of a rosary on me as both a reminder to say the prayers and a reassurance that Mama Mary has my back. Aside from the sacraments, intercessory prayer is one of my favorite elements of the Catholic faith. I still pray directly, of course. But I take comfort in knowing that I can ask the Blessed Mother to whisper into Jesus' ear on my behalf, especially since He has a hard time denying his mother's requests.

"Landry." I turn to face him. "I think we should pray together first."

He flinches. "I ... I don't ..."

I reach over and take his hand in mine, but he looks like he's barely managing not to tug it back. "I know this isn't a ceremony ordained by God or anything like that, and I realize it's somewhat ironic since we aren't doing this because we're *in* love. But this is still a great act of love and charity on your part, one that I'm unbelievably grateful for."

Landry's throat bobs, and he nods hesitantly, and I could swear his eyes even look a little glossy. "You'll have to say it, though—the prayer."

I smile and give his hand a slight squeeze before I use the other to make the sign of the cross, stifling a laugh at the way he adorably and awkwardly tries to use his left hand to mime the gesture. Then I repeat my affirmations, adding a request for God to bless us in our endeavor before leading Landry in the Our Father, Hail Mary, and Glory Be.

I sneak a peek at him and watch his lips twitch slightly, as if he's at least attempting the prayers, and that small effort is enough to reinforce our decision.

He lets go of my hand once we're done and swallows hard again. "Okay. I can't believe I'm saying this, but let's go get married."

"Okay," I affirm.

He walks around the car for my door, and I quickly flip down the visor mirror to check my appearance. Then I take the hand he offers while holding my bouquet in the other and let him lead me into the courthouse.

The next fifteen minutes or so are a blur, and I'm grateful Landry's so thorough in his planning, because those butterflies have started kicking my butt. My hands are trembling so badly that I can hear the rosary beads rattling in my bouquet. It's all I can do to follow his lead like a lost puppy.

Before I know it, we're standing in front of a judge and a clerk, holding hands and exchanging rings as we repeat our amended wedding vows. Strange as it sounds, making a promise to respect, honor, and support Landry for the rest of my life feels like the most natural part of all this. He doesn't waiver when it's his turn to stare into my eyes and make the same pledge, confirming my suspicions about his inherent goodness, and I choke back an unexpected sob when I realize there will always be some part of me that loves him. How could I feel any other way about the man who's willing to do this for me?

"By the power vested in me by the great state of Louisiana, I now pronounce you husband and wife." The judge smiles. "You may kiss your bride, son."

Landry's expression shifts to one of terror, killing the warm, fuzzy vibes we had going a second ago. I guess he hadn't thought this far ahead, though I've been lying awake nearly every night since we agreed to our marriage of convenience and wondering whether he'd kiss me at the altar—or the desk, I suppose.

The judge glances back and forth between us, confused by our hesitation, so I lean in and aim my lips at Landry's cheek. He must have the same idea, because he places a hand on my back and turns his face at the same time I close in, bumping his mouth awkwardly into mine. Our lips meet for a second, barely long enough to consider it a real kiss, albeit a closed-mouth one.

But a moment later, something different flashes across his dark eyes. He takes me by surprise and splays his hand over my spine, urging me closer so he can intentionally press his lips back to mine. I instinctively close my eyes and lean into the kiss, and he tilts his head to the side as he slips his tongue into my mouth. My free hand flies up to his chest as I take him in, but he pulls away abruptly, ending it as quickly as it began.

My cheeks burn after we part, and I roll my lips in, wishing they'd stop tingling. Landry clears his throat loudly and furrows his brow. I can't tell whether he's confused or embarrassed but knowing his aversion to any and all public displays of physical affection, I imagine it's the second. He must have decided we needed to make the kiss look realistic in front of our audience and regretted his decision as soon as I reciprocated too enthusiastically.

"Congratulations, Dr. and Mrs. Reed," the judge continues, grinning this time. He holds out his hand for Landry to shake, then turns his attention to the marriage certificate sitting on his desk. The clerk shows us where to sign before she jots down her own signature, and the bailiff at the door comes over to fill in the last witness line. I ask the clerk to take a couple of photos with my phone, just in case we need them later, and my heart races when Landry pulls me close to pose as a happy couple again. Then we're ushered out into the hallway to wait there for the official copies we'll need to add my name to Landry's health insurance policy.

"Well, that didn't take long," Landry mumbles absentmindedly.

"No, it didn't." I glance down at the plain, gold band resting on my left hand. I can't help the way my eyes immediately water. I know this is what I agreed to, and it's not like I expected or even hoped Landry would change his mind and want this to be a real marriage. I honestly couldn't consider this any more than a legal contract, either, despite my admiration of him. But that doesn't stop my chin from trembling as reality sets in.

Landry shoots me a pitying look, and I lose control of my tear ducts. "Dammit," he curses under his breath and darts into the nearest bathroom to retrieve a tissue. "You're already having regrets, aren't you?" he asks when he returns.

I try to cover up my sniffling and accept his offering. "No, no, I'm fine, just unexpectedly emotional." I pull away and wipe beneath my eyes. "I hadn't accounted for trapping my roommate into a marriage of convenience and guilting him into a courthouse wedding when I dreamed about this day as a little girl, you know," I say with a light chuckle, but Landry stares at me for a moment.

"Daisy ..." His voice is hoarse when he finally speaks up. "I meant what I said before. You're not trapping me into anything, and you're not a burden, okay?"

I nod, unable to meet his eyes. Then I hear him groan before he reaches out to wrap his arms around me. My body instantly melts into his while my mouth curls up into a smile. A hug and a kiss from him in the same day? I'm on a roll.

"This is the kind of stuff friends and family do for one another," he continues over my shoulder, reaching up to gently stroke my back.

Friends and family ...

It's too bad my husband will only ever see me as one if not both of those and not as a wife, a partner, or even a lover.

I let out a small whine, annoyed at myself for throwing an unwarranted pity party. I knew exactly what to expect from this arrangement. It's too late to feel sorry for myself now.

But it's my wedding day … and I may never get another one.

I cling to him a second longer, indulging in his intoxicatingly woodsy cologne and rugged chest muscles while I can—you know, just in case. He moves my hair over and away from my face, and his fingertips begin trailing lightly over my neck and shoulders as if he's tracing a pattern. I shiver, and he sighs.

"You okay?" he asks tentatively, probably mistaking that shiver for a sob.

"Mm-hmm," I squeak out. "You?"

He pulls away to check on me anyway before he answers. "I'm fine."

"Thank you, Landry," I breathe.

"Reed?" a voice calls out.

"I guess that's us," Landry says with a shy smile, making those butterflies in my stomach flutter around again. He leaves me standing there to retrieve a copy of our marriage certificate, and we're both silent as we walk to the car together and he drives us home.

A heavy awkwardness settles over everything by the time we find ourselves standing in the kitchen together. It's not the same demure apprehension that lingered between us the last time we stood in this same spot just over an hour ago. This time, there's a quiet, clumsy *what now?* hanging in the air.

I set my bouquet down and begin picking at one of the roses while he leans back against the counter, crossing his arms and drumming his fingers idly over his elbow. He stops and looks down at the ring on his left hand before he hides it behind the opposite arm.

"So, um, I guess I'm good to turn in that paperwork now," he offers after a while.

"Right," I return with a forced smile.

He nods absently. "What should we have for dinner tonight?"

I sigh. "I'm not even sure what I'm going to have for lunch."

He huffs out a laugh. "You're right. It's only eleven in the morning." I fidget uncomfortably, and he opens his mouth to speak again.

"There's something I've been meaning to ask you. What's 'marital debt?' "

"Hmm?" I squeak.

"You mentioned it before, but I'm not familiar with the phrase."

I feel the tips of my ears reddening. "Oh. Well, it's um ... are you sure you've never heard the term before?"

He shakes his head. "No. Is it a trad-Catholic thing?"

I shrug. "I guess you could say that."

"I almost asked Rowan what it meant the other day, but I figured it'd be suspicious out of context."

A small, strangled sound escapes my throat. "Please tell me you didn't?"

He lifts an eyebrow. "So it's ... *that* kind of debt?"

"I don't think the euphemism was intended to exclusively refer to the type of debt you'd be calling in right now if we would have gotten married for any other reason, but yeah ... pretty much." My stomach dips at the mere thought of what a real wedding night with Landry might look like.

His eyes flare slightly, but we're interrupted by his phone chiming before he can say more. "Sorry, it's Lo," he mumbles. "She wants to know when we were planning to tell her that we moved in together."

"Should we have asked her before we made that arrangement since this is technically still her house?" I cringe.

He shrugs and frowns down at the phone. "It shouldn't make a difference to her. She should be worrying about her babies and not about our living arrangements, anyway." But his face reddens, and he clenches his jaw as he continues reading. Then he growls under his breath as he types in a quick reply.

"Is she upset?" I venture.

He huffs and puts the phone away. "She's questioning my intentions for moving in with you."

"Oh," I say on a laugh. "No worries there."

My comment doesn't seem to register with him, though. He's too angry now. "Yeah, well, she doesn't have much room to talk in this situation."

"I'm sure if I explained why I need you to drive me around, she'd understand."

"I thought you didn't want anyone else to know about your last couple of seizures?"

I shrug. "She should know that you're doing this out of the kindness of your heart and not because you're trying to hook up with me. And I'm sure I can trust her, right?"

But he shakes his head. "Don't bother. There's nothing you can say to make my sister think I'm anything but a jerk." The way he says it so matter-of-factly makes my chest ache. "But, hey, at least you know she cares about you, right?" he adds sardonically.

I sigh. "Yeah. Look who's becoming the optimist now."

"I guess you're rubbing off on me," he replies, his tone still flat. "Anyway, back to lunch. How does this work now that we're married?"

"What do you mean?" I ask.

"Which one of us is supposed to make the other a sandwich?" he poses, stifling a smirk as he reaches up to loosen his tie.

A laugh escapes before I can stop myself. "Should we make fancy ones today?"

"Oh, you're right. While you're at it, I want extra jam on mine," he says with a grin, but he's already walking toward the fridge to get the ingredients. And I can't help the way my chest tightens against my will when he goes out of his way to make me feel better for the umpteenth time today.

He places a jar of strawberry preserves on the counter at the same time I reach for the bread, my left hand bumping his. We both freeze in place to stare down at the gold bands we slipped on earlier.

Landry coughs lightly before he jerks his hand back. "Guess we won't be needing these, right?" He removes his ring and holds it up with a rueful smile.

"Right," I agree quietly, and he wanders off, presumably to put the ring away.

I follow his lead, stopping in front of a small jewelry box on my dresser. I glance up to find a green ribbon hanging from a bulletin board, and I loop the ribbon through the ring instead.

By the time I return to the kitchen, Landry's already busy

spreading peanut butter over bread. I notice he's removed his tie and left the top buttons of his shirt undone when he cranes his neck to smile at me over his shoulder, reminding me of how much I like him already.

Did I really expect myself to walk away unscathed after living with him? Is it even possible *not* to fall for my husband?

"Here," he says, bringing me back from my thoughts. "I cut them into triangles, since you seemed to like that last time."

I take the plate from him, our fingers brushing again, and my mind flashes back to the feeling of his hand on my back, coaxing my body closer to his as he pressed his lips to mine. I glance up at his mouth and swallow hard.

"Thanks," I murmur, trying to tear my eyes away. But all I manage to do is shift my focus to the patch of exposed skin between his throat and his chest. It's really too bad he's not interested in collecting that debt.

"No worries, Mrs. Reed," he replies coyly before he turns back to the kitchen.

I sigh. Maybe it's my intentions Loren should be questioning.

landry

"Go on in, Daisy. Staff and families get in free," says the lady in the admissions ticket booth.

"Thanks, Mrs. Julie," Daisy answers. I tip my head in a polite nod as I follow closely behind her.

"Excuse me, sir," Mrs. Julie calls out.

I stop and clear my throat. I've never paid to get into a Camellia High athletics event in my life. "It's okay. I'm Landry Reed," I reassure her.

She glares at me. "Right. But your dad's not a coach anymore, and you can't get in for free under your sister's name or your brother-in-law's coaching card."

Ouch.

I may have gotten used to the moniker of "Coach Reed's son," but only being recognized as "Loren's brother" or "The Other Bourgeois' brother-in-law" has a little more of a sting to it.

"Dr. Reed is my ride tonight," Daisy explains sweetly, and I'm surprised at the effort required to keep my mind out of the gutter. Must be the high school setting messing with my hormones.

"Oh, well, I'm sure that's okay." Mrs. Julie's expression softens, and Daisy tugs me forward. I suppose it's a good thing no one knows about the latest updates to our roommate arrangement, or they'd be calling me "Daisy's husband" by now.

I stop once we reach the fence that separates the sidelines, filling my lungs with the all-too-familiar smell of fresh-cut grass, musty football equipment, and concession stand food. My mind is instantly flooded with memories of the time spent here with my dad and my teammates, both good and bad.

"Hey, Miss Daisy," a couple of cheerleaders drawl as they walk past us. One of them looks familiar and studies me more carefully than the rest until Tenley's nephew comes around to pull her into an embrace. Her friend drags her away when she and Ethan go in for a short kiss, and he continues grinning at her even after she's gone. Then he turns and acknowledges Daisy and me with a nod before he puts on his helmet and trots onto the field to join the kids warming up.

"Is that her boyfriend? Are they married?" I overhear another girl ask the others before she turns and bats a set of gaudy, fake eyelashes in a way that makes me feel uncomfortable.

Daisy glances up at me and stifles a smirk. "Should I tell them you're single?"

"God, no," I retort, making her laugh. "They're all young enough to be my patients."

"Come on, there's no harm in letting them crush, is there?" She nudges me, and my expression softens. I think there must be a deeper meaning behind it, but we're interrupted by a catcall.

"Ayo, Miss Day-zee! Came to watch me play?" says one uniformed kid among a small crowd of football players, and I place my hand on Daisy's lower back without thinking.

"She's here for me, you simp," his teammate retorts, shoving him playfully. And a growl nearly escapes my chest.

Instead of blurting out some inappropriate threat, I clench my jaw and curl my hand into the fabric of Daisy's dress possessively. She blinks a few times before she answers, obviously flustered, though I can't tell if it's because of the kids' calls or my reaction to them.

"I'm here for all of you," she says sweetly.

They laugh as one of them nods in my direction. "That your boyfriend or something?"

"Something," I answer for her this time.

"You look like you'd rather be watching a golf tournament than a football game, Pops," he continues, elbowing his teammate.

I reach up to adjust the collar of my polo while they carry on with their roast, though I don't understand most of the words they're using.

"Hey, see that sign over there, the one next to the concession stand?" I address the first kid again.

"The one with Coach JD and Coach Blake on it?"

"Yeah, that one," I retort dryly, then I tap my chest. "Number seventeen."

They all turn and squint at the billboard honoring our state championship run from about fifteen years ago. I ended up serving as a catch-all that year, alternating positions as a backup quarterback and wide receiver, as well as a middle linebacker.

"You're Landry Reed?" the kid finally surmises. Frankly, I'm a little disappointed that it takes him so long to read my name aloud.

"Well, *Doctor* Reed now." I feel my mouth curving into a smile.

"Hey, he must be Ms. Reed's brother," one kid tells the rest of them before he turns to me. "Wasn't your dad the coach?"

I sigh when he knocks me back down again. "Yeah."

He unexpectedly tosses a football my way, and I let go of Daisy to catch it. Then I step to the side and roll my shoulder around before throwing it back, depending on my muscle memory to keep me from looking like a total loser. The kid's eyebrows raise appreciatively when he wraps his hands around the ball after it spirals toward him.

"So you played with Coach JD, too?"

I laugh shortly. "Mm-hmm."

"That's cool, bruh," he replies just as JD walks by. "Hey, Coach, we just met your old teammate."

JD's grin falters when he turns and sees me. "Doc, Miss Daisy. Thanks for coming out to support us," he says mechanically before he marches on down the sideline. Blake and another assistant coach trail behind him, to my surprise, and Blake gives me a halfhearted nod before he tries to get away.

"What are you doing out here?" I call out to him. "Shouldn't you be at the hospital?"

He sighs before turning around and jogging over. "Loren kicked me out tonight."

"What the hell did you do?" I fire back.

"Not like that." He rolls his eyes. "She guilted me into coming to the game."

"And you listened?"

"Look, it doesn't matter how many times I tell her—she thinks I need to get back to doing the things I used to enjoy before I had her and the girls to keep me—" Blake stops abruptly and points an accusing finger at my face, and Daisy nudges me, presumably to warn me about my expression. "Don't you dare, Reed. You know damned well I was talking about coaching," he says defensively.

"Whatever," I mutter, flinching when Daisy elbows me harder.

He shakes his head and scowls at me. "What have I done to make you think I'd ever go back to being that guy?"

I run my tongue over my teeth before I shrug. "Nothing."

"Right. And for the record, it's absolutely *killing me* not to be with them right now. So you can just go f—" He stops and glances apologetically at Daisy. "Sorry. Go screw yourself, Landry."

"Thanks, Coach. Best of luck to you tonight," I retort sarcastically, but he's already sprinting off to join JD.

I turn to find Daisy frowning. "What? I didn't say a single thing to him. How was that my fault?"

She sighs. "You're right, you didn't say anything offensive. But you can't go around looking at your friends and family like you despise them and not expect them to think it's true."

"Technically, Blake's not a friend or a member of my family."

"Yet," she points out.

I roll my eyes. As far as I know, Loren and Blake's engagement still stands. But they don't seem eager to set a timeline on it yet.

"Come on, let's go get you some of that disgusting concession stand food," I tell Daisy, changing the subject.

Her face lights up. "Really?"

"Yeah." I can't help but smile back at her now. "You going with the greasy barbecue sauce burger or Hot Fries drenched in cheese?"

"Oh, definitely the second," she confirms. "And I'm gonna need one of those giant pickles the kids are always talking about."

I snort as I lead her to the concession stand. "You can have your pickle."

"Come on, don't tell me pickles are in the same category as corn dogs and lollipops?"

I chuckle out loud. "Not quite, but I'll pass this time. I've been plotting on a burger and some chili-cheese fries."

I approach the window and order our food, noticing that Daisy looks concerned beside me. "Hey, everything okay?" I ask when we turn to head back toward the bleachers. She hesitates, so I add, "You have to tell me the truth, remember?"

"You paid for my food," she says after a second. "But we're not on a date, are we?"

I clear my throat. "No. We're not."

"Then you'd only be doing that if you thought I couldn't afford my own dinner."

I shrug, fending off my annoyance. "No, I just—"

"You pity me because you know I'm broke and pathetic?"

My first instinct is to point out her lack of gratitude in response to my kind gesture, but the sad smile she flashes me doesn't align with that attitude. Instead, I open my mouth to tell her she's being ridiculous, since we both know she's on a much tighter budget than I am. But then I remember her whole reason for moving out here—to become self-sufficient. And as if having to depend on me for transportation and health insurance weren't enough, I just robbed her of her autonomy again.

I force a smile in return. "Of course not. I thought we agreed to share the responsibility for meals since neither of us can cook all that well. Dinner's on you next time, right?"

She nods, looking relieved. "Thank you."

More of Daisy's coworkers and students greet her as we walk on, and she doesn't hesitate to give each of them a friendly smile or address them by name. I recognize a few of my old classmates and acquaintances, but not many of them bother to acknowledge me.

We get to our seats just after kickoff, and I lean in close to explain what's happening in the game. I'd already prepped her with the basics of football on the short drive over.

"So Ethan is the running back on this play. The quarterback there is going to hand the ball off to him, like that, then Ethan's going to try to get as many yards as possible, if not a touchdown."

She nods in understanding before she flinches when number twenty-three absorbs a hard hit and spins away. "But it's not enough to hit him, right? They have to knock him down for the play to be over?"

"Or push him out of bounds." Ethan skirts the sidelines for a few more yards before he gets shoved past the white line on the edge of the field.

That was Robin on the carry for a gain of twelve yards and another Yellowjackets first down!

Daisy's eyes perk up at the sound of the announcer. "He's earned them a whole new set of downs, right?" I nod encouragingly, and she continues, "And since they're past the midpoint of the field—"

"The fifty-yard line," I correct her.

"The fifty-yard line," she repeats and smirks, "they're getting close enough to kick a field goal if they get to fourth down?"

"Exactly."

"See, told you I'm a fast learner," she says, lifting her chin smugly and making me chuckle.

"I guess you are. Coach Reed would be proud to have you for a daughter-in-law," I lean down to whisper near her ear, and I see her cheeks flush once I back away. She might have taken that one a little too much to heart, judging by the way she tucks her hair behind her ears as she stifles a grin.

I clear my throat awkwardly. "Any other football terms you're wondering about, while we're at it?"

"Oh, what about a Hail Mary catch?" she asks excitedly. "Whatever it is, I bet it's my favorite."

"Well, it's usually just a Hail Mary *pass*," I say with a soft laugh. "Because it's not often caught."

"Why not?"

"It's basically a last resort play where the quarterback just throws the football into the end zone or as close as he can get to it and prays one of his teammates comes up with it," I explain.

"Oh, well ... now that I think about it, it's kind of sweet that they named it that."

"How do you mean?"

She shrugs. "Even a big, tough football player knows to call on the Blessed Mother's intercession when he needs a miracle, right? Except, I like my version better. A catch sounds more optimistic."

I stare at her in appreciation. The way this woman's mind works is just ... well, admirable.

"I don't think I've ever met anyone who thinks the way you do, Daisy," I hear myself saying.

"Is that a good or a bad thing?" she ventures as her cheeks turn pink again. "Wait, don't answer that. I'm going to tell myself you meant it as a compliment."

"I don't give those away for free, so take it while you can, I guess," I reply, holding back a smile.

"Landry!"

The sound of Blake calling my name and waving frantically on the sidelines derails my thoughts. I furrow my brow and jog down to meet him, my stomach instantly turning with the dread of what he might have to say. Did something happen to Loren or one of the twins while he was here at the game? If so, I may never forgive the cocky son of a—

"Hey, Doc, we need your help down here," Blake tells me when I make it to bottom of the bleachers. "One of the guys just took a hard hit to the head, and he's showing signs of a concussion."

I hop down immediately. "Okay, but I thought you had paramedics on site for that stuff?"

"We do, but this wouldn't be his first concussion of the season," Blake explains as he walks me toward the bench. "And I'm worried. He's got some scouts looking at him, but we need someone qualified to convince him to sit his ass out for a while before he develops CTE."

"Gotcha." I nod as I approach the bench.

"Hey, Damien," Blake says to the kid, and I recognize him as one of Daisy's catcallers earlier. "This is Dr. Reed. You cool with letting him take a look at you?"

Damien's eyes flash to Blake's, but he keeps his head in his hands. "I don't need a doctor, Coach," he declares before he groans and spreads his feet to vomit on the grass.

"Looks like you do," I say. "But I'm not gonna do anything without your permission, kid. Are your parents here?"

"No." He spits on the ground and squints in pain. "You can examine me if you want, but I'm not going anywhere in that ambulance."

"Okay. Does your head hurt, Damien?" I ask as I kneel beside him in a patch of clean grass. I take his wrist to check his pulse. His heart rate is slightly elevated.

"Yes, sir," he rasps. "But I have to get back out there—"

"No. What you have to do is take care of yourself, or you won't be able to play at all before long," I tell him sternly. "Any numbness or tingling?"

"No, sir."

"Can you look up at me?"

He reluctantly tilts his head back and cracks his eyes open, and I can see that one of his pupils is larger than the other. I ask him to follow my finger, and his eye movements are jerky and delayed. He also confirms he's been experiencing tinnitus.

"To be honest, Doc, my ears have been ringing on and off since that last hit I took a few weeks ago," he admits after a while. "And sometimes things get blurry out of nowhere, but they always clear up later."

"I appreciate you telling me that, but I'm sorry, man. You probably know these are all symptoms of a serious concussion and that it's not safe for you to play right now."

"Yeah," he says, his eyelids drooping. "I know."

I sigh. "I know you don't want to hear this, but I'd really like you to come with me to the hospital to get some more tests done. I think you need a scan of your brain to be sure there's nothing too serious going on."

He tries to shake his head but ends up holding it in his hands again. "I don't want to go to the hospital."

"Damien," comes another voice from behind me. "You're not doing yourself any favors by staying here. You know damned well I'm not letting you play again until you run every possible test and a doctor says it's safe."

I turn to glare at JD over my shoulder. "He probably shouldn't have been playing in the first place."

"You're right," he admits, crossing his arms over his chest. "I should have noticed his symptoms were getting worse. And I should have made sure he got that scan the first time."

Damien cringes. "That ain't your fault, Coach. I told you I was better because I had to get back on the field. This is all I have."

JD crouches down beside me and places a hand on Damien's back. "Hey, it's all right to be scared. I know how much you love this. And even though it feels like football is everything right now, it won't always be that way. We have to put your health and safety first. Not to mention, your teammates are watching you. If it were any of them in the same position, you'd want them to take care of themselves, right?" Damien lets out a loud exhale but doesn't answer him. "As hard as this is, I need you to be a leader right now."

"Come on, Deculus," Blake adds, reaching in and taking Damien's helmet. "I'd tell you we don't have to turn on the siren or the lights, but you're probably into that sort of thing."

Damien smirks. "Think the ER nurses will be hot?"

"You can always pretend it's the concussion if you try to rizz them up and it doesn't work," JD offers, and Damien laughs softly and stands.

"All right. I'll go. But only if Doc rides with me and tells them what kind of tests to run."

I furrow my brow. "I can't tell the ER doctor what to do, but I can give him my recommendations."

Damien nods, and another kid helps him out of his pads. JD tells him they'll call his grandma to meet us at the ER, and the rest of his teammates come up to pat him reassuringly on the shoulder as we walk toward the ambulance parked on the other end of the field.

"Hang on a second. I'll be right back," I say before I jog over to the bleachers. Daisy's already descending the steps to meet me at the railing.

"Hey, sorry about this. It looks like I'm taking one of the kids to the ER, but I'll be back later," I tell her.

She smiles. "Damien Deculus?"

I nod. "Is he one of your students?"

Something brief flashes in her expression, but she covers it up quickly. "Yes. I hope he's okay?"

"He just needs some tests for now. Will you be all right here?"

"Don't worry about me. I'll hang out with Tenley and her mom or something until you get back."

I hesitate for a second. "Sorry I—"

"Landry, go," she says, shaking her head. "I'll be fine."

I nod and turn toward the field again, wondering why I feel so guilty for abandoning Daisy. I guess it's because she'd seemed so excited about coming to the game before, and we hadn't even gotten to eat our dinner.

I try to swallow the lump in my throat as I lead Damien onto the ambulance. After a quick talk with the EMTs, we head toward the hospital.

"You ever had a concussion, Doc?" Damien asks once we get down the block.

"Yeah, once. I got sacked as a freshman, and my head bounced off the ground. Hurt like hell for weeks."

He grunts. "I bet."

I stare at him for a second. "You're in Miss Daisy's class, aren't you?"

"Yeah," he replies, the corner of his mouth turning up in a smirk. "She's—"

"And you've been giving her a hard time."

He blinks. "I'm just—"

"But you're going to show her some respect from now on. And you're not going to let any of your classmates mess with her, either."

He swallows hard. "Yes, sir."

"Good," I tell him, forcing a smile.

"Is she your girlfriend?"

"She's like a little sister to me," I say.

Damien nods and holds out a fist, so I bump it with mine. "Aight, Doc. I gotchu."

We get to the emergency room a minute later, and I help get Damien checked in before they take him back for a CT scan, which thankfully doesn't show any major issues. The cocky, young resident pushes back at first when I insist on the scan, but the nurses are great and basically overrule him. Damien's elderly grandmother arrives after a while, and I explain everything that's been happening with him. She's sweet and grateful for my help, but I can tell she's been overwhelmed trying to raise him alone. I give her my number, and she agrees to let me know how he's doing throughout the weekend and to bring him to see me at the clinic next Monday.

The EMTs are kind enough to give me a ride back to the football field since they're headed there anyway, and Blake and JD thank me when I stop to give them an update on Damien before I return to the bleachers.

A smile spreads over Daisy's face when she sees me from her place in the row behind Tenley and her mom, Therese. "I'm so glad you're back. My nacho fries were getting cold and soggy," she tells me as she hands over my burger.

"You didn't have to wait for me to eat your food, Blondie," I reply, unable to resist smiling back at her.

"You're the manager of first-time experiences, remember? I couldn't do this without your supervision." She shrugs. "So, how's Damien?"

"He's all right, but he's going to have to take it easy for a while. He might need to apply for some temporary accommodations at school, too. I wouldn't be surprised if he suffers from headaches and brain fog for a while."

"Eh, the brain fog might not be a concussion thing," she mutters, and I laugh. "Thanks for going to help him. Camellia's lucky to have you around, you know."

"I agree," Tenley's mom turns to add, patting me affectionately on the knee. "How's the kid?"

"I'm thinking he'll be fine after a few weeks of rest," I say.

Tenley shoots me a smile as she rubs her belly absently. "That's good. I'm sure the whole team appreciates your help, especially JD and Blake."

"No worries. That's what I'm here for," I reply awkwardly before they turn their attention back to the game.

"All right, I'm starving," Daisy says, nudging me. "Can we eat now?"

"Yeah." I laugh. "*Bon appetite.*" I hold up my burger, and she taps her tray against it.

"Cheese and biscuits, that's the most disgustingly delicious thing I've ever eaten in my life!" she exclaims through a mouthful of cheese-covered Hot Fries. Then she hurriedly unwraps the pickle and takes a huge bite. "Mm, it's eben bedder togedder!"

I chuckle at her again, reaching over to swipe a napkin over the cheese on her chin. "Better than scrambled eggs and cold sandwiches?"

She shovels more into her mouth. "Absolu-ley."

"It's not steak and lobster, but ... you know, now that I think about it, I have been craving surf and turf," I muse. "Just thought I'd mention it, since you're buying dinner next time."

She giggles and bumps her shoulder into mine. "As long as neither of us has to cook it."

CHAPTER 13

daisy

I SHUT the Louisiana teacher certification test prep book with a sigh and set it down on the coffee table. It's a beautiful Saturday morning, yet here I am, studying for a test I'm not even sure I want to pass.

My phone buzzes, and I jump to answer it, eager for a distraction.

MAGNOLIA

DAISY COLETTE LAFLEUR

Why am I just finding out from Rowan now that you're living with LANDRY REED??

IRIS

What? You're living with a man?

I cringe. Maybe that study guide wasn't so bad after all.

VIOLET

At least he's a doctor.

MAGNOLIA

He's not just any doctor, Vi. He's a hot doctor. We're talking McDreamy/McSteamy hot.

IRIS

Are you living together as a couple? Or are you just roommates?

MARIGOLD

Calm down, ladies. Let's give her a chance to answer before we jump to conclusions.

ROSEMARY

Mari's right. Judge not lest we be judged, sisters. 

IRIS

Really, Rose?

ROSEMARY

Jk. 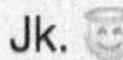

I'm here for the Doctor Landry McSteamy details.

gif of Patrick Dempsey from Grey's Anatomy

MAGNOLIA

Rosie, That's McDreamy, not McSteamy.

ROSEMARY

Tough crowd today.

I snort at Rosemary's reply. Even my consecrated Sister (with a capital *S*) can't deny that Landry's easy on the eyes.

VIOLET

I don't get it.

Daisy, did you move in with your hot doctor so he can watch over you? Or is it that you can't answer us right now because you're busy fornicating?

I groan. My parents hadn't even reacted this way when I broke the news to them about Landry and me deciding to share a house. They only traded amused looks as if they had been placing bets on how long it would take me to give up on living alone and reminded me that I could come home as soon as I was ready. Not *if* I was ready, but *when* I was ready.

Once they realized I was serious and that I was not in fact ready to admit defeat, my dad tried to give me a short lecture about the dangers of putting oneself in a state of unnecessary temptation. I cut in to reassure him that there would be no *danger* of anything happening between Landry and me, but he insisted on finishing his sermon with a reminder that pride often precedes the fall. I thanked him for the advice, even though I was sure it wasn't relevant to my situation. And I don't think my sisters will understand, either.

I also know they won't leave me alone if I don't answer them.

DAISY

Landry and I are renting separate rooms in his sister's old house. He's been very kind to me because, and I quote, "he owes it to Rowan to take good care of his baby sister." And that about sums it up.

MAGNOLIA

Oof. He best-friend's-baby-sister-zoned you?

MARIGOLD

Oh, honey. I hope this doesn't make you forget how beautiful you are, both inside and out.

IRIS

I still think this is a bad idea. You're at least going to walk in on one another naked at some point, and it's hard to come back from that.

ROSEMARY

I'm just relieved to hear that he's taking care of you, Daisy. You know we all love you and want you to be safe, happy, and holy. I'll be praying for you and your roommate to get along well.

VIOLET

So, no fornication, then?

I roll my eyes and set my phone down on top of that test prep guide. I glance toward the light streaming in from the front window, thinking I could use a little vitamin D. Normally, I'd have brought my book outside to study, but Landry said he was going out to wash the Jeep earlier, and I knew I'd end up talking to him if I went out there. I think I might have to take that risk, though, since I can't seem to focus inside.

I rise and make my way to the front door, halting in front of the window when I spot the shirtless man wielding the water hose.

"Mercy me," I hear myself saying on a gasp.

Maybe I should at least go out to water the flowers. I bet they're real thirsty.

I'm not even sure I'm conscious of what I'm doing as I shuffle out to the front porch and pick up my watering can. I gulp and allow my gaze to run over Landry's bare back, his muscles flexing as he reaches up to rinse the top of the car. His skin looks flushed beneath a layer of glistening moisture, the origins of which are unclear. Has he been sweating through his grueling labor as the sun blazes down upon him? Or has he simply gotten caught in the spray of the water hose, inadvertently drenching himself as he continues toiling away?

He answers my question when he turns the hose on himself, giving his sun-kissed shoulders a quick reprieve from the heat.

I hear myself whine as I continue gaping. Then I flinch when I realize my feet are wet, too, because I'm literally standing in a puddle. Apparently, I've been watering the same pot of hydrangeas for the last two minutes.

"Frick and frack," I mutter to myself.

"Hey, I didn't realize you were out here," Landry calls. Because of course he'd choose that particular moment to notice me. He halts the spray as he turns to shoot me a friendly smile and adjusts the backward cap on his head. "Everything okay?" he asks once he takes in my strange expression.

"Yep," I squeak. "Fine. Just ... you know, keeping everyone hydrated."

He chuckles softly. "Speaking of, mind grabbing me a water from inside? It's not easy to drink from the hose with a nozzle on there. Plus, it feels a little like eating off a stick."

"No problem," I manage before I scramble inside and return with a cold bottle. He's waiting at the edge of the porch when I walk outside again, and I nearly lose my own footing when he props one leg on the first step and brings his arm up to swipe at his forehead.

He takes the bottle and thanks me before unscrewing the cap and tilting his head back, his throat bobbing as he downs it within seconds. Then he lets loose a guttural, inherently masculine *ahh*, and my hand flies up to cover my mouth when I whimper quietly in response.

No need to look for a basal body temperature rise this month— peak ovulation day has just been confirmed.

My eyes run down his chest and catch on the edges of his lightly defined hip vee. The athletic shorts he's wearing are slung low enough to reveal the waistband of his boxers, and I shiver at the reminder that this man is technically bound to me. Well, legally bound, at least.

He furrows his brow when he catches me staring. "Don't worry, I'm going straight to the shower once I'm finished out here. I promise I won't get swamp ass on the couch."

I blink away the sudden image of Landry's face under the stream of water before my ovaries get a peek at him below the neck.

"Oh, um, you're fine," I choke out, and he looks amused. "I mean, I grew up on a farm, remember? I'm immune to the smell of hard work."

He chuckles. "Why does the image of Rowan shoveling horse shit and feeding pigs seem so hilarious to me?"

For the first time ever, I'm actually grateful when he shifts the conversation to mention my brother.

"We all had to do it," I say with a smile. "Even Dr. Athanasius."

Landry shakes his head. "And I always forget about his first name. Poor kid."

"My parents figured the more obscure the saint name, the closer to heaven, I guess." I shrug, and he laughs again.

He hands me the empty bottle and steps back, resting his hands on his hips, and it takes all of my willpower to keep from gawking again. "Hey, you got anything going on today?"

I shake my head quickly. "Nope. Free as a bird," I say, cringing inwardly. "Well, I'm supposed to be studying for my certification exam, but that's all."

"Great, because I was thinking we could hang out. You know, watch a movie, paint each other's toenails," he proposes with a sly grin.

I scoff and toss the empty water bottle at him. It bounces off his chest and hits the steps. "Very funny."

"Nah, but seriously ... wanna come with me to see the twins in a little bit?" he offers instead.

"Really?" I can't help the way my face lights up.

"Lo said she and Blake have an appointment with the priest or something, so we could take the day shift in the NICU," he continues, his smile growing more genuine.

I nod vehemently, suppressing a full-on squeal. I've only gotten to see videos and photos of Penny and Charley so far, but I absolutely adore them already.

"And after that, I was thinking we could grab some takeout. It's your turn to pay, if memory serves me."

"Okay," I agree, reaching up to tuck my hair behind my ears. My night's getting better by the second.

Landry takes a step up, and his eyelids lower. "Then, when we get home, there's something we could do ... together," he drawls, pausing to lick his lips. "Something I'm sure you haven't done with anyone else before. But I really think you need to try it with a partner at least once, and who better to teach you than your husband?"

My lips part as I take in a shuddery breath, and my heart feels like it's trying to do a somersault in my chest. "Yeah?"

Okay, I *know* he's just messing with me. Even though he's not usually this suggestive, I'm not stupid enough to think he's setting me up for anything more than the punchline of a joke. But I'm also desperate, so I play along, just in case.

His brows draw together as he leans in to whisper, "Daisy, will you let me help you study for your certification test?"

"You—you *canaille* little ... jerk!" I shriek, reaching out to shove him back. He absorbs my push off and barely budges as he tosses his head back and laughs. I cringe and shake out my sweat-covered hands.

"I thought I only had *jerkish tendencies*?" he reminds me.

"Kiss my grits, Landry," I fire back, stifling a smile. The truth is I'm still flattered, because he wouldn't go this far with his teasing if he didn't see me as an adult woman—one who makes him comfortable enough to be this flirty and silly.

He clicks his tongue and shakes his head. "The potty mouth on this one," he replies sarcastically.

I roll my eyes. "I'm only letting you get away with that because you're bringing me to meet the twins. If I don't get to hold a Bougie baby later, I'm gonna—"

"Gonna what?" he interrupts me. "Cuss me out? Beat my ass? Force me to eat scrambled eggs again?"

I lift my chin haughtily. "Maybe I'll just sneak a pair of my panties into your underwear stack."

He glares at me. "You wouldn't."

"Wouldn't I?" I tap my bottom lip, pretending to brew up an evil plan, and I could swear I see a flicker of something in his expression when his eyes follow my movement. "Or maybe I'll accidentally knock your toothbrush into the—"

"Daisy Colette!" he growls, and those silly butterflies flutter around at the way my name sounds in his deep, rumbly voice. "Don't you dare touch my toothbrush."

"Fine, but what if I," I pause to lean in and narrow my eyes ominously, "hugged you?"

"Oh, is that supposed to be a punishment?" he says on a laugh.

"For you, it is. At least, last I checked," I reply smugly, though my stomach dips again at his implications.

"Right, because if you were to hug me right now, *I'd* be the one grossed out?"

I scrunch up my nose. "Fair enough."

A cocky smirk takes over his face, and he lunges forward to wrap his arms around me, pressing my cheek against his bare chest.

"Lan-*dreee*!" I squeal, feigning disgust. "Eww! Let me go! You're so hairy and sweaty and ... just *ew*!"

"You said you were used to that smell," he reminds me and loosens his grip. I swipe at my face as he laughs one more time. "All right, Blondie. Go inside and clean yourself up. And stop distracting me. I have to finish this before we can go to the hospital."

I eye him carefully. "How am I the distraction in this scenario?"

He straightens and reaches up to scratch the back of his neck, then adjusts that sexy ball cap again. "You're too easy of a target," he replies, suddenly sounding less confident than he did a second ago. "And my ADHD kicks into high gear when I'm doing chores."

"Right," I say, pulling my hair over my shoulder and twisting it into a quick braid. "Is that how you plan to help me study later? By distracting me?"

Something shifts in his expression as he watches me. His lips part, and his chest rises and falls as if he's breathing heavier. I may not know a lot about men, and I'm not crazy enough to think he'll ever change his mind about relationships on my account. But there are times when Landry looks at me, and I could swear he's fighting against *something*, as if there's at least a trace of attraction in his eyes.

What if my dad and my sisters are right? What if a man and a woman can't coexist this way for an extended period of time without being drawn to one another? What if our close proximity is chipping away at his resolve, too, just at a much slower rate than it is for me?

He clears his throat. "We don't have to study together if you don't want to," he says, then he turns abruptly and walks back to his Jeep. "But I'm leaving for the hospital in thirty minutes," he adds, picking up the hose. "If you're not ready, I'll have to go without you."

My eyes water against my will. Maybe I should have just stopped at *I don't know a lot about men*.

Then again, Landry isn't like most men. If he weren't so kind and charitable, at least on the inside, I'd already have been forced to move back home with my parents.

Maybe it's not up to me to figure him out; maybe I'm simply meant to help him.

daisy

I FINISH my gardening before I go inside to ditch my sweat-stained dress and freshen up. The faint sound of running water travels through the wall as I dig through my closet. I give up on finding a clean dress after a while and dart out to check the laundry, assuming the coast is clear with Landry in the shower.

I'm bending over to sift through the dryer when I hear a strangled noise behind me.

"What the hell, Daisy?" Landry demands angrily, making me flinch and hit my head on the inside of the dryer.

This time I'm the one growling as I rub my head. I grab the first clean clothing item I find, the Camellia High Football T-shirt I got from work, and I pull it down over my bra. Landry's already turned so that his back is facing me by the time I stand.

"Sorry, I thought you were in the shower," I tell him.

"I turned it on but realized I'd forgotten my clothes," he mumbles.

"Then you only have yourself to blame for catching me in my underwear this time," I reply, shutting the dryer door with my hip. "And if you don't want to be scandalized by my panties again, I suggest you close your eyes while I walk past you."

I glare at him, but he does as told and keeps his eyes shut tightly, presumably until I slam my bedroom door behind me. I rifle through my dresser until I root out a pair of old jean shorts. The cutoffs hit me mid-thigh, so I rarely wear them in public. But I'm too frustrated to look for anything else today, so I slip them on.

Landry knocks on my door a few minutes later, and I finish re-braiding my hair before I swing it open.

"Are you rea—" His voice cuts off abruptly as his gaze runs over me, his eyes trailing down my legs and back again. "What are you wearing?" he asks with a frown.

I shrug. "I couldn't find a clean dress, and I had to change after *someone* got my other one all sweaty."

"But you never wear shorts," he mutters absently.

"Well, I'm wearing them now. Unless that's a problem? Are you going to start telling me what to wear now that we're married?" I cross my arms over my middle.

"No." He looks down at his feet as he continues. "I already feel bad enough for saying you should wear a sweater to work every day, as if it's your fault those boys can't stop ogling you."

I blink at him. I used to think I had plenty of patience, but this man is absolutely maddening.

"I don't even know how to reply to that," I blurt out.

"Wear whatever you want. I don't care," he grumbles before adding, "I mean, it's not my place to say anything."

"How flattering," I retort sarcastically as I step out from my room.

He sighs and walks ahead to open the front door for me, then backs away and gestures for me to go first. I think I hear him mumbling something, so I stop and turn my head. "What now?"

His eyes flutter up to mine suspiciously, and he shakes his head. "Nothing."

We're both silent on the drive to the hospital, which feels strange after the comfortable stride I thought we'd fallen into over the past month or so. Once we're in the NICU, Landry directs me to wash my hands thoroughly. He trades friendly greetings with the nurses, intro-ducing me as his roommate before he leads me toward a pair of pink-adorned bassinets. I watch carefully as he wheels one of the carts over to a set of rocking chairs.

His mouth turns up into a proud smile as he inclines his head in an invitation, and I peer over the edge to find the two babies snuggled up together. He knew they'd be in the same bed, I realize, and it only makes the girls (and Landry) that much cuter.

"What's your preference? Chunky and snuggly or a wide-eyed and wiggly?" he asks.

"Oh, let's start with Princess Pen," I reply, and his smile grows wider.

He reaches in to pick up the smaller of the two and hands her over to me. "Here you go, wide-eyed and wiggly."

My heart expands to fill my chest when I look down into her tiny, blue eyes. Penelope squeaks and squirms in my arms as promised, staring up at me the whole time as if we were having a silent conversation. I glance over at Landry after a while, and my breath catches in my throat at the sight of him with a baby lying on his chest. He strokes Charlotte's back and kisses the top of her head before leaning down to murmur into her little ear. Charley lets out a grunt and curls in, as if he's been tickling her with his beard, and he chuckles, making her bounce over his chest.

Forget the shirtless car washing—*this* is the kind of stuff that could tempt a woman to extend inappropriate offers to her platonic roommate. And all the hot-and-cold moods in the world couldn't stop me from thinking he's the sexiest man alive and fantasizing about what our fictional babies might look like.

That could also be my ovaries talking for me again.

"You good, Blondie?" he asks me after he catches me staring.

"Amazing," I say dreamily, unable to care whether he sees through me at this point. "Thank you for bringing me with you. They're beautiful, and I love them, even though they aren't really my nieces."

He shrugs. "Technically, they are. At least for now."

"You're right, they are." I smirk at him. "Does that mean I get to hold both of them before we go?"

"It does," he confirms. "And I think we'll get to feed them, too."

I let out a wistful sigh as I return to playing with Penny's tiny fingers. "This isn't even fair, you know. What's the recommended treatment for baby fever, Doc?"

He chuckles. "Sorry, that's more of your brother's specialty."

I roll my eyes, slightly disappointed he didn't take the opportunity to tease me. "Really, because I feel like you'd be more helpful in this situation," I mutter.

Landry snorts and continues staring down at Charley. "I'm not biting on that one. I've already pissed you off enough times today."

That makes my smile grow wider again.

We sit that way for a while longer before a nurse brings over a set of bottles, and Landry swaps babies with me. We're almost done with their feeding when he pulls out his phone to read a text.

"Son of a bitch, they're really going through with it," he mumbles to himself.

"What?" I ask.

"Loren and Blake—they're actually getting married ... in a month," he adds in disbelief.

"That's awesome though, right?"

He huffs. "I just ... I don't know. I guess I figured they'd stay engaged forever. I never imagined them throwing together an actual wedding, especially not this fast."

Penny coughs and chokes on her bottle then, and he shifts his attention back to her. I glance over every so often to find him looking uneasy. A nurse comes over to tell us it's almost bath time, so we finish the girls' feedings and get our goodbye snuggles. Landry still seems lost in thought as we walk out to the car.

"Hey, are you okay?" I ask when he cranks the Jeep and shifts into drive.

"Fine," he replies shortly.

"Are you sure? You don't—"

"I just need some time to wrap my head around this," he cuts me off.

I shake my head. "I don't understand why you're letting it bother you so much."

"Don't worry about it."

I frown at his curt tone. "But I hate seeing you so upset."

He pounds his fist lightly on the steering wheel. "I just can't see this going well, okay? My mind doesn't work the way yours does. You might be able to find the good in everyone and everything, but I only know how to panic and prepare for the worst-case scenario."

I reach over and place a hand over his where it rests on the gearshift. "Hey, nothing bad is going to happen, okay? They love one another, and they're going to get married and raise the twins together, and everything's going to be great."

He lets out a loud exhale. "How do you know that, though?"

My stomach clenches when his voice cracks. "I don't. But all this constant worrying is making you miserable. It has to be worse than allowing yourself to hope now and getting let down later, right?"

"You'd say that, since you haven't gotten let down enough times before," he replies.

"And you might think that, but you're probably wrong," I retort. "Look, I'm not saying you don't have the right to feel the way you do. But you have to change the way you react to these things if you want to fix your relationship with your family, especially with Loren."

He opens his mouth to say more but shakes his head and clenches his jaw instead. I figure that's at least a step in the right direction for him, since he's more apt to lash out than to talk through his feelings right about now.

The rest of the ride home is quiet, but I can't help feeling like he needs me to push him just a little further, like this is one of those times I'm meant to help him learn something about himself.

"Landry, wait," I begin once we're back inside the house. He stops and turns to face me. "I'm sorry. The last thing you need is me telling you what to do."

He stares at me before he answers. "Why are you apologizing to me after I was such a jerk to you just now?"

"Because I wanted to make you feel safe enough to tell me what's so scary about the idea of Loren getting married, but I ended up making you feel worse instead." I wait a second before adding, "So what are you worried might happen?"

He shrugs. "I guess ... I'm afraid they're only getting married because of the babies. I worry one or both of them will regret their decision later, that they'll grow resentful of one another and allow it to destroy their family."

"Like your parents?"

"Yeah," he says, crossing his arms over his chest.

"I suppose it's possible the same thing could happen with Blake and Loren. But I honestly don't think it will," I offer.

"Because you only look at the bright side," he says dryly.

"I'm not saying that to be optimistic," I correct him. "I'm saying it because they remind me of *my* parents, and because they're obviously meant to be together. I also think you have it backward. Blake didn't propose because of the twins; the twins only exist because Blake and Loren can't help how much they love one another. And even if I'm wrong, they still deserve the chance to figure it out on their own."

I pause and close in the space between us as I reach out and tug his arm. "You supported me when my family couldn't, and it's made all the difference. Just think what your love and encouragement could do for your sister now, when she needs it the most."

He licks his lips and stares down at me before finally letting his arms fall to his sides, and I wrap him up in a hug. I hear his shaky exhale as he reluctantly embraces me, eventually resting his chin over my head. We stand there for a full minute before he pulls away.

"Thank you, Daisy," he rasps.

I lift one shoulder. "Anytime."

"You, uh ..." He clears his throat before continuing. "Do you still want to grab dinner and take a crack at that study guide?"

"Of course, if you're feeling up to it," I reply, smiling hopefully.

His expression relaxes, though he doesn't return the smile. "Only if you're buying."

I snort out a laugh and shove him playfully. "Fine. But I'm

thinking something more along the lines of corndogs instead of surf and turf."

"Well, we can't exactly go out for steak and lobster with you dressed like that, can we?"

This time he shoots me a genuine smile before he inclines his head toward the door, making me sigh inwardly. Living with a man like Landry could be dangerous indeed.

daisy

"WHAT IN THE ..."

Loren blinks and turns her head to the side in confusion as she holds up another lacy, little number for our appraisal. She gasps when she realizes there's an opening where most undergarments make it a point to hold it together, then she stuffs it back into a gift bag.

"Tenley Jean! I can't believe you made me open this in front of our mamas and everything," Loren scolds her, making the others laugh.

I'd be lying if I said my own cheeks didn't feel warm after that one. This evening is proving to be quite educational for me.

Loren and Landry's older sister Lilley had put together a quirky *Pride and Prejudice* themed bridal shower earlier today, complete with tea, sandwiches, and scones. But now that the more distinguished guests had come and gone, including such acquaintances as the assistant district attorney's wife, the party has morphed into a less formal *Bridgerton* bachelorette soiree. The guys had all gone on some sporty excursion to celebrate Blake's last weekend as a free man, but the ladies were more comfortable hanging out at home, especially since the twins had only recently graduated from the NICU and Tenley was fresh out of the maternity ward with her brand-new baby boy.

And I've been enjoying every second of it. I guess I hadn't realized how much I've been missing my mom and sisters and the busyness of a full house.

Tenley smirks at Loren. "I told you I'd get you back for teasing me about my wedding dress."

"Yeah, well, joke's on you because I'll probably text you all the details after I wear it," Loren says, sticking her tongue out.

"Eh, it's good for business," Tenley replies smoothly, and Loren moves to toss a throw pillow her way before stopping abruptly.

"No fair, you've got a baby in your lap."

Tenley grins. "That's also my new excuse for lying around and letting JD handle everything."

I furrow my brow. Tenley's never struck me as anything less than amazing at multitasking and balancing motherhood with her busy career as a midwife, so it's surprising to hear her admit to relying on her husband for anything.

"Milk it while you can," Tenley's mom says. "Then again, you could probably sit on a throne all day and that man would gladly finish all of the chores in time to lay a bed of roses at your feet."

"And thank God, because I couldn't even keep a teenager alive without him, much less a newborn," Tenley mumbles.

"But I thought ..." I clamp my mouth shut once I realize I'm about to blurt my thoughts out loud.

Tenley raises a brow at me as she adjusts the baby in her arms. "Thought I'd know what I was doing with one of these things since I've been delivering them for the past decade?" She pauses to laugh. "I actually used to think I wasn't meant to have kids at all, but I guess I just needed the right guy to come along and show me I wasn't meant to do it alone."

I sigh wistfully, because I'm starting to think I understand what she means.

"Don't let her fool you," Loren chimes in. "She wasn't open to all this baby-making business until JD started coming up with reasons to take off his shirt around her."

Tenley shrugs. "There's a reason why our lawn is always so well kept, you know. And it's not because I care about the grass staying short."

The group cackles at her confession, and I stifle a smile when the image of Landry washing his Jeep flashes through my mind.

Loren opens my gift next, and everyone compliments the white linen gown I sewed for her. "You, um, might want to be careful with it. It's a bit see-through," I say quietly, and she bounces her eyebrows suggestively.

"Thank you, Daisy. It's beautiful. I can't wait to wear it and pretend I'm the protagonist in my favorite Regency romance novel," she announces, waving the gown dramatically and making the skirt twirl.

"I would have thought you'd grown out of playing pretend by now," Lilley begins. "But I suppose you aren't playing alone anymore."

Loren smirks. "I can't help that my fiancé makes the perfect male lead. He's just so smushy."

"Smushy?" Jada asks.

"Blake is the perfect combination of sexy and mushy," Loren replies contentedly.

Tenley hums. "It's a Bourgeois thing."

"Aaron is smushy, too. But he does the sexy part so quietly that no one suspects it. It makes it even better," Jada says with a wink.

"I suppose Emmett is all marshmallow and fluff," Lilley says thoughtfully, pausing to stand before she adds, "until the lights go out." Then she saunters out to the kitchen as if she just dropped the mic on us.

I laugh along with the others, grateful not to have the spotlight turned on me. I've got plenty of commentary to offer regarding my husband's sex appeal, but I'm not supposed to be thinking it, much less talking about it. That doesn't stop me from longing to dish about him to my sisters and friends, though.

Those of us without a baby to nurse join Lilley in cleaning up after that. Then a few more of the guests say good night, including Loren's mom, and we're left with the other half of the wedding party:

Loren, Tenley, Lilley, and Jada, Blake's good friend and legal secretary. I settle on the couch with one of the sleeping twins in my lap while Jada takes the other. Lilley hands each of us a glass of wine before she goes back into the kitchen and returns with a large teapot.

"All right, for our next bachelorette activity, we're playing a game called *Spill the Tea*," Lilley announces, looking pleased with herself as she presents the teapot filled with slips of paper. "Girls, you'll take turns picking a random question related to your love life in which you must answer truthfully. Lo-Lo, our blushing bride, you're first!"

Loren grins as she reaches into the pot, obviously loving this, as corny as it seems. And I kind of love her all the more for it.

"A proper lady never kisses and tells ... but there are no proper ladies present tonight, so tell us about your first kiss," she reads aloud. She bites her lip and bats her eyelashes before she answers. "There was this party when I was thirteen. I was hiding out in the pool house because I was tired of being a wallflower when the most popular boy in my class stumbled in looking upset because his younger brother had swooped in on his date. And since my own brother was busy making out with my best friend at the moment," Loren's eyes dart over to Tenley, who scoffs, "I suggested we get our first kisses out of the way, too. The boy agreed, and we kissed." She pauses to grin before she continues. "And it was so good that we kissed again. But we were young and stupid, and we spent the next eighteen years or so pretending we were rivals when we were secretly pining for one another." She shrugs shyly, holding the rest of us captive with her story. "But one night he let his guard down, and I let him kiss me again ... and then he knocked me up with freaking twins, and we lived happily ever after. The end," she finishes on a sarcastic tone, making everyone laugh hysterically.

"That man is such a sap," Jada says, sighing and reaching into the basket for the next paper. "Okay, let's see. A lady's secret garden must be kept safe from both the birds and the bees alike. Who gave you *the talk*, and how did it go?" She blows a raspberry. "I'd already found out more than I should have from some of my classmates, but my mom sat me down when I was about twelve and told me the rest. It was painfully awkward, especially because she used a lot of those corny euphemisms like *tending the garden* and *getting deflowered*, but at least she was honest about it."

"It's all fun and games until you're the one giving the talk though," Lilley says, casting a quick glance at her sister. I realize she's probably worried the mother-daughter aspect of Jada's answer might be triggering for Lo, so she swipes another question from the teapot. "It is a debutante's duty to appear charming and graceful at all times, especially when she's being called upon by an eligible bachelor. Provide us with a cautionary tale about your most embarrassing dating moment."

Lilley tells us a short story about getting gassy on her first official date with Emmett, which apparently reminds Tenley of JD on their first date. After another round of giggles and a topping off of our wine glasses, Lilley passes the teapot to me.

I shift Charley's weight in my arms before I dip my free hand into the pot for my own question, hoping I get something I can answer. But I gulp when I open the slip of paper. "Sometimes the mood strikes when we least expect it, whether we're in the garden at the ball, on the stairs within listening distance of the servants, or on the chaise lounge of the library during a house party. What is the most scandalous place you've ever made love?" My voice cracks by the end, and I can feel myself starting to sweat.

Truthfully, I'm not embarrassed to admit I'm a virgin. In fact, I'm proud of myself for keeping my vow and managing to stay chaste this long. My family taught me to see my sexuality as a privilege, one most gratifying when saved for marriage. I was also raised to deem any man who couldn't see my celibacy as a gift or respect my choice to wait as unworthy of me in the first place. And I wholeheartedly believe all that.

The fact that I still haven't found a man who loves me and agrees with that philosophy by the time I'm old enough to be invited to this kind of party with a bunch of other married and experienced women is the part I'm having trouble swallowing.

"I ... I, uh ... *C*," I spit out awkwardly.

Loren glares at me in confusion. "*C*?"

"Final answer." I nod vehemently.

"You know this wasn't a multiple-choice question, right? We're gonna need more than that." Loren smiles and stares expectantly.

I blink down at the paper, feeling my face heat and my eyes water.

"Hey, it's okay if you don't want to answer," Lilley says, reaching over to pat my arm softly. "If you're not having fun, honey, then we're not having fun."

The baby sighs in my arms, and I swallow hard again. "I just ..."

"Daisy," Tenley calls out across from me, and I glance up at her. "She's right. You don't have to talk about anything that makes you feel uncomfortable. But don't you dare think any of us are going to judge you for your answers, either, especially if you don't have one. Personally, I find that kind of thing pretty admirable for an unmarried woman."

"You do?" I ask, my voice still wobbly.

She nods. "Absolutely. In fact, I regretted not saving that to share with JD. We both did. So we did the next best thing and made the decision to save our first time together for our wedding night."

The tension in my stomach loosens just a bit. "You did?"

"Yep. And it was perfect."

"So that's why you only had a three-week long engagement," Jada says, snickering.

"Exactly," Loren pipes up, rolling her eyes. "And they skipped out on a wedding reception so they could leave the church and go straight home to play hide the sausage."

"First of all, we both know JD and I weren't the only couple running off to play that game," Tenley begins, making Loren blush. "And secondly, don't be so crude, Lo. We're talking about a sacramental act, the unitive and procreative joining of our bodies and souls ... which means we weren't just hiding the sausage, we were baking cream pies," she says, smirking.

Jada nearly chokes on her wine at that one, and I can't help but smile.

"See? You can't say anything more embarrassing than that," Loren points out.

I lift one shoulder in a shrug. "Then the truth is that I don't have any lovemaking experience to speak of … because I've been waiting to share it with my husband."

My next husband, hopefully.

I look around at their surprised expressions.

"Well, I agree with Tenley. I think that's pretty badass of you, Daisy," Loren volunteers. "And I have a whole new respect for all that chastity and celibacy stuff, since Blake and I have decided to wait until our wedding night, too." A collective hush falls over the room until everyone starts cackling. "Hey, I'm serious. You guys just said we weren't going to judge one another!" she protests.

"Hmm, it's a little late to make that claim, though, Mama," Jada says, lifting her arms to gesture to Penny.

"I mean, we're doing what Ten said. We've been waiting since the last time—the time we conceived the twins," Loren clarifies. "And it hasn't been easy, thank you very much."

"Aw, I imagine that's been *hard* on both of you, especially Blake," Tenley coos, barely getting it out without snorting.

"Or are you struggling because he's used to you being so *easy*?" Lilley adds.

"Both," Loren admits with a pout, and the rest of us laugh again.

"All right, Daisy, why don't you just pick another one?" Lilley tells me after we all settle down. "There should be plenty of other questions you'll be able to answer."

"Okay." I nod and reach in for a second scrap of paper. "This one says, when a lady and a gentleman are found in a compromising position, the result may be a hasty marriage or a duel for her honor. Tell us about a time when you were caught …" I trail off, realizing I can't answer this one, either. "Um, sorry."

"How about I take that one?" Tenley offers cheerfully, and I force a grateful smile. "The thing about having a teenager in the house is that he knows too much. *Pauvre bête,*" she goes on, shaking her head. "A while back, JD and I were home alone, compromising the couch, when Ethan surprised us by coming back early. We thought we'd spared him, but the poor kid accidentally slipped on my *caleçons* on the floor before he could make it out unscathed."

Her story elicits another round of riotous laughter, and Lilley prompts me to pick again after they settle down.

"Okay, but I'm giving up if I get another spicy one," I say, smiling. "Here it goes: Many claim love at first sight, but most of us know it's in his kiss. Tell us about your last kiss and whether you knew it was true love."

If I thought my expression had given me away before, I was wrong. My cheeks are on fire by the time I finish reading, and I'm pretty sure I audibly gasp at the end. I can't tell them that the last kiss I shared was at my wedding ... with Landry. But I can't lie to them, either. And I have to say *something* this time.

"Daisy?" Loren questions me after a second. "You okay?"

"Mm-hmm," I squeak. "Just thinking about my answer."

"Do you ... have an answer?" she whispers and smiles encouragingly, but I can tell she's only trying to save me from the embarrassment again.

"Mm-hmm," I repeat. "I mean, yes, I've been kissed before."

"Oh. Well, if you don't want to share—"

"I kissed Landry," I cringe and blurt out. "Or maybe he kissed me. I'm not sure."

Loren gasps, and Lilley clicks her tongue before declaring, "*Mais gah*, look who's spilling the good tea now."

daisy

My eyes dart around nervously, and it almost looks like they're leaning in closer now. "It wasn't—I mean, it was sort of an accident. I think we both went in for a cheek kiss, and ... anyway, I'm sure he didn't mean for it to happen."

Phew. Nice save, I tell myself.

"*Riiight*," Loren drags the word out, narrowing her eyes at me and stifling a smile. "Then it must have just been an awkward, little peck?"

I bite my lip, trying not to think about the feeling of Landry's warm mouth covering mine.

"Oh, Daisy, tell me you didn't make out with my brother," Loren teases as she bounces up and curls her knees beneath her.

I shake my head quickly, making Charley stir in my arms again. "No, it wasn't like that."

"Was there tongue?" Jada asks.

My face heats again, and I nod shyly.

"Then he definitely meant it," she declares.

But I feel so guilty now. It's as if I'm misrepresenting Landry since I can't explain that he only kissed me to make our courthouse wedding look more legit and not because he's actually into me.

"I think he only went along with it so I wouldn't feel so bad," I admit after a while. It's close enough to the truth. "We've already established that he doesn't see me that way."

"Daisy, honey, you're gorgeous. Anyone with eyes would see you *that* way," Lilley corrects me.

I shake my head again. "Not Landry. He thinks of me as Rowan's little sister, and that's all. Believe me."

"Bullshit," Loren interjects. "I'd bet my last dollar he hasn't stopped thinking about that kiss since it happened."

"If he's thought about it again, it's only because the whole thing was awkward and embarrassing," I hold fast. "He certainly hasn't brought it up or tried to kiss me again, and I've given him ample opportunity."

Loren gasps. "You totally have a Lando crush, don't you?"

My cheeks burn, but I ignore her accusation. It's not like I could deny it, even if I wanted to.

"Leave her alone, Lo-Lo. You might not want to hear this, but Landry is a catch. He's still relatively young and good looking. And he *is* a doctor—a pediatrician, which means he's good with kids," Lilley chimes in, the wine sloshing around inside her glass as she talks.

"But he's so ... *Landry*." Loren wrinkles her nose in distaste.

Tenley snorts. "Even I used to think that was a good thing."

"Wait, what?" I blurt out, and everyone's head turns in my direction.

She smiles softly as she adjusts the sleeping newborn in her lap. "I had a huge Landry crush of my own once upon a time."

"You did?" I ask, sounding way more desperate than I intend.

This time she laughs. "For the better part of junior high."

A wave of jealousy and longing hits me as I realize Loren was referring to Tenley and Landry as a couple in her story earlier. I know there's a good chance Landry will never feel the same way about me as I do about him. But hearing that someone like Tenley had her sights set on him just reinforces the idea that he's way out of my league.

"So what happened?" I venture.

Tenley looks a little forlorn. "I was going through a lot at the time, and I pushed him away, but none of it was his fault. Even worse, I pushed my best friend away, too." She glances at Loren, and they share a secret smile. Then I realize what Tenley's done by taking the heat off me again, and I couldn't hate her if I wanted to.

"Aw, Ten," Loren intones. "That's so cute, the way you think you've saved Daisy from having to confess to thinking my hairy, old, grumpy brother is ... *sexy*." She shivers in disgust.

I take another sip from my wine glass and inhale deeply. "Fine. If you really want to know, I do think Landry's sexy. In fact, I actually like all of those things you just said about him, even though he's not as grumpy as he pretends to be. At least not when he gets to sleep in and have his coffee first."

A relieved exhale breaks free once I'm done. I figured it would feel good to finally say that out loud, but I hadn't realized how badly I needed to talk about my crush to *someone*.

Lilley reaches out to stroke my arm again. "Then I'm glad he has you around to make his morning coffee," she tells me, warming my chest.

"Thanks," I reply before turning to Loren and measuring her reaction.

"So am I," she says, smiling. "He could use a little more sunshine in his life. In fact, maybe you could teach him a thing or two about gardening."

My eyes brighten. "I have been making him water my plants. I mean, I've been tending to my own garden for as long as I can remember, but it's nice to have his help sometimes. Especially while he's already got the hose out to wash his ..."

But I gasp and cover my face when I notice the way Loren's eyes are nearly bugging out of her head with the effort it's taking her not to laugh.

Her chin trembles as she replies. "I agree, wholeheartedly. We could all stand to benefit from him learning to plant a few daisies."

She slaps a hand over her own mouth when a loud snort escapes, and that's all it takes for the entire room to break out into a fit of cackles once again. Eventually, Loren wheezes out an apology as she swipes at the tears staining her cheeks.

"I'm so sorry, Daisy," she says breathlessly. "It was too easy."

I giggle as I tuck my hair behind my red-hot ears. "Understandable."

By the time everyone settles down and we get through another round of *Spill the Tea*, Tenley announces that it's time to call it a night. Jada says she's right behind her, and I text Landry for his ETA, hoping to avoid admitting I can't drive myself home.

But between the delirium and the wine, I'm afraid I end up coming off a little too flirty. I bite my lip as I await Landry's response, and those butterflies start bustling around as soon as his replies start to match my tone.

"Need a lift, Daisy?" Lilley offers, bringing me back.

"Oh, um, Landry said he'd take me home once they get back to town, but I guess I don't need to wait on them. That is, if it's not too much trouble for you."

I press my hands to my cheeks to cool them off, and Lilley smirks. "It's no trouble at all. And even if it were, I still wouldn't mind. But I think I might actually leave you here, because I like Tipsy Daisy's chances." She winks.

My face heats again, just as another message comes through from Landry. "Thanks. He says they'll be here soon, so I might as well just hang around a little longer, if it's okay with you?" I glance at Loren, hoping I haven't overstayed my welcome.

"Of course," she replies, standing up to embrace her older sister. "I'm also a huge fan of Tipsy Daisy. She's adorable and plenty sober enough to help me get the twins to bed after their last feeding. I could use the help, since they tend to fight their sleep when Blake isn't here to put them down."

Loren thanks Lilley for her party then, and I turn to pick up one of the babies, attempting to give them a little privacy when they get slightly emotional. Penny and I settle in a rocking chair, and Loren brings me a bottle before she grabs Charley.

"Thanks for letting me crash your bachelorette party," I offer after a while. "I hope you had fun, because I certainly did."

"This was the best, wasn't it?" she grins. "And I'm so glad you were here. I love having you around. We all do."

"I love it here, too." I shrug shyly. "You've all been so welcoming. I never want to leave."

"That's a pretty strong statement coming from the lady tasked with making Landry Reed's coffee every morning," she replies.

"What can I say? He sleeps in his underwear. I enjoy the view," I admit before I bring Penny up to burp her over my shoulder, and Loren giggles.

"And you're really not concerned about, you know, your policy?" she ventures.

I shake my head. "Like I said, Landry doesn't see me that way."

"Sometimes that kind of stuff can sneak up on you, though. All it takes is a moment of weakness, and … well." She gestures to Charley in her arms.

I laugh softly. "I'm sure we'll be fine. I'm kind of a professional virgin at this point, and Landry acts like a prude half of the time."

Although, I could swear he's flirting back with me for the other half.

"Hmm," she hums thoughtfully. "He does have a hard time conveying his affection. It's always been easier for him to take care of everyone than to come out and articulate his feelings for them. I guess if he worries about you to the point where he starts bossing you around and snapping at you, then you know he really loves you."

I huff. "Well, then, maybe I am one of his favorite people."

She smirks. "Welcome to the club."

"He loves you more than anyone, you know," I tell her.

She furrows her brow. "I'm not so sure. My brother is easier to love than to get along with most of the time."

I frown. "He does take really good care of me, for the record. And he may not seem very open with his emotions, but I think that's because he actually feels a lot more than he lets on."

"Does he know how you feel about him?" she asks carefully.

I sigh. "He thinks I have a crush, but that's all."

"Maybe you should make a move," she suggests, patting Charley on the back.

"Oh, I don't think he'd appreciate that," I say, shaking my head.

"Daisy, I know we all have our insecurities. But if my brother's are anything like mine, then it's going to take him a while to see himself as worthy of your love. You'll have to be persistent."

I nod. "Yeah. I guess I could see that."

"For what it's worth, I'm absolutely on board with Team Tipsy Daisy," she adds, gesturing to my phone, and I purse my lips as I consider her advice. "Well, Charley's out. Wish me luck."

She stands carefully and tiptoes toward the girls' bedroom. And I snatch my phone up and reply to Landry's last text before I lose the nerve.

landry

"Why did we have to come all the way to Baton Rouge for this?" I muse to myself.

"Because there's another surprise later," JD says, winking as he hands a credit card to our Top Golf waitress.

We've rented out a whole bay for our group, which consists of Blake, JD, Ethan, Blake's friend Aaron, Emmett, my dad, and myself. I must admit, I was a bit surprised to receive an invitation to Blake's bachelor party, and even more so by the venue. I certainly hadn't expected Blake the Snake to choose a guys' brunch at the driving range for his last foray as a single man. But then again, there's probably another leg of this itinerary later tonight, one that doesn't include all of us.

"Is that the part with the strip club?" Ethan asks hopefully.

"Sorry to disappoint you, Big E," Blake replies, patting him on the shoulder. "Even if I'd requested a trip to the local gentlemen's club, *Padre* would never," he whispers the last part and gestures toward JD. "Especially not with you."

JD rolls his eyes. "For the record, you specifically told me you didn't want that kind of party. And I quote, 'keep it low-key, just the guys, no strippers ... make sure I'm back in time to help Lo get the girls to bed.' "

Blake smirks and shrugs. "I did say that. And this is perfect. Thanks, man." Then he turns to me and gestures toward the selection of golf clubs. "Ready to get your ass handed to you, Lando?"

I furrow my brow. "Let me guess, you're both good at golf, too?"

JD snorts as he goes to pick out a club. "I usually just *Happy Gilmore* the hell out of it. But Blake's pretty good. E, you ever played before?"

"Only putt-putt," Ethan offers.

"Aaron's not half bad," Blake adds, gesturing to the guy he introduced earlier as his legal secretary's husband. Aaron smiles and joins JD to get a club for himself.

"Coach, how about you? Been hitting the greens since you retired?" JD calls out to my dad.

He grunts. "Golf is a rich man's sport. I mostly leave that stuff to my son-in-law."

I shake my head. Figures he'd talk about Blake before me.

"Emmett?" JD asks next.

Emmett cringes. "He means his other son-in-law. I play, but I'm not a competitor."

"Let's hope you swing a club better than you toss a washer, hmm?" Blake jokes, referring to the time when we played a team washerboard tournament earlier this year.

I let them all gather their clubs and set up the game without saying a word. When it's my turn, I walk up to the tee confidently and swing away. The ball lands on one of the targets in the far reaches of the range.

Blake lifts an eyebrow. "Damn, Doc. Beginner's luck?"

"Not likely," I mutter before I drive the next ball to hit the same target on the opposite side of the range. They all groan, and I turn to grin at them. "It's gonna be a long day, boys."

"Since when are you a pro golfer?" my dad asks quietly when I return to my seat.

"I'm not a pro, but I *am* a scratch golfer. And to be honest, I didn't think you'd care," I retort.

He huffs. "Nobody likes a cocky attitude."

I shrug and nod in Blake's direction. "So you say, but it doesn't seem to be true."

I don't get a real reply, though, not from Coach Reed. He simply grunts again and returns to ignoring me for the rest of the game.

"Now, Blake, I know you said you wanted to make it home early tonight, but I've already gotten your lovely bride's permission to have you home a little later than planned," JD explains as we make our way back to a large SUV. He'd apparently swiped Tenley's new ride so we could all squeeze into one vehicle.

Blake frowns, looking almost disappointed to hear he won't be going home. "Oh."

"Come on, bruh. It'll be worth it. Trust me."

"Don't let him take me to the Pink Pony Club," Blake whispers loudly to Ethan, making the rest of them laugh.

We leave Top Golf and head directly into a ridiculous traffic jam, one only made possible by a Baton Rouge game day. "There's a home game this weekend," I say aloud. "Why the hell are we bothering with this?"

"You'll see, man," JD returns cryptically.

I groan from my place in the third row beside Ethan, who turns to whisper to me, "He got us all sideline passes."

My brow lifts. "Seriously? How did he—oh. Right."

I'd forgotten how the Golden Boy had earned his crown for a second. But I suppose being a former collegiate and professional football player entitles him to lifelong perks such as these.

I keep my comments to myself for the rest of the ride, and everyone's excitement grows as we get closer to the stadium. And I have to admit, I'm just as guilty as the others, grinning like a kid in a candy store as we walk out onto the field. Any football fan would have a hard time not enjoying himself.

My dad goes over and pats JD on the shoulder affectionately, effectively ruining my good mood. "Not bad, kid."

"Eh, I couldn't have gotten here without you, Coach," JD says, making me roll my eyes. Ethan nudges me when he sees it, shooting me a secret smile and reminding me to silence my facial expressions.

I try to ignore them after that, though it isn't easy with the way people come over to greet both JD and Blake as if they're royalty. Emmett, Aaron, and Ethan are all starstruck, and my dad is practically preening at this point.

Shortly before the game starts, we're escorted to a luxury box suite to watch the rest of the game. I scoff at the spread of food and drinks as we walk in. I mean, I'm a freaking doctor, so I've been schmoozed before, and I've never seen this kind of treatment.

Blake comes over and pats me on the back heartily as he picks up a drink. "Having fun yet, bro?"

I clear my throat. "I can't imagine how much all of this cost."

"Hey, lighten up. JD called in a few favors. Enjoy yourself." He lifts another glass and puts it in my hand before he clinks his against it, and I sigh as I give in and take a sip. But the alcohol goes down too smoothly, so I set it down before I'm tempted to overindulge.

Most of us have our share of complimentary drinks but manage to remain remotely sober by the time we walk back to the SUV a few hours later—all except for Blake. He stumbles through the parking garage, and JD quietly ducks under his arm to help him slide into the back seat. This time I end up sitting between my two brothers-in-law for the long ride home.

Blake chuckles and snorts to himself when he picks up his phone.

"What's so funny?" I ask, already annoyed.

"Your sister," he replies with glossy eyes and a lazy smirk. Then another message comes through, and his expression changes. He swallows hard as he stares down at the phone, then clicks it off abruptly.

But the screen lights up again with a FaceTime call from Loren. Blake turns the phone over in his lap, cringing while it continues vibrating.

"Aren't you going to answer her?"

He blows out a breath. "Not now."

"You're really making her wait on you?"

"Trust me, it's for the best."

I frown at him. "You're such a douche."

"You really think I'm ignoring her right now because I'm having too much fun with *you*?" he poses, laughing incredulously. Then he shakes his head. "You have no idea what it's like for us, do you?"

"What?"

He casts a pitying glance my way. "You don't understand the power that woman has over me. There's nothing I wouldn't do for her," he slurs.

"Except answer the phone, right?"

He laughs again. "You know they threw her a lingerie shower tonight?"

"Oh." I'm not sure I like the way this is headed.

He leans in closer and gestures to the phone. "She's been sneaking away all evening to try on her gifts for me. And you don't really want to see what she does to me, do you?"

I shove him away, and he cackles loudly. "What is wrong with you?"

Blake grins widely. "A lot, although it's nothing a little alone time with your sister can't fix."

"You're disgusting."

He bounces his eyebrows. "Maybe. But it turns her on, so I'm leaning into it."

"Ugh. You don't deserve her," I mutter.

"We've already established that, haven't we?" He pats my thigh. "And for some reason, she loves me anyway. What else you got?"

I press my lips together, unable to think of any more insults, and he sighs when he senses I won't be continuing. "I'm fully aware that I'm the luckiest man in the world, Landry. No doubt about it. Not only do I have an amazing family and a great career, but I'm also charming and relatively easy on the eyes, or so I'm told." I grunt before he goes on. "Wanna know what the best part is, though?"

"Not really."

"I get to spend the rest of my life with the girl I fell in love with when I was only thirteen years old, the kind of woman who sends me sexy selfies in her *Lord of the Rings* themed lingerie, who isn't afraid to call me out on my bullshit but still loves me for who I am, and who makes me so hot that I can't even stop fantasizing about her while I'm riding in a car with her brother and dad," he explains, closing his eyes and tilting his head back as a smile creeps across his face.

I cringe. This is worse than usual. "You're drunk."

"I am," he confirms with a sigh. "And I miss my fiancée ... and my babies. I wanna go home." He lifts his head to yell into the front seat. "You'd better be taking me home, bruh. My babies can't go to sleep without me, remember? They need their daddy." He pokes himself in the chest, and it's almost endearing.

"Don't worry, dude. I'm having withdrawals of my own. I'll get us back soon enough," JD returns, sounding amused.

"Good, 'cause I miss my lady so much," Blake replies, sighing dreamily again. "Especially her smell. Have I ever told y'all how amazing Loren smells? Gah ..." He shakes his head and inhales. "Like roses ... and *really* good sex ..."

"Oh-kay, bro," JD cuts him off, but Ethan and Emmett are already snickering. "We all appreciate how much you love her, but can ya take the poetry down a notch?"

Blake squints and groans. "I don't know how you did it, man. These past weeks have felt like a lifetime, and the next few days aren't going to be any easier, are they?"

I glare at him, and JD chokes on his laughter before he answers. "No, but it'll be worth the wait, kid. You're almost there."

"But it's getting harder and harder every day ..." Blake seems to lose his train of thought when he pauses to snort at himself, and Ethan joins in again.

"You can't be serious," I mumble, but Blake's head lolls to the side and his eyes pop open.

"We're down to the last week," he continues. "It's been ten long months, Lando. Ten. Freaking. Months. Almost a year since the best night of my life, and only six days until she's mine forever and ever." Then he reaches up to swipe at his cheeks.

"Are you actually crying about not getting laid?" I ask incredulously. "To me? In front of my dad?"

"No. I'm mostly crying because I love her so much," he says, his head drifting over to my shoulder as he brings his pointer finger and thumb up for reference. "And maybe a little bit about not getting laid."

JD grins and reaches over to pat my dad on the arm. "He's a good man though, right?"

My dad grunts, but his mouth curls up into a half-smile. "He'll make a better husband than I ever was, that's for sure."

"I'm gonna try like hell, Coach," Blake vows before I have time to dwell on my dad's comment. "I didn't believe him before, but my brother was right. It's all so different once you realize she's *the one*, you know? But it's always been Lo. I'd wait a lifetime for her, because she's it for me." He sniffles and shakes his head. "She's my person. I just keep praying she won't change her mind, because I don't know what I'd do without her. And the girls, they're everything to me, all I've ever needed."

I curl my lip in distaste when he turns to rub his snot on my shirt. "You're pathetic," I say to him. But when I glance around the car, all I find are watery eyes and looks of admiration. I groan. "You guys aren't really buying this, are you?"

"Have some respect," my dad speaks up, his voice thick. "He's talking about your sister."

"I know, that's the freaking point!" I yell, throwing my hands up in exasperation.

Blake sighs and rolls his head back from my shoulder. "I'm sorry, Landry. I know you never wanted to see her with a selfish bastard like me, but I can't help myself. I think I was made just to love her," he drawls until his heartfelt apology ends in a yawn and a snore.

landry

BLAKE'S PHONE buzzes again in his lap, and it slides onto the floor when we take the next turn sharply. I instinctively lean over to pick it up, forgetting what he'd said earlier about Loren's last few messages. But once her name flashes across the screen alongside a tiny, thankfully incomprehensible image, I look away and gingerly slip it into the front pocket of Blake's button-down shirt. He hums and shifts his position to lean against the door.

At least he's not texting other women, right? I mean, I can't be the only one surprised to hear him admit they're waiting until their wedding night this time around, but his drunken declarations do seem pretty sincere. It's not like he's done anything but dote on Loren and the babies for the past few months, so I suppose he could mean everything he's saying.

I sigh, teetering on the edge of the line between loving and hating my future brother-in-law. But there's one bit that's keeping me from throwing in the towel and admitting that I approve of Blake the Snake marrying my sister.

You have no idea what it's like for us, do you?

I can't shake the way he looked at me as if I was the one to be pitied when he said it. Like he and Loren share something so undeniable that I'll never understand the secret to life unless I follow his lead and allow myself to fall hopelessly in love.

Yeah, okay.

That's why he's the one spending his bachelor party bawling like a baby in a car full of grown men, not to mention the celibacy part. I cast another poignant look over at him before I make myself comfortable and close my eyes.

You don't understand the power that woman has over me. There's nothing I wouldn't do for her.

The memory of Daisy's big, green eyes staring up at me while I slip a gold band onto her finger floods my mind. I groan and drag a hand over my face, trying to stop myself from reliving any more of that morning—especially the part when I involuntarily pulled her in for a very authentic, union-sealing kiss.

My own phone buzzes this time, and I sit up to check it. I'm grateful for the distraction until I realize it's a picture of Daisy and Loren, their faces pressed cheek-to-cheek while Loren holds up her gift.

DAISY

How's it going over there? You guys having any fun?

LANDRY

The groom just cried himself to sleep on my shoulder.

DAISY

So, best night of your life, then? 😄

LANDRY

I've had better.

Looks like you're having a good time, though.

DAISY

Your sisters might be the most entertaining people I've ever met.

And I'm learning a LOT from Tenley.

LANDRY

> Oh no. Please don't let them corrupt you.

DAISY

> Too late … 😊

> Think you'll be able to bring me home when you get back, or should I catch a ride with Lilley while I can?

LANDRY

> It sounds like you should get out of there before any more of your innocence is compromised.

DAISY

> Oh, stop it. We're only looking at fancy panties. Nothing to be afraid of.

LANDRY

DAISY

> I think I'll wait for you to get back. You know, just in case you might be missing me as much as I miss you.

My chest tightens, and I swallow hard.

LANDRY

> Have you been drinking?

DAISY

> Don't get mad, but …

> I may have sipped a glass of wine. 😬

LANDRY

> You shouldn't be mixing too much alcohol with your meds. You know better.

DAISY

> Dude, don't kill my vibe.

I accidentally chuckle out loud, then I look around nervously and make sure no one noticed before I continue.

LANDRY

Since when do you have a drinking vibe?

DAISY

I just wanted to be normal for one night.

I frown down at the phone. I know she only wants to be one of the girls, and even though having a drink wasn't the smartest choice, I guess I can't blame her this time.

LANDRY

Do you feel okay?

DAISY

I'm great. I promise.

Okay, I might be a little sad. But that's only because everyone else has been trading stories about their husbands, and I can't talk about mine.

LANDRY

I'll be there to pick you up soon.

DAISY

Thank you, fake husband/real roomie/accidental bestie.

"S'okay, Doc," Blake murmurs beside me. "Your secret's safe with me."

I furrow my brow and wipe the stupid smile off my face. "What secret?"

He smiles, his eyes still closed. "You've been driving Miss Daisy," he intones.

"What?"

He laughs shortly and attempts to open his eyes again. "Maybe you *do* know."

"Know what?"

"You can't say no to her, can you?"

I scoff at his accusation, but my heart rate quickens. "I have no idea what you're talking about."

"Better yet, you don't *want* to say no," he adds with a yawn. "That's how it starts, though, just a little bit of 'I'll make sure she has what she needs' and one or two thoughts of 'gah, she's cute.' Next thing you know, you're moving her into your house and sniffing her hair when no one's looking. Then it's all over. It's too late. You belong to her, and there's nothing you can do about it."

"What the hell are you trying to say?" I ask again, but he's already drifting back to sleep. So I slip my phone into my pocket and pout in silence ... for all of about five minutes.

Dammit.

LANDRY

> Think you can hold onto what's left of your virtue until I can get there to rescue you?

DAISY

> Are you asking me to save myself for you?

A wave of heat flashes over me, and I blink down at my phone. Thankfully, another message pops up before I have to dwell too long on the last one.

DAISY

> Sorry. That was the wine talking. 🙈

I smirk as I type in a response.

LANDRY

> Lay off the booze, Blondie. We'll be back in about thirty minutes.

DAISY

> *heart react*

The last leg of our drive feels like it takes forever, but JD manages to get us back to town in one piece. The other guys bid one another good night and express their gratitude for the invitation, leaving JD, Ethan, and me to help Blake stumble into his house.

"*Aaag-ness*! Daddy's home!" he calls out loudly, and everyone shushes him.

"Are you crazy? You're going to wake the girls," Loren comes around to scold him, looking amused. I frown when I don't see Daisy with her.

"Crazy 'bout you. Hmm, what are you wearing, Agnes?" Blake asks, regarding her carefully, and I roll my eyes when he calls her by her middle name again.

Loren tightens the belt of a silky robe. "New jammies."

He sighs and leans in, tugging her closer. "You look amazing, babe." Then he lets his forehead drop to hers and inhales deeply. I look away when it starts to feel like we're interrupting a private moment. I notice the rest of the house seems empty as Blake continues, "So sexy. And you smell so freaking good. Like—"

"All right, Gus Gus, we get it," JD interrupts him, to my relief. I'm glad I'm not the only one annoyed by their pet names. "Blake's been waxing poetic about your new nightwear all evening. We don't need any more details than we've already gotten," he tells Loren.

"Poetry, *pour moi*?" she asks Blake as she pulls away, and he shoots her a lazy smirk.

"Hey, where's Daisy?" I take the opportunity to ask before they get too mushy again.

"Passed out on the couch. She got really sleepy and asked if she could take a nap while she waited," Loren explains as Blake continues petting her arms and staring at her as if he can't believe she's real.

"What? Did she say she was feeling off? She didn't mention anything about having a seizure, did she?" I ask quickly.

"No," Loren replies. "She was tired, is all. Maybe a little tipsy."

"Heh. I'm a little tipsy," Blake admits.

"Yeah. We know," I mutter, coming around to the sofa to find

Daisy lying on her side. Her hair is messier than usual, and her cheeks are flushed. I kneel down beside her for a quick assessment. Her breathing seems normal, and she isn't showing any signs of having an episode.

"Daisy," I begin quietly. "Hey, are you all right?"

Her mouth curls up into a smile, and she takes a deep inhale. "Landry?" she rasps with her eyes still shut, and I'd be lying if I said I didn't like the way my name sounded on her lips.

I clear my throat. "I'm here. Are you okay?"

"Mm-hmm," she hums, stretching her limbs. "Just ready for bed."

"You hear that?" Loren intones behind us. "She wants you to take her to bed, Lando."

I glare at Ethan when he laughs. "Shut up, Lo."

Daisy finally opens her eyes and reaches out to cup my cheek, making me swallow hard. "It's okay. She's just teasing."

"I know," I say, clenching my jaw as she caresses it.

"Are you sure you didn't miss me?" she asks quietly, but I'm frozen. Her expression falls when she realizes I'm not going to answer her the way she wants. "I'm sorry. Can we go home now?"

"Yeah," I say on a sigh, but we're interrupted by the sound of my sister squealing behind me.

I turn in time to see Blake sweeping her up into his arms. "That's it. I'm done," he declares.

"What are you doing?" Loren asks, giggling.

"Taking you to bed, woman," Blake replies plainly. "You've been teasing me all night. Hell, you've been teasing me for the past ten months, and then eighteen years before that." He leans in and plants a sloppy, tongue-heavy kiss on her, and I choke back my disgust. "And I might just drop dead before I get the chance to bury myself in your—"

"Okay, I'll be taking that," JD steps in and pulls Loren from his arms while Ethan snickers nearby.

"Nooo," Blake whimpers and stomps his feet. "It's mine!"

"Not yet," JD tells him like he's talking to a child. "One more week before you can open your big-boy gifts, remember?"

Loren snorts from her place in JD's arms now, and I'm a little jealous. I'm supposed to be the big brother helping her make good decisions. Then I look down into Daisy's sad eyes, and I realize my sister can't be my priority anymore. She doesn't need me the way Daisy does.

"I'll take her," JD says to Ethan. "You got Blake?"

Ethan nods and steers Blake in the direction of his own bedroom, his protests growing more muffled as they disappear from sight.

"But I'm not dressed for a Coach JD tuck-in," Loren whines.

"I'll find you a flannel nightgown when we get to your room ... and a chastity belt," he mumbles and takes her down the hallway.

I offer a hand to Daisy once we're alone. But she only stares at it, her eyelids drooping. "I'm sorry. It was getting late, so I took my medicine," she slurs. "I think I might be stuck here."

I sigh and lean down to scoop her up, and she struggles to wrap her arms around my neck. I don't wait for the others to return before I carry her out to my Jeep. I lay her across the backseat, and she rolls over to her side, making it impossible for me to buckle her in. So I take my time driving us home.

Getting her out proves more difficult than I planned. From the way her head flops limply over my arm as we walk inside, I suspect the alcohol strengthened the effects of her medication. I bring her straight to her bed, pull the sheets back, and place her down gently before I drag the covers up over her.

She rolls to her side again and grunts when her hair seemingly gets caught beneath her shoulder, so I reach in to draw the full length of it out behind her. I don't think she drank enough to make herself sick, but just in case, I quickly pull her hair back into a makeshift braid and secure it with a hair tie I find on her nightstand.

She smiles and sighs in her sleep, and I turn to leave her there when something shiny catches my eye. I creep closer and reach out to examine the ring dangling from a ribbon on the wall, my chest expanding the second I realize it's her wedding band—the one I placed on her finger the day I married her.

I'd wait a lifetime for her, because she's it for me. She's my person.

I scoff when Blake's words echo in my head once more. Then I drop the ring before I hurry off to my own bedroom.

daisy

"LANDRY ... YOUR FACE," I whisper and nudge him in the shoulder, and his expression softens a second later. But I can almost hear him grinding his teeth as he watches his sister pose for a group picture around a baptismal font with her soon-to-be in-laws. Blake holds baby Jake up proudly, and JD pulls Charley's bonnet back to kiss the top of her head, then he turns and does the same to Penny from her spot in Tenley's arms.

Landry clears his throat. "He shouldn't be kissing the babies like that. Who knows what he could be passing on to the girls, especially with their preemie immune systems?"

"Oh, come on. They've been exposed to tons of new people in the past few days alone, and it won't be any better by the wedding next weekend. JD's probably doing them a favor right now by helping them build new immunities," I offer reassuringly.

"Right, in addition to all the bacteria that's been growing in that stagnant water Father Conrad just poured over their heads," he mutters.

I huff out a laugh. "It's holy water, silly."

"Let me guess, the priest's blessings give it antimicrobial properties?" he asks, cocking an eyebrow at me.

"Nah, that kind of miracle's reserved for the consecrated hosts," I retort. He shoots me another skeptical glare, making me laugh again. "It's not like they're drinking the water or getting kissed on the face, Landry. I'm sure they'll be fine."

He frowns but doesn't say anything else until a hand appears on his shoulder, and he jolts to attention.

"Hey, there, Landry," we hear Dr. Broussard's soft voice call from behind us. I'm slightly flattered when he tips his head in a smile and adds, "Hello, Miss Daisy." I didn't think he'd remember my name after only meeting me once.

"Hey, Doc," Landry turns and reaches back for a reluctant handshake, and we both trade greetings with Mrs. Broussard as she slides into the pew beside her husband.

"We didn't want to impose, but I couldn't pass up the opportunity to hang around after Mass and get a peek at those beautiful nieces and that adorable nephew of yours," Mrs. Broussard explains.

I stifle a smirk when Landry's nostrils flare at the mention of JD and Tenley's baby as his nephew.

"I know you're enjoying having those baby girls so close," Dr. Broussard directs at Landry before turning to me. "Dr. Reed's been scooping up all the brand-new patients before I can get to them. If I didn't know any better, I'd tell you to watch out. He might be coming down with a case of baby fever."

My cheeks heat. "Oh, well, um ... we're not ..." I purposefully leave the statement unfinished, hoping they form their own conclusions. I'm sure Landry wouldn't appreciate letting the Broussards go on thinking we're making babies together, but I also don't want to back myself into a corner and be forced to choose between lying in church or divulging the details of our secret marriage of convenience.

Dr. Broussard's eyebrows draw in together, though he's still smiling. "But I thought ..."

"Like I said before, we're roommates," Landry clarifies, his voice flat.

"My brother and Landry lived together in college," I volunteer awkwardly. "And now we live together, here. In Camellia. Well, not *together*, obviously, but in the same house."

"I suppose your brother can rest assured you're in good hands, then," Dr. Broussard replies, his smile looking less genuine now.

We make small talk for another minute before they excuse themselves, and Landry goes back to supervising while the rest of his family takes turns posing for photos with the girls in their frilly white dresses.

"Go ahead, I'll take your picture," I urge him forward after a while. He drags his feet for a second before he steps in to take Charley from Lilley's arms, and Loren smiles tentatively at him before she turns for me to get a few photos of them together.

Loren waves me over then, and Blake hands Penny to me before I realize what's going on. "Give me your phone," she demands.

"Oh, you don't have to—"

"I want a picture of the girls with their *N'oncle* Lan and their honorary *Tante* Daisy."

She smirks, seemingly pleased with herself as she takes a few steps back and lines up the shot. I peek at Landry from the corner of my eye. He's pressing his lips into a hard line and looking mighty uncomfortable again.

"Smile, Landry," Loren orders, and he lets out a quiet groan before he forces a softer expression.

I turn to him after Loren lowers my phone, his frown already returning. "Thanks for sharing this with me," I whisper quietly.

"You're already here," he mumbles, and my smile falters for a second. But I lift the corners of my mouth again, because I don't want to pile more guilt onto his shoulders. I'm sure he's only been including me in everything because he feels obligated to keep me around, even though I genuinely enjoy spending time with him and his family.

But he surprises me by reaching out to stop me. "I'm sorry. I didn't mean that the way it came out." He pauses and shakes his head. "I know how much you love the girls and wouldn't have wanted to miss their baptism."

"It's okay. I'm sure you're getting tired of having me tag along all the time."

He shrugs. "You help keep me in line."

The butterflies in my stomach get a kick out of that one, and I barely manage to stop myself from breaking out into a full grin as we walk back toward the pews.

"All right, we're heading over to Mom's," I hear Tenley say as we approach, and everyone begins gathering their things.

"Thank God. I'm starving," Blake whines.

"Because you're hungover as hell," Landry blurts out, and I prepare myself for the worst.

But Blake only cringes and rubs his head with a smile on his face. "I'm definitely that. Why'd you let me drink so much, anyway?" he asks Landry when he takes Charley to strap her into her car seat.

I watch as Landry's expression shifts to something dark, and Blake flinches once he realizes what he's said. "Ah, sorry, man. I was just kidding," he leans in and tells Landry quietly.

"What?" Loren turns and asks once she senses the tension between them.

"They were just saying that some of us had a little too much fun last night," I volunteer as I take a step closer to Landry, and he visibly relaxes. "Thanks for braiding my hair for me after I passed out on your couch, by the way," I continue, directing my comment at Loren. "I imagine it would have been a mess this morning if I'd have slept with it down."

Loren looks confused. "I didn't braid your hair, Rapunzel."

"Oh," I reply thoughtfully. "Then ... I wonder who did?"

"Yeah, I wonder," Loren echoes, smirking at her brother.

Blake raises an eyebrow, and I instinctively follow his lead to check Landry's reaction.

"I ... I just thought ..." Landry begins, and I could swear his ears are turning red. "You usually braid it before bed," he sputters, then he shrugs and drops his eyes to the ground.

"Score one for Tipsy Daisy," Loren mumbles, but I barely hear her.

I blink up at Landry in disbelief, because no matter how hard I try, I can't wrap my mind around the image of him braiding my hair.

I woke up this morning with a foggy recollection of him carrying me to bed. But the only parts I remember are the way his arms felt cradling me while my hand rested on the back of his neck. It was already an unbelievably tender and sweet act on his part, and not at all surprising for the Landry I know. But stopping to tend to my hair?

"You know how to braid?" I ask without thinking.

He coughs and crosses his arms over his chest. "Lilley taught me before she moved away for college. For Lo."

I'm still gaping at him when Blake chimes in. "Does that mean you would have held my hair back for me last night if I'd gotten sick, Lando?" he poses with a grin.

Landry growls, but Tenley's mom saves us by interrupting to remind Blake and Loren that she has lunch waiting for everyone back at her house.

"Landry, Daisy, y'all come on," she adds.

"Oh, we can't impose," I reply, thinking of Landry's comment from a few minutes ago.

"*Mais cher*, you're not imposing if you get an invitation. And you never need one around here, anyway." Mrs. T winks and squeezes my arm affectionately.

"Thank you," I tell her. "A good meal doesn't sound so bad, right, Landry?"

"Of course, he's coming," Mrs. T says, patting his shoulder next. Landry forces a smile and nods, and we're all ushered out to the parking lot.

"We don't have to go to lunch with everyone if you don't want to. I mean, I figure you might want some downtime after last night, especially since you'll be seeing everyone for the wedding festivities all this week and into next weekend," I begin rambling before he can crank the Jeep.

"Do you want to go?" he asks me.

"Well, yes. And not only because Tenley's mom is a good cook." I chuckle when I say it.

"Okay," he says. "We'll go. On one condition."

"What's that?" I ask curiously.

He sighs. "You forget the hair-braiding thing ever happened."

I bite my lip to hide my smile. "I'm not sure I can forget it, but I can pretend I didn't know it was you."

His lips twitch, but he keeps his face blank. "Good enough."

landry

I THROW BACK another glass of champagne while I watch my baby sister's first dance with her husband. They'd shown up late to their own wedding reception just now, both of them wearing smug expressions that could only mean one thing. I may have a hard time reading people, but it was pretty obvious that they'd managed to sneak in some "marital activities." And if it wasn't enough that I had to pretend not to notice, Blake's brother made sure we all knew exactly what took them so long to get here with the corny and inappropriate jokes he cracked during his wedding toast.

I'd say I should have been the one making that toast, but the truth is that I'm not capable of delivering a speech that manages to make everyone laugh and cry within the same sitting. And even if I were, I'd never do it as well as JD.

My eyes search the room until I find my mom again. She's sipping what I hope is the plain Coke I secured for her a while ago. She's spent the last eight years completely sober, to the best of my knowledge, but I'm still going to have to watch her all night. She and Tenley's mom are on babysitting duty, which I'm hoping will keep her occupied.

I'm still concerned about the twins being around all these people and their germs with their compromised preemie immune systems, though.

And I can't help but worry about Tenley and JD's baby boy being out here in the same cesspool, too. He *is* one of my patients.

Then there's Daisy. I also have to make sure she's safe and seizure-free.

I sigh, thinking I might need another drink.

"You gonna be okay, Lan?" I hear my older sister ask as she sits across from me at the empty table I've been occupying.

"Yeah," I reply shortly. "Just trying to let all this sink in."

It's a lie, though. I'm over the whole "allegedly reformed player marrying my sister" part. I'm honestly not even sure why I'm angry at this point.

Lilley chuckles. "Good, because it's a little late to object now," she says, gesturing to the dance floor.

Blake is leaning down to whisper something into Loren's ear as they continue dancing to Hoobastank's "The Reason," which seems nauseatingly cheesy now that I think about it, and she smiles and flut-ters her eyes before she turns to lay her head on his chest. Then I notice that her feet aren't even touching the ground anymore. He's holding her up while he sways and turns them in a circle. And she's just ... letting him.

It's been so hard to wrap my mind around this version of her, of them together. But even I can't deny that she looks happy.

I don't even think I'm upset anymore.

I want to be happy for Loren. I *want* to give in to that warmth creeping into my chest. I want to let go of the resentment and smile and celebrate with my family. I want to be friends with my sister again. I want her and Blake to know I love and support them, and I want them to enjoy my company.

But why do I still feel like shit? Why can't I stop brooding and lashing out all the time?

I huff and reach across the table to snatch a half-emptied glass of champagne and knock it back in one gulp. "Is that supposed to make me feel better?" I ask after a while.

"She's a grown woman, Landry," Lilley reminds me with a smile. "She's a mama with her own family to care for and a husband who's more than happy to take care of her. You're off the hook ... not that she was ever your responsibility in the first place."

"Sure, she wasn't," I mutter under my breath.

Lilley sighs. "I'm sorry you felt that way. But you chose to—"

"Someone had to do it," I cut her off.

I catch the way she winces before she presses her lips into a hard line. "It wasn't your job." Then she pauses and reaches out to brush her hand over mine. "You did it well, though. Be proud of yourself. Of Loren."

"I am proud of her. She's a good mom." I clear my throat awkwardly before adding, "And so are you, Lil."

She tugs her hand back. "Wow. That sounded painful."

"What do you mean?" I ask, furrowing my brow.

"It just seems like the things that bring everyone else joy make you miserable instead," she mumbles, shaking her head.

I nod silently before I spot another glass left unattended. I take a sip before starting again. "Well, I'm doing my best. I don't know what you want from me."

"I just want to see you happy," she says quietly. "We all do."

I scoff and drain the rest of the glass. "Is this an intervention or something?"

"Maybe," she replies.

"Look, I'm trying to be nicer. I really am. It's just ... I usually have a lot on my mind, and I get frustrated when the people I'm trying to protect work against me."

She shakes her head and regards me, a mixture of pity and concern lining her expression. "Landry, don't take this the wrong way, but have you thought about getting help?"

"What do you mean, *help*?"

"Therapy? You know, get some techniques for managing those feelings so they don't eat away at you. It's never too late for you to learn more about yourself. Maybe there's more to it than just the ADHD stuff. And who knows, you might feel better once you get a diagnosis and figure out how to work with your brain instead of fighting it."

"Oh, so there's something wrong with me now?" I shoot her a wry smile.

She glares at me. "You know that's not what I meant."

"And you don't think I recognize there's more than ADD going on up here?" I retort, gesturing to my head. "I'm a doctor, too."

"Exactly! And you should know better than anyone that it's not good to feel this way all the time!" She throws her hands up in exasperation before she softens her tone and adds, "Then again, doctors usually make the worst patients, don't we?"

But she's wrong, because I don't feel this way all the time. I like my career. I like my patients, and I like helping people. I enjoy going to work most days, even if I haven't managed to befriend all my coworkers. And I don't wake up every morning intending to be a miserable grump.

In fact, lately ... I don't wake up miserable at all.

I think it's this crap—these confrontational interactions with my family that I dread to the point of putting me in a bad mood. This is the source of that underlying anger and resentment I can't seem to shake.

"Is that what you did, Lil? Your therapist help you work through all that guilt when you moved away and left us behind?" I mumble after a while. But I regret it as soon as I look up and see the way her eyes are watering. I shake my head. "Sorry, that came out wrong."

She bites her lip and nods softly. "You know, I never had what you and Lo have. I didn't have anyone to cling to when things first started getting bad at home. But I've always been grateful the two of you had one another, and I'd hate to see you ruin that bond because you're too scared and stubborn to allow yourself to heal or move on or ... whatever the hell it is you need to be happy."

My chest feels like it's being squeezed, and I involuntarily reach up to rub it. "I don't think I know *how* to be happy," I say after a while, my voice cracking.

"Then let someone help you figure it out." She turns her head and gestures in Daisy's direction.

Daisy's eyes instantly meet mine, and they're filled with concern.

Then she offers me a sad smile, and I clear my throat and look away when my eyes begin to sting.

"You deserve it, Landry," Lilley adds with a light sniffle.

I stand abruptly, because I can't take any more. "I'm going to get a drink. Thanks for the session, Doc."

But Daisy follows me to the bar, and I curse under my breath.

"Hey, is everything okay?" she asks, placing a gentle hand on my forearm.

"Fine," I retort as I lift my arm to pick up a fresh glass of champagne. But I frown when I realize I actually felt better before I shirked the contact.

"Landry," she begins.

"I said I'm fine," I repeat before she can continue. I turn and spot my sister dancing with my dad, then I throw the glass back and down its contents. "Loving and supportive, right?" I mutter before I hand Daisy the empty champagne flute and march toward the dance floor.

The song comes to an end as I wait with my hands in my pockets. My dad lets Loren go and casts a wary glance my way before he walks off, and I force a smile when I offer a hand to her.

"Never thought I'd be the most popular girl at the dance, but here we are," Loren says, grinning, and I soften my expression as she places her hand in mine.

"You're certainly the prettiest, Lo-Lo," I tell her, and she laughs. "Even if you are bratty enough to need two dresses."

She cocks an eyebrow at me. "Who says that wasn't just an excuse to go home and let my husband undress me before the reception?"

I groan, and she snickers, pleased with herself. "I guess you were right when you said you didn't need my help fending off the creeps," I begin again. "You've certainly managed to turn the douchey quarterback into a sappy family man."

Her smile fades. "I didn't do anything. Blake's always been a great guy. It's just that none of us wanted to see it."

"Yeah, maybe," I say as we continue dancing. My eyes drift over to the crowd, and I spot Lilley watching us, though I can't read her expression. Then I notice Daisy beside her, and I turn my attention back to Loren.

"Either way, you're a beautiful bride and an even better mom. I'm proud of you," I choke out after a while.

"Thank you, Landry." Loren squeezes me tightly just as the song ends, and I rest my chin over her head as I welcome the embrace. "I love you."

"I love you, too."

"But I still think you'd be happier if you gave this stuff a shot." She pulls back and looks up at me. "You know who would also make a lovely bride?" She inclines her head in Daisy's general direction, and my stomach turns.

"Don't do that right now," I mumble and let her go. I should have known she'd add a *but* after that.

"Do what?" She grins mischievously. "Get you to loosen up and see what's right in front of you?"

I blink, my head suddenly getting thick. I probably should have eaten before having a few drinks. "Whatever."

"Landry ..." she steps forward and reaches out for me when I sway on my feet.

But I push her away, and everything gets foggier. "Let it go, Lo."

"Fine," she says on a sigh, then she turns into the next set of waiting arms as I head back to the bar.

CHAPTER 21

daisy

A series of loud taps on the microphone and a short screech from the feedback grabs the attention of most of the guests at the wedding reception.

"Hey, everyone," a deep voice slurs. "I've got something to say."

The music trails off as we all turn to stare at Landry, watching as he chokes on a swig from a champagne bottle. "You already got the good toast from the Golden Boy over there, but it's my turn to speak," he says, gesturing to the side where JD stands beside Blake and Loren.

I cringe. Something tells me this isn't going to end well.

"I'm sure you're all aware that I'm not the easiest person in the world to get along with, but ..." he shrugs before he continues, "neither is my sister. I mean, I love you, Lo-Lo. I'd die for you and everything, but gah, you can be an ungrateful brat."

Everyone turns to see Loren's reaction. She's observing Landry with a blank expression while Blake clenches his jaw and tightens his grip around her as if he's preparing for the worst. And now I'm wondering whether I should cut in and stop this before he goes too far.

Landry laughs sardonically over the mic and sways a little as he turns to address the guests directly. "But she's my baby sister, you know? I have to take care of her. So when I found out that she and Blake the Snake were an item, well ... y'all can only imagine what went through my mind."

We all fidget uncomfortably. "I mean, this is the same guy who's famous for screwing his way through one of the biggest college campuses in the country, right?" He gestures in Blake's direction as he says it, and now Loren's emotionless stare shifts into an angry glare.

"But, I mean, he gave all that up for you, Lo-Lo, so he must *really* love you."

My stomach turns when Loren's eyes drop to her feet and Blake runs a hand through his hair, looking mortified. If only Rowan was here, he'd know what to do right now. I glance around the crowd, looking for someone else to help, but they all just look on in a combination of horror and secondary embarrassment.

"And even though this son of a bitch almost got my sister killed when he knocked her up, at least he had the courtesy to marry her, right?" Landry says, waving the hand holding the empty bottle.

That's when JD steps forward, and so do I. He may be a nice guy, but I don't know anyone with that much self-control. And even though I know it's not my place to butt in, I imagine the situation will only escalate unless I put a stop to it now.

"All right, Landry," I croon when I reach his side and tug on his arm. "I think you've said enough."

He lets me take the bottle, but he yanks his arm back. "No, I'm not finished. I need them all to know I'm okay with this," he tells me, gesturing at the bride and groom again. "That I'm happy for them. Because I know he loves her. Blake's always had a thing for Lo. I knew it when I caught them together in middle school, and then again in high school. They tried to pretend nothing was going on every time, but I'm not an idiot, okay?" He pokes himself in the chest. "This was inevitable."

"Come on, Lan. I think they get it," I plead again.

"I'm trying to be loving and supportive though," he whines, then he turns and addresses the crowd again. "This is what you all wanted, right, for me to play nice?"

"The young lady's right, son. You've said enough."

I glance up to find Landry's father on the other side of him. He holds out a hand expectantly, and Landry reluctantly drops the mic into his palm. Then Landry turns to face Loren, blinking away the moisture in his eyes.

"I'm sorry," he says, even though she probably can't hear him anymore. "I tried."

My chin quivers when I read the sadness and regret in his expression, and I struggle to hide the way my voice cracks when I urge him on again.

"Let's go, buddy. I think it's past your bedtime." I wrap my arm around his waist, and he surprises me by draping his arm over my shoulders and leaning into me. Then he looks down and furrows his brow.

"I'm sorry, Daze," he tells me, and I'd be lying if I said I didn't like the way he shortens my name. "I don't mean to be such an ass, you know."

Loren shoots me an anguished look as I struggle to turn Landry around. "I know," I say, trying to coax him toward the door.

JD nudges my arm a second later. "Why don't you bring the car around?" he asks as Ethan comes to take my place as Landry's crutch.

"Oh, well, I actually ... I guess I'll need to find his keys," I reply awkwardly.

"Think they're still in one of his pockets?" JD asks.

"Nuh-unh. You can keep those big ole paws to yourself, Golden Boy," Landry grumbles, making JD snort. "If anyone's shoving a hand down my pants, it'd better be Blondie."

"For the first time, we're in complete agreement, Doc," JD retorts dryly.

"I guess that means I'm conducting this search, then," I say to myself, and they stop at the door for me to reach gingerly into Landry's right pocket.

"Who says I wasn't talking 'bout Tenley?" Landry chimes in,

making JD's nostrils flare and Ethan snicker quietly. "S'okay if you wanna hit me, man," he continues. "I was kinda hoping you'd just do us all a solid and knock me out this time. We both know you've always wanted to, and I bet you haven't had a reason to make those ridiculous pythons look useful in a while."

I watch the muscles in JD's jaw tick as I continue digging around, but I come up empty. "I'd rather leave you conscious so you can lie awake and wallow in self-pity once you realize how much you've hurt your sister tonight," he replies after a second.

"Hmm. You might be smarter than you look," Landry mutters.

"I do get more use out of my muscles than my brain, though, since my wife likes being lifted so much," JD adds. Ethan makes a loud gagging sound, and I bite my lip to keep myself from smiling too hard. But Landry's apparently too preoccupied with keeping his balance to catch it, and he stumbles when I go to slip my hand into his left pocket.

He catches his footing again and cocks an eyebrow while I sift through the empty space. "This is taking you a while. Find anything you like down there, sugar?"

I sigh. His nicknames are becoming less endearing by the minute.

"Hey, now," he squirms. "Be careful before you start the wrong engine."

I glare at him angrily as I pull my hand back. "Both pockets are empty."

"Oh, yeah," Landry starts with a laugh. "Left my keys in the Jeep. Guess I forgot."

I growl, and his expression transforms into something more remorseful again.

But then I remember our predicament. I need to come up with something fast if I want to make it home without having to drive us there myself.

"I, uh, I'm actually not sure it's a good idea for me to get behind the wheel, either, now that I think about it ..." I say slowly, hoping they'll assume I've also had too much to drink.

"I only had a sip of champagne during the toast. I could drive you both home in Doc's Jeep and have Mawmaw pick me up on her way out," Ethan volunteers after a second. I turn to study him, thinking it's a suspiciously generous offer, but he shrugs and admits he's been dying to check out Landry's ride. JD eyeballs him along with me. "I'll be careful, I promise."

"And you're sure you only drank that one sip of champagne all night?" JD grills him.

"One small sip, I swear," Ethan replies, smirking. "After that, I switched to Jack and Coke."

Landry chuckles as JD reaches around him to knock Ethan in the back of his head.

"Ow!" Ethan objects. "Okay, I know this dude's getting under your skin, but touch grass, bro. He's not really trying to get with Aunt Ten. He just wants to make someone else feel as lame as he does."

JD grunts as we approach the Jeep.

"He's right," Landry slurs. "Don't worry. I know Tenley would never stoop to my level again, even if she weren't happily married."

"Again?" Ethan asks, perking up.

JD pretends it's an accident when he bumps into Landry, crushing Ethan against a car. The kid groans and promptly drops the subject.

"Either way, I'm not brave enough to hit on her now," Landry continues, squinting his eyes and pointing a finger at JD. "Not because you scare me though. It's *her* I'm afraid of."

I can't help but giggle softly at that one, and JD even bites back a smile while he lowers Landry into the backseat. Then I go around the other side and slide in next to him.

CHAPTER 22

daisy

"STRAIGHT THERE, no detours. Drive under the speed limit and stop for ten seconds at every intersection. I'll get Therese to meet you there," JD instructs Ethan.

Ethan nods from his place in the driver's seat and snatches the keys from the cupholder, grinning a little too eagerly for my liking. Then he pulls out his phone and poses for a selfie. "Aye-aye, sir. Sure you don't want me to pass by the drive-thru liquor store, first?"

"Are you done being a smartass yet?" JD growls.

"Eh ... mostly."

"Good. Now hand your phone over to Miss Daisy and don't touch it again until you text to let me know you're all home safely."

"Fine," Ethan concedes and passes his phone back to me.

JD walks back inside, and Ethan continues adjusting the seat and fiddling with the mirrors. Landry laughs to himself, his head lolling back as we pull out of the parking lot of the reception hall.

"What's so funny?" I ask, still annoyed with him.

"How much would it take for that dude to act like half the douchebag I am on a good day?"

"You could have threatened me," Ethan pipes up. "That'll do it."

"Don't give him any ideas," I tell Ethan, and he chuckles.

177

"I just wanted a good reason to hate one of them, for once," Landry goes on. "They've been taking everything important from me for as long as I can remember. My QB1 spot, the college scouts ... Tenley, Loren, my dad, the twins ... even Lilley and Emmett like him better than me. Next thing you know, Blake'll be my mom's new favorite, too."

I frown as he heaves out a sigh. His eyes are closed, and he runs a hand through his hair before it drops between us. Then he lets out a sardonic laugh. "I take that back. I'll be stuck looking after my mom forever while my sisters get to live their own lives with their husbands and their kids and never have to worry about our mother relapsing."

I glance up, and Ethan's eyes meet mine in the rearview mirror. He reaches out to turn the radio louder when we stop at the town's only traffic light.

"You're only thirty-three, Landry. It's not too late for you to start a family of your own," I offer reassuringly.

"Pfft," he blows a loud raspberry with his lips. "I'll never have a real wife ..." My heart speeds up as I wait for him to say more and expose our fake marriage. "Or kids. No one can stand me. And all that soulmate shit is a load of crap, anyway."

I cover his hand with mine, and he turns his wrist to intertwine our fingers. "You don't mean that," I whisper.

"I do," he replies, his voice thick. "Why do you think I've been so hard on Blake? I know he thinks he's doing the right thing, but marriages never last. And if they do, it's only because they're both too stubborn to admit they're miserable later."

"That's not true." I squeeze his hand, scolding him. He squeezes mine back weakly, and it almost breaks my heart. "My parents have been happily married for nearly forty years, and you know half of my siblings are just as content. Lilley and Emmett are happy, too, aren't they?"

"Stubborn, not happy. And your parents may be the only exception. Must be all the weird, hippie sex."

Ethan covers up his laugh with a cough.

"They did make a lot of babies, but I think you've got it back-wards," I say, stifling my own amusement. "They kept having kids *because* they were in love. Oh, take a right up ahead, please," I direct Ethan.

"Oh, sorry. I thought ..."

"Landry and I are both staying at his sister's old house. We're, um, roommates."

Ethan's brow rises, but he keeps his thoughts to himself. And Landry stays quiet so long that I would have assumed he'd passed out if he weren't slowly stroking my thumb. I bite my lip and attempt to hide the way it makes me shiver.

"Thanks again for doing this, Ethan," I begin, because I can't stand the awkward silence. "If I'd have known my designated driver would get this sauced, I wouldn't have ..." I leave things ambiguous again, hoping he draws his own conclusions.

"No worries, Miss Daisy. Just don't tell Dr. Reed I'm the one who drove his Jeep if he finds anything wrong with it later."

I laugh softly. "Where's Caidence? I didn't see her tonight," I remark as he pulls into the driveway and puts the car in park.

He reaches back to exchange the keys for his phone again, and I notice he looks sad. "She couldn't make it. Well, not as a guest, anyway. She had to help her parents with their catering business."

I nod and offer him a small smile before turning back to my charge. "Landry, hey, we're home now. It's time to go inside," I croon near his ear.

He stirs and groans as Ethan comes around and opens the door. "We're home?" Landry asks, seemingly lost.

"Yeah. Let's get you to bed."

"Okay." He pulls himself up and out of the backseat with Ethan's help, then he stops abruptly and squints at him. "You know, I wasn't always this pathetic."

"Really?" Ethan asks, obviously humoring him.

"Yeah. Your Aunt Ten had a huge crush on me when we were growing up."

"No cap?" Ethan continues.

"What?"

"He means 'no kidding,' " I translate for Landry, and he nods and starts walking again.

"Oh yeah, no cap. I'm pretty sure I was her first—"

"Landry!" I turn to interrupt him in my rush to unlock the front door.

"Kiss. I was gonna say *kiss*." Landry glares at me as he defends himself.

Ethan laughs. "So what happened?

"With Tenley? Oh, I tried to feel her up in front of everyone at a party, and she barely even acknowledged me again after that."

The confession surprises me since Landry seems so anti-PDA.

"I was actually referring to the low point you seem to have hit in your life in general, but yeah, that tracks," Ethan clarifies as we move Landry into the house.

"As for the rest, I guess it's just finally getting too hard to keep up," Landry mutters. "I've never been able to make my dad proud or keep my mom and my sister safe. And the only time I can hold a conversation without offending someone is when I'm talking to one of my patients."

There's a tiny ache in my chest after he says it. Because I know Landry's infamous negativity isn't just a character quirk; it's a symptom of something bigger.

"Kids tell the truth, you know. They don't have a filter, and it's so much easier to read them than to guess what adults are really thinking," Landry continues as I lead us to his bedroom. "Except for you, Daisy. You're honest. Well, you try anyway." I don't respond as we steer him into the tiny bedroom, and he plops down onto his bed.

"You, uh, might want to help him with his tux," Ethan volunteers, his eyes darting around the room and landing on the dresser. "JD mentioned having to return the rentals tomorrow."

"Oh right, good idea," I say, following Ethan's gaze. My lips part in a slight gasp when I see Landry's wedding band sitting there, but I move to block the ring from Ethan's line of sight. "Come on, let's get you changed."

"Trying to get into my pants again, Blondie?" Landry's mood takes a sudden upturn, and he bounces his eyebrows suggestively at me.

Ethan snorts loudly, and I bite my lip and will my cheeks not to redden any more than they already have. "You can undress yourself, and I'll come back to collect the pieces once you've changed into your pajamas."

"Aw, we both know I never wear pajamas."

"Landry ..." I struggle to camouflage my humiliation with a menacing glare.

"Sorry, I probably shouldn't be saying that in front of Tenley's kid," he says, looking remorseful. "He might find out about our arrangement."

Ethan covers up another laugh, and I clear my throat.

"The kid has a name. And he already knows that we're room-mates," I tell Landry, making eye contact again and hoping he gets the message. "But you shouldn't be saying things like that at all."

"You're right. I'm not even supposed to be thinking it, am I?" He sticks his lip out in a childish pout, and my insides start to feel all warm and tingly. "For the record, though, you're the only one I want putting her hands down my pants. You're my Blondie."

I roll my lips in and nod while I help him out of his jacket and begin loosening his tie. But I can't allow myself to stop and think about what he's implying. All I can do now is move things along and pray I'm minimizing the damage.

"You know why I call you that? It's because I like your hair," Landry says, gazing up at me. "It's so long ... and it always looks so soft and shiny. And when you braid it, you remind me of Rapunzel."

"That's nice." I hand the tie over to Ethan, who smirks and adds it to the pile accumulating on the dresser. "Come on, let's get your shirt."

He brings his hands up to the buttons but stops and blinks at me a few times. "You're so pretty."

I swallow hard and begin unfastening his shirt. "Mm-hmm."

"I'm not supposed to be saying or thinking that either, but it's true. And you know what else? I like your freckles." He reaches up and brushes a knuckle over my cheek, and I feel my face flush with heat at the contact. "Especially the ones that go all the way down your back."

I let out an audible gasp, and Ethan chokes on his spit and tries to cover it up with a cough. "Okay, Landry, that's enough," I tell him, my eyes nearly bugging out of my head.

"What? I mean it. They're sexy," he adds, shrugging. My stomach swoops much, much lower than I'm used to.

"*Aaand* I think that's my cue to hang out in the other room," Ethan announces, his voice jarring me from my daze. "I'll be waiting on the couch and pretending not to listen if you need me."

"Thanks, Ethan." I shoot him an apologetic smile. "Just so you know, he didn't mean—"

"Not my business," Ethan replies, turning his lips to the side before he walks out of Landry's bedroom.

"I'm sorry, I'm doing it again, saying too much," Landry whines as I push his shirt back over his shoulders. I'm quickly reminded that he has very nice collarbones, located just above his very solid chest and

…

Oh hello, objectively attractive ab muscles. Haven't seen you guys in a while!

"At least I didn't tell him that we're married, right?" he whispers.

"Shh, he's still here," I scold him, my eyes darting around nervously, even though I doubt Ethan hears him from the other room.

"Oh, sorry," he mouths, and I shake my head and force myself to turn away. Sometimes I wish my husband weren't so gosh darn hot.

"It's okay. But you can take off your own pants. Just leave them with the rest of your clothes for now. I'll help you get everything together in the morning."

"Sure you don't need to check my pockets again?" I hear him

drawl from behind me. The bed squeaks, and I hear the rustling of his clothing.

"It can wait until you're not wearing them anymore," I say as I move to leave him in the room.

He chuckles softly, tossing his slacks onto the dresser before he brushes my arm and stumbles past me in nothing but his underwear. "Where's the fun in that, wifey?"

I bite my lip as I take in his form. Might as well get a good look in while I can, right? It's not like he'll remember me checking him out this time. "Wait, Landry, where are you going?"

"Gotta take a leak," he mumbles. Then he stops and turns to shoot me a cocky smirk. "Wanna help? I'm not sure I can trust my aim right now."

Ethan guffaws loudly from the living room, and I roll my eyes. "You're on your own this time, buddy," I barely manage to spit out.

"It was worth a shot," he says before he sticks an arm out to brace himself against the wall, and I shove him and urge him on before he ducks clumsily into the bathroom. But I instantly regret the contact with his warm skin when my stomach dips again.

"I hate to interrupt, but I think my ride's here," Ethan calls out.

I shuffle back into the living room to bid him good night and thank him again. "And tell Mrs. T thanks for me."

"No worries. She won't mind once she hears about all this," he says with a cheeky smile before he closes the front door behind him.

I don't even get the chance to stress about what he means to tell his grandmother because there's a loud thump in the bathroom.

"Landry? You okay in there?" I yell. I round the corner just in time to watch him staggering into my room and falling face-down onto my bed. "Landry?" I poke his shoulder. "This isn't your bed."

"But mine's too far. Can't we just share this one?" His voice is muffled by the blankets. "Married people sleep together."

"Not in our case," I remind him.

He lifts his head and smiles, patting the empty space beside him. "Hmm. Just think of it as a payment toward that marital debt. Night-

night, 'Punzel," he murmurs before his cheek hits the pillow. Then the only sounds he makes are obnoxiously loud snores.

I groan in frustration. I'm tired. It's past time for me to take my epilepsy medicine, and I know I'm more likely to have a seizure tomorrow if I don't get a decent amount of sleep tonight. I change into my pajamas and return from the bathroom to find Landry hasn't budged, but I don't have the energy to do anything about it. I slip beneath the covers and drift off to sleep beside him in no time at all.

landry

I can't feel my arm.

It's the first thought I have that morning, though it's quickly followed by *ouch, my head.*

I keep my eyes closed while I gather my whereabouts. My arm is numb because it's pinned beneath something—someone. I attempt to adjust my position and realize I'm spooning the culprit, my other arm draped over her side while my body curves around hers. I flex my hand and curl my palm over the nearest body part. It's soft and squishy and—yep, this is definitely a woman. She's warm. And she smells amazing, like ... honeysuckles and lavender essential oils.

Lavender?

My heart begins racing for a second, panic setting in. But my bed buddy distracts me when she squirms, rubbing her butt against me and making my breath hitch. The contact feels so good that I know this can't be real, especially since neither of us would actually allow it to happen.

I must be dreaming.

And since this is only a dream, there's no harm in enjoying it, right? I mean, sure, facing my roommate is going to be awkward after this. But I can't exactly control what happens in my sleep, and she'll be none the wiser.

Might as well just let Dream Landry get this out of his system.

It's also been a while since I've gotten this close to a woman in real life, and I'd be lying if I said I didn't like the way this seems to be going, even though Daisy's still wearing clothes.

Not for long, if I can help it.

I bury my face in the back of her neck, and she gasps when my hand slips beneath her nightgown. My lips curl up into a cocky grin before I move to press a kiss over her freckled shoulder. I knew she'd be into—

"Oh, *shhit*," I blurt out as soon as my eyes crack open, only to discover that I'm surrounded by a mass of actual blonde waves. I mumble a few more curses under my breath as I loosen my hold on her and back away.

Daisy clears her throat beside me, and I squint through the painful throbbing in my head after all that sudden movement. "Um, good morning?" she offers hesitantly when I finally open my eyes again.

"Oh God, what have I done?" I mutter to myself.

She snorts and adjusts her gown. "Gee, thanks."

"No, I didn't mean it like *that*," I spit out awkwardly. "It's just ... I didn't realize we were almost ... but you're Rowan's little sister, and I could never ..."

She sits up. "Not helping."

"I'm sorry, Daisy." I cringe and prop myself up on my elbows, waiting for my head to settle before starting again. "Can you please explain what I'm doing in your bed?"

"You mean you don't remember any of it?"

"Not a thing," I say, careful not to shake my head or nod.

"I can't believe you've forgotten all about the most passionate night of my life," she replies, furrowing her brow.

"Passionate?" I gulp.

She nods sadly and reaches out to grab my forearm, her eyes wide. "After you took to the microphone to announce our marriage and proclaim your feelings for me at your sister's wedding reception, you brought me home to consummate our union and made such beautiful, sweet love to me all night. Tell me you remember, Landry?"

"I ... I ..." The room begins spinning as real panic sets in. I lift the sheets to make sure I'm still wearing underwear. At least the aftereffects of her pushing her backside against me have dissipated. "Daisy," I breathe. "I don't know what happened, but—"

She cuts me off with another loud snort before she bursts into a fit of obnoxious laughter. "I wish you could see your face right now," she barely gets out. "You know I'm just messing with you, right?"

"So, we didn't ..." I narrow my eyes at her. Her giggling is starting to irritate me.

"Of course not," she reassures me. "You got ridiculously drunk at the wedding reception, so I brought you home. Then you ended up passing out here on your way back from the bathroom, and I didn't have the energy to drag you to your own bed."

"Oh."

"To be fair, you *were* lying on top of the covers when I fell asleep. So the cuddling thing must have been Drunk Landry's doing."

"We weren't *cuddling*."

She glares at me. "Oh, right. What's the name for that thing two people do in bed, you know, when the guy wraps his arms around the girl and she snuggles up close to him?" She snaps her fingers and pretends to search her mind.

"Okay, so we cuddled," I admit with a groan. "But it was more of a platonic, mostly clothed snuggle between friendly roommates of the opposite sex ... who coincidentally happen to be married."

"Then what was your hand doing on my right boob a minute ago?" she poses, cocking an eyebrow. "Not to mention, it didn't *feel* platonic when you pushed your—"

"That was an involuntary reaction to you grinding your ass against me, thank you very much," I retort angrily.

"Eh, fair enough," she concedes with an unapologetic shrug.

I glare at her in surprise. "Were you ... trying to seduce me?"

"Seduce you?" She laughs loudly again. "Need I remind you that *you* stumbled into *my* bed?"

"I was drunk!"

"Which is why I let you stay," she says matter-of-factly. "And why I'll spare you the embarrassing report of the stuff you actually did say and do."

"Wait, what?" I sit up straighter, and it suddenly feels like I'm on a boat over water.

She waves me off with a hand. "You were in your feelings a little. Nothing bad *really* happened, except for the part when you embarrassed the hell out of your sister during that very uncharitable wedding toast ... and then again when you made some borderline inappropriate comments about my boss's wife in a misguided attempt to start a fight."

"A fight? With your boss?" I squint my eyes as I think. Then I reach up to examine my face, searching for evidence. "I survived a fight with JD Bourgeois?"

"He refused to hit you, but you definitely deserved it, especially after the unkind things you said about his brother in front of all their closest friends and family."

"Oh." I scratch my head as I run through a hazy memory of that impromptu wedding toast. "What else?"

"Drunk Landry's significantly more ... flirty." She stifles a smirk. "Nothing I couldn't handle, though."

I frown. "I can't believe I got that drunk on freaking champagne."

"You are much more of a lightweight than I expected," Daisy tells me.

"It's because I don't drink very often. My mom's an alcoholic, remember?"

"Right," she says softly. "If it makes you feel any better, she looked great last night. She stayed quiet and kept to herself."

"Good." I breathe a sigh of relief. "I guess I showed her up though."

Daisy shrugs again. "You definitely have some sucking up to do. In fact, I think you ought to just issue an apology to everyone with the last name of Reed or Bourgeois in this town. All the Robins, too."

I groan and let my head fall back against the headboard, making it pound again. "Wait, how did we even get home?"

"I am a capable adult, you know," she replies defensively, throwing the covers back. I avert my eyes when her gown rides up and exposes her long legs as she rises from the bed.

"You shouldn't have been driving, either. I was supposed to be taking care of you."

"Look, I got us home safely, all right?"

"But you could have gotten hurt, and—"

"It's late. You should get moving." She cuts me off as she begins flittering around the room. "I'm sure you have things to do today, like returning your tuxedo."

"Shit. I'm actually supposed to go around and pick them up from everyone in the wedding party, then drop them off at the rental place." I run my fingers through my hair and growl in frustration.

"Hmm, and I don't imagine any of them will be particularly happy to see you today," she muses while she pulls a dress from her closet. "It's probably best if you drive me around while I make the pickups."

I shake my head. "I don't want you to—"

"I'll put the coffee on," she continues, ignoring me. "I suggest you have a couple of aspirin with yours and do whatever's necessary to fix your mood before we go." Then she stops abruptly and adds, "But do it in your own room, if you don't mind."

I roll my eyes and force myself out of bed, moving slowly to keep my head from imploding. Meanwhile, it sounds like Daisy's purposefully slamming cabinet doors and tossing metal pans around the kitchen.

She walks by me again, and I remember I'm standing there in nothing but my underwear. I cover myself with my hands, though modesty seems like a moot point after everything else that's transpired this morning.

But she barely glances my way. "You'd better get dressed. You've got a busy day ahead of you, Doc," Daisy mutters dryly, darting into the bathroom and letting the door shut loudly behind her.

I whimper at the noise and shuffle into the kitchen. I should probably stop by my bedroom to slip on a pair of gym shorts first, but she doesn't seem as bothered by my semi-nudity anymore, so I settle for pouring myself a cup of coffee and throwing back a couple of OTC pain relievers.

I sit on the first stool at the kitchen counter, still trying to make sense of everything that just happened. I don't get it. Why am I struggling so much to figure out basic human interaction, especially at my age?

What am I supposed to think now? Daisy has said before that she could ignore her initial attraction to me, but I'm pretty certain she was into it when we were spooning this morning. She wasn't shy about admitting to her participation, either.

But now she's claiming she wasn't trying to lure me into actually *doing* anything with her, and I'm more confused than ever.

It doesn't matter, though. All I should feel is relief, because our arrangement would be ruined if anything were to happen between us, and I like the way things are now. We're both better off forgetting the whole thing. I should just drop it.

That's what I'm going to do—drop the subject.

But it's bothering me more than it should. I mean, I'm a generically attractive heterosexual male with all my parts in working order. And I'm a doctor, for goodness' sake. I get the look from women all the time. Hell, I get the look from *Daisy* all the time.

I glance down at myself. I could probably use some grooming, but I'm in decent shape. So, why wasn't she ogling me in my underwear just now? Better yet, why *didn't* anything happen between us last night?

Not that anything *should* have happened. I'm grateful it didn't. Married roommates or not, we could never hook up, not only because of our age difference and the fact that she's my best friend's baby sister, but also because I'm well aware of the LaFleur family values.

Still, I'd allegedly flirted with her before stripping down and sneaking into her bed last night. If she's even remotely attracted to me, she'd at least have entertained the idea, right?

I'm still sitting at the small bar in the kitchen trying to figure things out when she walks in.

"Why aren't you dressed?" She stops and glares at me.

I huff. "Why do you care?"

"Because we have places to go. And because we're not supposed to be lying around in our underwear." She turns her eyes to the coffee pot and walks past me.

"Daisy, do you not find me attractive anymore?"

Well, shit. Way to be subtle, man.

She freezes for a second and clears her throat before she goes back to pouring her coffee. "What difference would it make?"

I frown down at my mug. "You know I hate it when I misinterpret a situation, and everything about this is confusing the hell out of me."

Her expression softens as she comes around to sit beside me. "I'm feeling pretty weird about everything, too. But I'm not sure honesty can fix it this time."

I groan. "My head hurts too much to keep beating around the bush."

"You're not going to let this go, are you?" she asks, taking a sip of her coffee and sighing. I'm momentarily distracted by her reaction, but I can't stop to acknowledge how cute she looks when she does that.

"I can't," is all I say.

She puts her mug down and stares at me. "Fine. If you really want to know, yes, I still think you're attractive. Even more so now that I've gotten to know you. But we agreed that those feelings don't have a place in our relationship. And even though most of what you said last night implies the opposite, I knew you didn't mean it. So taking you up on one of Drunk Landry's numerous offers would have been a betrayal of your trust."

"I made offers?" I ask, purposefully ignoring the first part of her confession.

"Oh yeah." She nods.

I gulp. "Sorry about that, then."

"Don't be," she says plainly. "I was actually relieved to hear that some part of you finds me attractive, too, even if it's only while you're wearing champagne goggles."

"Relieved?" I furrow my brow and study her reaction. It's not the same version of relief I felt before.

"It's not like it matters, but yeah. I liked hearing you don't find me completely appalling and that you at least have the capacity to think of me as a woman and not just as Rowan's little sister."

"Oh." Our previous conversations run through my mind again. "I'm sorry if I've been making you feel bad, but I had to establish those boundaries from the start. I ... I couldn't see any other way to make sure I'd never end up in a position to take advantage of you."

She smirks. "From the start? You mean, the first time you walked in on me in my underwear?"

I clear my throat and attempt to ignore the image she calls to mind. "Maybe."

"Hey, I thought we weren't allowed to give cryptic answers like that?"

"I'm not trying to be cryptic. I honestly don't know the answer because I forced myself to compartmentalize half-naked Daisy within the part of my brain reserved for examining patients," I reply defensively.

"Hmm. You tried, anyway," she remarks, taking another sip.

"Now that's a cryptic answer," I say, narrowing my eyes at her.

"Let's just say last night's pickup lines implied otherwise. You weren't terribly crude or anything, but ... you did use the word *sexy*."

I cringe. "I did?"

"You did." She looks amused.

I open my mouth to speak again, but she cuts me off.

"Look, I'm only teasing you. Please don't make me repeat the rest. If you don't remember saying it, then you probably didn't mean it, anyway. And I'd rather not have to admit to spending the last eight hours thinking you did."

"See, now that's confusing," I point out. "I can't understand why you wouldn't want to know the truth, one way or the other. It's always the guessing that bothers me most."

"I know exactly how you feel after you freaked out about waking up in bed with me this morning," she mumbles, staring down at her cup. "Then again, none of that coincides with you telling me that you like my shiny hair and then asking me to put my hand down your pants, so …"

"Shit." My face heats up. "I'm sorry about that, too."

"It's fine." She shrugs. But I don't think it's really all that fine, and there's a part of my brain warning me to stop now before I upset her even more. The problem is that part is being overruled by the impulsive side again.

"Daisy, why'd you, you know, encourage me when we were spooning just now? What'd you think would come of it?" I blurt out.

Her eyes lower again. "You already know I haven't had much dating experience. But I still managed to grow into the body of an adult woman with a fully functioning reproductive system, despite not getting the chance to use it." She stops and sighs. "So when you presented me with an educational opportunity this morning, I guess I thought I'd make the most of it."

My heart rate quickens. "And I almost … I mean, we could have …"

She huffs. "Don't flatter yourself. A few seconds of incidental groping hasn't managed to shift my core values. I still intend to save the real thing for my future husband. All I'm saying is I temporarily let my curiosity get the best of me when my female body reacted naturally to the contact you initiated with your male parts. So if anything, I'm sorry for … using you, I guess."

My brow lifts. I haven't heard much of Daisy's tougher side before, but I'm a little impressed. I can see how she's been surviving in a high school classroom now that she's less afraid to assert herself this way.

"Wow," I say after a while. "No matter how many ways I might have rehearsed this conversation in my mind, I never would have seen that last part coming. I don't know if I've ever felt so ... *dirty*." I turn to shoot her a smirk, and she elbows me playfully.

"Are you satisfied now?"

"Not really," I mumble. "But a few more minutes of what you call 'cuddling' could have fixed that." I don't mean to sound so suggestive, but it comes out before I can stop myself. And then I watch as her smile grows wider.

Dammit.

I like making her smile. And I can tell she likes it when I flirt with her, even for the simple fact that she's craving the attention in general. Maybe it's not so wrong of me to give her this, then. She deserves the chance to practice within a safe environment. And I'm as safe as she'll ever get.

"Hey, I thought we're supposed to keep things honest and transparent?" she continues, sounding more coy this time.

I scrunch up my nose. "Who says I wasn't? It's been a while for me, too."

She giggles, and I realize I've forgotten all about my hangover now. Because that sound is the opposite of irritating.

"Is that your excuse for fondling me?"

"I'm sorry. I only went for it because I thought I was dreaming," I divulge hesitantly.

Her brow shoots up. "Really? And you're admitting that?"

"You shared something personal at the risk of embarrassment. I figured I should do the same," I tell her with a shrug. But I suspect it's because she makes it so easy for me to let my guard down. "For solidarity."

"As if it wasn't enough that we're stuck in a secret marriage, now we know all of one another's most mortifying secrets." She clinks her mug against mine before she downs the last of her coffee.

"But why do I get the feeling you've got more dirt on me than I think?" I ask before I empty my own cup.

"Let's see, I'm a twenty-five-year-old virgin, and I just confessed to letting my best friend cop a feel, even though I know he's not into me.

And I'm still smiling like this because I think I have the upper hand." She points to the grin on her face.

I puff out my cheeks and blow out a breath, trying not to dwell on the fact that she just called me her best friend. "Right. Tread carefully. Got it."

She laughs again, and I find myself staring at her for a second longer than I should. I clear my throat and stand. "I should get dressed."

"And in the interest of full transparency, I'm warning you now that I'm going to respectfully look away until you've reached an acceptable distance before sneaking a peek at you in your underwear again," she announces.

"Then as your best friend and platonic husband, I hereby consent to your objective appreciation of my male form as the opportunity presents itself," I say, stifling a grin and walking backward toward my bedroom.

Her eyes run over my body before she lifts a finger and gestures for me to turn around. "I'm done with this side. Can we flip to the back?"

I spin on my heels and walk on. But my smile doesn't fade for a while.

landry

DAISY TAKES one for the team by going in to pick up JD's tux at our first stop of the morning, and my dad brings his out to the car next. He doesn't say much, of course, only asks if I'm proud of myself after the way I behaved last night.

"Of course not," I tell him with a sigh. "I'm on my way to apologize to Loren." Then he grunts and walks away.

I received similar messages from both my mom and Lilley this morning, though my mom at least cared enough to ask how I was feeling before she recommended that I check in with my sister. Lilley's message, however, sounded more like "I hope you woke up feeling shittier than our new brother-in-law did during your toast last night, asshole."

It's nothing I don't deserve, I know. And once I got Daisy to reenact my big speech, I actually wished my hangover had been worse.

Now I'm sitting here in Blake's driveway, staring at the front door.

"Good luck," Daisy says, reaching over to pat my thigh.

"You're not coming in with me?" I whine. "You know I'm not good at apologies."

She shakes her head. "I think you need to handle this one on your own, big boy. Especially if you want to continue playing *N'oncle* Lan to those baby girls."

I take a deep, fortifying inhale. "You're right. I just wish I knew what to say to make up for this."

"Be honest, speak from your heart," she says plainly.

"And never get to see my nieces again?" I reply, smirking.

"Come on, Landry. You're obviously sorry for what you said. So tell her that, nothing more and nothing less. She doesn't need to know why you said it, only that you know it was wrong and you're sorry for hurting them."

"But I didn't mean to hurt them. I was trying to be nice, and it came out wrong."

"Stop worrying about being misunderstood. This is about making Loren and Blake feel better." I furrow a brow at her, and she sighs, shifting her position in the passenger seat to face me. "Think of it as triage or first aid. You're going in to stop the bleeding, and you can treat the minor scrapes and cuts later."

I shake my head. "How do you do it? You always know the right thing to say."

She blushes and smiles shyly, obviously pleased. "If only that were true."

"Maybe you just speak my language, then," I mumble, and she turns her eyes to mine. My chest warms, so I clear my throat and force myself to look away. "Okay. I'm going in. Wish me luck."

I don't wait for her to reply before I get out and walk up to the front door. I knock a few times, but there's no answer, so I pull out my phone to text Loren. I'd sent her a message earlier saying I'd be there in a while to pick up Blake's tuxedo, but she'd left me on *read*.

I knock one more time before I cross my arms and shift my weight, preparing to leave, but the door swings open to reveal my sister wearing a robe and looking disheveled.

"Um, hi. Good morning. I'm here for—"

She glares and shoves a garment bag at my chest. I take it, and her eyes flutter, a momentary crack in her resolve to stay mad at me. Then she spins on her heels and swings the door closed behind her.

"Lo, wait," I call out, stepping forward to hold it open. "Can we talk for a second?"

"I'm a little busy." She crosses her arms and refuses to face me again.

"I know, but—"

"Can't keep my husband waiting," she says as Blake rounds the corner in a pair of shorts. He ignores me and shoots Loren a secret smile that makes me want to gag, but I fight to keep my expression neutral.

"Coming back to bed, Agnes?" he asks in a sultry tone, tilting his head in an invitation.

I lift my sunglasses and cringe at the pain. "I won't keep you long, I promise. I just want to apologize for last night. Then I'll leave you to get back to ..." I force myself to smile, "your honeymoon activities."

Blake leans down for a kiss, sliding his hand around to cup Loren's backside before he pulls away and shoots me a look. I expect to see his trademark cocky grin aimed my way, but I get a silent "hurt her and die" warning instead. It only adds to my overwhelming sense of guilt, and I lower my gaze as I agree to his unspoken terms with a nod.

"I'll be in the kitchen if you need me," he says quietly before he saunters away.

Loren turns to face me again. "You've got thirty seconds."

I frown. "You okay? You look—"

She holds up a finger. "I look like someone who needs to get rid of her dickhead brother so she can get back to having sex. Twenty seconds."

I wince. "Right, sorry. Um, look, Lo. I just wanted to apologize for what I said last night. It was completely inappropriate, and ..." I bite back the urge to add something in my defense, to tell her I only said it because I'm always worrying about her. But Daisy was right before; my reasons don't matter right now.

"There's no excuse for it, and I've never regretted anything more. I was wrong. I'm sorry for hurting you, and even though you deserve to stay angry with me forever after this, especially after all the other times I've been an ass, I hope you can forgive me one day." I gulp as my voice gets thicker. "I love you, and I'm so glad you're happy, you know, with Blake."

She turns her lips to the side and looks away as her eyes start to water. "Okay."

I nod and blow out a breath. "Thank you for hearing me out. I'll get out of your way now, so you can finish your ..." I gesture with an awkward wave.

This time a smile creeps across her face. "Sex? With Blake?" she volunteers, staring me down and looking for my reaction. "My husband and the father of my children, the man, the myth, the legend, also known as Blake 'the Snake' Bourgeois?"

I force my expression to remain neutral as she narrows her eyes at me, daring me to flinch. "Yeah, that guy," I choke out.

"The same man who cried when he saw me in my wedding dress yesterday, who punched you in the face when we were kids because you hurt my feelings, and who's currently in the kitchen fixing *me* a sandwich?" she poses, lifting an eyebrow.

"Yep. That's the one," I grind out. "Just ... freaking ... *love* that guy."

"Good, so do I. Thanks for coming by and for volunteering to return the tuxes. Hope your hangover lasts three days," she returns. Then she grins and flips me off as she steps toward the door.

I can't help but smirk. "Love you, too, Lo-Lo."

"Agnes, you wanna pickle on this sandwich or what?" Blake calls out loudly.

"Only if it's slathered in peanut butter," she returns, shutting the door in my face. Then I hear what sounds like muffled footsteps and a squeal from Loren, and I shiver in disgust.

Daisy looks like she's about to explode by the time I return to the Jeep. "How did it go?" she asks before I can sit.

"Better than expected," I say with a sigh. "I may be scarred for life, but it sounds like she's willing to forgive me."

"I'm proud of you, Landry," she continues before she cringes. "Sorry, I forgot—"

"No, thank you for helping me get it right this time. I appreciate your help," I tell her, and she smiles shyly.

landry

ROBIN, ETHAN P.

I check the name on the chart twice before opening it. Sure enough, it's Tenley's nephew. I'm already Jake's pediatrician, but I'm surprised to see Ethan on my caseload. I sift through his records quickly to make sure he doesn't have any preexisting conditions I should know about, then knock softly on the exam room door before letting myself in.

"Hey, there," I say awkwardly when I find Tenley sitting in a chair with baby Jake in her arms while Ethan lies back on the exam table. He barely glances up from his phone to nod at me until Tenley reaches over and backhands his thigh. He groans and reluctantly sits up.

"Hi." Tenley turns and shoots me an apologetic smile, and I wonder if they didn't give me the wrong chart by mistake.

"What brings you guys in today?" I ask as I take a seat on a rolling stool. "Is something wrong with the little guy?"

"No, Jake's fine. Well, he has been a little fussy since he spiked a random fever the other day, but I didn't notice any other symptoms. We're actually here because of Ethan's ankle. It's been giving him trouble for just over a year now." The baby grunts and stirs in her arms, and she sighs when she adjusts him, sounding exhausted.

"And you want me to take a look," I offer, still distracted by the baby's increasingly loud protests.

"I'm sorry," she mumbles, draping a blanket over her chest. "He's so stinking greedy. Anyway, all we need is an orthopedic referral, if you don't mind. Our health insurance requires it," she continues as she works beneath the blanket. A second later, I can hear smacking and gulping.

I glance at Ethan, who seems bored and completely unbothered. "Uh, yeah, sure, I can do that. But I don't think that's necessary with the hospital's insurance," I tell them. I only know because I looked up the details of the policy for Daisy.

"Oh, he has the state employee health insurance," she replies. I blink a few times, so she clarifies, "He's on JD's policy. We all are. He said it made more sense for his retirement."

"Is that even possible? JD's not his dad or anything," I retort without thinking.

Ethan snorts, and Tenley narrows her eyes slightly. "Not that it's any of your business—but yes. JD and I share domicile custody, which basically makes him one of Ethan's guardians. In fact, thanks to our family lawyer, JD legally outranks Ethan's biological father."

I clear my throat and look away, kicking myself for putting my foot in my mouth again. "Sorry. I, uh, I'm sure I'd have known all that had I taken the time to read through his chart more thoroughly."

"It's fine, Doc," Ethan volunteers. "We're not exactly a normal family. One minute I was living with my grandparents, and the next, I'm begging my football coach to stop walking around the house in his drawers."

I laugh shortly. "Well, if there's anyone who understands what it's like being the coach's kid, you're looking at him."

Ethan smirks at me, to my surprise. "Or is that just something guys your age do? Go around in their underwear in front of all their roommates?"

I blink. "Uh, I don't know. I can't say it's a common practice for me."

"See, he respects his roommate's wishes," Ethan says to Tenley. "It's not so hard."

She clicks her tongue. "You're not a roommate, you're a tax deduction. And give JD a break. The last time that happened, it was the middle of the night, and he was delirious from trying to soothe a crying baby. You're more likely to get accidentally flashed with a boob around the house these days, anyway."

"Ew. Who wants to see *your* boobs? Right, Doc?" Ethan turns and nods to me.

My eyes widen and flash to Tenley's, and she immediately reaches out to slap Ethan's arm. "Stop that," she scolds him through her teeth.

Ethan shrugs, still staring me down. "I mean, unless he's seen 'em before?"

Tenley's jaw lowers. "Ethan Paul Robin, what has gotten into you?"

"The tea," he replies, leaning back and crossing his arms.

I glance back between the two of them. "What's ... *the tea*?"

Tenley narrows her eyes at him. "Gossip. He must have heard we dated a long, long time ago. And I imagine he thinks it's funny."

"Oh. Why would that be funny?" I ask dryly.

Now they both turn to look at me. "Because it's awkward," Ethan says. "And because it pisses JD off."

"JD has nothing to be upset about," she mutters. "We were in junior high when that happened, and we're all mature adults now. Right, Dr. Reed?"

"Technically, I was in high school."

Tenley glares at me. "So, how about that referral, Doc?"

"Yep," I say, realizing she's annoyed at me, too. "Just let one of the receptionists know which orthopedic you'd like Ethan to see, and I'll sign off on it. Anything else I can do for you today?"

"There is this one spot on my lower back—a weird freckle. Mind taking a look at it?" Ethan ventures, a smile playing at his lips. "You remember, right? I mentioned it to you the other night on the way back from the wedding reception."

I inhale when it hits me. Ethan was the one who brought Daisy and me home after my sister's wedding when I was too drunk to drive myself. That means ... he must have heard some of the stuff I said to her.

"I think you've managed to jog my memory," I say quietly.

Just then, baby Jake fusses again, squeaking until he releases what sounds like a full load into his diaper. Tenley whimpers, clutching the blanket against them.

"I think that was another blowout." She turns to Ethan. "I'll meet you out front after I change Jake. Behave yourself, or else."

"Yes, ma'am," he croons. She shoots me another apologetic look before she shuffles out of the room with the diaper bag, leaving me alone with Ethan.

"What do you want, kid?" I ask.

He raises his brow. "What's going on with you and Miss Daisy?"

I recoil. "None of your damned business."

He blinks, refusing to back down. "You don't remember anything from that night, do you?"

"Not much," I admit reluctantly.

He leans forward conspiratorially. "You asked her to follow you into the bathroom to help you with your aim ... in front of me ... after you called her a *sexy Rapunzel*."

"What?" I shake my head in disbelief. "I never said—"

"Bruh, you totally did." He sits back and crosses his arms over his chest. "Ask her if you don't believe me."

"There's nothing going on between us besides the fact that we're roommates. And even if I'd actually said any of those things, I meant it as a joke."

"Then how do you know what she looks like naked?"

I gulp. Not only because he's got me cornered, but also because I'm picturing Daisy in her underwear again.

"This is a completely inappropriate discussion."

"It is," Ethan confirms. "Which is exactly why you never should have said all that crap in front of me in the first place."

I stare at him for a second longer. "What do you want?" I ask again.

He sighs. "Look, as entertaining as it is for me to watch you mess with JD and Blake, do us all a favor and give it up. It's impossible to resent them forever. Trust me."

I furrow my brow. "That's it? You want me to pretend I like the Bourgeois brothers?"

"No, I want you to quit making yourself and everyone around you miserable by trying to one up them."

My stomach turns with guilt. "Why are you telling me this?"

"Because I get it, you know, being torn between loving and hating them, knowing how good they really are and realizing you'll never measure up to them." He sniffs indignantly. "And even though it's not exactly the same, I think I understand how you felt about Blake marrying your sister. You don't need to worry about her, though. He's loyal."

"What the hell would you know about Blake Bourgeois and my sister?" It almost comes out as a growl. But I'm over Blake and Loren's marriage, if I'm being honest. It's the way this kid just called me out on most of my biggest insecurities that's making me consider breaking the Hippocratic oath at the moment.

"A lot more than I know about you and Miss Daisy," he retorts with a grin. "Or should I say *Mrs. Reed*?"

My nostrils flare as panic shoots through me, but I clamp my jaw shut and stop to reassess the situation before I speak again. "So what, you just go around minding the adults' business?" I pose, buying myself some time.

He shrugs. "Yeah, kinda. Well, technically, they just sort of forget I'm around or post crap in the wrong group text, but here we are. Just know that whatever Blake's done in the past, he's not that guy anymore. I've watched him change, all because of Loren and those babies. But that's how these guys operate. Once they decide they care about someone, that's it. There's nothing they wouldn't do for the people they love."

"So what's it to you whether I go on hating my brother-in-law forever?"

"Look, believe it or not, Blake's done as much for me as anyone else. And that shit you said at the wedding really hurt him, especially because it was true and he's been killing himself to get past all that. You owe him an apology."

"I've already apologized to my sister."

"You owe Blake an apology," he repeats slowly, his voice stern. "And although I personally find it hilarious because I've never seen anyone get under JD's skin the way you do, you should apologize to him, too."

I clear my throat. "For ..."

He smiles. "For the borderline disrespectful comments you made about his wife while you were drunk, particularly when you implied you still had a thing for her and wouldn't let something as silly as her being married stand in your way."

I gulp. Daisy had warned me about that part. "I must not have said anything too bad about Tenley if I'm still alive," I blurt my thoughts aloud.

"Actually, you have me to thank for that," Ethan offers smugly. "Like I said, it was fun to watch. I've never seen JD so close to losing his temper. Congratulations."

"Shit," I say, then sigh. "For the record, the only feelings I have toward your aunt are respect ... and maybe a healthy fear."

He nods in agreement. "You did tell me as much on the ride home. But I'd like you to make sure JD knows it, too."

"This is exactly why I don't drink," I mumble under my breath.

"No kidding. If that's the stuff you say after a few glasses of champagne, I'd love to see you high."

I glare at Ethan. "It was more than a few glasses. And while I appreciate your candidness, I think it's time for you to go, kid."

"I really do have a weird mole on my back, though," he says with a grin.

I let out a loud exhale. "Fine, turn around."

I examine Ethan and reassure him that the birthmark on his lower back is in fact normal before walking him back to the front desk.

"Good talk, Doc. Glad we got all that settled. I was really worried about that back freckle."

"Yeah," I say.

"It's a good thing I came to you, since you're somewhat of a back freckle expert, right?"

I grunt, and he continues.

"And you won't mind relaying the good news to both of my uncles?"

"Sure," I force out, holding back a smirk. The little shit is clever, I'll give him that.

"All done?" Tenley asks when she emerges from the bathroom with her baby in a sling.

"For now, at least," Ethan mumbles, pulling out his phone again.

She shakes her head, looking exasperated with him, then she turns to me. "Thanks, Dr. Reed."

"Why does that keep sounding so weird when you say it?" I say without thinking, but I quickly follow up with a friendly smile.

She huffs, but her expression softens. "You're right. This business of growing up and getting old is all really strange, isn't it?"

"It really is," I confirm, earning a side-eyed glare from Ethan. Then something else odd catches my attention, and I lean in to study the baby's ruddy cheeks. "Tenley, didn't you say Jake had been running a fever and acting fussier than usual?"

"Yes, why?" She glares at me warily.

"Mind if I take a look?"

She nods and lifts him out of the sling for me, and I click my tongue to get his attention while I run through a quick exam. I unzip the top half of his onesie, and his bottom lip trembles until I pretend to tickle his chubby shoulders while I check for more evidence of the same rash I found on his cheeks.

"Hmm," I hum. "I think I know why he's been so grumpy. Well, besides the obvious case of being a coach's son."

"What is it?" Tenley asks hesitantly.

"Roseola," I tell her, though I keep my eyes trained on Jake's as I run my finger along the sides of his face and point out the red splotches, hoping to distract him from the fact that he's not staring back at his mama.

"Isn't he young for that?"

"Yes, but it's viral, so it'll pass quickly. They normally run a high temp for a few days, maybe get some swollen lymph nodes here," I add, tickling under his chin and making him squirm. "Then the rash comes out, and they start to feel better."

"Oh," she says, surprised. "That actually makes a lot of sense. I was worried he was going through another growth spurt already, but I bet he's just been comfort nursing."

I nod. "His throat could have been sore, too. An oatmeal bath and a little hydrocortisone cream will keep him from getting too itchy. Otherwise, the worst should already be behind him."

I tug on his zipper again, and he blinks up at me as he lets out a loud burp.

"Already back to normal," Ethan muses behind us, and Tenley smiles, looking more relieved. Then she hands Jake off to Ethan to take care of their bill.

"Hey, Cheryl," I begin, leaning over the desk toward the billing receptionist. "Would you mind making a note of Jake's diagnosis in his chart?"

"Of course, Doc. But it's not actually *Jake*, is it?"

"Yes, sorry. It's short for *Joseph Drake the Fourth*," Tenley answers, already digging for her wallet.

"You can write off their copays, too," I add, and Cheryl nods as she clicks on a keyboard.

"Oh, you don't have to do that," Tenley says quickly.

I shrug. "I guess we're technically family now, right?"

She stops and nods. "I guess so. Thanks, Landry."

"Yeah, thanks, *N'oncle*," Ethan echoes sarcastically behind me. I'm tempted to jerk my elbow back, but then I remember he's holding Jake.

"See you around, Ethan," I say through my teeth instead.

Dr. Broussard comes up then and greets Tenley. They make small talk for a few minutes until Jake fusses again, and Dr. Broussard turns to me once they go.

"If you don't have another patient waiting, there's someone I'd like you to meet," he tells me, holding up a hefty chart.

I take it and flip through the patient's files. They detail the story of a ten-year-old boy named David who's been struggling to regulate his Type 1 diabetes symptoms since infancy. But things seem to have taken a positive turn in the last few months, which is probably why I haven't seen him around.

"What changed?" I mumble to myself as I skim over his latest test results. My eyes catch on a mention of his DAD, and I realize what's been making the difference for him. "He got a diabetic alert dog?"

"Yes," Dr. Broussard confirms. "It took a while to make it happen, but David's dog can scent the ketones and isoprene in his blood stream and alert him before his glucose levels spike or drop, giving them enough time to adjust his insulin or get some carbs into his system. It's been a game changer for them, and David can finally do some of the things he's always wanted, including playing sports."

I hum thoughtfully. "I imagine it gives his parents some peace of mind."

"As well as his pediatrician," he adds, smiling.

One of the medical assistants opens the door then, and a gangly boy wearing goggles for glasses charges in with a chocolate labradoodle hot on his heels. A woman with similar features trails behind.

"Hey, David!" Dr. Broussard greets him.

"Hey, Dr. B," the boy returns, reaching up to deliver a high five and marching on as if he owns the place.

I chuckle to myself and follow them into the exam room, where Dr. Broussard introduces me and David tells me about his best friend, Mack. Mack sits up from his place at David's feet as soon as he hears his name and turns to give the boy's hand an affectionate lick.

David's mom answers a few of my questions about their lives with a service animal and tells me about the overall improvement in

David's health, such as his recent weight gain. David proudly relays that he's grown an inch and gained a few pounds since his last visit, and we talk about football for a few minutes before they go. Then I ask Dr. Broussard more about the nonprofit organization that trains and places dogs like Mack and the application process.

I see a few more patients before the end of the day, including another toddler with Roseola, and I get home later that afternoon to find Daisy watering her plants on the front porch. She grins and waves at me as if she's genuinely happy to see me.

She may be the only person who's ever made me feel that way, but I shouldn't have let myself get used to it. For the first time in a while, I'm reminded that our time is limited. Things are going to have to change soon.

Daisy should get the all-clear to drive in a couple of months, barring any more episodes. She's also been preparing for her certification exam so she can qualify for that permanent teaching position and full benefits. And once she doesn't need me to taxi her around or share my health insurance, there won't be any reasons left for us to live together or stay married.

An unexpected pang of regret pierces my chest at the thought of divorcing her, of leaving this home we've made together over the last few months, of leaving Daisy. It's going to be much, much harder than I thought.

I groan and run my hand through my hair. I never should have let her go through with this in the first place. It was selfish of me to make that offer to marry her knowing she didn't have any other options aside from running home to her parents. Rowan was right before—I needed someone new to take care of, and helping Daisy was like switching from one addiction to another. I'd stopped smoking only to start drinking. And I'm not sure I have the willpower to quit this time.

landry

"WELL, hey, you two. Go on in and enjoy the game."

I'm almost suspicious of the friendly reception when we walk up to the entrance of the Camellia High football field. I lead Daisy past the ticket booth, nodding politely to some of the familiar faces we cross as we make our way toward the bleachers.

"Hey, Doc," Ethan calls out, making me cringe. I never told Daisy about his little blackmailing scheme, and I'd been doing my best to avoid him. "Hey, Miss Daisy," he adds as he approaches.

I clear my throat and offer an awkward fist bump. "Good luck out there, kid."

"Thanks. I was actually coming over to see if you'd gotten the chance to deliver that message we spoke about before." His gaze locks onto mine, even as he pulls his helmet down, and Daisy looks on curiously.

"Uh, no. Not yet."

"Why not?" he demands.

"Haven't had the opportunity. Been busy doing grown-man shit," I retort, and Daisy nudges me.

"No time like the present, right?" He tilts his head to gesture behind him as JD and Blake strut down the sideline together. I consider fulfilling my end of our agreement for a second, jogging over to offer an apology for the way I acted at my sister's wedding reception and even for all of the times I was a jerk to both of them before that.

Then I glance around at all the witnesses surrounding us. It can wait.

"I'll get around to it when I'm ready," I say gruffly.

Ethan snickers. "Sure hope you're ready soon. I'd hate for—"

"Don't worry about me. Just have yourself a good game, two-three." I tap the top of his helmet, and he narrows his eyes at me one more time before he gives me a short nod and jogs off.

"What's that about?" Daisy asks.

"Guy stuff," I reply as I urge Daisy forward, and I watch as my sister bounds down the bleachers with one of the twins in her arms.

Tenley's already leaning over the railing with a baby strapped to her chest while JD effortlessly pulls himself up the metal stands to give her a kiss. Blake repeats the same moves, except he hops up to straddle the railing as he greets both babies, since Tenley's mom has come down with the other twin. All it takes is a subtle tilt of his head for Loren to grab him by the shirt and shove her tongue down his throat.

I scoff, though they at least have the decency to break it up after a few seconds, unlike JD and Tenley, who are still whispering to one another and squashing poor baby Jake each time they lean in for another kiss. For some reason, I can't look away, though. I continue watching, reading Blake's lips as he says, "I love you." Loren says something back that shifts his expression to something smug, and I'm grateful I can't make out her words.

Blake leans over and plants a kiss on Mrs. T's cheek, then swings his leg back over the railing to hop down, dragging JD along with him, to Tenley's dismay. JD smiles and waves to his mother-in-law before he joins Blake and the other coaches.

"Aren't they adorable?" Daisy asks wistfully, bringing me back.

I grunt. "It just seems so ... unnecessary."

She frowns. "I think it's nice. Why should they hide their affection in public? It's not like they're being inappropriate."

"I beg to differ," I return with a sneer.

"You're such a fuddy-duddy," she mumbles, pulling my arm toward the bleachers.

"I'm a fuddy-duddy because I don't do public make out sessions?" I ask sarcastically.

"At this point, I'd be surprised if you did *any* make out sessions," she retorts bitterly, and I take a second to think about what it signifies.

"Right. Well, I'm not exactly in a position to go out looking for a casual hookup at the moment," I say after a while, calling her bluff.

She sighs. "I know, Landry. I meant that it's okay for you to be happy for your sister. Isn't that what we all want for our siblings? For them to find their soulmates, then fall in love and get married, have babies, and live happily ever after?"

I frown as she continues hauling me up the stairs. Loren smiles when she sees me, though her face doesn't light up the way it did for Blake a minute ago, and she lifts Charley's pudgy hand to wave at me. My heart admittedly softens as Daisy squeals with delight and waves back, but I tug her to a stop before she can take the next step.

"Is that what you think we all need to be happy?" I ask her abruptly.

She hesitates before she answers, and I'm afraid I've upset her for a second. "I'm sure that looks different for everyone," she begins. "But, yeah, some form of true love and acceptance is required, I think, whether it's from a spouse or a child or even a community."

"And what about Rosemary? She'll never be married." I'm referring to one of her sisters who joined a religious community a few years ago and seems to be happily living out her life as a nun in training.

"She *is* married," Daisy corrects me. "To Jesus."

"Is that how that works?"

"Yes, but come on, we can talk about this—"

"Wait, is that what *you* need to be happy?" I'm not sure why I have to know her answer right now, but I do.

She smirks. "To become a consecrated virgin? Or to marry a man who wants to make out with me at a high school football game?"

"The second. And to have babies," I clarify.

"While I'm grateful for my friends and family, yeah, I'd still love to get married for real and have kids one day," she says.

"But I thought you wanted to be independent?"

She shrugs shyly. "I don't know. I'm starting to think independence is overrated."

"Hmm," I hum thoughtfully. "Wait, can you even have children? Safely, I mean."

Her eyes flicker away, but she answers the question. "My neurologist says I should be able to handle pregnancy, so long as I take a few precautions. It's the postpartum time that's more likely to be dangerous, so I'd need a lot of help from my husband."

"Oh. Well, that's ... good."

"Yeah, sure," she murmurs, continuing up the bleachers.

"So once you and I go our separate ways, you'll start dating ... in Camellia?" I blurt out the question without thinking, and my stomach instantly turns at the thought of having to see Daisy with someone else. I imagine it'd be just as disturbing as when Loren and Blake first got together. Maybe even ... worse.

Daisy's answer pulls me up from that dangerous rabbit hole. "I suppose I'll have to start dating if I want to find a loving and supportive husband. Although at this point, I'd settle for someone who takes care of me half as well as you do, as long as I can squeeze a little PDA out of him every now and again."

"You shouldn't have to settle," I say flatly, ignoring the way the very idea of being forced to watch her with another man makes me see red. "We'll find you another one of those douchey Bourgeois brothers. You deserve the annoyingly wholesome yet inappropriately handsy man of your dreams."

She shakes her head and rolls her eyes at me. "Well, since you're volunteering to help, it'd be nice if he was a Catholic, too," she adds, and I let out a short laugh as we reach the others.

Loren turns and plops Charley into my lap as soon as I sit behind her, and I'm instantly reminded of how much I love being an uncle. I lift Charley to nibble at her neck and belly, making her giggle. It's the sweetest sound in the world.

Daisy nudges me before she leans over and whispers in my ear. "Deny it all you want, but I still think all that stuff would make you happy, too."

"What?"

She smirks as she reaches out to tickle Charley, and I can't help the way Charley's belly laugh makes me melt again. "You want *this*," Daisy repeats. "Babies."

I shrug and try to keep my expression neutral. "So I like kids. We get along. They're easier to figure out than adults. That doesn't mean I'll never be content without having them."

"That's exactly what it means, Landry," she replies.

"I'm a pediatrician and an uncle. I'm already surrounded by babies. I don't need a soulmate to make me happy. I have a fulfilling career *and* a family." I gulp and avoid her gaze, but it's not because I'm lying. I'm worried she'll point out the holes in my plan, especially since she knows exactly how my family feels about me.

"Mm-hmm. And what happens once you retire? What are you going to do when these girls grow up and go off to live their own lives, just like Lilley's kids will? Who's going to keep you company when you're old and lonely?"

I frown as I stare at Charlotte. It's hard to imagine her growing up and moving away or starting a family of her own one day, but it's likely it will happen. I readjust her position in my lap and kiss the top of her head.

"I'm a single doctor who never spends his money. I'll use my fat retirement checks to pay people to take care of me. And my great nieces and nephews will visit me on occasion to secure a piece of my inheritance, regardless of how grumpy and senile I get."

She snorts and pats my shoulder affectionately. "Maybe I'll encourage my future grandkids to check on you and try to weasel their way into your will, too."

"You keep mentioning all these children and grandchildren," I say, shooting her a side-eyed smile. "But you know it's gonna take more than a little PDA to make some of those, right? Better choose your second husband wisely."

I watch her carefully as she gets visibly flustered. "Just when I think I understand you, you go and say something like that. And you claim other people are hard to read," she tells me.

"What do you mean?" I ask, my smile widening.

"It's just that you ... well, to be honest, you come off as a prude half the time. But every once in a while, you throw in one of *those* comments in your sexy-doctor voice," she says, lowering her tone, "and I'm not sure what to think about you."

I narrow my eyes at her. "And just how much time have you spent thinking about my sexy-doctor voice, Blondie?"

Her lips part in shock, and her eyelashes flutter. I can't tell whether she's guilty or embarrassed, but I've obviously hit a nerve. "Don't make me answer that," Daisy pleads quietly, and a wave of heat surges through me, just as Charley begins to whine.

I clear my throat and bounce the fussy baby over my knee a few times. What the heck am I even doing right now? That felt dangerously close to legit flirting, and the absolute last thing I should be doing is flirting with my wife. Because she's also my much younger, very naive, overly romantic, extremely vulnerable, practically untouched best friend's baby sister, as well as my roommate.

"I'm sorry," I whisper after a moment, but my apology is drowned out by cheers when the football team busts through a huge banner and stampedes onto the field.

"What?" she asks, squinting.

"I said I'm sorry," I reply a little louder.

Daisy shakes her head. "You're *what*?"

"I'm sorry for making you think I'm so sexy!" I yell, just as the crowd quiets down and stands for the National Anthem.

A handful of heads turn to gape at me, and I cringe. "Sorry for that, too," I add. Daisy covers her mouth, but a snort and a giggle still escape from behind her hand.

"Landry Nicholas! Give. Me. *That*!" Loren shrieks, snatching Charley from my lap. But she's barely disguising her own amusement.

I scowl in return. "What, I'm not allowed to say 'sexy' in front of your offspring? As if their parents haven't said worse."

She scoffs. "You should have heard the offer I just made to their daddy in exchange for getting them both to sleep after this game," she declares, making me groan. "But you're not allowed to use my babies to pick up women, especially since you're already a pediatrician. Charley's too cute, so it creates an unfair advantage, and Daisy deserves a level playing field."

"But ... I'm not ..." I shake my head. "Nothing's going on between Daisy and me. That's why I apologized for accidentally flirting with her."

I realize I've said too much, because my sister's smirk stretches across her face like an evil villain formulating a master plan. I half expect her to cackle, and—*dammit*, there she goes.

"Oh, dearest brother, there is no *accidental flirting*," she corrects me. "Only involuntary seduction."

"No," I reply forcefully. "None of that. There will be absolutely *zero* seduction happening here."

Loren purses her lips and glances at Daisy, and my eyes dart over reflexively to find my wife tucking her hair behind her ear and staring back at me with her eyes wide, her cheeks rosy, and her lips pouty.

Whoa, hold on—why do her lips look so pouty? Better yet, why am I looking at her lips in the first place? And why do I keep calling her *my wife* inside my head?

I swallow hard and force my gaze away, but I need something better to distract me before I do something stupid, like allow myself to be attracted to Daisy. And if I so much as think about her mouth again, I'm totally done for.

Her mouth ...

Hand-foot-mouth disease ... oral candidiasis ... erythema infectiosum ...

There. Nothing sexy about childhood viruses and infections.

"Landry?"

"Huh?" I straighten.

"I'm just teasing," Loren says, adjusting Charley in her arms. "Loosen up, all right?"

I roll my shoulders back. "Who says I'm uptight?"

"That constipated look on your face, for one." I roll my eyes, and she mumbles, "Unless that's just sexual frustration," under her breath.

"Enough, Lo," I growl.

"Fine. You're no fun." Then she turns to Daisy and cups her hand around her mouth as she adds, "Maybe I'll train you to become an involuntary seductress. You could always use your skills to hook someone better than my lame-ass brother."

I keep my eyes trained on the field and pretend I don't hear when Daisy giggles through her reply. "I'm open to learning, especially from the best."

landry

WE GET through most of the game when the twins start getting too fussy, so I volunteer to take them on a walk to the concession stand. Daisy comes along and gets a barbecue burger this time. I laugh when she says it's amazing but not as life changing as the cheesy Hot Fries with a pickle on the side.

The crowd gets loud after a few exciting plays in a row, making Penny crankier than before. Loren decides to throw in the towel after that, and I insist on walking her out to her minivan. Daisy follows and seems happy to help buckle Pen into her seat, even with her doing that back-arching thing babies do when they get overly sleepy and refuse to cooperate with anything. I see it a lot in my line of work, especially when I have to dole out shots.

After we send Loren off, Daisy agrees that we might as well head home, to my relief. I'm not interested in waiting around for Ethan to get off the field again.

"Thanks for bringing me to the game tonight," Daisy says as we climb the front porch steps. "I had a lot of fun."

"Yeah. Me, too," I tell her with a smile.

"And thank you for teaching me about football. I'm really starting to enjoy it."

"Good."

We stand there awkwardly for a second until it starts to feel like the end of a date, and I quickly jam my key into the lock and let us both inside. I clear my throat before announcing that I need to shower, and she reassures me that it's okay for me to go first.

"Good night, Landry," she calls over her shoulder as she heads toward her bedroom.

"Good night, Daisy," I reply, watching her walk away.

I barely make it back to my room after showering when my phone dings a few times in a row, and I flip it over to find a group text thread.

UNKNOWN

ay whats up fam

JD

Wtf are you texting me? You're literally sitting on the other side of the couch rn.

BLAKE

Hang on. If this is a group text, then I'm gonna need to put my phone on silent. I can't risk waking these babies, or all my efforts to get laid tonight will have been in vain.

UNKNOWN

tmi man

so im gathering all you dudes together bc i need some help

JD

Whatever it is, I'm in.

gif of the Diamond Dogs from Ted Lasso

What the actual hell? Is that … Ethan? Panic rises in my chest as the messages continue to bounce up, and I take a second to punch in a response.

LANDRY

Um. Why am I here?

ETHAN

i need to apologize to a friend but idk how bros
say sry

JD

And you invited Dr. Douchebag?

I scoff. Ethan's sadly mistaken if he thinks this is going to go over well.

LANDRY

Fancy language for you, Golden Boy.

Especially since I circumcised your kid a few
weeks ago.

JD

Wait until I finish changing this shitty diaper ...

BLAKE

Calm your tits, ladies. Let's hear what the kid has
to say.

ETHAN

i added him to the chat bc i'd like to hear from
someone who doesn't have to ask his wife for
permission to stay up past his bedtime

JD

Since we live in the same house, you tell me:
Does it sound like my wife minds any of the
things I do late at night?

BLAKE

You walked right into that one, kid.

ETHAN

ftr this dude is literally texting with one hand while
wiping baby crap with the other

JD

Yeah, changing the baby I made … with your aunt.

Bc it's like that.

ETHAN

I roll my eyes along with Ethan.

JD

Keep on. I'll make another one.

BLAKE

Big talk coming from a guy no more than four weeks into a six-week dry spell …

JD

gif of little boy smiling and crying

BLAKE

Come back to me once you survive nine months of pelvic rest, you big titty baby.

This time I gag a little, but the messages just keep popping up.

JD

I'm not a baby, but … 😊

ETHAN

you walked right into that one kid

BLAKE

gif of man tipping a cowboy hat

LANDRY

WHY AM I HERE?

ETHAN

to show us how a real man apologizes to his bros

LANDRY

You've got to be freaking kidding me.

ETHAN

the bro chat is sacred

i would never joke around in here

BLAKE

Liar

Liar

I groan, figuring I might as well get this over with. Ethan won't let it go until I apologize, and doing it over text messages has to be easier than doing it in person. I try to think of it like jumping into a cold lake or ripping off a Band-Aid at once.

LANDRY

Fine.

Hypothetically speaking, if I were in Ethan's position, I guess I'd say …

I'm sorry for being an asshole. You didn't deserve the things I said about you in that wedding toast … or at the hospital.

So thank you for being loyal to my sister, even though I've been a dick to you since we were kids. I'm actually really happy for both of you. I just don't know how to show it.

Or something like that.

BLAKE

gif of old man crying and biting fist

JD

gif of The Rock raising an eyebrow

ETHAN

ok ok i see you doc

that's not half bad

but i'm not just talking about an actual bro

like what if it was your bro's bro's feelings you
hurt kwim

hypothetically speaking of course

I groan louder before I type out the next apology.

LANDRY

I would begrudgingly add that I'm also sorry for
being a douche to him over the years and
especially for disrespecting his wife, which I only
did to piss him off. I'd reassure him that I hold her
in very high regard, both personally and
professionally, and that I would never intentionally
cross a line.

ETHAN

anything else?

LANDRY

The truth is that I don't hate any of them, even
though I want to. It's really myself I can't stand
most of the time.

I hit send on that last message and cringe. Maybe I got a little too honest on that one. My phone rings a second later.

"Why the hell are you calling me right now?" I answer gruffly.

"Because I wanted to prepare you for when my sappy-ass brother calls to accept your weird apology," Blake replies, though his voice sounds suspiciously thick.

"Gah, what is wrong with you people? He wouldn't really—"

The call waiting beep interrupts me. Sure enough, JD's number flashes on the screen when I pull it back.

"Told you," Blake says. "No point in trying to ignore him. He won't leave you alone until you let him do his thing."

"Ugh," I groan. "Is it too late to take it all back?"

"Yep, you're stuck. Hope you like cheesy dad jokes and bro hugs.

He's your problem now." Blake chuckles when I curse under my breath. "But there's nothing he wouldn't do for you, either."

"I guess that's why he's the twins' godfather, huh?"

Blake laughs shortly. "You know, he asked me to be Jake's *Parrain* before he knew Loren was pregnant. He told me he trusted me more than any person in the world, that he knew I'd be a great father one day. And he was right—I *am* a great dad. But sometimes I wonder whether I'd have had the confidence to be this good without my brother's encouragement, because he was the first person to believe in me."

I swallow hard and try to hide the way his words make my breath hitch in my throat. It's hard to imagine myself as part of a family like theirs, one so supportive and openly affectionate.

"I'm sorry I didn't recognize that same opportunity when I had it, Landry. I want you to know that I appreciate your apology, even though I owe you the same. I'm grateful for everything you've done for Loren and the girls, and there's no one else I trust more with their safety. You're an amazing uncle, and you'd make a great father, too."

I frown. "Did Daisy put you up to this?"

"Absolutely not. But I'm very interested in your reasons for asking that question," he says quickly, his tone perking up. The call waiting tone sounds in my ear again, and I can feel my stress level rising.

"Um, well, I—"

"Never mind. Lo just walked in, and she's giving me *the look*. Talk to you later, Lando." Then he hangs up. I pull the phone back to find JD's number lighting up the screen again at the same time a text from Ethan comes through.

ETHAN

dude you might as well answer him

do it now over the phone so you don't have to hug him

LANDRY

How did you get my number anyway?

ETHAN

don't worry about that doc

just answer the phone

I growl under my breath and accept the call. "Can't you leave well enough alone, JD?"

"I literally cannot. In fact, that's kind of my thing," he replies, sounding somewhat amused.

"Look, I apologized, okay, what more—"

"I'm sorry, too, Landry. I haven't always been very nice to you. But thanks for being the bigger man."

I sigh and shake my head at the irony of that statement. "Yeah, no worries."

"I'd really like it if we could be friends after this."

I snort. "Are you really asking me to be your friend? What is this, first grade?"

"No," he retorts defensively. "But grown men are allowed to be open with their feelings. It's healthy."

"Oh, is it?"

"Yeah. Unless one wants to convey certain feelings about his bro's wife. Then he's signing his own death warrant. But, you know, other than that, I'm here for you."

I choke on a laugh, unable to help myself this time. "Yeah, man. I'm probably never taking you up on that offer, nor am I going to return the favor, but I appreciate it."

"Anytime, brother," he says, and I could swear I hear him sniffling. "I might hug you next time I see you, though."

"The hell you will."

He chuckles. "We'll see."

"Dude, I'm hanging up now."

"Fine, good night—"

I tap the red icon and end the call, then I laugh to myself as I toss my phone aside.

CHAPTER 28

daisy

I TURN on my favorite playlist as I make my way to the dryer with an empty basket on my hip. After filling it with clean laundry, I bring it to my room for folding.

I make a separate pile for Landry's boxers and take it back to the laundry nook, trading the stack of underwear for a fresh towel since I think I might have used the last one yesterday. I smile to myself as I pop the towel back into the dryer for a minute to get it extra warm and fluffy, singing along before I return to my room for a changing of clothes and fling open the bathroom door.

Then I freeze in place. My jaw lowers, and I blink a few times as I stare blankly. Because standing before me in all his soaking wet glory is my husband.

It's the first time I've ever seen a grown man naked, at least in real life. And let me tell you, the biology textbooks haven't done this one justice. John Denver continues crooning in my ears while my eyes run over Landry's body, which is still covered in water droplets. And muscles. *Lots* of muscles.

Country roads, take me home, to the place I belong ...

I bite my lip as my gaze trails down his abdomen, all roads leading to the same focal point, and I'm pretty sure I tilt my head to the side as I take in the view.

"Wow. There it is," I blurt out, and Landry moves to cover himself with his hands.

"Daisy?" I vaguely hear him call, but his voice sounds muffled. Then I remember I'm wearing my noise-cancelling earbuds, and I quickly shift everything to one arm so I can use my free hand to remove them.

"DAY-ZAY!"

I flinch. "What?"

"I've been yelling at you for a whole minute! I need a towel," he grinds out.

"Oh right, sorry," I say, begrudgingly offering him the warm one in my arms.

He growls in frustration. "Can you bring it a little closer to me? I don't want to drip all over the floor."

I guess I was subconsciously hoping he'd reach out and uncover himself again. I stifle a smirk as I step forward, and he clears his throat.

"Um, do you mind?" he asks when I hesitate to turn away. But I notice his lips twitching once I finally drag my gaze up to his face. "A little privacy would be nice, too."

"I thought you said it was okay if I checked you out," I mumble, my cheeks flushing.

He scoffs and wraps the towel around his waist. "I wasn't exactly offering to pose buck-ass naked for you." Then he shivers. "Ooohh, it's so warm."

I giggle at the abrupt change in his tone. "You're welcome."

"Thanks," he says, his mouth curling up into a smile. "Still waiting on that privacy, though."

"Fine, I guess I've gotta heat up a fresh towel, anyway," I reply before I reluctantly leave him in the bathroom.

I'm bending over to slam the dryer door closed when I feel Landry brush up beside me. "Thanks again for the towel," he says quietly, dropping his dirty clothes into the washer. "I may never settle for a room-temperature one again."

"Consider it your payment for the anatomy lesson," I retort, and he chuckles out loud, to my surprise. I stand up straight and glare at him. "I'm glad you find me so entertaining."

"I'm sorry," he replies and smirks. "It was my fault. I'm starting to wonder how many times this is going to happen before we learn our lesson about locking doors and knocking before entering."

"Yeah," I tell him, blushing again. "And I can't seem to remember my manners every time it happens. At least you manage to look away when you walk in on me."

"That's only because if I stare, it's creepy. But when you stare, it's just … cute."

My stomach dips. "Is it?"

He shrugs. "It *was* kind of adorable when you turned your head to the side like a confused puppy."

"I did not look like a confused puppy," I whine, covering my face.

"You were certainly surprised. I just wasn't sure whether it was bigger or smaller than you expected."

I groan behind my hands. "I'm going to pretend that was meant to be rhetorical."

"Full transparency, remember?" I bring my hands down to find his expression entirely too smug for a man who doesn't already know what I'm thinking.

"Well, it's definitely not *smaller* than I imagined," I say.

He furrows his brow, trying to conceal his grin. "You've been imagining it?"

"No," I squeal in protest and reach out to shove him in the chest. "I only think about your butt that way." He throws his head back and laughs loudly, and I smile. I love funny, flirty Landry, even when he's teasing me.

"Should I have just turned around, then?"

I lift a shoulder, my confidence growing as I feed off his attention. "I don't know. Would I have liked it?"

He clicks his tongue. "It's probably hairier than you think back there."

"It's all pretty fuzzy, if we're being honest," I say and gesture over his chest.

"Hey, that's a sign of healthy testosterone levels," he retorts, crossing his arms but still grinning playfully.

"Too bad you let it all go to waste."

He stops abruptly, and his expression turns serious. "What's that supposed to mean?"

"Nothing," I say, trying not to let him hear the sadness in my voice. "I'm going to take a shower."

But he sidesteps and blocks my exit with his body. "Daisy." His voice is deep and demanding, and this time I'm the one who shivers.

How am I supposed to explain that I'm just feeling sorry for myself while concealing enough of my desperation to keep from making him uncomfortable?

I lick my lips before I begin. "It's just that ... well, I guess there's a part of me that feels guilty, like I'm holding you back from dating or ... whatever it is you normally go for."

He fixes his gaze on me as he processes the shift in our conversation. "I told you before we got married that I wasn't really dating."

"You've dated in the past, though, haven't you?"

"Yes, but I always made it clear I wasn't looking for anything serious."

"Maybe I'm worried you'll start to feel like you're missing out on ... on the other half of that equation."

His eyes run over me as he considers it. "You mean sex."

I nod. "Any kind of physical relationship, I guess."

He sighs and reaches up to run his hand through his hair, and I'm momentarily distracted by the way his muscles flex. "Despite the way some men act, we *can* survive without sex. It's not impossible."

"I know that," I retort. "But I don't imagine you *want* to. I mean, it's obviously different for me, but I'm still looking forward to it ... one day."

He narrows his eyes. "So, you feel like I'm holding *you* back?"

"No, of course not," I say too quickly. "I just mean that I ... you know what, never mind. Forget I said anything."

"Daisy, wait," he calls before I can scurry away. "You've never been shy before, but if there's something you want to ask me, you don't have to be embarrassed about it."

Think you'd ever be willing to match my desperation? Feel like putting all that wasted masculinity to use and taking this fake marriage to the next level? What's it gonna take for you to see me as a viable option or a real wife?

A number of questions run through my mind, most of them sounding more like propositions, but I'm not sure I'll ever be brave enough to ask them.

"I don't doubt your mom was pretty thorough in whatever you guys call the homeschool version of sex-ed, but ..." He shrugs and smirks. "If you can't ask your platonic husband about this kind of stuff, who can you, right?"

"You think I'm working up the courage to ask you questions about sex?" I venture, crossing my arms over my stomach when it flutters again. "Landry, you do realize I have four married sisters and two sisters-in-law who've been pregnant a combined total of seventeen times between them, right? And that's not counting the stuff I hear from your sister and Tenley. Because contrary to popular belief, Catholics aren't prudes. We may wait until we're married to have sex, but we certainly aren't shy about it. So, don't worry, despite my lack of firsthand experience, I'm far from ignorant. Not to mention, I've been charting my own cycles since I hit puberty. I probably understand more about women's health than you do."

His expression grows cockier. "Well, I am a doctor, Blondie. The MD at the end of my name says I know a good bit, too. And I haven't received many complaints in the past, if you get my drift."

I groan, partially because he's annoying me, and partially because he's hot as heck right now, which is equally irritating. "Yeah, well, did you learn how to be an ass in medical school? Because I'm starting to believe you really are a professional."

He pulls back, dropping his smug expression when he realizes I've actually cussed at him. "I'm sorry. I didn't mean to ..." He swallows hard. "I thought we were just kidding around. But ... I guess I read the situation wrong."

I frown. It'd be easier to stay angry at him if he'd stop being so insightful and sweet. "You did," is all I say.

"I wasn't making fun of you or your lack of experience. I just thought I'd keep things light to make you feel more comfortable about opening up. I want you to know you can trust me with anything." He pauses and waits for me to nod before he adds, "And I promise I won't tease you about stuff like this again."

"Okay," I whisper, my chin trembling against my will. I'm starting to regret all those apology-tutoring sessions.

"No, please don't …" He shakes his head, looking entirely too contrite. "I really am sorry. What can I do to make you feel better?"

A short make out session would do the trick. Or even an admission that you see me as an actual adult woman.

"Don't worry about it," I mumble instead. "This whole conversation took a wrong turn from the beginning."

"Then let's start over, please. I hate leaving you upset like this." He reaches for my hand, practically begging me to forgive him.

I wipe a tear from my cheek. "I'm not even sure what I meant in the first place anymore," I lie.

"Hey, look at me. If this has anything to do with you thinking you're holding me back from something better, then you're wrong. Maybe our relationship isn't conventional, and I know you're still looking forward to finding the man you're really supposed to marry, but for now, I like things the way they are. In fact, it's kind of perfect, if you ask me." He shrugs shyly before he continues. "You make me feel comfortable, like I can really be myself. And I've never felt that way with anyone else, not even with Rowan or my own family. We can be completely honest with one another, and we're both good at sensing what the other needs. I mean, who really needs sex or romance or any of the other shit that goes along with a traditional marriage when it's this easy?"

My lips part in shock, yet he's smiling at me as if it's the best thing he's ever said. He might think he's just given me the greatest compliment in the world as opposed to twisting a knife into my heart, but I'm leaning toward the latter.

"People who want kids, I suppose," I spit out awkwardly.

"What?" he asks, furrowing his brow.

"As you so often like to remind me, you can't make babies without having sex. So yeah, Landry, *I* need those things, eventually."

His smile falters. "Of course, you deserve it—and I'll do anything to make sure you get all that one day. I just meant that *we* don't need ... I mean, this works for now, right?" He gestures between us, and I absorb another invisible blow to the chest.

I shake my head. "I'm very grateful for everything you've done for me. But this is not enough, for either of us. It shouldn't be. And you're obviously not as good as you think at sensing what I need."

He stares back at me, his face panic-stricken. "I'm not?" he asks after a while.

"Not even close," I whisper before I turn on my heels to march away.

landry

MY HEAD POUNDS when I roll over in bed the next morning. At least I don't have to go into the clinic today. And I'm not on call, since I told the other doctors I was going out of town for Thanksgiving.

Then my tonsils rub together when I try to swallow, and I whimper.

I'm definitely sick.

There was a strep outbreak in Camellia this week, and judging from the imaginary hammer hitting my head and shards of glass lodged in my throat, I've picked it up from one of my patients.

I attempt to sit up in bed, but the room immediately spins, and I'm forced to fall back onto my pillow.

I'm still breathing through the dizzy spell when my phone pings on my nightstand. It takes me a second to get to it, despite the short distance. There's a message from Daisy. She's letting me know that Rowan's on his way to pick her up and take her to Baton Rouge to spend Thanksgiving with her family and not to expect her back until later this weekend.

I sigh and rub a hand over my face. I was supposed to bring her there myself, but I suppose she wasn't in the mood to spend a two-hour car ride with me after our awkward interaction last night. I'm still not sure where I went wrong, but I really upset her this time.

Eh, maybe that's not the whole truth. I think I know *what* I said to upset her. I'm just at a loss as to how to fix it or make it up to her. It turns out that Daisy's much more sensitive about the whole virginity thing than she's been letting on. She'd joked about it before, so I thought it was fair game. But I was wrong—very wrong.

To top it all off, the whole conversation only started because she'd walked in on me fresh out of the shower. It should have felt uncomfortable, but her reaction to seeing me was entirely too … flattering. It was also a reminder of my responsibility to protect her innocence, at least when it comes to our relationship.

It's probably for the best that she's gotten Rowan to bring her home, anyway. My back is starting to ache as much as my head, and Daisy doesn't need to catch this, too. I'm still thinking over my reply to her when there's a soft knock at the door.

"Come in," I rasp, wincing at the pain in my throat again.

"Landry?"

I cough and try again, but my voice only gets worse. I end up having to text her.

She opens the door carefully and keeps her eyes on the ground. "Everything okay?"

"Fine. Just a sore throat," I strain to get out.

"You don't sound fine." She looks up, and her brows draw in closer. "And you look terrible."

I shake my head, but it makes me feel drunk again, and I have to close my eyes and lean back against the headboard to keep from falling out of bed.

"Do you have a fever?" she asks, her voice filled with concern. I feel her hand on my forehead a second later, and I reach up to push it away.

"No, stay back. I'm contagious," I force out.

"Oh gosh, you're burning up," she exclaims. "Have you taken anything yet?"

"No," I say as I realize I'm shivering. She clicks her tongue in annoyance and stomps out of the room, and I close my eyes again.

Just before I drift off to sleep, the light flickers on. I flinch, and the movement makes my whole body ache.

"Come on, sit up and take this. We have to break your fever," Daisy says. Her hands are on my shoulders, pulling me up to a seated position, but her voice sounds distant.

"Just let me sleep," I whine.

There's a beeping sound before she redoubles her efforts. "Your temp is almost a hundred and three degrees. If you can't man up and take this ibuprofen, I'll have to replace these blankets with ice packs."

My teeth chatter when I whimper in protest.

"Then get your bubble butt up and take these meds right now," she demands.

I'd smile at that if I wasn't struggling just to comply. I barely manage to lift my head as she puts the pills in my mouth and brings a cup to my lips. It takes all I have to swallow it down.

"I know you're already cold, but you need this," she says and drapes a damp cloth over my forehead.

"Thank you, Daisy," I whisper. And it's the last thing I remember before I'm out again.

* * *

The next time I wake up, I find myself drenched in sweat. I groan and push the dampened sheets away, noticing the smell of eucalyptus in the air. My head's still thick, but it's not as bad as before, and my muscles are weak but less achy.

"Hey, how are you feeling?" Daisy asks before I open my eyes.

I peek through a small crack in my eyelids to find her sitting at the edge of my bed. "Better," I wheeze. "What are you still doing here?"

She lifts the washcloth from my head and replaces it with a fresh one. "I couldn't just leave you here to die," she replies dryly. "We did say 'in sickness and in health.' "

"I wasn't ..." I stop and cover my mouth to cough before I continue. My throat still feels horrible. "I'm not dying. It's probably just strep throat. And the last thing you need is to catch it."

"You were so pitiful earlier that I considered calling someone to help me get you to the emergency room."

I roll my eyes, but even that movement hurts. "It was just a fever. Obviously, the ibuprofen did its job."

"When's the last time you ate or drank anything, besides sipping water with your medicine?"

"That depends. How long have I been asleep?"

She frowns. "You took that first dose around nine in the morning. I woke you up at eleven to give you some acetaminophen because you were still running a temp. It's nearly one in the afternoon now."

"Well, shit," I mutter. "I guess I haven't had anything since yesterday."

"You're probably dehydrated. And I'm guessing you need antibiotics."

I sigh. "Yeah. But it's Thanksgiving. Pharmacy's closed."

"What about an injection? Can you get one from the clinic?"

"It can wait until tomorrow."

She eyes me skeptically. "No, it can't. What if I get sick, too?"

She's right, even though I suspect she's using herself as bait. She knows I won't risk letting her spike a fever because it could cause a seizure.

I swallow and cringe. "I'll get dressed and go in a minute."

"You can't drive yourself. You're barely past the point of delirium, and you're as pale as a ghost."

"I can't send someone else for it. I have to go myself," I say, coughing again.

"Just let me drive this time," she suggests. "I'm only a couple of months away from being cleared again."

"It's not worth the risk."

"Yes, it is," she holds.

"What about Rowan?"

"I told him not to come after I saw you this morning," she admits quietly. "I couldn't leave you like that."

"But if I weren't sick, you'd have left my ass behind, right?" I ask her, forcing a smile, and she smirks back at me. I lift my arm to adjust my position and realize how terrible I smell. I groan and scrunch my nose. "You could have at least given me a sponge bath while I was out. It's not like you haven't seen it all, anyway. And I bet it would have made for an interesting dream."

She doesn't seem to think it's as funny as I hoped though. "Get dressed. The only thing I'm looking forward to giving you today is a shot," she says, standing and averting her eyes.

I laugh softly, but she ignores me and moves to check the essential oil diffuser she must have brought in before she leaves me alone in the room.

I exhale and run my hand through my sticky hair. She's still upset with me from before, but she stayed behind to take care of me anyway. I guess she felt like she owed it to me after the way I've been taking care of her.

I move slowly as I climb out of bed and slip into a pair of sweatpants and a T-shirt. I can't imagine it's cold enough outside for a jacket, and it isn't worth the energy to find one.

"Ready?" she asks when I stagger into the kitchen to meet her, and I nod. "Here." She hands me a bottle of cloudy water. "Drink that first."

I eye her skeptically. "What's in it?"

"Electrolyte mix. It helps me stay hydrated and keeps the seizures away."

"Right. Thanks." I unscrew the cap and gulp down two-thirds of the bottle, stopping to catch my breath before going for the last bit. She stares me down and scrutinizes me the whole time, and I'm not sure how to feel about it. Being told what to do is new for me. But ... I also like seeing this side of her. I don't think I mind being bossed around by Daisy as much as I should.

I squeeze my eyes closed, bracing myself to swallow the last of the drink, and when they open again, her expression softens. "What's next, Doc?" I ask her, drawing a hint of a smile from her this time.

She dangles a set of car keys in the air. "Now I get to chauffeur you around for a change."

"Can't we just ask my sister to take me?"

"And expose them and therefore the twins to whatever this is? Not to mention, I'd have to tell her why I can't just drive you myself."

"Shit. You're right," I concede. "Wait, I never let them know I wasn't going to make it to dinner today. Although I'd honestly be surprised if they cared."

She clicks her tongue. "Of course they care. I've been texting Loren about you since this morning, and your mom called your phone to check on you a couple of hours ago. I figured you wouldn't mind if I answered it and gave her an update."

"Oh," is all I say.

"Well, *allons*," she calls, gesturing to the front door. "Let's go, kid."

I smirk and follow orders, though I nearly change my mind as soon as I step outside and face the sunlight. I groan loudly, but Daisy only rolls her eyes and urges me on to her little green Volkswagen.

"I can barely even fit in this thing," I complain as I fold into the car.

"Oh, get over it. You don't hear me griping about having to hike up my dresses to climb into your Jeep, do you?"

"I guess not," I say quietly and ignore the image of her pulling up her skirt to reveal her legs as I flip down the visor. She hands me a pair of girly sunglasses, but I don't hesitate to put them on. I catch her holding back a grin as she slips on another pair of pastel purple shades before she cranks her car and pulls out of the driveway.

"Daisy, if you—"

"I'll pull over if anything feels off," she interrupts me and reaches out to raise the volume on the radio. Then she thinks better of it, probably because of my head, and turns down the John Denver song.

"You've missed this, haven't you?" I ask after a while. "Take a right at the red light."

"Yes, I have. And I know where I'm going, thank you."

"For what it's worth, you're a surprisingly good driver for someone who hasn't been behind the wheel in a few months. Then again, you're driving a glorified Barbie car, so ..."

She reaches out to backhand my arm, and I chuckle until it turns into a cough. Then her back tire scrapes the curb on the turn into the parking lot before she pulls up too far and catches her bumper on the cement divider. She winces adorably each time we hear the grating of plastic over concrete, and I stifle my laughter.

"How am I supposed to park straight with you watching me like that?" she poses.

"I'm not watching you," I reply, amused. "I'm just being a passenger."

She furrows her brow, but she's still smiling. "You haven't stopped staring at me since we left the house. I know you're worried, but I told you, I'm fine. That six-month rule is just an arbitrary line in the sand, isn't it?"

I lick my lips, my mouth suddenly feeling dry. "Sorry. I guess I didn't realize I was doing that."

"Come on." Her cheeks darken, and she looks away. "We breaking into this joint or what?"

I laugh again before getting myself out of the car and leading her around to the staff entrance. I punch in a code and open the door for her before we slip into a supply closet to grab a strep test.

"Think you can stomach it?" I ask, holding up a long cotton swab and a tongue depressor.

She rolls her eyes and takes them both. "I spent half my childhood as a patient, getting poked and prodded, and the other half growing up on a farm. I've stuck worse things into grosser orifices, especially of the non-human variety."

I nod approvingly and sit on the nearest table before tilting my head back and thrusting my tongue out. She doesn't hesitate to go in and rub the swab over my tonsils, and I gag exaggeratedly, holding my throat when she backs away.

"Damn, woman," I spit out between coughs. "That's the wrong orifice."

"You said to swab your throat, didn't you?"

"Yeah, but you didn't have to go deep enough to touch my asshole from this end."

She glares at me before she follows my instructions to set up the test. "You should probably be wearing a mask and gloves," I say after a while. "Especially if you're going to give me an injection."

"I'm sure it's too late for that. Might as well just have my prescription on standby for when I start showing symptoms," she replies with a shrug as she sits on the table across from me.

"You might not catch it, since it's not like we've been sharing drinks or swapping spit. But I'm not just talking about the strep cooties."

She crosses her arms over her middle. "Shouldn't you have told me about your other cooties before we got married?"

I huff. "I've never actually had an STD, for the record. I just meant that you should always wear gloves around sharp objects in a medical setting. You never know what's lurking around."

"Oh." She relaxes a little.

"I didn't think that would matter, anyway, since we don't have the kind of marriage in which we could actually trade STDs."

Her eyes dart down again, and a lightbulb goes off above my head. I think I'm starting to understand how I might make up for hurting her last night.

"There's always the possibility of a blood-borne pathogen transfer during a kitchen accident. In fact, I was pretty close to drawing blood the day you moved in," she mumbles.

"This is true." I watch her expression carefully as I continue. "Or in the unfortunate event we run into one another outside the shower again but neither of us has a warm towel handy."

Her face reddens again. "We can't have that, can we?" she remarks, but instead of sounding sarcastic, her tone seems ... sad.

I replay yesterday's conversation in my head again, especially the last part when I told her that we have the perfect relationship because we don't have to bother with anything physical.

I really am the world's biggest idiot.

Because even though I meant what I said and have absolutely no intention of changing our dynamic, Daisy obviously wants more. Or at least she thinks she wants more. My guess is that she's just longing for the romantic aspect and not necessarily for me, although I could see how she might mistake our mutual feelings of fondness, trust, and familiarity for something deeper. Hell, at this point, if I weren't so vigilant about not letting my thoughts of Daisy drift into more-than-friends territory, I'm sure I'd be tempted to—

The timer beeps just then, letting us know the test is ready to read. I watch as she clears her throat and hops down from the table.

"Two lines means it's positive, even if the test line is faint," I volunteer as she studies the strip.

"Well, congratulations. It's a boy," she replies, holding it up so I can see the positive result.

"Figured." I rise to my feet to track down a syringe and a vial of penicillin. I attempt to draw up the medicine myself, but my hands are trembling, and I realize I've gotten weaker since we arrived.

"You'll have to do it," I say on a sigh, handing it over to her. "Have you ever given an injection before?"

"No, but I've been on the receiving end of plenty, so I'm sure I'll manage. Do I really need gloves?" she asks as she takes the vial and syringe.

"Nah. This would probably kill most cooties of the STD-variety, anyway."

She laughs and waits for my instructions to draw up the correct dosage while I find an alcohol pad, then I explain how to administer the shot. I'm about to reach for my sleeve when another stupid impulsive idea overtakes my already foggy brain, and I turn to face the table instead.

"You'll need to wipe the injection site with that alcohol pad first," I turn to instruct over my shoulder.

She stares at me in confusion. "Okay. Don't I need your arm for that?"

I shake my head, barely holding back a smile. "Not enough fatty tissue there. Since you're an amateur, it's probably best if you hit me with it from behind."

Daisy rears back and blinks a few times. "Y-you want me to put in your butt?"

"More or less." I reach behind me to lift my shirt and pull my pants down on one side. Then I take the alcohol pad and wipe the upper edge of my left cheek. "See where I'm wiping? You can stick me right there, where my hip ends and my ass cheek begins."

"Mm-hmm," she squeaks, and I watch with amusement as her eyes run over the area I've exposed.

"Daisy?"

"Yeah, I'm, um ... can you show me again, just in case? I feel like this is too important to mess up."

I chuckle softly and reach back to grab her free hand, then press her index finger into the right spot. "Right about there. Just disinfect the site again before you administer the injection, okay?"

She nods quickly, her eyes still glued to the space. "Got it."

I lean farther down, planting my elbows on the table. Although I'm not sure what I'm trying to accomplish with my tactics besides either grossing her out or giving her a small thrill. "This any better?"

"Uh, yeah, that's ... that works."

She blinks and shakes her head with her fingertip still pinned to my butt cheek, and it takes all I have not to laugh again. Eventually, she reaches for the alcohol and moves her finger to clean the spot, then she inhales deeply behind me. "Ready?"

"Yeah, go for it. Make sure you take all your resentment out while you're at it—" But I interrupt myself to blurt out a four-letter word when Daisy literally jams the needle between my glute muscles.

"Whoopsie," she intones as she pulls the plunger back and pushes it down. "Didn't mean to stick you that hard, but I wanted to make sure it took." Then she presses a bit of gauze to the injection site to keep the medicine from working its way out, just like a pro.

"Sorry for the language, but I think you might have hit bone."

"Oh, no." She giggles. "Plenty of fatty tissue here, like you said."

I scoff, and she replaces the gauze with a Band-Aid. "For the record, you lied to me before," she continues, pulling my boxers and my pants up one at a time and making me gulp hard, which fortunately makes my throat hurt enough to distract me from the feeling of her hands on my skin. In fact, it's not until this exact moment that I realize I'm literally bent over the table, baring my ass for her. We're on a whole different level of trust now.

"Wait, I didn't … when did I lie?" And now I'm the one who's flustered.

"You said I wouldn't like the view from back here because it was too hairy," she reminds me, leaning in to whisper next to my ear.

I swallow again and wince at the pain. "If you think that's completely hairless, then you need to get your eyes checked, Blondie."

"It's not as bad as you made it sound, though," she replies before turning and backing away, leaving me to either force my tonsils together on purpose or start reciting a list of common *streptococcus* infection sites.

"I know you don't want a sucker, so am I supposed to give you a sticker now?"

"What?" I ask, rising from my position at the table.

"You were a big boy today, Landry. You deserve a reward," she adds with a smirk, and I groan.

daisy

"THANK YOU," Landry says as I tuck him into bed.

"No problem," I mumble somewhat bitterly while I set a glass of water and his next dose of medicine on the side table.

He tries to clear his throat and winces before he reaches out to grab my arm. "I mean it. No one has ever ..." He shakes his head before he continues. "I can't remember the last time anyone's taken such good care of me."

But I catch what he didn't mean to say. "Your parents never tended to you when you were sick?" I ask, furrowing my brow.

He shrugs, his hand still wrapped around my forearm. "Not this well, no."

My insides feel heavy. "How did that work, then?"

"After Lilley left home, I did most of that stuff for Loren and myself, I guess."

"Oh," I say softly. "Well, I'm sorry."

"It is what it is," he replies. "But I'm grateful for your help, especially since I'm probably not your favorite person at the moment."

I press my lips together before I answer. "Is this supposed to be your attempt at another apology for last night?"

He smiles ruefully, and his thumb softly strokes my arm. "Maybe."

"The sympathy card was a dirty move," I pull away and cross both arms over my chest.

"To be fair, I only planned on playing the current-sickness card. I was forced to put down the shitty-childhood card when you called my hand."

"Mm-hmm." I glare at him skeptically. "That all you got?"

He pats the bed beside him, and I reluctantly sit at the edge. "I think I understand what I said to hurt you last night."

"You do?" My heart immediately begins beating faster, making my head pound.

"Is it because I made it sound like I could never want a physical relationship with you?"

My eyes grow wide. "Maybe."

"Look, Daisy, I know this probably isn't what you want to hear, but ..." He pauses and exhales before he goes on. "It's not like I don't think of you as attractive or sexy because you *aren't* those things ... I just can't allow myself to think about you in that way at all, you know?"

"Right," I say, forcing a smile even though it feels like he's getting ready to push that knife back into place. "Because I'm Rowan's baby sister."

"Yes. But it's also because I can't trust myself around you," he blurts out, his expression pained. And my breath hitches in my throat.

"Why wouldn't you be able to trust yourself around me?" I venture after a second, my heart racing now.

He licks his lips. "Because I don't have a lot of willpower, especially once I get fixated on some impulsive idea. And besides that, you and I don't even want the same things. I can't allow anything to happen between us because any way you spin it, I'd be taking advantage of you."

I'm sure he's right. The responsible part of my brain agrees wholeheartedly.

But every other part of me just wants to pull back the sheets and slide into bed next to him, then cling to him long enough to make him believe he's worth my love and attention.

"Landry," I begin, my voice thick, "it's not just that."

"It's not?"

"I mean, yes, it does hurt my pride to hear you can't even be enticed to see me as more than your friend, particularly when you throw in the fact that you were my brother's friend first. And you know how much I hate being treated like a child and being told what's best for me." He frowns, but I go on. "But what upsets me the most is the way you refuse to see *yourself* as more than my friend. You like to make excuses for me because you don't think I could be attracted to you as you are. It's gotta be my lack of options, right? Or you think my only motivation for wanting a physical relationship with you is to settle a debt. I mean, a man like you, one who's selfless and caring and loyal, he couldn't possibly be good enough for a girl like me—an overly sheltered virgin with a health problem. She must think she owes him something. No way anyone could stand him long enough to marry him and have his kids, even if she were as desperate as I am, right?"

He swallows and closes his eyes to wince. "I'm sorry, Daisy," he whispers. "That's not what I think of you at all. I'm just trying to protect you."

I sniffle and wipe my nose on my sleeve, noticing a burning in the back of my throat for the first time. "But who's taking care of you?"

He opens his eyes and studies me carefully, then he reaches up to brush his hand over my forehead. "Oh, shit. You're hot."

"What?" I blink.

He sighs and shakes his head. "You're burning up. Does your head hurt yet?"

"I'm fine. If anything, I'm ... cold."

He glares at me expectantly. "You have fever chills. That's not just the afterglow from getting to stab a needle into my bare ass."

An unexpected laugh bubbles out of me. "Well, we both know it doesn't take much to excite me."

He presses his lips together, looking more concerned than entertained. "Open up and say *ah*."

I pout for a second before I stick out my tongue, and he grunts.

"Come on," he says, scooting over and inviting me into the bed alongside him. I follow his lead tentatively, but he gets up as soon as I move to lie down.

"Where are you going?"

"To get your injection ready," he replies matter-of-factly.

"Injection?" I sit up quickly.

"Good thing we brought the rest of that vial of penicillin home. You're not allergic, are you?"

"No." I bite my lip, watching him as he walks across the room and confidently draws the medicine into a fresh syringe like the hot doctor he is.

Stupid, sexy, capable Dr. McDreamy.

He returns a second later, flicking the side of the syringe. "Ready?"

"Sure," I say with a shrug before moving to stand at the edge of the bed. Then I bend at the waist and begin gathering my skirt in my hands.

"Whoa, whoa, whoa!" Landry exclaims.

"What? I thought you were giving me a shot?" I turn my head to him.

"In the arm," he wheezes, his eyes huge and round. He gulps and cringes again, but he doesn't look away. "Can you please, please, put your dress down?"

"Whatever you want, doctor." I oblige and turn around to sit on the bed this time. "As long as you tell me why we have different injection sites."

"Impetigo, rheumatic fever, post-streptococcal glomeru-lonephritis ..." he mumbles and squeezes his eyes shut.

"What?"

"Just reviewing the types of streptococcal infections, you know, so I don't miss any symptoms," he says quickly without looking directly at me, then he turns to grab an alcohol wipe.

"Landry?"

"Your sleeve, Daisy."

I slide the cap sleeve of my dress down my arm as slowly and deliberately as possible, and his gaze follows my movements. Then I angle my body to offer him my bare shoulder while I tilt my head down and look up at him from beneath my lashes. "Like this?"

"Yeah, that's ... perfect." The way his half-lidded eyes run over me reawakens the butterflies in my stomach after their last foray when Landry and I played doctor at the clinic. Then again, that could also be the fever chills.

"I'm ready when you are," I say quietly, trying to hide the way my teeth are chattering.

He nods, but it takes him a second to move again. I flinch when he rubs the cold alcohol pad against my skin.

"So, are you going to tell me why you're afraid to put it in my butt or not?" I pose.

He turns his head to cough. "I'm not afraid. It's just not necessary this time," he says before he reaches in to pinch the back of my arm. "Females tend to have more fat around their upper arms than men do."

"And your arm muscles are too big for a shot?"

"Exactly. Okay, three, two ..." He pokes the needle through my skin, and I do my best to stay still. Once he's done with the syringe, his touch grows more tender as he smooths a Band-Aid over my arm and gingerly slides my sleeve up into place. "Hopefully you won't get much worse since we caught it early."

I nod. "Thank you."

"Thank me by taking some of that ibuprofen and getting yourself to bed."

I pout when I stand, ignoring the way my head throbs. "I can't believe you're kicking me out. We've already shared cooties, and I figured you'd want to keep an eye on me."

He laughs shortly. "You really want to snuggle up in these musty sheets?"

"Fair enough," I say, my throat starting to burn again. "My bed definitely smells better. And it's bigger."

He narrows his eyes at me before he grabs the medicine off the side table, then he ushers me forward. We turn the corner to my room, and he sets everything down beside my bed before he hands me a couple of pills and a glass of water. I swallow them obediently, and he pulls the sheets back, tilting his head in a gesture. At least he's tucking me in.

But as soon as I slip beneath the covers, he surprises me by sliding in beside me. He grabs a spare pillow and plants it firmly in the space between us. "Only because I need to keep an eye on you all night. You're more likely to have a seizure if your temperature spikes."

"Right, Doc," I confirm, stifling my smile. "Whatever you need to tell yourself."

He exhales loudly before he reaches up to flick the switch on the lamp beside my bed. "Good night, Daisy. Wake me up if you start feeling funny, especially if you get really hot."

"Hmm, ditto."

He chuckles. "That's not what I meant, and you know it."

"Says the man who sacrificed his left butt cheek for the sake of my pride today," I mutter before I settle in next to our border pillow.

"If you knew why I was doing it, then why'd you stab me so hard?" he asks through a yawn and a subsequent whimper.

"Thought you might be into that kinda thing."

He groans. "That better be the fever talking."

"If I agree, will you kiss me and make it better?"

"Stop flirting and go to sleep."

"Fine." He can't stop me from grinning at him in the dark though. "Happy Thanksgiving, Landry."

"Happy Thanksgiving."

We're both quiet after that, and although I don't remember drifting off to sleep, I wake a few hours later to find myself snuggled up to Landry's chest, that extra pillow lying on the ground beside him.

landry

"YOU SHOULD GET DOWN with me. I mean, if you want," Daisy offers quietly as I drive up to her coworker's house. Festive lights and decorations line the path from the driveway to the back of the house, and I can hear faint Christmas music from the car.

I smile. "I'm not a Camellia High faculty member."

"As the husband of a faculty member, you're entitled to be my date."

"I'm not the kind of husband that's entitled to anything," I correct her, but I try to keep my expression light to avoid hurting her feelings again. Although, I might need the reminder more than she does.

Things have felt different between Daisy and me for the past few weeks or so. I thought we'd hit a sweet spot in our relationship where we could live comfortably and platonically until it was time for our annulment. But ever since we got sick together and I had to let Daisy doctor me up, her confidence has grown around me. Not that it's a bad thing—I'm proud of her. It honestly warms my heart to see Daisy maturing into this more capable, self-assured version of herself. But the way she's started cracking suggestive jokes at my expense and making it seem like *she's* the one taking care of *me* is becoming some-what problematic. It's like we've swapped roles, and now I'm the awkward one around the house. It's also getting harder to keep myself from seeing her as the competent adult she's obviously become, and I'm afraid it'll only take one more crack in the mental fortress I've built around "Potentially Attractive Adult Daisy" for the whole damn thing to come crashing down.

"I don't mean *that* kind of date," she mumbles, bringing me back. "But Mrs. Julie said we could each bring a guest. And there will be plenty of food. You might as well get a free meal for your trouble."

I shake my head. "I'm good, thanks. You go have a fun time. Just call me when you're ready."

Her shoulders droop. "I'd probably have more fun if I didn't have to walk in alone or feel guilty about making you drive back to pick me up later."

"Maybe you could ask Blake or JD for a ride home," I suggest, but she frowns. "I'm not even dressed for a party."

"It's casual. Just take off your tie."

She sticks out her bottom lip in a pout, preparing to give me that look—the one she knows I can't refuse.

Aaaand ... yep. There it is.

"Just for a minute? Pleeease?" She looks up at me from beneath her lashes. "It's not like I can go out and find a real date, you know?"

I heave out a sigh. Why am I such a sucker? What happened to my resolve, my fortitude, my freaking backbone?

She blinks at me again, and there's more determination in her big green eyes than I have in my whole body.

"A minute. That's all."

She lets out one of her trademark squeals while her face breaks out into an ear-splitting grin, and I'm overcome with an unexpected spark of attraction. I look away quickly, pretending to concern myself with my tie, but she rises to her knees and leans over to loosen it for me.

"You need this, Doc. It'll get you into the Christmas spirit. And since you aren't having a holiday party at work ..."

I clear my throat. "Actually, there's a big hospital party this weekend. I just hadn't planned on going."

"Why not?" she frowns and drags my tie out from my collar.

"I, uh … I didn't want to go alone either, I guess." I wasn't planning on admitting that to anyone, but I need a distraction from the feeling of Daisy's fingers moving deftly over the buttons at my neck.

Shit.

I inhale deeply, then immediately realize it's a mistake because she smells so damned good and feminine and … Daisy-ish.

Measles, mumps, rubella … roseola, varicella …

"I'll go with you, silly," she says as she opens my collar. "Hmm, one button or two?"

I continue holding my breath while she leans back and surveys my chest, then loosens another button and regards it again.

"Did you trim your chest hair?"

"What?" My voice cracks, and my ears heat up.

"I like it," she remarks with a smirk before she reaches out to pat the skin she's exposed. "Two buttons it is."

Respiratory syncytial virus, laryngotracheobronchitis, pertussis …

"What's *pertussis*?"

I straighten in my seat. Have I been saying that out loud?

"Uh, it's uh … whooping cough."

"Why are you whispering about whooping cough?" she asks again, her expression amused.

I shake my head. "It's … something I forgot to chart earlier," I lie. Which I'm not supposed to be doing. But I also cannot under any circumstances explain my default method of deflection to her. The very idea that I need a distraction would be all the encouragement she needs to start tempting me on purpose.

"See—all the more reason to let loose tonight," she continues, finally moving back to the passenger side, to my relief.

"Yeah, I guess," I mutter before getting out of the Jeep and going around to open her door. Daisy smiles happily as she wraps her hands around my bicep, and I remind myself that I'm not allowed to enjoy the feeling of her at my side as I lead her on to the gathering in the back.

"Well, fancy meeting the two of you here … *together*," a familiar voice drawls. I yank my arm free and look up, my stomach immediately twisting into knots when I see Blake approaching.

"Did we miss anything?" Daisy returns cheerfully when he makes his way over, and my eyes scan the crowd for my sister. She'd never let me hear the end of it if she were to see us walking in arm-in-arm.

"It just got a helluva lot more interesting from where I'm standing, that's for sure," Blake proclaims with a wide grin. "So what are you doing out here, Lando?"

I shove my hands in my pockets. "You know … official roommate business."

"The kind that requires you to get dressed up and escort your roomie to a work party?" He leans in and brushes a kiss over Daisy's cheek. "You look lovely tonight, by the way."

I grunt but don't say anything. "What, I figure someone ought to compliment the young lady, in case her date forgets to do it," Blake replies with a sly grin. Daisy casts a remorseful glance my way before thanking him.

"You're awfully quiet, brother. Don't you have anything to say for yourself?" Blake asks after a while.

"I'm not your brother," I grumble.

"Ah, that's where you're wrong, Doc. I happen to be well-versed in the law. And the fact that your sister and nieces bear my last name, share my DNA, and sleep in my bed definitely makes us brothers by law." Blake tilts his head from side to side before he brings his drink up to his mouth and takes a sip. "Kinda the same way you and Dr. Rowan would become legal bros if you and Daisy were to end up tying the knot one day."

Daisy's eyes grow wide, but I clench my jaw, too annoyed to panic with her. "Technically, Loren wouldn't share your DNA unless she developed fetal microchimerism and the twins left behind your half of their genetic material," I say automatically.

"Sperm transfers DNA, doesn't it?" Blake poses.

"Yes," I answer hesitantly.

Blake cocks an eyebrow. "Well, then she's definitely walking around with a healthy dose of my genetic—"

"Enough," I interrupt him, my blood starting to boil. Whatever it is that makes me so powerless against Daisy has got to be the same stuff that Blake's always used to get under my skin. I may have learned to tolerate and respect my brother-in-law, but that doesn't mean I've stopped imagining how satisfying a right hook to his chin would feel most of the time.

Blake only grins harder. "There he is. I was starting to worry you'd gone soft."

"All right, you can stop now. This isn't a date. I'm only here to take care of her," I blurt out, my tone much harsher than necessary. Blake frowns as Daisy and I trade embarrassed glances.

"It was my idea," she admits softly. "He didn't want to come, but I begged him not to make me walk in alone." I can see her eyes watering and her chin quivering as she says it.

Maybe that newfound confidence doesn't run as deep as I assumed.

I sigh. "Daisy, don't—"

"Dammit, Landry," Blake curses under his breath and steps in to place a comforting hand on Daisy's back. "You know, you lose all your brownie points when you act like an ass, even when you're doing something nice."

"It's okay," she says, sniffling. "He doesn't realize you weren't being literal, that as unlikely as it is for me to show up with a real date, no one would ever be silly enough to believe Landry would stoop to my level."

Blake gives her a look that I can't quite read as she pulls away from his embrace. It's not pity—maybe empathy or understanding—and it reminds me that Loren really did put him through the ringer. I don't know if I like what it implies about my relationship with Daisy, but I don't have time to overanalyze that kind of stuff right now, and I'm not about to ask Blake for his thoughts.

"Daze ..." My voice is hoarse when I finally speak up. "I'm sorry. I didn't mean that the way it came out."

She sniffs one more time and nods, and I instinctively reach out for her hand as I continue. "You know it's the other way around, right? You're the one who's too fun and beautiful to waste your time on an old grump like me. Okay?"

Her eyes are still downcast as she uses her free hand to wipe the moisture from her cheeks. "Yeah, sure."

"I mean it. That's why I didn't ask you to come to the hospital party with me. I figured everyone would think I was delusional if I showed up with you on my arm. Or they'd all assume you were only with me for my money."

To my relief, that one elicits a small laugh from her, and I smile at the sound of it.

"Well," Blake begins, bringing me back. "This keeps getting more interesting by the minute."

I glower at him as Loren walks up, and he bounces his eyebrows suggestively and shoots me a cocky smirk. If I didn't know any better, I'd swear he just set me up.

"Heyyy, you two look *noice*," my sister slurs and tucks herself under her husband's arm.

I snort out a laugh. "Yeah. And you sound like you're *feeling* pretty nice, Lo-Lo."

She giggles and casts a sultry glance up at Blake, and I barely manage to hide my disgust. "Oh, I'm feeling verryyy nice, thanks to this drink my husband fixed me." She reaches up to tap her cup against his, and he smiles down at her. "You should make one of these for old Land-*oh*," she tells him, puckering her lips as she drags out my name. "It'll help dislodge that stick up his ass."

Daisy stifles a laugh, and I huff. "Should you be drinking while you're still breastfeeding?"

Loren scoffs and waves me off. "Re-laaxx, Doc. I'm only having one drink, and I just pumped a half-hour ago. It'll be out of my system by the next feeding."

"Don't worry, I'm monitoring the situation very closely," Blake leans in and says quietly before raising his voice again. "And of course I don't mind mixing a cocktail for you, bro. I can even make it a little weaker than my wife's, if you prefer. After all, I'm not trying to get *you* drunk enough for a DNA swap later. Although, your roommate might—"

I growl, and he cuts himself off mid-sentence, grinning at me all the while. "I was just going to say she might appreciate the lubrication if she's going to try to remove that aforementioned branch before the end of the night."

"All right, boys, play nice," Daisy chimes in and places a hand on my forearm, instantly calming me. "And for the record, Landry doesn't have a big stick or a tree branch up his butt. It's more like an itty, bitty splinter."

My sister sprays us all when she bursts into laughter mid-sip, which Daisy apparently takes as a compliment. She aims a satisfied smirk at me, and I can't even be mad at her for that one. I smile in return and nudge her playfully.

"I'm sorry," Loren apologizes and wipes her chin. "Can you say that last part again?"

"It's more like an itty, bitty splinter?" Daisy shrugs.

"Uh, that's what she said," JD pops in over Loren's shoulder to deliver, and I groan.

"It's like his calling card," Loren explains as her brother-in-law and his wife join us. "If you set up a wood joke, he will—"

"No one wants to hear that one, Agnes." Blake slips a hand over her mouth before she can finish, then winces when she bites him. " Save that enthusiasm for later, huh?" he tells her, narrowing his eyes and shaking his hand out.

I gag to myself.

"She's not wrong, though. In fact, it doesn't take much," Tenley says with a snort, and JD reaches down to smack her lightly on the butt, making her giggle before he turns to me.

"Sorry if that one was at your expense, Doc. The opportunity was too good to pass up."

I glare at JD strangely. "Well, we *have* shared a locker room before, so I don't think I need to remind you that it's bigger than a splinter."

Daisy gasps quietly beside me, and my smile creeps back. Because she knows it, too.

"Ay, I may have seen the lumber, but my wife hasn't. So keep your tree trunk to yourself, man," JD adds. Tenley bites her lip and rolls her eyes while the rest of them stifle their laughter, and I grin.

"Wait, you haven't actually seen it, have you?" he turns and whispers to Tenley, but he's not doing a good job of keeping a straight face.

"I wouldn't tease him if I were you," Tenley mumbles. "It took you two months to accomplish what he did in ten minutes."

JD huffs and pouts while Blake tugs Tenley closer and plants a kiss on her cheek. "Have I ever mentioned how glad I am that you married my brother?" I'm surprised again by their ease with one another. I've never taken Tenley for an affectionate person, and that's coming from someone who's actually tried being physically affectionate with her before. "I've got to make the lumberjack over there a drink. After that burn, you've earned one, too, Ten," Blake continues.

"Well, you heard the man," JD agrees quickly, shoving his wife forward. "We're officially six weeks post-delivery. I need you as drunk as Lo."

"Geez, don't you guys ever think about anything but sex?" I mutter.

JD and Blake glance at one another and shrug. "We married up. Can you blame us?" JD replies, making Tenley roll her eyes again. Then she simpers at him as if she's got the same thing on her mind, and he leans down for a short kiss before the four of them walk on together.

Meanwhile, I stand there confused, watching it all unfold.

"Everything okay?" Daisy whispers when I don't move.

"Yeah," I say after a second. "It's just ... weird."

"What's weird?"

"All of it ... my sister and her husband being so nice, the Golden Boy cracking inappropriate jokes and not looking at me as if he wants to knock my head off my shoulders, Tenley bringing up that time we dated as kids ... it's all a little foreign to me," I admit.

She smiles softly. "I think that means you're in their club now."

I furrow my brow. "It's never been this easy before. What's changed?"

"They're probably saying the same things they always have. You're just reacting differently," she offers with a shrug.

"Come on, Lando. I need you to bear witness to all this. Your sister makes dirty jokes when she hits the sauce too hard, and I can't be held responsible when I fall for her methods of seduction again," Blake calls after me, and I snort out a laugh as Daisy tugs me forward.

I cautiously sip the drink Blake fixes for me, reminding myself that I can't afford another incident like the one at their wedding reception last month. Daisy hesitates when she gets ahold of a spiked hot chocolate, but I reassure her that I'm fine to look after her. She brings the cup to her lips, I suppose to test the temperature, then takes a longer drink. She glances up at me and stifles an adorable smirk, looking pleased with herself, and I can't help but return the smile.

Not long after she finishes her drink, Daisy mentions being cold and rubs her hands over her arms. I lead her away from the rest of our crew to join the crowd gathering around a firepit near the edge of the patio. She leans into me, I assume to soak up some of my body heat, and I automatically wrap an arm around her to help her warm up more quickly.

Daisy laughs as she chats up her friend Claire with my arm draped over her shoulders. After a while, she reaches up and wraps her fingers around my forearm, tugging it in closer. It's the kind of thing teenagers would do in public. In fact, I'd usually scoff if I saw adults my age acting like this. I imagine it must be the alcohol making her more friendly, especially since she doesn't drink often.

I'm plotting on how to slink away without hurting her feelings when she brushes her fingernails lightly up my forearm as she continues talking. And it makes me shiver.

I force a friendly smile and pretend I'm paying attention to what they're saying while she does it again, and my stomach dips.

Oh, no. This is bad.

I ... like it.

The way she's being so openly affectionate as she talks me up to her coworker, the feel of her gentle strokes over my arm …

I like all of it.

"You guys get cold?" Blake's voice knocks me back into consciousness, and I tug my arm back a bit too quickly to avoid looking guilty.

I clear my throat and glance down at the drink in my other hand. Maybe this thing is stronger than I thought. "Uh, yeah, Daisy's just trying to warm up."

Because that's all it was. And just like the morning after the wedding, I'm certain what I felt just now was only a natural reaction to her physical contact.

"Who needs hot chocolate and a bonfire when you have a hot date?" Blake mumbles so quietly that I'm the only one who hears it.

I shoot him a dangerous glare and put a little more space between Daisy and me, and her eyes dart around nervously when she notices the distance. She crosses her arms over her middle as she continues talking to her friend, but it's obvious that my overreaction embarrassed her.

"Want me to grab you another drink?" I lean in to ask in an attempt to smooth things over.

She lifts her empty cup and forces an uncomfortable smile. "Um, no thanks, I'm fine."

I sigh when she purposefully turns her back to me. This must be one of those times when "I'm fine" is actually code for "I'm pissed and it's all your fault."

Blake coughs lightly, grabbing my attention, and his smug expression confirms my suspicions.

He tilts his head encouragingly in Daisy's direction. I shake mine in response. He nods, I mouth a silent *no*. He rolls his eyes and steps forward to grab my arm and force my hand toward Daisy's backside, and I barely manage to move it up in time to catch the small of her back instead of her ass.

Then Blake spins around and pretends to take a drink, leaving me to face Daisy on my own.

Her round eyes meet mine questioningly, and I open and close my mouth a few times before I spit out an awkward response.

"Um, sorry, can I talk to you for a second?"

"Oh, sure," she replies carefully. And I search my mind frantically for my next move as she excuses herself from her previous conversation.

I use the hand still planted on her back to lead her toward the patio, buying my time before I have to speak again.

"So, uh, just now," I begin, furrowing my brow when I catch my brother-in-law puckering his lips at me over Daisy's shoulder. "I didn't mean to—"

But I'm interrupted when the host of the party walks by and pats my arm. "Uh-oh, looks like you guys are standing under the mistletoe," Mrs. Julie announces. "You know what that means!"

Daisy and I both glance up at the same time to find the bunch of greenery hanging from the edge of the awning above us. My stomach dips immediately.

"Guess you gotta give your date a kiss now, Doc," Blake says, smirking.

Loren grins and sidles up to him. "He's right," she chimes in, her eyes glossy. "It's tradition."

I clear my throat uncomfortably and look down to Daisy. She's already blushing and looking adorably shy. But I can't come out and ask her what she's thinking right now, so I'll have to sort it out.

My heart rate picks up as I continue to survey her expression. I think back on our previous conversations, and my memory flickers over her saying she wants a man who isn't afraid of a little PDA, as well as all the times she's seemingly enjoyed our harmless flirting, especially over the past month. And I imagine she'll be devastated if I leave her hanging in front of her coworkers, even though she's already preparing herself for a letdown.

Maybe it's the slight buzz that fuels me on, or maybe it's the warmth still lingering in my chest from earlier, but I swallow hard and channel Impulsive Landry as I grab Daisy's hand and yank her closer. "Well then, we can't break tradition. Right?"

CHAPTER 32

landry

DAISY BLINKS at me before giving the slightest nod. Then I bring my left hand to her hip and slide my right around her neck, cradling the back of her head as I drag her in and press my lips to hers. She's stiff at first, I guess because she's in shock, but only a second passes before I feel her hands on my chest. She tilts her head to the side and parts her soft lips for me, and I immediately slip my tongue inside.

Damn, she tastes good—like hot chocolate and marshmallows and everything sweet.

My fingers twist into her silky, blonde hair as I continue kissing her, and I'm instantly aware of the different parts of me that we're awakening. But I don't want to stop. Allowing myself to give in to this one urge was as good as throwing the doors wide open, because all of the other compulsive ideas I've been struggling to keep locked away suddenly come flooding in.

Forget whooping cough. There's no diverting my thoughts from this.

Because I like kissing Daisy. I like it a *lot*.

I'd like to try kissing her neck, too, to move my mouth down that line of freckles ...

Her hands push lightly against my chest, and she pulls away, surprising me. When I open my eyes, she's licking her lips and staring at my mouth, and she's still close enough that I'm already struggling to resist pulling her back in.

"Are you two done or what?" I hear my sister's voice in the distance. Then she bumps her hip clumsily into my thigh. "Move over, lovebirds. I want a turn."

I stumble, pulling Daisy with me. But Loren and Blake are both grinning widely at me before they turn to give one another a relatively modest kiss, at least by their standards.

Daisy clears her throat, and I turn my attention back to her. "Um, thank you?" she whispers, but it sounds more like a question.

I run a hand through my hair, unsure of what to say now. I might have been able to play off that first awkward kiss at our wedding, but this is a lot harder to explain. Coming back from *this* kiss isn't going to be so simple. Not only have I opened myself up to a new level of temptation, but I've also contradicted Daisy's assumptions about me having an aversion to physical contact. The truth is that I don't mind it one bit when Daisy touches me, and I sure as shit don't hate kissing her.

Gah, what am I doing? I can't let this—

"Landry?" she asks quietly. "Are you okay?"

I realize I'm frowning and attempt to soften my expression. "Yeah, of course. Are you?"

She shrugs and forces a smile. "Mm-hmm."

I sigh. I know I'm confusing the hell out of her.

"I think I'm ready to go," I begin. "I mean, if you want to stay, I can come back for you later ..."

"No, that's fine. You can take me home now," she says quickly, and I have to shake my head lightly to erase the thoughts she conjures up.

"Then we should probably get out of here before—"

"Whoa, where are you running off to now?" Loren calls, and I roll my eyes.

"Home. It's been a long day," I mumble as she and Blake approach.

"You mean it's gonna be a long night?" she retorts, and Daisy blushes again.

"Lo," I growl. "Don't start."

She lifts her hands up in surrender. "Fine. This is me respectfully butting out of your love life. See how that works?"

I grind my teeth together and inhale deeply, trying to avoid biting her head off. I know my sister means well and that I deserve to be teased after all the crap I've pulled with her and her boyfriends over the years, but she doesn't understand that this is a touchy situation right now.

"Yeah. Good night," I manage in a somewhat neutral tone, and I catch Blake winking at Daisy out of the corner of my eye.

I lead her on to my Jeep, and the ride home is quiet. But there's a different kind of tension in the air now. By the time we make it into the house, I feel like crawling out of my own skin. I want to stop Daisy and talk this out, for her to reassure me that it was just a chemical reaction and that she didn't feel the same things I did during that kiss. I *need* to know we're okay and that things can go back to normal between us. But I'm scared I'll hurt her, and I'm even more afraid of having to admit that I want to kiss her again.

"Landry, wait." Daisy reaches out to grab my sleeve once we're inside, and I turn to face her. "I have a confession to make," she begins, her eyes drifting down. "I ... I don't know how to say this, but ... I enjoyed it. You know, when you kissed me in front of everyone."

I press my lips into a hard line, trying to keep my expression blank. "You mean you enjoyed being physically affectionate with someone in public?"

She shakes her head softly, though I expect her to laugh. "Well, yeah, that's definitely part of it. But ..." She bites her lip, and I gulp, because I want to bite it, too. "It felt like more than an opportunity or a favor this time. I may not have a lot to compare it to, but I *have* been kissed before. And this was a really good kiss, at least for me."

"Hmm," I hum, pretending to consider what she's saying, when I'm really just trying to drag my eyes away from her mouth. "Aside from the peer pressure aspect, I guess it wasn't half-bad."

"So you enjoyed it, too?"

I shrug, trying to look aloof. "I certainly didn't hate it."

This time I elicit the smallest of smiles from her, and she crosses her arms as she glances coyly at me. "Your tolerance for PDA has improved, at least."

"You make it easy for me," I reply without thinking. But I shouldn't be flirting with her like this anymore, not when we can't keep this up. "And I figured you'd have wanted more than a little peck, at least in front of your coworkers."

Her shoulders sag. "You only kissed me like that in front of everyone because you felt sorry for me, then?"

"Not exactly. But I didn't want to embarrass you more than I already had." My voice cracks.

Then she shakes her head and steps forward. "Hold on. I want to see something. Just humor me for a second, okay?" She stands so close that our bodies are nearly touching, and I can't help the way my breathing quickens. Her hands slide up my chest, and she curls her fingers into my shirt. And it all makes my heart beat so fast that I'd swear I was staring out the side of a plane and preparing to jump.

She waits for my consent, but I barely get an "Okay" out before her lips are on mine again. It only takes a second for all of my logic and reason to evaporate. The only thing on my mind is the silky softness of her hair between my fingers, the heat from her body pressing into mine, and the chocolatey sweetness of her tongue in my mouth. A low moan escapes her throat, spurring me on. My mind wanders into dangerous territory, and I can't help but imagine what it would be like if we were lying in bed together, her bare skin against mine, the things I could do to her and the sounds she would make.

It's not just that, though. Kissing Daisy feels good in ways I've never experienced before. There's also a different kind of warmth coursing through me. It's a mix of comfort and relief washing over me, but stronger. It feels like she's ... consoling me.

But she breaks away and steps back, and that restlessness immediately returns. My chest heaves as I force myself to let go of her, and my head pounds from the leftover adrenaline. I growl and run my hands through my hair, already disgusted with my lack of self-control.

"I'm sorry," she chokes out.

When I glance up, she looks apologetic, and I realize she thinks I'm angry with her for kissing me. "No, I'm the one who's sorry. I'm frustrated with myself, Daisy, not with you," I choke out.

"Because you kissed me back, even though no one was around to see it?"

"Yes." I breathe out a sigh. "Because now that I've given in to my impulses, I'm worried I won't be able to get that version of myself under control again."

"I thought we agreed to be honest, though. Now that we've acknowledged our," she pauses and shrugs shyly, "physical chemistry, wouldn't it make things more awkward if we tried to ignore it?"

I shake my head, trying to rid myself of the wildly inappropriate thoughts I had a minute ago. "You don't understand. I can't risk letting that guy out around you. In fact—*shit*. I promised Rowan I wouldn't."

Yes, that's it. Think of everyone you're letting down, I tell myself.

She frowns and crosses her arms again. "Let me guess—you're going to say that was all a natural reaction to me forcing myself on you?"

"Of course. I mean, it makes perfect sense, right? I haven't gotten much action in a while, and you're still eager to gain experience. It stands to reason that we'd both enjoy the physical connection for what it is. It doesn't have to signify anything." Maybe if I'm convincing enough, I'll believe it, too.

"Yeah. That tracks," she mutters bitterly.

"We can work around this," I continue, ignoring the pang of guilt in my chest. "We'll just have to be more careful and cut out anything that could lead to it happening again."

"So no more mistletoe." Her voice is dry and sarcastic. Because I did that to her. I didn't just break my promise to keep anything from happening between us; I made her bitter. I broke her spirit.

"Right," I say, forcing a smile. Regardless of whether I can control my feelings after this, I can't let her see what she does to me, or she won't let me leave when the time comes. The only way to protect her is to remind her that I'm not what she needs.

She shrugs and looks away. "Yeah, well thanks for being my date tonight. I appreciate the effort you put into your performance."

She's pissed. Good.

I hate that I'm making her feel so bad. But I absolutely cannot, under any circumstances, set her straight.

"My pleasure, Blondie," I mumble.

"And don't worry, I won't impose on you again." She turns on her heels and stomps off to her bedroom, and I lean against the wall, letting my head fall back and heaving out a sigh. Because every cell in my body wants to go after her and make sure she knows that she's my favorite imposition.

daisy

"THAT'S why Jeremy wasn't at the Christmas party the other night," Claire admits with a shrug.

"I'm sorry, Claire," I tell my friend when she confesses that she and her husband are officially calling it quits. Then I reach out and pat her shoulder. "That stinks."

She only gives herself a second of vulnerability before she hardens her expression again. "Yeah, well, people get divorced all the time, right?"

There's a pang in my chest when she says it, because I'd all but forgotten that I'm about to become a member of that divorcées club, right alongside Claire.

"Yeah, it happens," I reply with a shrug, trying to hide the emotion in my voice.

"Anyway, how are things going with your hot doctor?"

I force a laugh, but my mind is still reeling with the thought of Landry moving out and leaving me alone in a month. "They're not," I tell her.

She grunts. "Didn't the two of you leave the party in a hurry after that steamy kiss? I figured it was safe to say he took you home to finish what he'd started under the mistletoe."

My cheeks heat. "We left because Landry was embarrassed. And he only kissed me because he didn't want to make me feel bad in front of everyone else."

"Lame," she grumbles, and I can't help but smile. "You tell him I think he's full of shit. And a tease."

I press my lips together, stifling my amusement. "I'll certainly relay the message."

"Well, have a good break," Claire says after the bell rings. "Let me know how your test goes."

"Yeah," I reply, though I'm not confident of my answer. "Merry Christmas."

"Call me if you need a ride. Or if you feel like going out and making your hot doctor jealous," she adds as she leaves me in the classroom.

My phone chimes, so I take it out, just in case it's Landry. Then again, I don't mind making him wait on me today, anyway.

MAGNOLIA

> Daisy, what are you bringing to Christmas dinner
> this weekend?

I frown at the screen after reading my sister's text. Because I'm twenty-five, married, gainfully employed, and I still cannot cook. I can sew. I can garden. I can clean. I can interpret classical literature, manage a financial budget, and make friends practically anywhere I go, yet I can't cook a casserole to save my life.

IRIS

> She probably doesn't have time to cook with
> her job.

> Don't bring anything store bought, Daisy. I don't
> want my kids to find out that junk food exists.

This time I roll my eyes. Iris has never been one to sugarcoat anything, literally or figuratively. You think I'd be used to that kind of blunt honesty by now.

MARIGOLD

Bring whatever you want, Daisy. Or don't bring anything at all. Your presence is all we need. 😊

ROSEMARY

I second that and add that I can't wait to see all of your faces and love on your sweet bébés all weekend! 🩶

VIOLET

I didn't know Daisy could cook?

IRIS

Good point. Can you actually cook anything, Daisy?

I pout as I type in a response.

DAISY

A woman's worth is based on more than her culinary talents, you know.

MAGNOLIA

And the way to a man's heart is through his stomach, so I'm guessing you're still single?

DAISY

gif of a little boy crossing his arms and pouting

Sore subject, Mags.

Landry and I will stop on the way and pick up something homemade. And who cares what I'm bringing when we all know Mari's making her famous pecan divinity candy, right?

IRIS

Wait, so you're bringing the hungry doctor?

Please tell us he's not just hungry …

DAISY

He doesn't care much for my cooking, I'm afraid. 😔

MAGNOLIA

Oh, sweetie. I'm sorry. Why don't we practice
baking while you're home?

VIOLET

Hey, congratulations on not fornicating, Daisy!
Well done! 🏆

I snort after that last message and put my phone away. Then I take one last look around Loren's classroom before I stuff the last of my things in my school tote and head for the door. By the time I return from the break, I'll have my very own space. Mrs. Joanie has been prepping me to take over for the past couple of months, and Claire helped me set up a date between Christmas and New Year's for my certification test. I should be giddy with excitement for this new venture, yet I can't seem to channel any of my usual enthusiasm.

Maybe it's because I'm afraid I can't pull it off. Even Mrs. Joanie's instruction doesn't seem to be enough to turn me into a good cook. But I'll get by with the few basic recipes she's been teaching me during our planning time.

I don't even think it's a fear of failure.

If I'm afraid of anything, it's that the start of this new job means the end of my arrangement with Landry.

Somewhere along the way, he must have planted a small seed of hope. We arrived at a point in which we'd shared too many flirty exchanges, moments of vulnerability, and stolen glances for my heart to accept that we could never be more than friends. So, in all Daisy fashion, I started tending to that seed.

Then Landry kissed me again, leaving me defenseless as that flower bloomed overnight, just before he crushed it underfoot.

Silly me, thinking it would mean something to him.

No, scratch that. I'm only silly for hoping he'd acknowledge what's so obviously grown between us. But deny it all he wants, there's more to us than friendship.

I flinch as I step outside and raise my arm to shield my eyes from the bright sunlight. It's only a few days before Christmas, after all. Plenty of time left to run the air conditioner in South Louisiana.

My eyes adjust to the light, so I drop my hand. And the first thing I see is Landry grinning at me from the front seat of his Jeep.

I'm supposed to be mad at him, but I can't help the way he always reawakens those butterflies in my stomach. I smile back at him and pick up my pace, and he leans over to open my door for me.

"Hey," I greet him as I slide into the seat.

"Hey." His smile grows wider, as if he's relieved to see me. And I'd be lying if I said I didn't think he was the most handsome man I'd ever seen. There's just something about him that makes me think I'll never feel the same way about anyone else as long as I live.

I clear my throat awkwardly. "I'm sorry. I didn't realize you were in a hurry."

He shakes his head and shrugs. "I'm not."

So he opened my door because he simply couldn't wait a second longer to be near me?

I'm not crazy, right? I can't be reading too much into our interactions. Maybe my feelings for him are more developed, but he's got to want—

"I guess I might be trying to suck up just a little," he admits after a second.

"For what?"

He shrugs again. "You seem like you're still upset with me after your Christmas party."

My shoulders droop as I'm reminded of the second half of that night, when he kissed me back like his life depended on it and told me it could never happen again in the same breath.

"Yeah, I guess I am."

"Anything else I can do to make you feel better?" he asks, staring expectantly.

"No," I return, trying to hide the sadness in my voice. "I mean, we agreed to be honest with one another, and we've both been holding up our end of the deal, right?"

His throat works as he swallows hard, and he chokes out a

hoarse, "Yeah." It sounds like another lie, just like the one he's been selling me about not being into any kind of physical affection. But everything about his body language the other night led me to believe he thoroughly enjoyed having my hands on him ... and my lips.

"Then I suppose I'm more disappointed than upset."

"I'm sorry," he rasps.

"Don't be," I tell him, forcing a smile.

He sighs and turns his attention back to the road, and I remember my sisters' group text from earlier. "Are you still able to bring me to the homestead this weekend? I can always ask Rowan to pick me up if you're going to be busy."

"Would you rather go with your brother?" he asks carefully.

"Not really," I admit. "But I can't monopolize your time forever."

"You're not monopolizing my time," he says with a soft chuckle. "I'm volunteering it at this point. Besides, I was admittedly looking forward to a good, hot meal."

I frown. "Yeah. It's not like you get that at home."

He laughs again. "Unless you're trying to uninvite me?"

"Of course not. I just thought you wanted us to cut back on the time we spend together."

"What?"

"You said we should minimize the opportunities for ... mistletoe incidents," I say carefully.

Something flashes in his eyes. "I meant that we shouldn't take any chances around Camellia. I don't think we'll be in danger in front of your folks."

I study him for a second longer, noticing the way his cheeks are looking a little darker than usual against his short beard. "Okay then. The invitation is always open."

He smiles. "You know, there's a reason I always took Rowan up on that offer. What's better than hanging out with your family and stuffing my face with your dad's famous duck gumbo and your mom's homemade bread pudding?"

"Maybe I need to learn her recipe," I mumble.

"Nah, I'd make myself sick if we ate that stuff every day," he muses.

"Is that why you never invited Rowan to come home with you to Camellia all those years?" I ask after a while.

He lifts a shoulder, but his eyes stay on the road. "I guess I was a little embarrassed for him to see my family all together. Someone always ends up arguing, and by someone, I mean Lo and me. We're not the worst, but your family is just so ... different."

Now I feel guilty about harboring that little bit of resentment toward him. "Well, you know my family is always happy to have you."

"Yeah. They may not love me, but they tolerate me better than my own," he says on another sardonic laugh. "Speaking of, Loren asked if you'd be coming to the Reed family Christmas. I told her you were planning to stay in Baton Rouge for a few days, but I wanted you to know the invitation stands."

He gulps again, and his hands tense over the steering wheel.

"Do you ... want me to come with you?" I'm almost breathless as I pose the question. He's making me an offer that he's never even extended to Rowan. That has to mean something, doesn't it?

He turns into the driveway and shrugs before he responds. "I know you miss your family. I don't want you to cut your time with them short on my account."

"Okay," I say. "Tell Loren thanks for the invitation, though."

He's silent as he comes around to open my door and offers to take my heavy bag, and I'm reminded that he's a nicer person than most of us give him credit for. Maybe that's all this is. Maybe he's been right all along—nothing good can come of my attraction to him.

I guess it's too bad I'm already in love with him.

And since it seems pretty unlikely he'd ever admit it even if he did fall for me, I might as well enjoy this while I can. That's why I hang back a few steps and allow myself to check out his butt as he climbs the porch steps in front of me.

"Daisy?"

"Hmm?"

He groans. "Don't do that." He stops when he gets to the top of the stairs, and I realize he's watching me over his shoulder.

"Do what?" I squeak.

"Make this any harder than it already is," he says, his tone sad. Then he cringes, and I have to cover my mouth when I snort.

"Last I checked, there was plenty of fatty tissue there," I barely manage to get out before the giggling takes over.

"Fine. I walked into that one." He backs away and gestures for me to go into the house first, stifling a grin of his own.

landry

"Look who showed up after all," Dr. Broussard says cheerfully when I approach.

"Yeah, well, here I am. Merry Christmas, everyone." I force a smile and reach out to shake hands with the crowd clustered near one of the tables in the town's biggest event hall. There are only a couple of rental options for a decent-sized gathering in Camellia, so the group that owns the hospital and its satellite health clinics is hosting their annual Christmas party in the multipurpose building where my sister's wedding reception was held last month. It's also the same place that houses the high school prom, the town's Cajun heritage festival, some of our Mardi Gras festivities, and a small annual rodeo.

Dr. Broussard gestures to a glass of champagne, but I politely decline. I've done enough drinking lately to last a while.

"Where's your sweet, little friend?" Mrs. Broussard asks.

I clear my throat. "Oh, um, Daisy's at home, getting ready for her teaching certification exam."

"And I was looking forward to seeing her," Mrs. Broussard says, sounding genuinely disappointed. As if I wasn't already feeling bad enough for leaving her at home. "Tell her we wish her good luck on her test."

I nod politely, thinking I might want a drink after all. I excuse myself to find the open bar and request a plain Sprite. At least it'll give me something to sip on and hold in my hands.

"Hey, Landry," Tenley greets me when she and JD approach the bar. She surprises me by pulling me in for a friendly hug.

She steps away, and I stick out my hand before JD can get any funny ideas. He chuckles and shakes it. "You're good, bro. I'm saving my hug for a rainy day," he reassures me with a pat on the shoulder.

"Where's Daisy?" Tenley asks.

I sigh. "At home, studying for her test."

JD hums in disapproval. "I'm sure she'll do fine. She's been preparing for a while. You should get her to take a break and come out with you. I bet she would love this."

I look away, the guilt making my stomach turn. "Yeah. She would have. But, you know, we're not ..."

"Not what?" He furrows his brow.

The bartender hands over my drink then, and Tenley quietly excuses herself to visit the ladies' room while JD puts in their order. Then he turns and looks at me expectantly again.

I shrug. "Wouldn't it be inappropriate if Daisy and I kept going to every event in town together since we're just roommates?"

He rears back, looking surprised. "What do you mean, you're just roommates?"

"Daisy and I are friends. That's all."

He scoffs. "Bullshit. You were certainly acting like more than friends when I saw you at the last Christmas party."

"That was an accident," I spit out before I realize I'm sounding like a jerk. "I mean, we only kissed because of the mistletoe or whatever," I add in a softer tone and take a sip from my drink.

He frowns. "You guys kissed? I was only talking about the way you seemed so comfortable together."

"She gets handsy when she drinks. I didn't want to hurt her feelings," I fib.

"You forget I've seen you drunk, too. And I'm pretty sure *you're* the one who gets handsy when he drinks," JD points out smugly.

"All I did was run my mouth." But the feel of Daisy's soft body under my hands the morning after the wedding reception flashes through my mind, and I cough awkwardly.

"Yeah, and you also hit on Daisy in front of all of us. Not to mention, the two of you are inseparable. A man doesn't spend every waking moment with a woman unless he's either trying to hook up with her or he likes her so much that he can't stay away."

"Well, in our case it's neither. You don't know a damn thing about Daisy and me, and it's none of your business, anyway," I retort, getting defensive again.

But JD laughs. "You're right, it's not. But the longer we stand here, the more you're convincing me that you're already in love with her."

My stomach flips again, and he grins as he reaches over to get his drinks from the bartender before dropping a tip in the jar. A growl threatens to escape my throat when I open my mouth to deny his accusation, so I have no choice but to snap my jaw closed and continue fuming at him in silence.

"Easy, loverboy," JD drawls. "Your secret's safe with me."

I think I see where Ethan gets it.

"You ... I ... I'm not," I begin again, but that condescending look on his face keeps distracting me. "Look, I don't do that shit, all right? So don't go giving her any ideas."

His expression shifts. "What are you talking about?"

"I don't ..." But he's got me so worked up that I have to stop and breathe before I can go on. "I don't do relationships. And I can't have Daisy thinking there's a chance something might happen with us, because I'd only be letting her down."

Well, that came out surprisingly honest.

"Man, you can't just pick and choose which people to love and how much. That ain't the way life works," he says matter-of-factly before he takes a drink. "Just look at the way I gained a wife and two kids in the span of a year if you need a testament to that. Hell, I should get Ten to tell you—"

"You should just drop it and leave me the hell alone," I mutter.

"Eh, but where's the fun in that?" he muses and shoots me another self-satisfied grin as Tenley joins us.

"What's wrong?" she asks, glancing back and forth between us.

"Landry thinks he friend zoned Daisy, but it's giving *for now*," JD tells her and hands over her drink.

"Ooh. How fun!" She takes a sip and smirks at me.

That growl rumbles up from my chest this time. "No, it's not *fun*. Nothing's going on."

"What about that kiss you shared?" she asks, tilting her chin up and inspecting my reaction. "I bet you're thinking about it right now, aren't you?"

Well, I wasn't before, but now ...

"He says they only kissed at the faculty party because of the mistletoe," JD volunteers on my behalf.

"I wasn't talking about the faculty party." Tenley eyes me more carefully.

I feel my face reddening. "What did Daisy tell you?"

"So you have kissed before?" I look away and curse under my breath while JD snickers beside her.

"I didn't need Daisy to tell me anything. I was working off a hunch, and apparently, I was right."

My nostrils flare again. "People kiss all the time, Tenley. It's not like they end up together, right?" I gesture toward the two of them, and she frowns.

"Only after they start kissing the right person," she declares, and I don't like the sympathetic look in her eyes.

Another partygoer bumps into me before I can reply, causing my drink to slosh up over the side of my glass and down the front of my shirt. I mutter another curse.

"Oh, Dr. Reed, I'm so sorry," croons a gray-haired lady apologetically, and I immediately regret the four-letter word I just uttered.

"No worries," I tell her. She looks familiar, but I can't remember where I should know her from.

"Nurse Tenley, Coach JD, Merry Christmas to you," she says.

"Merry Christmas to you, Mrs. Ardoin. How are things down there in the business offices?" Tenley asks politely.

The business offices? Wait, that's where she's from. She's the human resources manager of the hospital group. She takes care of the intake paperwork, including the benefits applications. Which means she knows—

"All alone, Dr. Reed?"

"Mm-hmm." My heart begins beating faster, and my eyes dart around us, searching for an out.

"Where's your wife tonight? I can't imagine you newlyweds would want to—"

"I'm sorry, I've gotta go get cleaned up," I cut her off and make a beeline for the door. I don't stop until I reach the safety of my Jeep.

After I slam the door behind me, I drop my head to the steering wheel for a second as I take a few deep breaths. I have to go so far as to picture Daisy beside me in the passenger seat offering some overly sweet affirmation and patting my back before I can calm myself enough to drive home.

"Well, you're back early," Daisy mutters when I walk into the house. She yanks her arm as if she's pulling a needle through fabric, though I can't tell if she's sewing or cross stitching from here.

I press my lips together and nod, though the sight of her is enough to make me feel slightly better. "I saw my opportunity to sneak out after an unfortunate soda accident and took it. But it's not like I wanted to go in the first place."

"You said you didn't want to go alone. Weren't JD and Tenley there?" she asks, sounding only remotely interested in my answer.

"Yeah, but ..."

She lifts a brow at my damp shirt when I come around to join her in the living room. "I thought you were friends now?"

"I still felt like a third wheel," I tell her, and she makes room for me to sit beside her on the couch.

"I could see that," she replies, smirking down at her work. My chest tightens when I realize it's my lab coat. She's stitching the pocket I ripped the other day. I hadn't even told her about it, but she must have noticed the tear when she was doing our laundry.

"And I ..." I swallow hard. "I realized I'd rather be here ... with you."

She stops, and her eyelashes flutter before she turns her big, green eyes to me. "You did?"

I nod, trying to ignore the urge to touch her in some way. I settle for letting my thigh rest against hers, and it instantly grounds me. "How's your studying going?"

"Ugh, it's not," she groans and lets her head fall back against the couch. "Why am I taking this test again?"

"So you can get a raise and benefits, divorce my old ass and kick me out of your house, and become the best home ec teacher Camellia's ever had, all own your own," I say, unable to hold back a small smile.

"I'm not even sure I want any of that anymore," she mumbles, closing her eyes.

My heart jumps up into my throat. "What?"

"Landry, I don't want to teach home ec. I don't want to teach at all, at least not in a school setting. I can't even cook, for goodness sakes!" She exhales before her eyes pop open again. "Son of a nutcracker, it felt good to say that out loud!"

I chuckle hesitantly, hoping that's all she meant. "Good. I mean, I'm glad you finally figured that out. So what are you gonna do instead?"

"I don't know," she whines and sticks out her bottom lip. "I just know I don't want to go back to living with my parents. I feel like ... like Camellia might be my home now."

I look away when I realize I've been torn between wanting her to have her independence and needing her to return to the safety of her family. Whether it's for my safety or hers, I'm not sure anymore.

"I'd still like to work with kids. Maybe I can apply for a job as a babysitter or a nanny?" she thinks aloud. "I should be able to drive myself around soon. But, I don't know if anyone would feel comfortable letting me stay at home alone with a baby or a toddler," she says sadly.

"Have you ever thought about getting a service animal to help?" I pose. "I know it would make me feel a lot better about leaving you by yourself."

She smiles. "Of course. But they're not easy to get, and I certainly can't afford one myself."

"There are foundations that sponsor that sort of thing." I watch her expression carefully.

"As much as I'd love having a seizure alert or even a seizure response dog, it doesn't seem fair to go out looking for a sponsorship when there are so many kids with epilepsy who probably need it more than I do." She shrugs. "Besides, I just remembered that I can't become a nanny, anyway. I wouldn't get health insurance, would I?"

"Not around here, I'm afraid. I don't even think there are any daycares big enough to offer the salary and benefits you'd need to survive on your own. Especially once I move out and you go back to paying full rent." I barely catch the way she winces at the last part before I continue. "What if you applied to teach at the elementary school instead?"

She shrugs. "I suppose teaching is my only option. Unless we find some other rich doctor willing to marry me and turn me into a stay-at-home mom between now and the end of the year."

I laugh shortly, trying to disguise my disdain of that idea. "Should I start asking around on your behalf?"

"No." She sighs and sits up to trade my lab coat for the study guide on the table. "I guess it's time to accept my fate and make the best of it. At least I get to work at a great school, and I love my little house. And my roommate is kind of amazing, especially since he's willing to stay up late to braid my hair and paint my toenails." She slings her legs over mine and drops her feet into my lap, wiggling her toes.

I shake my head and bite back a smile. Little does she know that I'd happily accept a night of nail polish with her over a party with anyone else.

"Daisy," I begin, barely aware of where I'm going with this. "I'd really like it if you came with me to my dad's house on Christmas Eve. I think ... I think it would make it a lot easier for me to get through the night without, you know ..."

"Of course I'll go with you," she replies, tucking her hair behind her ears. "All you had to do was ask."

I nod and squeeze her foot affectionately. "Thank you."

She giggles and squirms, and the corners of my mouth turn up once I realize she's been hiding something from me. "Wait a minute. Are you telling me," I pause to run my fingers over the bottom of her other foot, and she squeals as she attempts to escape, "after all this time, you're ticklish? What happened to full transparency, hmm?" I continue pinning her ankles against my lap with one hand while I tickle her feet with the other, and she's breathless in no time.

"Okay, okay, stop!" she wheezes, reaching up to wrench her legs from my grasp. "Wait, ew, your shirt's still all wet." She tugs her hand back and wipes it on the couch.

"Told you so," I retort with a laugh.

"Give it here," she demands. "I was about to put this lab coat in the wash, so I might as well take your shirt, too. You'll probably want to wear that one again before Christmas, since it's such a pretty green."

"It's fine. I'll wash it later."

"Just hand it over," she insists as she leans up and begins unfastening my shirt, her slender fingers making quick work of the buttons.

My chest starts heaving by the time she gets to the third button, and she pauses there to drag her eyes up to mine. Her eyelashes flutter and her lips part when she realizes what she's done.

And dammit if she doesn't keep going.

I barely hold back a whimper as the fabric loosens over my chest, but she continues, her gaze darting back and forth between my eyes and the next bit of skin she exposes.

Then she climbs up to her knees before fisting her hands into the sides of my shirt, tugging upward until she untucks the hem. She grabs me by the lapels, and I'm afraid I'm going to spontaneously combust any second. I garner every bit of willpower I've got and attempt to stop her by covering her hands with mine and holding her in place. But it backfires, because my skin burns at the contact.

"Daisy," I rasp, my eyelids heavy.

"I've undressed you before, you know," she tells me, her voice taking on a sultry tone, and I don't know why I free her hands, but I do. She moves them up to my shoulders, peeling my shirt away and forcing the sleeves down my arms. I automatically lean up when she lets go of one side to wrench it out from behind me while her mouth looms only inches from mine.

Something rumbles in my chest against my will, just as I surrender the last remnants of my self-control. I can already taste her by the time I concede, reaching out to grasp her by the hips and tilting my chin up to her.

But I'm too late. She backs away and rises to her feet, leaving me struggling to catch my breath. And the sight of my rumpled shirt in her hands makes the last of the blood drain from my head and gather in a more central region.

"What else is dirty?"

"Wha-what?" I sputter.

"Anything else you want me to wash now?" she asks, smirking and reminding me that she still has the upper hand. Because she's not anyone's little sister. She's a grown woman, and she's not going to let me forget it.

"Um, I might have gotten some of that soda on my pants," I mumble without thinking. Then I stop and squeeze my eyes shut. "I mean, no—NO. Just the shirt, thanks."

"Landry? Are you okay?"

"Mm-hmm," I intone, grabbing the nearest throw pillow and clutching it tightly in front of my middle.

"Well, I guess I'm not the only one who's ticklish," she declares, and I wait for the sounds of her snickering to fade before I open my eyes and grin.

landry

"SO WE'RE STICKING to the game plan, right?" Daisy asks when we drive up to her parents' house. "No mistletoe today."

"Right. Because we're roommates and platonic friends," I agree with a resolute nod.

"Friends who just happen to be married," she mumbles under her breath.

"Right," I say again, less confidently. "But no one needs to know that last part."

"You do realize they're going to ask us a million times if there's anything else going on between us, don't you?" she poses with another hint of sarcasm. "Especially once they see us interacting and looking so comfortable with one another."

I shrug. "I figured as much. But we'll just explain to them how we get along well, and that's all."

"Yeah, that's all," she whispers, and I can't tell if she looks more angry, disappointed, or hurt.

"Daisy?" I call out before she reaches for her door. "Is everything okay?"

"Mm-hmm," she murmurs unconvincingly and forces a fake smile, but I still see something in her expression that makes me suspect she's got more on her mind than she's letting on. Then again, after the last few weeks, I should probably be wary of asking her to divulge the rest.

Dammit.

I sigh and reach out for her arm, unable to ignore the compulsive need to know more. "You're not being completely honest with me right now, are you?"

She twists her lips to the side before she answers. "Maybe not. But neither are you." I straighten up in my seat and frown at her as she continues. "And I guess I'm feeling guilty about lying to my family. Withholding the truth about something this important feels an awful lot like a big, fat lie of omission, especially when I know we're not just platonic roommates or friends who got legally married for the insurance benefits. We don't just 'get along well, and that's all,' do we?"

"No," I choke out after a while. "But that's all that was supposed to happen."

"I'm so sorry to have inconvenienced you, then," she mutters, and I hate the way I've been rubbing off on her.

"Daisy," I say on another exhale. "That's not what I meant. You … you know I care about you, right?"

She turns and stares out the window. "Yeah, I know."

I look down and realize I'm softly stroking the back of her hand with my thumb. I'm not even sure when I took her hand in mine, but it seems like it's become involuntary lately. She curls her fingers in and squeezes, and I like the way it feels so much that I pretend not to notice so we can continue the contact.

"Then you understand why it has to be this way, especially since I'm not sure your brother would ever forgive me for taking advantage of you. I can't be responsible for driving a wedge between you and your family over Christmas dinner."

"That sounds like the kind of cop out the old Landry would use," she says quietly. "And you know Rowan would be supportive if you told him the truth. The problem is that you don't want to face it yourself."

"Look, I'm sorry," I begin, my voice cracking again. "I don't know how to be better. I've been trying, I swear, and you are the absolute last person I want to hurt."

She scoffs but doesn't say anything, so I continue, clasping her hand tighter, "I owe you more than you think, Blondie, and I never would have been able to start working on myself without your help. But I'm nowhere near the man you need me to be. Please try to understand why I can't ..." I shake my head, willing away the ache in my chest. "I just can't allow it."

She bites her lip and stares down at our intertwined hands. "I understand, even though I still think you're wrong. I wish you could see yourself the way I see you."

I hum. "I do, too."

"Then maybe I won't stop trying until you do." She shrugs and shoots me a smug look as she says the last part.

I can't help it when a short laugh escapes, which only seems to boost her confidence, because she gives my hand one more squeeze before she turns and climbs out of the car. I sigh to myself before giving in and following her.

We both grab a share of the heap of presents from the backseat and stagger into the house where a handful of her nieces and nephews happily relieve us of our burden and begin stacking the gift boxes and bags in front of the Christmas tree in the living room. Her dad comes over next, kissing Daisy on the cheek and slapping me gently on the back when he gives out hugs. It's not the first time I've been over for a LaFleur holiday event, so I've already prepared myself for their customary overly affectionate greetings. But when Mr. LaFleur adds that he's so glad we're *both* here today, I admittedly have to swallow the lump in my throat.

Daisy leads us into the kitchen to see her mom after that, and Mrs. LaFleur embraces each of us much the same, except she adds a kiss to my cheek as well. Then she holds us both at arms' length and studies us carefully. "*Mais la.* Aren't they feeding you down there in Camellia? You're both looking too *maigre* for my liking. Can't either of you cook?"

Daisy and I trade amused glances when she presents the pies we stopped and picked up from the bakery on the way here. "I've been trying. But you're looking at the world's first home ec teacher who can't cook anything beyond scrambled eggs," she admits, and her mom chuckles.

"*Pas bon*," Mrs. LaFleur replies and clicks her tongue. "I'll have to send you home with the leftovers, I guess." She pats Daisy's butt. "Put some meat on that *fesse*."

I snort out a laugh, though I don't think there's anything wrong with Daisy's backside, and I'm redirected toward the living room while she gets a baking lesson. Rowan and his brothers are sitting with his dad where they're flipping the TV channels to find a football game.

"Oh, hey, you guys made it. Thanks for driving Daisy over," Rowan says, standing to shake my hand. There's an instant tightness in my chest as I attempt to stifle my guilty conscience.

"Yeah, no worries," I reply quietly. "I always enjoy a visit to the homestead."

Rowan smiles and nods, oblivious to the fact that I've broken all of my promises, despite my best attempts. He may be the nicest guy on the planet, but I can't imagine he'd be thrilled to hear that I'm technically his brother-in-law, much less that I've had to resort to reciting a list of childhood diseases in my mind to fend off the impulse to pull Daisy in and kiss her so hard she sees stars.

I heave out a guilty sigh and continue to greet the rest of the clan before I join Rowan on one of the couches. His brother Heath and I are chatting about the college football game on TV when Daisy appears, and I can't help the way my eyes follow her as she walks over to sit beside one of her sisters. I force myself to look away, only to find Rowan watching me carefully. That pressure in my chest returns as the panic sets in.

Rowan continues staring at me, even after I pretend to turn my attention back to the conversation with Heath. I don't know why I'm so worried about his reaction, since it's not like he's got a single mean or vindictive bone in his body. And Daisy was right before—Rowan wouldn't hold it against me if I truly had feelings for her. But I gave him my word, and I can't imagine disappointing him, not after all of the times he's taken up for me or been the only person to tolerate me for the past fifteen years. I also know exactly how terrifying it is to watch your baby sister fall for the one guy you fear could hurt her the most.

"Wait, did I just hear Landry say he wanted to volunteer to be Saint Nick this year?" Rowan calls out loudly, a cocky expression plastered across his face.

I groan. "You must have mistaken my voice for Heath's."

"No, I'm pretty sure that wasn't me," the second-oldest brother declares.

"Come on, man," Rowan continues. "Do it for the kids."

I cringe. "Do I have to?"

"Yes, you do," I hear Daisy's voice ring out from across the room. "Landry *Nicholas*."

I turn to face her, and she's giving me those puppy-dog eyes, the ones she knows I can't resist. I press my lips into a hard line, trying to save face and at least give Rowan and the rest of them the impression that I'm somewhat capable of holding my own against her.

"Fine," I say flatly. "But I'll need your help with some of the kids' names." Then I accidentally smile when she claps and squeals with delight. Rowan lifts a skeptical brow at me when I reluctantly stand and head over to the tree while Daisy climbs nimbly over the pile of children gathering on the floor around me.

"Want me to say the prayer?" she whispers. I'd almost forgotten about that part of their family tradition—the LaFleurs pray together before and after everything they do. And I mean *everything*—every meal, every competitive event, every medical procedure. It seemed so strange to me at first, maybe even annoying, especially when Rowan used to insist on praying a whole rosary aloud before any big exams or practicals in school. But now that I've come to expect it, it's sort of endearing. And I'm honestly a little disappointed that Rowan never asked me to join him the way Daisy does. I guess he was worried I'd lash out at him.

I clear my throat. "Sure. Thanks," I answer her, and I turn and motion the Sign of the Cross as she begins a short prayer. The family mimes the same motion at the end, and the kids' excitement is even more palpable now that we're done with that piece of business. I imagine it's like Pavlov's bell for them.

"Okay, Santa, take it away," Daisy says with a wide smile. She hands me a box and tilts her head to one side, signaling which direction to face.

"All right, then. Where's Big Ben?" I turn to the left and lift the box, and Daisy's four-year-old nephew stands and lifts his hands triumphantly.

"Right he-yah!"

I can't help the grin that spreads across my face as I step through the obstacle course of cross-legged children to deliver Ben's gift. Meanwhile, Daisy's already started calling out more names, and I quickly realize she's saving all of the kids' gifts for me to announce.

A few minutes later, gift wrap and tissue paper are flying through the air as I hand the last box over to little Zélie, and I bite my lip when I turn to grab the small bag I'd asked one of the kids to hide behind the tree earlier. I'm starting to second guess my gift for Daisy, or at least my decision to give it to her today. It feels more personal than I thought before, especially now that we're surrounded by everyone. But before I can talk myself out of it, I feel her tapping me on the shoulder.

"Merry Christmas, Dr. Reed," she says quietly and hands me a wrapped box, a knowing smile on her face.

"Merry Christmas, Mrs. Reed," I lean down and whisper before giving her my gift, and my stomach flutters when her cheeks redden. She narrows her eyes at me, issuing a silent warning before she scrambles across the room to her spot on the couch. I sigh and move to stand behind the other sofa, figuring I've done enough interfering with their family moment, and I try and fail not to watch as Daisy digs through the gift bag and pulls out a stuffed puppy and a card.

She opens the card before she stands abruptly, letting the bag fall to the floor. "Wait. You ... you got me a *service dog*?" Daisy yells breathlessly.

Everyone stops moving at that moment, and I attempt to keep my expression neutral when I nod. "I hope that's okay," I croak out.

"Do you have any idea how hard it is to get a seizure alert dog? And how *expensive*?" She's still shouting even though the room's fallen silent.

I look around and notice all eyes on us. "Actually, this is an SRD. And I was only able to find one because Dr. Broussard knew the right people. He also pulled a few strings with one of the foundations—"

But the next thing that comes out probably sounds closer to an "oof" as Daisy practically bowls me over. She wraps her arms around my waist and presses her cheek against my chest, and I hesitate for a second before I return the hug.

And damn if it isn't the best, most sincere hug I've ever had in my life.

"Thank you, Landry," she says, her voice thick. "This is literally the most thoughtful thing anyone has ever done for me."

Her arms tighten around me as a sense of relief floods my chest, and I bow my head to hers. "It's not much. I just wanted to help you gain your independence and keep you safe."

"It's the best gift ever." She sniffles, and I fight the urge to kiss the top of her head when I feel her body shaking within my arms. "And now I feel even worse about that conversation we had on the way in."

I laugh shortly. "Eh, my idea's seeming a little more 'old Landry' the longer I think about it," I say, and she giggles as I reach up to wipe the moisture from her cheeks. "There are still a few more hurdles before she's yours. But the trainer wants to start bringing her by the house next week to make sure it's a good fit for both of you."

"She?" Daisy pulls away and looks up at me.

I grin and gesture to the card in her hands. "Did you even read that thing?"

"I was too excited!" she admits, making everyone laugh, and I'm reminded we aren't alone again. She lifts the card to her face and scans it, her lips moving as she reads. "Her name is Juniper?" An incredulous laugh bubbles out of her. "It's perfect. She's already a LaFleur!"

I shrug. "I thought so, too."

She stares up at me adoringly, awakening butterflies within me I never knew existed, and I'm only seconds away from needing to start one of those childhood disease lists again. Meanwhile, the rest of the family coos their approval before returning to their own gifts.

"I can't believe you did this for me. And all I got you was a couple of lousy ties."

"After everything you've had to put up with for the past few months of living with my grumpy ass, I figured it was the least I could do. And it'll make me feel better to know you won't be alone later," I explain quietly.

Her smile falters, and she looks away and blinks a few times. "Right. Good thinking."

Dammit. I've upset her again, but I can't ask her why. Maybe I should have waited until we were back home to give her this.

"Just promise me your next husband won't mind you keeping the dog in the divorce," I add in an attempt to lighten the mood. She laughs shortly before leaning in to hug me again.

"Thank you. I mean it." This time she embraces me like it's the last time she'll ever see me, reminding me that getting through the last piece of our arrangement is going to be harder than I imagined. I wrap my arms around her and rest my chin on her head, pushing away the dread and relishing in her warmth once more until I look up to find Rowan watching us carefully.

"Hey, um, I think your brother's starting to suspect something," I mumble quietly, trying not to move my lips. "Maybe we shouldn't—"

"Let him think whatever he wants," Daisy retorts. "We know what is and isn't going on between us. That's all that matters."

"Right." But the way Rowan's jaw flexes when he looks away still worries me.

Daisy finally loosens her grip and wipes her cheeks on the back of her hand before she demands I open my gift, even though she's already ruined the surprise.

"The kids are going to love this, thank you," I tell her, holding up the Minecraft-patterned tie.

She shrugs. "I thought they might like seeing old Doc Reed's sillier side."

"Did you do the embroidery yourself?"

"Yeah," she admits shyly.

"You did an amazing job. I'm impressed."

"There's another one," she prompts me again, looking nervous now.

I move the tissue paper around and find a pop of mint green. I let out a soft chuckle when I recognize the significance. "It's just like the one I borrowed from Blake."

"It's actually the original tie," she says. "I asked Loren if I could buy Blake a new one. I told her it held sentimental value for us, so she made the swap for me."

I run my fingers over the silky fabric, and my eyes begin to sting.

She shakes her head before she continues. "It's silly, I know, but—"

"It's perfect," I say on a gulp.

Then I wrap her up in another hug so that she can't see what the thought of leaving her does to me.

landry

"OH NO, you can't get out on the road now," Mrs. LaFleur begins.

"It's just a little sleet," I say. "I'm driving a Jeep. We'll be fine."

Ironically, we'd left the air conditioner on at home. It was muggy and seventy degrees out when we left for Baton Rouge earlier today. Neither Daisy nor I realized such a severe cold front was coming through tonight, and now the forecast is calling for snow flurries.

Just another Louisiana "winter."

"You may be all right, Landry, but I'm not so sure I trust the rest of these *couillons* who've never driven in the ice, especially when more of them have been drinking than usual." Daisy's dad crosses his arms and gives me a serious look, and I'm still trying to sort it out when she speaks up.

"Dad's right. We should stay," she tells me quietly. "We'll leave early in the morning so we can make it back for Christmas Eve with your family tomorrow afternoon."

I sigh, realizing she's trying to decode her dad's message for me: *You're not leaving with my daughter tonight.* "Okay," I agree reluctantly.

Rowan clears his throat and tilts his head. "My drive isn't as far, but I think I'll hang around, too. Come on, Lan. We'll make sure the guys' room is ready." I nod and follow him, casting one more glance at Daisy before I go.

Everyone else left after dinner and the adults' gift exchange game in which Daisy traded a frying pan for a towel warmer and I ended up with a fancy sandwich press. I can't remember the last time I laughed so hard.

"So," Rowan begins as soon as the door closes behind us. "Want to tell me what the heck is going on with you and my sister?"

I cringe. He's caught me with my guard down, and I'm afraid I'm going to say too much.

"It's definitely not what it looks like, that I can promise you."

"I seem to remember you making me a similar promise a while back, but I'm not sure you've kept it," he replies, crossing his arms over his chest. But he's still smiling, and I don't know what that means. Is he angry? Does he think we'd make a cute couple? I can't tell. So I do what I do best—or worst, I guess. I blurt out the truth.

"Daisy and I got married."

He blinks at me in disbelief. "You did *what*?"

"Not long after I moved in, I found out that she was having some trouble getting health insurance." I purposefully leave out the part about Daisy's seizures out of respect for her privacy, though I imagine it might have made our argument more compelling. "So we came up with this plan to get married—on paper only—just until her benefits kicked in, and we'd get the marriage annulled. No one else knows about it. But I swear, nothing's going on."

He narrows his eyes at me. "Nothing besides a fake wedding, you mean?"

"Okay, we might have kissed a few times. And we slept together once or twice, but—"

"You did WHAT?" he repeats more loudly this time, and his face turns beet red.

My eyes widen. "Shit—no! I'm sorry, I mean, we ended up in the same bed, but that's all ..." I lick my lips and begin again. "Okay, so maybe I accidentally groped her a little bit, and we've seen each other naked—but not on purpose. There was no sex, I swear. In fact,

Daisy's still a virgin." He furrows his brow, and I raise my hands in defeat. "You know what, I'm just going to stop talking now."

I let out a loud exhale as I plop down at the foot of one of the beds in the room, and Rowan sits across from me on the other.

"You're telling me that you secretly married my beautiful, sweet, innocent baby sister and have since been sleeping in the same bed, accidentally making out, and looking at one another naked throughout your cohabitation, but neither of you has any romantic interest in the other?"

I bite my lip as I consider keeping this next part to myself, but the truth is, now that I've gotten some of it off my chest, I'm already eager for the chance to get my friend's advice again. And I did promise Daisy I wouldn't lie about it.

"Daisy has expressed her interest in the romance stuff, but it's probably more of a crush than anything. She doesn't have a lot of life experience, and I'm right there, sleeping in the next room and sharing a bathroom. I mean, you know how it is with roommates—you either develop a certain comfortability and get along great, or you don't and find another roommate. And we just happened to get one another right away, I guess."

Rowan studies my face for a while before he speaks again. "You like her, too, don't you?"

"I don't know. I haven't even allowed myself to entertain the thought. It just wouldn't be right." But it's not the whole truth, and I wonder whether he can see the guilt in my expression.

"Why not?" He leans back and narrows his eyes, seemingly buying my fib. "I know you don't care about the epilepsy. Is it because she's my sister?"

I lift one shoulder in a shrug. "That's one reason, yeah. More importantly, we don't want the same things, and it wouldn't be fair to her. At first, I worried about her feeling like she owed me, but it didn't take me long to realize she deserves so much more than my cynical, old ass could ever give her. And just by acknowledging any feelings I might have for her, I'd risk letting her settle for a shitty life with the first man who offered. I wouldn't want my sister to get stuck with someone like me, and I know you want better for her, too."

"It sounds like you already care about her more than you're willing to admit."

"I do care about her, very much. I'd probably do anything she asked so long as it doesn't put her at risk. But you and I both know I'm not built for a relationship. That's why I could never ..." I shake my head and look down at my feet.

"Landry, do you not hear yourself right now?" he asks warily. "Because you're not saying anything to make me believe you're not already *in* a relationship with her and trying to talk your way around it."

I furrow my brow. "That's not what I'm saying at all."

He sighs. "No, but it sounds a lot like you're putting aside your own wants and needs to protect hers, despite the fact that you obviously both feel *something* for one another."

"It's still not enough. We both know I'm not capable of making her happy."

"Bro, have you seriously not noticed the way she looks at you? She clearly thinks you're the *only* person capable of that." He smirks and shakes his head while I attempt to process what he's saying. "Didn't you hear Cyprien telling the two of you to 'get a room' when she ran sobbing into your arms to thank you for the Christmas gift—which, by the way, was the most thoughtful, least douchey thing you've ever done to the best of my knowledge. I mean, assuming it wasn't just a move to get into her—"

I shoot him an angry glare, and he stops mid-sentence.

"I didn't think so," Rowan continues, still smiling. "But I'm also unconvinced that you're not leading her on, even if you don't realize it. Like it or not, man, Daisy's not going to accept your excuses for much longer. And if you're as worried about breaking her heart as you say you are, you've got to quit martyring yourself and hiding your true feelings."

I run my fingers through my hair as I let his words sink in. "Shit. You might be right," I finally say. "I can't bear the idea of hurting her, but ..." I mutter another curse under my breath. "I've already let things go too far, haven't I?"

"Normally I'd say a marriage license means you've gone too far to turn back now, even if it's not a valid sacramental marriage ... or a consummated one." He narrows his eyes at me. "Which, as you said, it's not, right?"

"I may not buy into the idea of saving yourself for 'the one' or the whole institution of marriage in general, but I can respect what it means to Daisy and the rest of your family," I say dryly.

He stands and backhands my shoulder lightly. "Good. But here's a tip: Don't admit to the guy that used to share a bedroom wall with you that you've been tempted to violate his baby sister while you're sharing a bedroom wall with *her*."

I feel my face heat up. "I didn't admit to that at all."

"And how did you end up in bed together again?" Rowan cocks an eyebrow at me.

I clear my throat. "I accidentally got drunk after Lo's wedding and somehow ended up passing out in her room."

"Right. And was this before or after you 'accidentally' saw her naked?" he continues, making air quotes with his fingers.

"Technically, I've only ever seen her in her underwear." He glares at me again. "After," I say with a sigh, thinking about the comments I'd supposedly made about her body that night and how eager I was to make the most out of what I thought was a dream the next morning.

"That's what I thought," Rowan says with a smirk. "So I'm just going to go on record saying that it's only a matter of time before something else happens. If you're worried about protecting her from yourself, then you probably shouldn't be living with her."

I nod reluctantly, instantly overcome with guilt. "Yeah, you're right."

"Talk to her, Lan. Think about how you really feel and tell her the whole truth. She deserves to know."

"I will," I tell him. Then I channel some of that relationship building stuff Daisy's been teaching me before I add, "Thanks for understanding, man. I honestly never meant for things to happen this way."

Rowan blinks at me, seeming surprised. "Of course. You know I'm not just saying this because I love Daisy, right? You're just as much my brother as the rest of those guys are," he says, gesturing to a wall covered with photos of the Lafleur boys. "I want you to be happy, too. Even if that means sacrificing my favorite sister."

I laugh awkwardly. "Thanks, I guess. Either way, I promise I'll do whatever's best for Daisy in the end."

"I'm sure you will."

daisy

I SMILE to myself when I tap on the bedroom door down the hall from my old one. Landry emerges a few seconds later in a pair of pajama pants that are a few inches too short for him. I point to his ankles and giggle as he pulls a tight T-shirt over his head.

"Shh," he scolds me quietly before he steps out of the room and closes the door behind him. "Your brother's still awake, you know."

I lift my chin tauntingly and shrug. "So? What's he gonna do? Tell my parents that I snuck out of the house with my own husband?"

Landry smirks at me, triggering a wave of butterflies in my stomach. "Exactly what have I agreed to?"

Gah, he's sexy, even in his ill-fitting pajamas.

Could he just play along this once and fulfill a few of my teenage girl dreams, especially the ones involving me sneaking out of my bedroom in the middle of the night to meet up with a boy who looks this good with sleep-mussed hair?

I step forward and use his shoulders to spin him around. Then I stifle a laugh at the way the flannel pants stretch awkwardly over his rear end.

"Yep, just as I suspected. Still hot." I reach out to smack his butt, and he turns back to face me with widened eyes after he flinches and covers himself with his hands.

He glares at me strangely, his expression still amused. "What's gotten into you tonight?"

I shrug again, trying to downplay my embarrassment. Maybe I went too far with the butt slap, but I'm feeling braver than usual, especially after basically confessing my feelings earlier today.

"I don't know. It just ... feels different now." I pause and bite my lip, debating whether to go on. "Let's go out and wait for the snow."

"Daisy, it's freezing out there."

"I know a place where we can start a fire. And I've always wanted to sneak out with a boy at night."

"A boy?" He narrows his eyes at me, but I give him my most convincing eyes and pouty lip.

"Pleeease?"

"Fine," he says with a sigh. "But only if you put on another layer of clothes first."

I glance down. "I'm already wearing a long-sleeved shirt." Then I remember that I'm not wearing a bra, and it *is* pretty chilly, even in this hallway.

Landry clears his throat uncomfortably. "Find a hoodie, a jacket, or something, Daisy."

By the time I look up again, he's turned his gaze away, but I can tell he *wants* to check me out. And that's good enough for me. "All right," I say, biting back a smile. "I'll meet you in the kitchen in a minute."

He agrees, and I dart back to my room and grab the first jacket I find in the closet, as well as a throw blanket from my bed. Then I tiptoe down the stairs, scoop up my boots near the front door, and enter the kitchen to find him waiting for me, already wearing his coat and shoes. This time his eyes betray him, and I catch him glancing at my chest before I pull the sweatshirt down.

"Ready?" I ask, snatching a lighter from the junk drawer.

He nods and forces a smile, but he looks less than enthusiastic. I imagine he's worried I'll get too cold.

I lead him outside and through the farm to a rocky firepit at the edge of the woods. I dig the lighter out of my pocket as he gathers a few small logs nearby, and he starts a fire while I spread the small blanket on the ground for us to sit.

My teeth chatter quietly while I wait for the flames to grow. "Do you really think it'll snow tonight?" I ask absently.

"No," he says flatly. "At least not enough for it to stick."

"Always a cynic," I say, bumping his shoulder with mine. He doesn't reply, only smiles. "I was hoping to get at least a few inches tonight."

His eyebrows shoot up, and he bites his lip before I realize what I've said.

"Of snow! A few inches of snow," I clarify.

"Right," he agrees, shooting me a sexy smirk. And I'm forced to change the subject before I embarrass myself any further.

"So how much does my brother know about us now?"

His smile falters. "What makes you think we talked about you?"

"That guilty look on your face, for starters," I reply, poking him in the jaw.

"I'm sorry, I folded," he admits. "I told him almost everything, including the conversation we had on the way here. But I left out the seizures you had a few months ago."

"Oh," I breathe. "He knows we're married?"

"Yes. I couldn't bring myself to lie to his face, even if I hadn't promised you I'd tell him the truth."

I smile, my relief outweighing my nerves now. "And what did Rowan have to say about everything?"

Landry sighs. "He said you were right, that I owe it to you to consider how I really feel. He pointed out that it would be inappropriate for us to continue living in the same house after all this. And he told me he just wants both of us to be happy."

"Wow. That's all really *Rowan* of him."

He laughs shortly, staring into the fire. "No kidding."

I want to prompt him to say more, especially about those feelings he can't seem to wrap his mind around, but we sit in the cold silence for a few minutes before I work up the courage to speak again. "I know I said it already, but I'm really grateful for your gift."

His expression softens. "It's more for me than anyone. I don't want to have to worry so much about you once you're living on your own."

I reach over and wrap my chilled fingers around his, ignoring the way he brings up moving out again. He doesn't resist the contact, but he doesn't seem to welcome it the way he did earlier today. "But it means you believe in me, that it's worth the trouble of helping me because I'm actually capable of taking care of myself. That's a much more important gift than you know."

"You shouldn't have to thank me for that," he finally replies. "You're capable of anything you set your mind to, Daisy."

The stillness stretches between us again, the only sound being the wind blowing through the trees.

"I feel like there's something else on your mind," I venture. "But you're waiting for me to invoke our full-transparency clause."

He huffs out a short laugh. "Yeah. Same."

"I've been trying to tell you what I'm thinking. You don't seem to want to hear it," I mutter and tug my hand back.

"I'm sorry. You're right. I've been afraid." He turns to face me, and my stomach flutters again.

"I'm afraid, too. I'm worried I'll say the wrong thing and scare you away. But I like being your roommate, and I don't want you to move out just yet."

"I like living with you, too," he says.

"Then ... you should stay," I add hesitantly.

"I can't stay forever though."

I swallow hard. "Can't you?"

He laughs softly. "Not unless I want to turn you into a cynical, old grump like me."

"Only if I don't turn you into a cheerful and bubbly optimist first," I retort, and he laughs again. My heart rate picks up as I push forward. "I mean it, though. Didn't you say the other day that we pretty much had the perfect relationship, minus the physical part?"

He sighs. "I never should have said that. I'm sorry."

"It might have hurt a little, but you were being honest. And in a way, you were right. It seems like that's all that's missing …" I struggle to hide the way my breathing quickens as I leave the offer hanging between us. He's still quiet, so I turn to look at him. He's staring at the fire, the muscles in his jaw ticking.

"Landry?"

He licks his lips. "Sorry. I'm processing."

"Should I be more transparent?" I ask.

"I think I get it. I'm still working on my response."

I laugh. "Would it help if I took off a few layers?"

He blows out a breath and shakes his head. "God, no. When I said 'response,' I really meant 'restraint.' "

I can't help the smile that spreads across my face. "But you don't need to hold back with me. I like you, Landry, as more than a friend. In fact, I think I might *more* than like you. And it's not just because of all the nice things you do for me, although I admire the way you care so much. I think you're funny, and I genuinely enjoy being with you, especially when you let your guard down. And I'm pretty sure you at least like me, too."

"Shit," he curses, scaring those butterflies away. "I was worried you might say something like that."

"Worried because you don't feel the same?" I ask, my voice thick.

He doesn't answer right away, leaving the pops and crackles of the fire to fill the silence.

"Regardless of whether there's something more than friendship between us, I can't give you the things you want and deserve, like a real marriage … and babies."

"You don't know that. How would a real marriage be so different from what we have now?" I demand.

"I just can't do it, Daisy. I'm too afraid of hurting you."

"And you don't think this hurts?"

He cringes. "I'm sorry. But I'm going to have to move out at some point, one way or another, and we both have a better chance of making it out of this unharmed if we leave things as they are."

I shake my head. "Who says you have to move out? Rowan?"

"I do," he replies flatly.

I use my sleeve to wipe my nose. I can't tell whether I've started crying or the cold is getting to me now, but I have to force myself to stop sniffling before I can go on. "You know, you keep saying 'it's not you, it's me,' but I don't believe you anymore. So what is it? The epilepsy? The age difference? Or is it because I'm Rowan's sister that you can't see a future with me?"

He closes his eyes and sighs again. "I care too much to do this with you. Just ... let it go, okay?"

"No, I told you, I won't just *let it go*." I cross my arms angrily over my chest. "I have a right to the truth, and you know it."

He groans. "It's because I'm an asshole, and it's only a matter of time before I *really* hurt you. I can't be the man you deserve, the one who doesn't overthink everything just to get it wrong anyway, who isn't afraid to kiss you in public, who believes in love and marriage and all the other shit you do. Despite what you've fooled yourself into believing, I'm not capable of making you happy." He turns to face me, and I swear I see tears in his eyes. "I don't even know how to be anything less than unpleasant, and I can't let you waste any more of your time on me."

"You're not an asshole, dammit," I fire back, and he flinches. "Stop saying that. There's nothing wrong with you, and it isn't your fault that your friends and family didn't get you growing up. Mine never really got me, either. Yet somehow, you do, and I get you, too. It seems like most people spend their whole lives searching for the exact thing we've accidentally stumbled upon, but you won't let us be that person for one another. Why not?"

"I'm trying to save you," he says, his voice cracking. "You don't understand what being stuck in a miserable relationship can do to someone. You haven't seen or experienced half of the shit I've been through. And I could never risk making you feel that bad."

"I understand more than you think. You just don't trust me enough to know my own mind, even though I thought you might have been the only person who did." He's quiet so I continue. "And you know what? Maybe *I'm* not the one being naive. So your parents taught you how marriage could go badly. Mine showed me that it could be amazing. It doesn't mean that I expect my relationships to be just like theirs, and neither should you."

"What do you want from me, Daisy?" He turns his body to face mine. "You want me to admit that I like you? That I'm constantly having to stop myself from fantasizing about being with you for real? That I've never wished I was a better person as hard as I do now?" His eyes are pleading, begging me to stop. "None of that would make a difference, even if it were true."

My heart races, and it's hard for me to breathe. But I'm not stopping to dwell on a small bit of hope, not when I can sense how close he is to giving in completely. "I want you to actually consider whether you feel that way, and I want you to tell me the truth. Because I believe that stuff makes all the difference."

"And what if I don't actually feel what you want me to? What then?"

"You owe me the truth," I repeat. "That's all."

"I'm not sure I can give you that right now," he mumbles, looking away.

I inhale deeply, garnering all the courage I have left. "Sure you can. Kiss me."

"What?" He recoils.

"You said it wasn't unpleasant when we kissed before, but it was purely physical, nothing meaningful, because you couldn't allow it to be anything more than that. So kiss me now, while no one's watching, and think about what it makes you feel."

His throat bobs as he swallows hard, and I think he's actually considering my offer. "You don't know what you're asking of me."

"Because you're afraid you'll feel something?"

He shakes his head. "I know I will."

My stomach dips. "But ... I thought you said—"

"I had to protect you," he cuts me off.

"You're not a monster," I say incredulously. "It's okay for you to admit you're attracted to me."

He inhales. "Impulse control has never been my strong suit, Blondie."

"So you've said," I taunt him. "But I haven't seen much of that guy yet. I'm starting to think he doesn't exist."

He turns and stares at me in a way that makes me think I'd be sweating, even without the fire blazing in front of us. "You really want me to kiss you, Daisy? You want me to show you what I'm like when I'm not holding back?" he asks, his tone shifting. His eyes are darker than I've ever seen them.

"I dare you," I whisper.

He growls as he reaches out to pull me in and captures my mouth with his, and I gasp against his lips. I instinctively reach up to clutch at his arms as he tilts his head to the side and presses his mouth against mine more forcefully, guiding me to open up for him. In one smooth motion, his tongue slips in through my parted lips, and I'm hyper-aware of the heat already building inside me, my body's involuntary reactions to his, and the powerful urge to draw him in closer.

Fisting his shirt in my hands, I drag him toward me while I rise to my knees, eliciting a low groan from deep within his chest, and he grips the back of my neck. A part of me is waiting, fearing the second he pulls away. The other half is savoring every second of this and reveling in the fact that he seems to be enjoying it, too.

Landry continues, his kisses growing hungrier as his hands become entangled in my hair, and I match his intensity. My fingertips dig themselves into his muscles while he dips his tongue into my mouth and swallows each of my desperate whines.

"I knew it. You taste so damned good," he mumbles against my lips. "It only makes it that much harder not to imagine what the rest of you might taste like."

A shiver runs through me when I realize I've unlocked a new level of Landry's personality. He's not just sweet—he's spicy.

He's *smushy*.

"Why don't you see for yourself?" I spit out after a while.

He whimpers and shifts our positions so that I'm lying on my back as he hovers over me. "Is that another dare?" he rasps.

"Yes," I say, gulping, and he immediately moves his lips down to my neck.

"Hmm," he hums and drags his tongue over my skin before his teeth scrape the same sensitive spot. "This checks out. But there are other places I'm still curious about."

I smile and tilt my head back. "Other places?"

His hand slips beneath my shirt then, and I know I shouldn't let this go on. I'm leading us both into a very, very near occasion of sin. But at this point, I can't imagine Landry isn't the man I've been saving myself for all these years. Maybe I haven't ventured this far into physical intimacy before, but I've never even felt the desire to do this with anyone else. And that has to mean something.

"Gah, you're so soft … so perfect," he murmurs. "So sexy it hurts." He barely gets that last bit out before devouring my mouth again, and I'm slightly disappointed he's not continuing his taste test. Besides the time when Landry was drunk, I've never been called sexy before, and he's definitely making me feel sexy right now.

I work up the nerve to drag my hands over him, and he groans when I grasp his backside and pull him down. He pushes himself against me when my back arches up to meet him. Then I slide my hands up his shirt, and he flinches, making us both stop and giggle.

"Shit, that's cold," he says, staring down at me and smiling.

"Hey, you're not supposed to be holding back right now," I scold him playfully. "You didn't hear me complaining when your popsicle fingers started crawling around in my shirt."

His smile grows cockier. "Oh, I heard you, Blondie." Then he leans down and nips at my bottom lip. "But it didn't sound like you were complaining."

"Then why'd you stop?" I muse.

"I have to stop at some point, don't I?" I'm sure the question was meant to be rhetorical, but the way he brings his lips back to that sensitive spot near my ear makes me think he wants an answer.

"No one's stopping you, Landry," I breathe. "In fact, I'd rather you didn't."

But my response has the opposite effect, because he pulls away and stares down at me, looking confused. "Is this all you want from me, then?"

I blink up at him. "No, of course not."

His chest heaves as he continues. "But I haven't even told you how I feel."

"I think I know," I say, giving him a soft smile.

"No," he replies, shaking his head. "You don't understand men at all, how easy it would be for me to go through with this, especially if I *didn't* care."

"You're not like that, though," I say quietly. "I know you, and you could never—"

"You don't know anything," he cuts me off and moves to sit back on his heels. "You have no idea what I've done or what I'm capable of. The only kind of sex I've ever had is the detached kind. And I've told you over and over again that I don't buy in to love or marriage. What did you expect?"

I tug my sweatshirt down and rise up on my elbows, my face heating up. "I guess I was hoping you'd feel something different with me."

He looks away. "Yeah, well, I told you I'd never live up to your expectations," he mutters to himself. "Come on. It's late. And there's not going to be any snow. You should get back to bed before you catch something."

"No." I frown. "I'm not ready to go yet."

He blows out a breath. "Suit yourself then. I'll see you in the morning." Then he actually gets up and walks away, leaving me alone at the edge of the woods, just as the first few snowflakes fall.

landry

"So, um, how long are we pretending I didn't hear you creeping back in at two in the morning?" Rowan asks as he makes his bed.

"Indefinitely," I growl from across the room.

"You and Daisy didn't go off together to talk things out?"

I shake my head. "We did. But she didn't take it very well."

"What do you mean?"

"Does it look like I want to relive that conversation right now? Sometimes I wonder whether I'm really the one who can't read people," I retort angrily, but Rowan only crosses his arms and continues staring expectantly.

"If you really want to know," I concede after a while, "I tried letting her down easy, like you suggested. I gave her all the reasons why we couldn't have a romantic relationship, but she shot each of them down." I leave out the accidental make out session for his sake, but just thinking about kissing Daisy admittedly makes my stomach dip. I clear my throat, hoping he can't read my thoughts on my face. "I'm afraid I only made things worse."

"Come on, Landry," Rowan scolds me. "That's not what I meant when I said you're too far in to keep leading her on. You were supposed to realize how much you actually *do* like her and tell her you wanted to be together for real!"

I frown. "Oh. Well, that's not exactly what I got from our conversation."

"Gah, for one of the smartest people I've ever known, you can be so dense sometimes, man."

"I'm sorry," I mumble, staring down at my lap. Then I glance up at him. "You know what, maybe you're the one who should be apologizing this time."

"Me?"

"Yeah. We've been friends for over a decade, and you still haven't figured out that I need you to be very literal in times like this. Yet, Daisy picked up on that within a few hours."

He huffs out an incredulous laugh. "And you can be painfully oblivious to the stuff right in front of you because you don't *want* to have to acknowledge your feelings or think about what it all means."

It instantly brings me back to the day almost a year ago when Blake told me the same thing about Loren in a parking lot outside of Rowan's clinic.

"I'm too stubborn," I mutter. "I know. But I'm not sure how to turn it off. I've been trying, but I don't know how to be different."

Rowan shrugs, his expression softening as he sits at the foot of the bed. "You've already started changing just by being open to the idea. Now take it one conversation, one interaction at a time."

I nod.

"You don't have to tell me, but would you at least allow yourself to consider how you really feel about her?" he adds.

Warmth and longing instantly fill my chest in equal proportions. "I'm not sure I have a choice in that anymore. The feelings are already there ... I just have to accept them. But it's probably going to take me a while to articulate it."

He smiles. "That's okay, as long as you tell her you're working on it. In the meantime, keep showing her."

"And what if we're never on the same page as far as commitment goes?" I pose.

"You've gotta quit saying you don't believe in marriage when you're already married."

"This doesn't exactly count, though."

He scoffs. "Even if it wasn't in church, it's legally binding, so it's still something. You made vows, didn't you?"

I open my mouth to argue, but my jaw snaps closed when I realize he's right. "Yeah, we did. Daisy insisted we write our own vows, though. Instead of 'love, cherish, and obey,' we used words like 'respect, honor, and support,' stuff we figured we'd both be able to uphold after we went our separate ways."

"You mean, after you divorce her?" Rowan glares at me as he waits for his words to sink in.

"Yeah, I guess," I mumble and drag a hand down my face. It's not like I haven't considered the divorce part. But it's already hitting differently after hearing another human say it out loud.

"What have I done?" I mutter behind my palm. "I've ruined her life, haven't I?"

My chest starts to tighten, making it harder for me to breathe. But Rowan moves to sit beside me and puts a hand on my shoulder. "Hey, it's okay, Lan."

"No, it's not. I swore to myself I'd never get married because I didn't want to make anyone feel like they were trapped or stuck with me and because I never wanted to have to go through a divorce. And here I am, doing exactly that, but with Daisy of all people. She's the last person in the world I want to hurt."

"No one's saying it has to be that way, though. Maybe you don't have to get divorced, right?"

"I can't ..." I stop and struggle to catch my breath again. Then I close my eyes and summon the memory of Daisy telling me to stop stressing over the worst possible outcome because it's more torturous than hoping for the best and getting let down in the end. I remind myself that she's just across the hall from me now and that there's still a chance I can fix some of the damage I've done.

"Landry?"

I let out a long exhale and open my eyes. "I'm sorry. I never gave the idea of marriage a fair chance before this, so I didn't think it would bother me when Daisy and I made it to this point. But I was wrong."

Rowan's mouth turns up on one side. "I'll spare you the jokes about admitting you were wrong if you tell me what part you were wrong about."

I huff. "All of it."

"Are you saying you're no longer opposed to a real marriage and everything that comes with it?" he ventures carefully.

"I guess I'm saying ... I don't know anymore. Maybe I should at least reconsider it before I make any more decisions about our future."

For the first time, I allow myself to think about what I want and not just what's safe or what I deserve. If I could have things like an actual loving relationship, long-term commitment, and kids of my own, would I want them?

Aside from the risks involved, why wouldn't I want all of it?

Didn't Daisy say that we all crave some form of love and acceptance? Isn't that what I've been missing all these years?

I guess I figured if I couldn't get that from my own family, it was pointless to try with anyone else. But she's already lived with me and accepted me for who I am, flaws and all, and she's still offering her love, without conditions. All I'd have to do is love her in return, in my own way.

"What's going on in there, man?" Rowan asks after a while.

I cringe and scratch the back of my neck. "A whole lot of shit I never imagined. And you know it's already a dumpster fire in here most days," I tell him.

He laughs softly. "I've always pictured the inside of your head as more of a circus—organized chaos."

"Not far off, but I think it's less fun," I reply, smirking.

"A browser window with too many tabs open?"

I snort. "And one of the tabs is blasting music, but I can't figure out where it's coming from to turn it off."

"So how many of those open tabs are reserved for my sister?"

"All of them—I mean, only the wholesome ones." I barely get it out with a straight face before he shoves me.

"In all the time we've known one another, this is the deepest heart-to-heart discussion we've ever had," Rowan declares as he stands. "Don't you think that's pretty significant?"

I roll my eyes. "Are you going to get all mushy and talk about all the ways Daisy's changed me?"

"I was actually going to say it's funny how this whole thing panned out. You thought you were in it to help Daisy, but you ended up learning about trust and love from her, just before those feelings seem to have developed for you. It's almost as if the Holy Spirit took both of your strengths and weaknesses into account before He nudged you together on purpose."

I laugh. "Maybe. It would make sense if that's how this works, since you're still single. Because what could you possibly have left to learn?" I blurt out, realizing how hurtful it sounds a second too late. "Sorry, man. I meant that as a compliment."

He nods, his smile looking sadder now, and I'm immediately overcome with guilt. My intentions don't seem to matter this time. He needs first aid, not an explanation.

"I mean, I'm sorry. That was insensitive, and I shouldn't have said it," I tell him firmly.

"Nah, it is what it is, right? I'll find someone if and when God wills it," he replies. "And probably when I least expect it."

"Yeah. For what it's worth, I wish I had more sisters to spare," I say, making him laugh.

"It doesn't have to be an even trade. Just promise me you'll take good care of mine."

I have to swallow the unexpected emotion in my throat before I can reply. "Always."

"And you have to let her take care of you," he adds with a smirk, and I agree.

daisy

LANDRY COUGHS quietly as he merges onto the interstate. I sigh and shift my position in the passenger seat, then pick up my phone again.

Okay, so maybe I'm fishing for a reaction from him. I know we both hate letting any kind of conflict simmer, so his unusually calm and collected demeanor this morning is making me feel exceptionally anxious. But I'm in love with him, and I need him to quit being so stubborn and admit that he loves me, too. And I really want to skip to the part where we kiss and make up.

"I'm sorry," he begins awkwardly, and I sigh inwardly. "About last night." He glances my way, his expression contrite.

"I'm not surprised to hear you say that," I return bitterly when I realize he's only apologizing for the parts I enjoyed.

"Look who's sounding cynical now." He smirks.

I roll my eyes. "You can't blame me for assuming you'd regret kissing me again."

His face falls. "But I shouldn't have been kissing you after the other stuff I'd just said, and I certainly shouldn't have let it go that far."

I huff out another loud sigh. "Right, because I'm just a silly, little girl who can't think for herself. And you're the Big Bad Wolf who's come to seduce me."

"Daisy ..."

"What, Landry? Do you want me to lie and say I've changed my mind? I'm frustrated, and I'm annoyed with you, yes. But it doesn't mean I've stopped liking you." I pause for a second. "That's not how love works. And I'm sorry if my feelings for you are inconvenient, but—"

"All right, enough!" he yells, pounding his fist lightly on the steering wheel.

I clamp my mouth shut and glare at him, surprised to see him smiling.

"I'm perfectly capable of putting my own foot in my mouth, if you'd give me a chance," he continues while I cross my arms and pout. "But I'm trying to tell you that you were right. I have been refusing to acknowledge your feelings ... and my own. And last night was only a mistake because I shouldn't have allowed anything physical to happen between us before I was able to admit all that to you."

"Oh," I breathe as a glimmer of hope surfaces.

"I'm also sorry for leaving you alone and for all the dumb stuff I said—for being an ass in general. I don't really think you're silly or naive, and no one is more grateful for your ability to see the good in people than I am."

"Thank you for that."

He hesitates before he begins again. "The thing is, I'm still pretty confused. It turns out that the way I feel about you doesn't exactly align with the rest of my beliefs. So I might need a little more time to make sense of everything, to figure out where we should go from here. Is that okay?"

"Yeah. Okay," I reply in a small voice. He reaches over and opens his hand, and I drop my palm into his. "But, for the record, we are talking about *romantic* feelings, right, and not just more of the friendly kind?"

"Definitely romantic." He glances at me from the side and brings my hand up to his lips to kiss my knuckles, making me shiver.

"So it's really the extent of these romantic feelings that you're struggling with?" I venture.

"I guess you could say that."

"If it helps, just know that I don't have any expectations," I tell him as he lets our hands fall to rest between us. His thumb strokes the inside of my wrist, and I have to clear my throat before I can continue. "You don't have to commit to anything serious if you're not ready."

He laughs shortly. "More serious than marriage?"

"You know what I mean." I smirk at him and give his hand a squeeze. "We based our friendship on honesty, and that's something I never want to change. So don't be afraid to tell me the truth, even if you don't feel as strongly as I do."

He heaves out a sigh and continues rubbing circles over my wrist as he exits the interstate and pulls up at the nearest gas station. Then he puts the Jeep in park and turns to face me.

"You're not going to let me go without saying more, are you?"

I cringe. "I'm sorry. I can be patient, I promise."

He smiles, looking nervous. "The truth is ... I think you're amazing. You're like sunshine, so bright and full of joy. You're also the only person in the whole world who gets me, who's willing to meet me where I am." He pauses and swallows hard before he continues. "When I'm around you—hell, every time I think of you—I get all warm and fuzzy inside. And that scares the shit out of me, because it's never happened before, and because I never expected to like it this much. It probably sounds stupid, but I think I've been afraid to acknowledge the way you make me feel because I knew that once I did, I wouldn't be able to stop myself from acting on it. And I can't bear the thought of letting you down." He exhales in relief before he adds, "That's all I've got so far."

"Wow," I say, my voice thick, and he laughs softly. I try to ignore the stinging sensation in my eyes, but they're growing waterier by the second. "Landry Reed, are you telling me that I give you the warm fuzzies?"

He shrugs shyly. "I don't know. Maybe."

"I didn't think you were capable of getting the warm fuzzies," I say, chuckling and sniffling at the same time.

"Neither did I," he mumbles under his breath. "But you're giving them to me again ... right now."

"Oh, sorry." My brow lifts and I tug my hand back. "Is this better?"

He stares at me for a full beat before he shakes his head. "No. You're still doing it." His voice sounds hoarse.

"Want me to stop?" I ask, smirking at him.

"Never," he rasps. He reaches out and brushes his hand over my cheek, and I blink at him a few times as a wave of heat runs through me. For a second, I think he's going to pull me in for a kiss. Instead, he tucks my hair behind my ear and continues gazing at me, looking more vulnerable than ever.

"I don't know if I can give you all the things you want, the things you deserve," he continues. "But the longer I know you, the more I find myself wanting to change, to at least try to be better, even if it's just for you."

I nod, trying to resist the urge to climb into his lap and ask him to stay there forever. His dark eyelashes flutter as his eyes dart down to my mouth. I watch his throat bob again, and I gulp along with him. "Thank you for being patient with me," he says quietly, taking my hand in his again. Then he dips his head to kiss my wrist before pulling away and letting my hand fall.

"Of course," I mutter disappointedly.

He clears his throat and looks down. "I think I'll top off before we head home. Do you need anything inside?"

"No, I'm fine, thanks." I offer him a forced smile before he nods and steps out of the car, then I groan aloud once he leaves me alone and pout inwardly until he returns.

I paste on another smile as he opens the door, because I really have no reason to be upset. I should be grateful that the man I love has finally admitted that he has feelings for me, even if he mostly cited the fact that I'm nice to him as his reasoning. It's not that I don't appreciate all the sweet stuff he said about me. But after being friend zoned first, I guess I've been hoping for a little more evidence of Landry's attraction to me. I mean, last night helped boost my confidence a little, but I'd still like an actual declaration.

Then again, I also promised I'd be patient with him. And I ought to know better than anyone that Landry needs more direct cues than the average guy, which isn't saying much.

I realize I've accidentally let out a frustrated huff a second too late. But Landry turns to me with a grin and holds out a convenience store bag.

"Don't worry, I've been taking notes."

I furrow my brow in confusion as I take the bag. "What's this?"

"When a woman says she doesn't want anything from the store, she really means she's too hangry to figure out what she wants, right?" He recites the line proudly as I dig around and find some jerky, my favorite brand of iced tea, and a pack of trail mix.

I bite my lip, feeling guilty. "Landry?"

"Hmm?"

"For someone who has a hard time articulating his affection, you already do a pretty fantastic job of making me feel very well-liked, if not loved."

His lips twitch, but he keeps his expression blank. "It's probably one of those at least."

"Thank you," I say and lean up and press a kiss to his cheek. Then I watch as his eyes flutter closed, and he inhales deeply, as if he's savoring the contact.

"You're welcome," he returns, and I scoot back to my side with a silly grin while he pulls out of the parking lot.

"Aren't you going to say a rosary?" he asks after a while.

"Right. I guess I forgot since I was a little distracted." I pull up my purse and begin digging around for my favorite green rosary.

"Will you teach me?"

My brow shoots up. "Hmm?"

"I, um, I never really learned before. But if you wanted to teach me, we could say it together sometimes."

I blink up at him. "You want to pray together?"

"Only if you—"

"Yes," I cut him off. "Absolutely."

He shoots me an adorable grin, and it takes me a second to gather my thoughts again. I only thought Landry was everything I wanted in a man before, but we're making it official now. If he thinks he's going to ask me to pray together and still get rid of me, he's definitely the gullible one here.

I attempt to clear the emotion from my throat before I begin our lesson, but I can't help the way my voice cracks every so often after that.

We make it back home just after lunch, and my heart begins racing as he pulls into the driveway. We're still sharing a home, and we're still married, yet things are going to be different now. I'm grateful when he grabs my bags out the back and opens all the doors for me so that he can't see the way my hands are trembling.

Landry silently follows me into my bedroom, and I struggle to keep my breathing steady. By the time he drops my bags down onto my bed and turns to face me, I'm forced to lean against the door frame for support.

"Thanks," I say awkwardly. He nods and locks his gaze onto me again, and I think I might swoon like one of those women in Loren's Regency romances if he doesn't turn that smolder away soon.

"So, um, do you still want me to tag along tonight? It's okay if you'd rather spend some time alone with your family," I pose, my voice shaky.

"No, I definitely want you …" He clears his throat after he trails off. "I mean, I'd still like you to come with me."

My eyebrows lift, and I can't help but wonder if I'm reading too much into what he's saying. "Oh, good. Would you like to go to Mass together first?"

"Yeah, that works," he says, taking a step toward me.

"And what should I wear later?"

He exhales loudly. "It'll be pretty casual, so whatever you're comfortable in. We can always run home to change after Mass."

"You want to come back home and 'change' before we go to your dad's place?" I ask, using air quotes. "Won't that look a little suspicious, especially if we show up looking cozier than usual?"

Landry laughs, momentarily distracting me from the way he's moving closer. "You've never been this flirty with anyone else, have you?" He says it more like a statement, daring me to deny it.

I blush a little, and my breathing picks up again at the abrupt shift in our conversation. "No. I've never been brave enough to talk to any other guy the way I talk to you."

"I think I like that," he says after a while, making me shiver.

"The flirting?"

"Yeah. And the idea that I'm the only man who gets to see this side of you."

My cheeks flush even darker. "You make me feel safe, I guess."

"So do you. For the first time in my life." He pauses, and his shoulders rise and fall. "You were right before, when you said that the way we get one another seems ... rare. I'm not sure yet what that means for us, but I promise I'm not going to take it for granted anymore."

My heart skips a beat, and I smile at him again.

"Daisy, I ... I think I might ..." He cringes and shakes his head. "I want to say it out loud, but I can't. Because I'm not supposed to feel that way about you."

An incredulous laugh bubbles out of me. "As your wife, I'd like to think I'm the only person you should be saying this stuff to."

"Everything else—all the things I shouldn't say—they all just come flying out before I can filter myself. Why is this so hard?" Then he pulls away and runs his fingers through his hair in frustration. "What's wrong with me?"

"Hey, look at me," I demand, and he obeys, but his eyes are still filled with doubt. "There's nothing wrong with you. Just like there's nothing wrong with me, right? Our brains work differently, that's all. And that's okay, because I like your brain the way it is. We can be different together."

"This is what I mean. You're too good. I can't let you waste yourself on me," he says with a rueful smile.

"Well, you're wrong, because I don't know that I've ever met anyone as kind and generous as you," I whisper, furrowing my brow. "You deserve the world, Landry. You deserve to be taken care of, too." I reach out to pull him in closer again. "You just have to let me."

He stares at me with half-lidded eyes as he closes in the last few inches of space between us and leans down to brush his nose over mine. "I have another confession to make."

"Hmm?" I tilt my chin up instinctively, and his eyes dart down to my mouth, but he doesn't take me up on my invitation.

"Although I'm glad we did it, I only asked you to pray that rosary together because I needed a distraction. And I don't remember most of the drive home because I was so busy fighting the urge to pull the car over and drag you into my lap."

I inhale sharply. "Oh."

"But I didn't want you to think I only said how I felt to pressure you ... you know?"

I shake my head. "I don't think that at all."

"Good, because I'm *dying* to kiss you right now. Only, I'm afraid I don't have as much patience or self-control as you do," he continues, backing away.

My stomach dips, and I grab him before he can move too far. "I don't have a problem with that."

"I mean it. You'll have to put the brakes on."

I nod, maybe a little too eagerly. "I can handle it."

I watch his throat work as he stretches an arm over me to brace himself and pins me against the door frame. My chest begins heaving when he leans down and rests his forehead against mine, until he finally gives in and allows our lips to meet. He starts off slowly and tenderly, but it isn't long before his hands are traveling over me and his body is pressing against mine.

I arch my back up from the wall and clutch desperately at his shirt sleeves, and he hums his approval into my mouth. Then he palms my thighs and moves to lift me in front of him before abruptly dropping his hands and taking a step back, to my disappointment.

"I'm sorry," he begins, cringing and licking his swollen lips, "but I should go … I just … I need to be somewhere else for a little while."

"You're not going anywhere," I reply breathlessly, yanking him down to me. He gives me another short kiss before he backs away again.

"You don't understand. This is why I couldn't even consider letting anything happen between us before. It's all I can think about now. It's only been a few hours, and I'm already struggling with this self-regulation stuff."

"So, you *do* want me the way I want you?" I ask hesitantly.

"I don't know if I can accurately convey my enthusiasm without using language you wouldn't appreciate," he replies, his tone deep. "But, yes, I want you."

I shiver as another flash of heat runs through me. "I was a little worried you were still just going along with all the flirting and kissing because you felt sorry for me," I admit.

He groans again and reaches behind me to trail a fingertip down my back. "Shit, Daisy. I've been fighting this since the moment I walked in on you in the kitchen. Do you have any idea how hard it's been to keep myself from thinking about you? From fantasizing about your sexy freckles … to keep my hands to myself when you're right there, looking so damned hot all the time?"

He leans in to kiss me again but stops short, and I'm slightly concerned that he may have just taken my virginity without even touching me.

"I'm sorry. I think all that pent-up attraction from the past few months is hitting me at once. And if we keep going, I'm not sure I'll be able to stop," he warns me, his voice rough and his fingers digging into my sides beneath the hem of my shirt. "At least, not unless you ask me to."

"Then don't," I say softly and brush my lips over his again.

"I need you to set some boundaries," he pleads between kisses. "Now, before I push you too far, especially while we're home alone with nothing and no one to stop us."

"And what if I've changed my mind? What if I don't want to wait—"

He stops abruptly. "You finish that offer, and I'm not touching you again. Do you understand me?" His eyes flash to mine, and I can see the anger and disgust in his expression.

I shrink back into the door frame. "Would it really be so bad for you?"

"I'd never be able to forgive myself if I let you break that vow, much less if I were to risk your health and safety by getting you pregnant. So, yes, it would be the worst, the most selfish thing I could do."

"But even if I got cleared by my doctor to have a baby, you still don't believe in marriage. So I guess that means we'll just never have a physical relationship?" I fire back.

"Hey, I'm working on it, okay? You told me you'd give me some time to wrap my head around all this, and it hasn't even been twenty-four hours," he reminds me, ironically sounding much more composed than I do at the moment.

I frown. He's right. I did promise him that much. "Okay."

He locks his eyes onto mine. "Full transparency?"

I nod, furrowing my brow, and he brings a hand up to my cheek. "I wasn't lying when I told you sex has never been very meaningful for me. But this already feels different. And even though I know it can't happen right away, I think I'm already nervous because I want to make it perfect for you. I'm sure you've had plenty of time to imagine what it'll be like, and I'm worried I won't live up to your expectations."

"And I told *you* that I don't have any expectations," I reply, though it's not completely true. Because he's been the only man my imagination casts in that role for some time now.

He ignores me, his chest rising and falling as he continues gazing down at me with a stormy look on his face. "I'm also afraid of hurting you. You know, physically."

I force a smile, though I feel a bit like a melted popsicle. "I've spent my whole life being handled like I was breakable. You're the first person to treat me like an adult, and the only one who doesn't sugarcoat everything just to spare me. I can't have you going soft on me now."

His throat bobs as he leans down to kiss me again. "Daisy?" he asks when he pulls away.

"Hmm?" I can't even open my eyes at this point.

"I think I was wrong when I assumed it would bother you—the fact that I haven't saved myself the way you have. But you like that I know what I'm doing, don't you? You like that I'm older and more experienced."

"Maybe," I barely get out. I'm also having a difficult time staying on my feet, and I'm afraid I might slump down the wall like that slushy popsicle sliding off its stick.

His mouth curls up into a cocky smirk. "And having a husband who's confident and trustworthy but who's also not afraid to get a little rough with you ... that turns you on, doesn't it, Blondie?"

My stomach swoops. "Yes. I like it," I whisper. Okay, so it's more like a whimper at this point. But Landry would rather eat a popsicle without the stick anyway, right?

He stares down at me and licks his lips before his expression shifts unexpectedly. "Nuh-uh." He shakes his head and backs away slightly. "I'm ... I've gotta ..." Then he clears his throat and puts a few feet of space between us.

"What's wrong?" I ask, frowning.

"Big Bad Wolf," he chokes out, poking himself in the chest. "I'm going to lock myself in my room. Please don't follow me."

I follow orders and stay behind, stifling a grin and studying his bubble butt as I watch him scamper off to his own bedroom.

CHAPTER 40

daisy

I SMILE BACK at Charley when she coos at me from over Blake's shoulder in the pew in front of us. It makes me feel so nice to be recognized by her that I think my heart could burst. That is, until she turns her eyes to Landry beside me, and her entire face lights up. She immediately begins bouncing excitedly and reaches out for him, and his expression mirrors hers as he leans forward to take her into his arms. Then Penny whines from her spot in Loren's lap when she notices she's been abandoned, and he turns to scoop her up, too.

No offense to Father Conrad, since I'm sure he's gearing up to deliver a lovely homily, on this, the Super Bowl of Masses. But it's hard to concentrate on anything else but Landry and the twins now, and I can't imagine God would have made babies this cute unless he were trying to give us a taste of true joy and happiness, right?

Though I must admit, at this point in my life there is a very fine line between lust and baby fever. And the man sitting beside me is currently giving me a healthy dose of both.

It's a good thing I made it to confession earlier today.

I'm teasing Penny and making her giggle by yanking her pacifier out of her mouth and giving it back when Landry leans down and whispers near my ear, "Aren't you supposed to be paying attention?"

"Shh," I scold him. "Let me have this."

His brow lifts. "I thought you said *no expectations.*"

I gasp and nudge him. "I meant that you have to share these babies with me in case I never get to have my own," I say through my teeth, trying not to smirk.

"Never say never, Blondie," he mumbles, staring intently at my mouth.

And we've officially crossed that line.

I clear my throat and turn my attention back to my game with Penny, and Loren turns to shoot us a knowing look under the guise of checking on the twins.

Penny eventually climbs into my lap and falls asleep in my arms, allowing me to participate in the rest of the Mass, and I admittedly enjoy holding her on the walk up to the communion rail. It's almost as sweet as the sight of Landry and Charley smiling at me when I return to our pew, as if they're both happy to see me. A girl could get used to all this.

I reluctantly return my borrowed baby once Mass is over, and Blake leans around Charley to smirk at me when he notices Landry's hand resting on the small of my back.

"We'll meet y'all at Dad's in a few. We're going home to change," Landry tells Loren.

"To 'change,' riiighhtt ..." She shifts Penny in her arms so she can free her hands to make air quotes, and I tell Landry *I told you so* in side-eye. But to my surprise, he simply grins at his sister's assumptions.

"I'd need more than a few minutes for that," he replies evenly, his hand fisting into the back of my dress and making me weak in the knees again. I should probably elbow him or at least scold him for the comment, but I can't bring myself to do anything beyond making another deposit in that bank of Landry fantasies. It's funny how it seems to have grown exponentially overnight.

"That's not church-parking-lot-appropriate humor, bro," Blake says, his brow lifting appreciatively. "I like it."

"Not sure I'm a fan myself," Loren mumbles as she wrinkles her nose in distaste. Then she narrows her eyes as she glances back and forth between us. "And I thought you were staying with your parents for the holidays, Daisy. I'm not sure what's changed, but I'm glad you're joining us after all."

I feel my cheeks flush. "Thank you for inviting me."

Loren nods, and the four of us stand there for a moment before Landry blurts out, "Daisy made bread pudding," and drags me awkwardly to the Jeep.

I giggle at him when we climb inside, and he turns to smirk at me. "Come on, that was smooth, right?"

"Sure," I snort. "They'll never suspect a thing."

He takes me home to change into something more comfortable, as promised, but the only thing I bother swapping is my shoes once I realize he's waiting outside my bedroom door.

"I've got an idea," he says as soon as I emerge, holding up his phone. There's a three-minute timer on the screen. "We can't do much in three minutes, right?"

I bite my lip and start the timer before I throw my arms around his neck and press my mouth to his. He hums in appreciation as he kisses me back, and we only reset the timer twice before we come up for air.

"We'd better ..." I begin, licking my lips.

He nods and gulps. "Can't forget the bread pudding."

I grin. My mom wrote down her recipe for me yesterday, and Landry and I spent the earlier part of our afternoon figuring it out ... I think. I hope, anyway.

He grabs the warm baking dish from the oven after already having loaded all the gifts, and I run to the bathroom for a quick touchup on my lipstick before we go. I don't usually wear much makeup, but it is Christmas Eve, after all.

"Aren't you going to ask about our game plan this time?" Landry smirks as we pull up at his dad's house a few minutes later.

I let out a shaky exhale. "I think you're getting way too good at this."

"At what?" he asks, clearly amused by my nervousness.

"At reading my mind," I reply quietly.

He chuckles and grabs my hand. "I would say it's because I'm making the effort now, but I think it's just a result of not having to hide how closely I watch you."

Oh, gimme a break!

How the heck am I supposed to keep my composure and not react to stuff like this?

I know Landry's not usually afraid to say what's on his mind, but the idea that he's been struggling to keep himself from developing romantic feelings for me all this time is sort of terrifying. Because now that he's suddenly open to those feelings, he hasn't been holding back with his affection. He's come a long way practically overnight, but I don't know how I'll recover if he never changes his mind about commitment and marriage after giving me so much hope.

I take in another deep breath, and he furrows his brow. "Did I say something wrong?"

There he goes again, paying attention.

"No. It's just ... it's getting harder to rein in my optimism. You're giving me the warm fuzzies, too, you know."

"I'm sorry," he says, laughing again. "I guess I hadn't realized how much I've been suppressing for the past few months."

"Months?" I squeak out.

He shrugs shyly. "I kept trying to convince myself it was all just appreciation and familiarity. But I'm afraid it's so much more than that."

"It is?"

"I still don't know where we go from here, Daze, and maybe we should keep our marriage to ourselves for a little longer, at least until we figure things out. But I'm not going to be able to hide my feelings for you anymore."

I nod eagerly. "I'm fine with that plan, as long as it involves more kissing."

He smiles as he leans in to press his lips to mine. "That's definitely included in the plan," he says once he pulls away. Then he comes around to open my door and piles the dish and the gifts in one arm so he can take my hand with the other.

We walk into the house with our fingers intertwined, and the noisy kitchen quiets as everyone's attention lands on us.

"Um, Merry Christmas," I offer awkwardly.

A grin spreads across Lilley's face. "Merry Christmas, you two," she returns, stepping forward to take the dessert from Landry and gesturing to our clasped hands. "What's this about?"

Landry clears his throat and glances at me. "Exactly what it looks like."

"Looks like you asked your teacher to bring you to the potty," Loren quips from the other side of the kitchen. Landry grunts, and my cheeks redden as everyone snickers behind her.

He lets go of my hand to set the presents down. I watch carefully, expecting to see him upset, but he's actually smiling when he turns and curls an arm around my back.

"That's not a bad idea. Maybe we'll sneak away later." He shoots me a sexy smirk as he says it, then he leans down to whisper near my ear. "We'll call it *Plan A*, and you can decide how long to set the timer."

I look away in an attempt to keep my face from flushing any darker and find Blake stifling another laugh at my reaction to Landry's smushy side. But it's not just his sexy offer that's got me so flustered; the fact that he doesn't seem to mind Loren making a joke at his expense feels like a pretty big turning point.

"Hey now, I thought you were enforcing a zero-seduction policy?" Loren continues. "And telling spicy secrets is way worse than accidentally flirting."

Landry shrugs. "The policy has changed."

"Since when?" Loren asks, blinking at me in surprise. I can only imagine what assumptions she's making about us, since she also knows about my full-chastity policy.

Landry narrows his eyes at her. "Since before it was any of your damned business, Lo-Lo."

She scoffs. "Fine. I'll just ask Daisy about it when you're not around. Maybe she'll have an explanation for the two of you going home 'to change' after Mass and showing up in the exact same outfits."

He sighs, but a cocky smile creeps across his face.

"Hey, let's just all take a second to be grateful that Landry's finally getting laid," Emmett mumbles quietly, making the rest of them choke back their laughter while the tips of my ears begin to burn. Landry shoots me an apologetic look, but I do my best to weather the storm, because I don't want him to think their teasing bothers me.

Lilley swats at her husband's shoulder. "That's not funny," she scolds him, though she's biting back a smile.

"At least someone's getting laid this week," Blake grumbles and forces a frown, and Loren rolls her eyes.

"Well, pardon me for ovulating, sir," she retorts, and he walks up behind her, wraps her up in his arms, and places a kiss on her neck. I wait for Landry to express his disgust, but he doesn't even grunt or growl. In fact, he laughs at them.

Landry's mom comes into the kitchen, interrupting my thoughts. She holds Charley in her arms while Lilley's daughter follows, carrying Penny.

"Oh, Daisy, I'm so glad you're here," Ms. Lana says as soon as she sees me, and I think I see something pass across Loren's face.

"Thanks for having me. Um, I made—I mean, we *tried* to make my mom's famous bread pudding," I reply, gesturing toward the dish Lilley set down on the stove earlier.

"My favorite. How are your parents?" she asks warmly as she hands Charley back to Loren and goes to the stove. Loren forces a smile and clutches Charley close, and Blake rubs her arm as if he's comforting her. I thought things had been going well for Loren and her mom lately, but maybe I was wrong.

"My parents? Oh, they're great," I reply absently.

"This smells amazing." Ms. Lana turns to smile at us. "Did you help, Lan?"

"Yeah," he says flatly, his eyes fixed on Loren.

"Now that everyone's here, are we ready to open gifts?" Lilley asks when she senses the tension. The others fake their enthusiasm and pile into the small living room where Landry's dad is already stationed in his recliner. He barely glances away from the football game he's watching with Lilley's son when we pass him.

Landry leads me over to another chair in the far corner of the room and pulls me down onto his lap after he sits. I do my best to maintain my composure as he cups his hand around my side and slips his thumb beneath the hem of my blouse. He rubs gentle circles over my lower back, making me shiver, and I make a mental note to add more separate skirt-and-shirt combos to my wardrobe. But I don't think he intends for the contact to be sexy, judging by his lengthy exhale.

I scoot in closer and drape my arm around his shoulders, and he looks up at me with a sad smile, confirming my suspicions. He's never had an aversion to my touch at all. In fact, I think he might need the physical contact to ground him.

I use my fingertips to mimic his movements over the back of his neck, and I watch as his whole body relaxes. My insides turn all warm and gooey again when the realization hits me—physical touch must be one of Landry's love languages.

Well, I'll be—

The sound of a throat clearing makes me flinch. "Santa, Mrs. Claus," Blake drawls as he hands me a small stack of presents, and I'm forced to use both of my arms to take them. "As you were," he leans in and says quietly with a wink.

After all of the gifts have been opened, everyone goes into the kitchen to serve dinner before returning to the living room, and I'm relieved this isn't a formal table gathering. Landry sits on the floor, giving me the chair. But all he does is move his food around on his plate, and I can tell he's counting down the minutes until we can go.

Once I'm done, he stands and takes our dishes to the kitchen while the rest of his family has dessert. The bread pudding gets rave reviews from everyone. Well, everyone except Landry's dad. Despite the way he finished off a decent-sized serving, he grunts disapprovingly after Ms. Lana reminds the whole family that Landry helped me bake it.

We take another turn playing with the twins, which seems to cheer Landry up a bit, as does the college football debate he has with his nephew and Blake. Until his dad chimes in to contradict him.

I can't help it when I roll my eyes and let out an exasperated sigh. I don't usually let this kind of stuff get to me, but there's only so much I can take.

I might be channeling my inner Landry when I lean over to drape my arms over his shoulders and whisper, "When are you gonna take me home, Santa?" a little too loudly.

His eyebrows nearly reach his hairline, and he tilts his head back to blink up at me, looking dazed. "Say the word, Blondie."

I smirk and tuck my hair behind my ears, and he wastes no time in standing and going around the room to dole out goodbyes. His dad rises to shake his hand, which doesn't impress me much. But the last straw is when I overhear the man telling his son, "Don't screw that up —you know how you are."

I walk up to Landry's father and wrap my arms around his middle, catching him off guard. "Merry Christmas, Coach Reed. Thank you for raising such an amazing man. But you know how he is, right?"

He furrows his brow as I step away, and Landry shakes his head at me, smirking in amusement.

Ms. Lana and Lilley each pull me in for a hug, and Lilley gives me an extra squeeze. "I'm so glad he has you," she says, making me smile.

Loren comes over to say good night and invites us to the Bourgeois Christmas dinner at her house tomorrow evening. "Hey, is everything okay?" she adds quietly, concern lining her face.

"Yeah, it's great," I reassure her.

"Good," she replies, offering a rueful smile. "I'm glad. It's just ... he can be impatient. Don't let him pressure you into anything, all right?"

I frown at her, torn between appreciating her effort to protect me and resenting her assumptions about Landry. "We're fine, but thanks."

She nods, looking slightly embarrassed now, and Landry shoots her a look as he leads me out.

He holds my hand on the short drive home, stopping to place a kiss over my knuckles once we're back inside the house.

"Thank you for tonight," he says softly.

I reach up and stroke his cheek, my fingers scraping against his short beard. "Landry?"

"Hmm?"

I take a deep breath and gaze into his eyes. "I love you."

He stares back at me for a second, his brow furrowed. "Daisy ..."

"You don't have to say anything. I just wanted you to know that you are loved." I wasn't planning on saying it yet, but I feel like he needs to hear it tonight. And it's the truth.

Landry's chest rises and falls until he leans in and kisses me softly, his hands entangling in my hair. But that sense of urgency and hunger quickly returns, and now I find myself thinking about my cycle and whether I'm past my window of fertility while I literally crush my body against his. It's like I can't get close enough.

My family was right—there's no way I'm coming away from living with Landry unscathed, and neither is my virginity at this rate. Chastity is a good and holy virtue, I know. And I don't just think that because I was taught to avoid premarital sex. I truly believe in all the ways a relationship can prosper from treating physical intimacy with reverence and temperance. But it's all fun and games until you find yourself facing real temptation. And it may have taken me nearly twenty-six years to get to this point, but I'm not sure I can last the next five minutes without begging Landry to take—

"Sorry," he says, pulling away and hissing. "That was not the appropriate response to what you said, was it?"

I blink at him, wondering if I accidentally took my anti-seizure meds too early because I've never felt this drunk before. "I think it was a lovely way to convey your gratitude," I slur, and he chuckles.

"Then you'll understand I mean it as a compliment when I tell you I'm running off to take a cold shower now." He smirks and kisses me on the lips once more before he leaves me whimpering in the kitchen.

I barely talk myself out of knocking on the bathroom door to offer him a warm towel, but I realize my desperation is showing and lock myself inside my bedroom to wait for my turn in the shower instead.

When I emerge, I find him sitting on the couch with a bowl of popcorn. He smirks and inclines his head in an invitation to join him, and I don't even bother trying to hide my smile as I plop down beside him with my hairbrush.

"Sorry, I had to wash my hair," I tell him as I flip my damp locks over the arm of the sofa to brush them out.

"Can I help?" he asks, gesturing to the brush.

My brow lifts. "Uh, sure."

He motions for me to sit on the floor between his knees, then he takes the brush and guides it through my hair until it no longer catches on any tangles. I shiver when he uses both of his hands to section my hair before weaving it into a thick braid. He holds a hand out over my shoulder, and I wordlessly drop an elastic band into his palm. Once he secures the braid, he pushes it to the side and leans down to press his lips to the back of my neck. I tilt my head as his mouth trails over my shoulder, and he wraps his arms around my middle to drag me closer to him.

My eyelids flutter closed, mimicking the butterfly wings flapping around inside me, and I lean back into him. After he takes his time kissing his way across my shoulders, Landry cups my cheeks in his hands and lifts my chin so that I'm looking up at his face. He plants an upside-down kiss on my forehead, then my nose, and finally my lips, and I reach up to hold him in place for a while.

"Daisy," he breathes when he pulls away, and my name has never sounded so good. He squeezes his eyes shut tightly. "You make me feel ..." He shakes his head before he opens his eyes again. "So much."

And I can tell by the way he says it, by the way he moves his hands so tenderly over me, that he wants me to know he loves me, too.

daisy

CHRISTMAS MORNING CONSISTS of coffee and eggs, snuggles, and lazy kisses around the house. And it feels like I'm floating on air.

Landry and I have to use the timer a few times to keep ourselves in check, especially after we forget about the batch of peanut butter cookies I was baking in the oven. Thankfully, he's better than I am about realizing when it's time to take a break, and he insists on making another bread pudding together so we'll have something edible to bring to his sister's later. He also admits that we could both use the distraction.

"Are we going to live off of this one recipe forever now?" he muses as he slides another pan into the oven, and my heart swells at the "forever" he's so casually slipped in.

I haven't used the L-word again, mostly because I don't want him to feel pressured to say it back before he's ready. But I'm almost afraid to learn he isn't there yet, because I can't imagine his affection having any room to grow. He's already been making me feel so loved and adored.

The oven door swings shut, and Landry turns to lean back against the counter in our tiny kitchen. He crosses his arms and smirks at me while I take him in.

"What?" he asks, shaking his head.

My face warms, and I shrug. "Nothing. It's just ... you're so cute."

He snorts, but his cheeks darken, too. "No, you're cute. I'm ... what's the opposite of cute?"

"Sexy?" I offer.

He lifts his brow in appreciation. "Am I?"

I don't even bother with a verbal answer as I close in the space between us again.

"You'll have to start a separate timer on your phone for this," he mumbles in between kisses. "Mine's already set for the oven."

"Can't we just use the same one for both?"

A rumble resonates from deep within his chest, and he grasps my hips firmly as he moves his mouth to my jaw. "I don't know. I can do a *lot* in forty-five minutes, Blondie."

I shiver at the thought of what he might accomplish with that much time. "Fine, just let me get my phone out."

"Go ahead. Don't mind me," he says as he continues down my neck.

I giggle. "Right, because you're making it so easy for me to concentrate."

He groans and nips at my shoulder. "Okay, I'll quit for now. But I'm not sorry for making you think I'm so sexy," he teases when he straightens.

I shove him playfully. "How do we manage our jobs and everything after this? What do normal married couples do?"

"*It*, probably." He grins, and I attempt to reprimand him with a glare, but I'm unable to stop myself from smiling. "They go on a honeymoon to get it out of their systems, I suppose," he adds, reaching out to hook his fingers through mine. "But I think that could backfire in our case. I have a feeling it's going to take more than a week of being trapped in a hotel room together to reconcile this much attraction."

That one nearly knocks the wind out of me, and it takes me a second to remember how my lungs are supposed to work.

Oh, right. They're involuntary.

"So what are we supposed to do in the meantime?" I choke out.

He bites his lip and shakes his head, his eyes locked onto mine. "Hell if I know."

"Maybe we need a diversion. Going back to work might be for the best," I offer, still trying to regulate my breathing. "And I should probably be studying for my certification test next week."

He furrows his brow. "You're still planning on taking the home ec position?"

"I haven't found a better option," I reply with a shrug.

"Hmm. Where's that study guide?" he demands, his tone shifting. I point to the book on the coffee table, and he marches over to the living room to retrieve it.

He holds the book up in front of me when he returns. "Daisy, do you want to keep teaching?"

"No," I whisper, shaking my head. "But I—"

He interrupts me by taking the book in both hands and splitting it down the spine with barely a strain. Then he turns and dumps it into the trash can behind him.

"Landry, what are you doing?" I cry, my eyes wide.

"I'm not letting you force yourself into a career that isn't making you happy," he says plainly.

I cringe. "No, I mean, that wasn't my study guide! I borrowed it from Claire."

"Oh." He lets out a loud exhale. "I'll buy her another one. But only if you promise not to take that test … or that job."

"I can't promise you either of those," I say, laughing incredulously.

"Yes, you can." He steps forward and takes my hand again. "Let me handle the financial stuff until you figure out what you really want to do."

I swallow hard. "I can't ask you to do that. Not when we're just …"

He frowns. "I know you can take care of yourself, and I'm not trying to rob you of your independence. But we're still married, at least for now, and I took a vow to support you. Let me help you, please."

I let go of his hand and take a step back. My chin trembles, and it takes me a couple of tries before I can speak again without my voice cracking. "Do you really want to help me? Or are you doing this to make yourself feel better about divorcing me in a month or two?"

"Daisy," he begins. "I may not have all that long-term stuff figured out yet, but I meant it when I said I was reconsidering my stance on commitment for you." Then he pauses and shakes his head. "No, that didn't come out right. Being with you makes me want to rethink commitment for my own sake. And I think we should hold off on a divorce until we make absolutely certain it's the right decision."

I blink at him as his words settle. "So you basically want a Josephite marriage until you come around to deciding what's best for both of us?"

"A what?"

I barely suppress an eye roll. "You want to skip ahead to the part where we act like a married couple in every way except we'll have to remain celibate while you figure out whether you can handle commitment?"

He cringes. "Well, when you put it that way ..."

"Look, I know what you're trying to do. You want to keep me on your insurance as long as you can, but ..." I trail off when I see his expression fall.

"It's not about that," he says sadly, shaking his head. "Well, it's not just about that. And it doesn't have anything to do with the extent of my feelings for you, if I'm being honest. I just need more time to consider what a lifetime with me might do to you. I can't bear the thought of killing your spirit, Daisy, and it sounds like that's exactly what I'm doing."

I sigh and step forward to take his hand in mine again. "You're right, I'm not being very optimistic right now. But the truth is that I'm scared, too, because I've never wanted anything as badly as I want this with you. And even though I wholeheartedly trust you to take care of me, regardless of what happens between us, allowing myself to depend on you for everything is only going to make it that much harder if things don't work out in the end. I'm not trying to force you to make any kind of declarations before you're ready, but I can't keep letting you save me if you can't promise me forever."

He squeezes my hand. "I'm sorry. I get it, though. I think I may finally be trending in the right direction but trying to force things out of order. And if it seems like I'm giving you all kinds of mixed signals, it's only because I don't know what the hell I'm doing."

I laugh softly. "At least you're trying."

He nods. "How about we table the job discussion for now?"

"No, I think I've made my decision ... somewhat," I say, lifting my chin. "I'm going tell them I'd like to continue working as a substitute teacher for now, at least until they find a permanent replacement for Mrs. Joanie. That is, if you're okay with leaving me on your policy until I figure things out."

He looks relieved. "Of course."

"I realized it wouldn't be fair for me to take the position, anyway, since I'll probably need some time to get everything settled with my service dog. And I think I should make that my priority for now, even if it means being patient and accepting help, because having an SRD could open up more possibilities for me in the future."

"Look at you, adulting like a pro." He grins and wraps me up in a hug.

"I know, right?" I say with a laugh.

"I'm so proud of you," he adds and kisses the top of my head.

"Thank you," I mumble, my eyes watering. "I'm a little proud of myself, too."

He laughs and pulls away, stopping for a short kiss on the lips this time. But I fist my hands in his shirt and hold him there, and one small kiss leads to another. And before we know it, he's lifting me and setting me down on the countertop, and I'm tugging his shirt up over his head. His hands slide up my bare thighs, his fingertips edging beneath the cuff of the cutoff shorts he asked me to put on this morning, and I'm not sure whether I'm more annoyed or relieved when the alarm begins blaring on his phone this time.

CHAPTER 42

daisy

AFTER THAT, we manage to break out of our little love bubble long enough to get dressed and head to Loren and Blake's, though I suspect we're only going because we're worried about what might happen if we stay home alone any longer.

Blake greets us at the door, chuckling when we arrive with another pan of bread pudding. "Sorry, it's all I've got for now," I tell him.

"I'm just honored by your presence and pleasantly surprised the two of you managed to come up for air long enough to make anything at all," he says with a smug smile.

Landry lifts a shoulder. "We have to eat sometime."

Blake snorts and pats him on the back, and the two of them trade knowing looks as we walk inside. Loren studies me carefully once we make our way into the kitchen, and I offer her a reassuring smile before I ask after the twins.

"They're napping," she replies. "I figured I'd let their highnesses sleep until the others arrive." As if on command, a baby cries out through the monitor on the counter, and Loren scampers off to retrieve her.

I turn to face Landry once we're left to ourselves, and he flashes me a wolfish smile before closing in the space and pressing his lips to mine.

"Maybe we should have set a timer," I whisper, giggling when he moves his mouth down to my neck for the umpteenth time today. Then I open my eyes to find that the rest of the dinner party has arrived.

"Landry, um, we're not alone anymore," I say quickly. He lifts his head before he turns to lean against the cabinet beside me, a smug look crossing his face, and I feel my cheeks heating up when I see Ethan and Caidence snickering in the background.

"Sorry." He shrugs, making his apology less authentic.

"Are you, though?" Tenley asks, seemingly amused.

"You could have done that before you got here," Loren adds dryly as she adjusts Penny in her arms.

Landry shrugs again and drapes his arm around my back. "Maybe we did. And maybe I just wanted to give you a taste of your own medicine, Lo-Lo."

She scoffs, but Blake chuckles lightly. "Go ahead, Lando. I don't mind if you guys want to make out in our kitchen, so long as you remember that your sister and I have already violated every surface of this house."

Landry groans as I stifle a laugh. But then I notice JD scowling at Landry and raising a hand as he speaks.

"I'm sorry. Maybe it's none of my business—"

"It's not," Landry cuts him off.

But JD shakes his head and continues, despite Tenley nudging him in the side. "Aren't you married, dude? What about your wife?"

My stomach drops to the floor, and Landry's hand tightens into the back of my dress.

"Relax, bro," Ethan pipes up, slipping by to grab a cookie from a platter. "You're looking at her."

Tenley glances apologetically before shifting into a warning glower for Ethan. "Sorry. For some reason, this one thinks he's grown enough to chime in on adult conversations." Ethan rolls his eyes exaggeratedly.

"You're not ... *married*," Loren declares after a while. "You can't be."

Landry clears his throat before he speaks. "Actually, Ethan's right." He pauses and loosens his grip on me. "Daisy and I are legally married. We have been for a while."

Loren blinks at him. "A while?"

"Since August."

She continues staring at him as she adjusts the baby in her arms, obviously having a hard time with the news. "You got married five months ago, and you never told us? Then, you attempted to sabotage my wedding while using the excuse that you were only trying to protect me from a man that didn't believe in commitment?"

"I wasn't trying to sabotage your wedding," Landry replies, his voice thick. "And I'm sorry again about what I said in that toast. But none of that has anything to do with Daisy and me."

Blake steps up behind Loren and places a comforting hand on her back. "Hey, it's okay," he says softly. "Maybe you should hear him out."

"No," Loren holds. "He's been horrible to you since we were kids, and from the second he found out about us, he tried to convince me that you were only out to prey on me. Yet, here he is, the guy who swears all relationships are doomed, tricking someone as unsuspecting and innocent as Daisy into marrying him."

Landry clenches his jaw so hard that I can see the muscles contracting beneath his beard. But he doesn't reply. I imagine he's probably weighing what he wants to say first, and I'm struck with a sense of pride again.

"For what it's worth, Landry didn't trick me," I chime in. "If anything, I'm the one who trapped him."

"Let me guess," Loren begins, handing Penny off to Blake. "He found out you weren't in the habit of giving away your milk for free, so he figured he'd get around that by buying the cow while it was convenient?"

Landry swallows hard. "I'm sorry for giving you and Blake a hard time, Lo. I really am. But I'm not going to stand here and let you talk about my wife like that."

My lips part in an audible gasp, but I do my best to hide my reaction to Landry calling me his wife and defending me in front of Loren. I'm sure it was only a knee-jerk response, and I shouldn't read that much into it. Still, I can't help the small thrill it sends through me.

Everyone else seems to brush right over the comment, and Loren crosses her arms, her frown growing deeper. "Oh, so you can say whatever horrible things you want about my husband, on a freaking microphone in front of all of our closest friends and family, no less, but I'm not allowed to use a harmless euphemism in front of your *wife*?" she rants bitterly. Then she turns to me and softens her expression. "No offense, Daisy. I didn't mean the cow part literally. And even if you were a cow, you'd be a very lovely one—the prettiest and friendliest heifer there ever was, I'm sure."

"Um, thanks, I think," I offer quietly, but it falls on deaf ears.

Landry's chest heaves as he continues staring Loren down. "You are a piece of work, you know that? I have spent the majority of my life taking care of you and trying to keep you out of trouble, while you've always gone out of your way to make my job harder." He pauses and lets go of me to gesture in the direction of Blake before he continues. "Do you want to know why I've always hated him? It's because Dad liked him more than he loved me, because even my own father recognized that I'd never measure up to the freaking Bourgeois brothers. Coach Reed only trusted me with two things as a kid: to play quarterback and to protect you. But as hard as I tried, I failed at both. And Blake just had to make sure everyone knew he could do it better. So where does that leave me, Lo? What use am I to the rest of you now that Mom doesn't need me to babysit her, and you don't need me to keep her away from you?"

The room falls silent except for the sound of Landry's labored breathing. I reach out to take his hand again, but he pulls his arm away, and I feel my shoulders droop. Charley cries off in the distance, breaking the awkward silence.

"We'll get that," JD says flatly before shoving Ethan forward. Tenley and Caidence go with them, leaving the rest of us alone in the kitchen.

"What do you mean you had to keep Mom away from me?" Loren asks quietly.

Landry licks his lips and looks away. "Dad was always worried about her embarrassing you in public."

"So you took it upon yourselves to stop her from being there for me, especially when I needed her the most?"

"It was for the best, trust me," he mutters.

Loren shakes her head. "You didn't have the right to—"

"No, it was worse," Landry says, cutting her off. "Dad made it my responsibility."

"Am I supposed to thank you for that?" she continues. Then her expression hardens, and her chin trembles as she chokes out, "Did you keep her from coming to my high school graduation?"

"No," Landry replies. "She made that decision herself. But after the way she acted at mine the year before, you should be glad she stayed in rehab."

"Yeah, well, you don't get to tell people what to do and how to feel," she says, and Blake comes up beside her. "And you don't get to accuse others of the same shit you're guilty of doing."

"I'm not trying to do any of that. I just don't know how else to show you I care," Landry replies, already sounding defeated.

"It sounds like you're just butthurt because we chose someone else to be the twins' godfather and we didn't get your permission to get married," Loren mutters, and Landry scoffs.

"Lo, babe," Blake finally speaks up, his voice thick. "I know you're upset, but you're saying some hurtful things—things you'll probably regret later, when you know the whole truth."

"What else don't I know?" Loren demands.

"Do you really want me to say this now, in front of everyone?" Blake asks, lowering his voice. And I have to admit, I'm getting a bit curious myself. Loren nods, and he sighs. "I didn't ask for your brother's permission, but I did get his blessing before I proposed to you.

And I'm pretty sure he married Daisy because she needed his help." He turns to Landry. "Right?"

I cross my arms over my middle and look away, feeling embarrassed.

"How do you know that?" Landry asks.

"I work at the courthouse, remember? The clerks that filed your marriage license told me as soon as it happened," Blake explains. "I already knew about Daisy's epilepsy, and I noticed that she never drives herself anywhere, so I figured she needed you to be her emergency medical contact or something, maybe to bypass her family. Although I never understood why you had to get married for that. I could have just helped you with the power of attorney paperwork, had you asked."

"Wait, you knew they were married this whole time, and you never told me?" Loren rears back.

Blake opens and closes his mouth a few times before he speaks. "Look, it wasn't my story to tell, and I assumed they had their reasons for keeping it quiet. Not to mention, I'm literally in the business of not spilling other peoples' secrets."

"Or maybe it's because you feel sorry for him. Now that you and JD have worked out your brother complex, you've started to think my shit with Landry hasn't been so one-sided after all."

"Maybe," Blake says on an exhale.

Landry huffs loudly. "That's great. As if it's not enough that everyone barely tolerates me, now I have your pity on top of that."

Loren stops shortly, looking wounded. "Wait, what did you just say?"

"I'm so sick of feeling like this," Landry continues quietly, the sadness in his eyes making my chest ache. "Like I'm just a burden to the people I love most."

I want to correct him, to tell him that he could never be a burden to me and that I can love him enough for everyone. But it's not my place. It's not my love he needs right now.

Loren sniffles and reaches up to wipe a tear from her cheek.

"Landry, you're my brother. Of course I love you, even when you say or do stuff that upsets me."

He shrugs and looks downcast again. "I guess I've always wished someone could say that to me without having to add the 'but' at the end. You know, a while back I got this stupid notion I could fix that. I thought with Daisy's help I could make it easier for my family to love me as much as I love them. But I've obviously failed at that, too, and this feels even shittier than being alone." He turns to leave, stopping shortly. "I'm sorry, Daisy. Will you be okay to get a ride home?"

I exhale shakily, ignoring the urge to correct him again. It's hard to believe a man who's still worried about me more than himself needs to prove his worth to his family. But I know if I were to tell him again that I love him right now, he'd only convince himself that I pity him, too.

"You don't want me to come with you?" I ask carefully.

"I think I need some time to myself."

My chest tightens. "Okay." I step forward to reach for his hand again. He lets me hold it for a second and shoots me an apologetic look before he drops it. "Will you let me know you're okay?" I whisper.

"Yes," he says stiffly, and I can tell he's struggling to hold it together. So I nod and back away, letting him go.

"Don't tell me you're going after him," Loren warns Blake. He frowns but lifts his free hand in surrender.

"I'll go."

We all turn to see JD walk into the kitchen with Charley in his arms. "This is my fault. I shouldn't have said anything in the first place." Then he glances my way and mumbles an apology.

"No, I'll go," Tenley says on a sigh when she walks up beside him. She leans up and kisses JD on the cheek. "You're all too extroverted to understand."

I should probably be grateful she's willing to help Landry, but jealousy swirls in my stomach instead. If Landry says he wants to be alone, what makes her think she can make him feel any better?

My eyes narrow as I watch her walk out the door.

"Whoa, you all right, Miss Daisy?" Ethan asks when he returns to the scene in the kitchen.

I clear my throat as I feel my face heating agin. "No, I'm not," I reply after a second before turning to Loren, who's still crying. "I needed health insurance," I tell her. "I didn't know that I wasn't going to qualify for benefits until I got a permanent teaching position, and your brother literally saved my life by marrying me and putting me on his policy so I didn't have to go without my epilepsy medication."

Loren cringes. "Of course. I'm sorry."

"Besides that, he's been voluntarily driving me around because I was too embarrassed to admit I'd had a seizure. I knew my family would force me to move back home. That's why he moved in with me, to make sure I was safe. Do you want to know the only things he's ever asked for in return?"

She bites her lip, and I continue. "He asked me if we could be open and honest with one another, because he's exhausted from a lifetime of trying to fit in and failing to read people correctly. He wanted me to teach him how to be nicer, especially to you, because he was so desperate to play a bigger part in your life. And he practically begged me not to fall for him, because he'd convinced himself he'd do me more harm than good. At first, I couldn't understand why he was so stubborn and cynical about relationships, especially since he so obviously wants to feel loved and accepted and to have a family of his own. I think I get it now, though, and it has a lot less to do with your parents getting divorced than with the way his family has always treated him."

"Wow," Loren breathes after a second. "Thank you for settling the 'am I the asshole' debate once and for all."

I shrug and smile. "You called me a cow first."

"A cute one, though," she reminds me, smiling through her tears.

My bottom lip trembles, and I step forward to wrap her up in a hug. She accepts it and murmurs "Sorry, Bessie" over my shoulder.

"So, um, I guess this makes us sisters?" Loren asks when I pull away.

"Legally, yes. But Landry and I haven't been living as husband

and wife all this time," I admit. "Only as roommates. Well, until yesterday, I guess."

"I really am sorry. I shouldn't have started all that just now. And I'm happy for both of you."

"It's okay. But I'm not the one you should be apologizing to," I tell her.

CHAPTER 43

landry

"LANDRY, WAIT!"

I stop in my tracks when an unexpected voice calls after me. I turn, surprised to find Tenley jogging my way. She slows down as soon as she realizes I've stopped, clutching the potato in the baby sling that's strapped over her chest and trying to catch her breath as she approaches.

"Sorry, I just ... I'm not much of a runner." She waves a hand in the air and gasps.

"What do you need, Tenley?"

The baby grunts and squirms, and she pats his butt before she continues. "I wanted to make sure you were okay, I guess."

"Since when do you care whether I'm okay?" I spit out, and she flinches. "Sorry, I'm not in the mood for this right now."

"I know," she says, "and you don't have to worry about hurting my feelings. I'm here for solidarity ... and to apologize."

"Solidarity?" I cock an eyebrow at her. "What the hell would you know about ..." But I trail off when I realize what she's trying to say.

"I always thought I was terrible at expressing my emotions and recognizing that in others, too. It turns out I was just scared." She shrugs and drops her hands to her sides. "I was so afraid of failing that

I kept pushing everyone away, and in doing that, I hurt them more than I thought."

"Well, looks like you're managing just fine now. Congratulations," I say sarcastically, gesturing to the baby. "I don't know what any of that has to do with me."

She rolls her eyes. "Yeah, you do."

I frown and cross my arms. "Are you really trying to offer me advice right now?"

"I'm trying to prove to you that it's not too late to pull your head out of your ass and see how much everyone in that house cares about you, despite the way you've convinced yourself otherwise."

"Now you're blaming me for this?" I ask incredulously.

She throws her head back and groans. "I'm not saying any of this is your fault. But you don't have to keep punishing yourself for wanting something different. You deserve to feel loved and safe and understood as much as the rest of us, but you have to give your friends and family a chance to make you feel that way."

By the time she finishes her rant, I realize her teeth are chattering, and she's rubbing her hands over her baby, presumably to keep him warm. I turn and open the door to my Jeep, which I've already used the remote to start a few minutes before.

"Come on, you're freezing," I tell her, gesturing for her to sit inside.

She peers at me curiously. "Thanks," she finally says before she climbs into the seat. "Aren't you going to get in?"

"Is that okay?" I shove my hands in my pockets while I wait for her consent.

"Of course, Landry," she replies, glaring at me. "I'm not worried about being alone in an enclosed space with you. And like you said before, we're family now, aren't we?"

I sigh and nod before going around to the driver's seat, then I turn up the heat as soon as I close the door behind me.

"This was very kind and intuitive of you, you know," she comments after a while. "I don't think you're as bad at reading people as you think you are."

"I'm a doctor," I say with a scoff. "I can't just look the other way when someone gets sick or needs my help."

"Is that why you married Daisy?"

I purse my lips and look down at my lap. "She needed the health insurance. I couldn't let her go without."

"You could have, but you didn't. And I'm sure she's very grateful."

"Yeah, well, believe it or not, I didn't do it so I could collect a debt from her later."

"I know you didn't, and so does Loren."

"I'm not sure anyone thinks that much of me," I mutter.

She laughs softly. "Well, I used to think you walked on water. You probably couldn't have convinced thirteen-year-old Tenley Robin that Landry Reed was anything less than future-husband material."

I roll my eyes. "Until he made a total ass of himself in front of everyone in Camellia and proved he was a terrible kisser, right?"

"No," she says to my surprise. "Your fall from grace actually had very little to do with you and a lot more to do with the guilt I felt after ditching Lo and throwing myself at you on the same day I found out my dad had cancer."

"What do you mean?"

"You weren't the bad kisser, Landry—I was. I was also the one who practically begged you to make a move and got upset when you followed my lead, and that wasn't fair of me. I'm not flattering myself by thinking any of this had a lasting effect on you or that you even remember it at all. But I'm still sorry for setting you up the way I did," she offers, reaching over to pat my hand. "You knew about my crush for a long time, and you were only ever kind to me. You deserved better."

I furrow my brow. "Well, um, thank you for that. But I still regret the way I treated you that night. I'm sorry, too."

"See? That wasn't so hard, was it?" She smiles.

"What?"

"We're all bad at this, Landry. It's not just you. The thing is, we can't stop trying to love and understand one another. And it's never too late to apologize or explain how you really feel."

I frown again. "Did Daisy put you up to this?"

"I actually came out here to spare you from having to deal with my husband," she admits, chuckling. "He can't stand lingering conflict, and the guilt is already eating him alive. But I didn't think he'd have been well-received right about now, especially since he seems to think he owes you a hug."

I snort. "Yeah, thanks."

"And that last bit of advice was mostly paraphrased from what your sister told me that time I was in a similar predicament. But Daisy *is* pretty upset back there. She must care a whole lot about you."

"Yeah," I breathe. "I'm afraid she does."

"Trust me, it's so much easier once you stop letting your fears get in the way and just embrace it."

"So I'm told," I mumble.

"Once you allow yourself to finish falling for that sweet, little ball of sunshine in there, give me a call. I'm told I teach a very entertaining NFP class for marriage prep."

"NFP?"

"Natural family planning ... you know, Catholic sex-ed," she says with a cocky grin. "You'll need it if you want to get your marriage convalidated in the Church. And I promise I'll only mention that time I let you get to second base in front of your wife again if it's relevant."

I can't help the laugh that bursts out of me that time. "You know you don't make a very good case for yourself with one of those things strapped across you."

"Of course I do," she says with a shrug. "It means my husband and I are doing it right."

I cringe. "Maybe you guys are a better match than I originally thought."

Tenley turns to reach for the door. "Yep. And from the looks of it, I've managed to make you feel uncomfortable enough to distract you and keep you from dwelling on your problems. Which is exactly what JD would have done."

"Thanks for trying, anyway," I tell her with a sad smile.

"We introverts have to stick together," she replies. Then baby Jake stirs and lets out a loud grunt, and she sighs. "I'll see you back inside?"

I press my lips together. "I don't think so."

She nods. "I understand. Can I tell them where you'll be?"

"I think I'm going to my dad's. After all, he won't bother talking to me."

Jake whimpers in his sling, and Tenley opens the door this time. "I'm sorry, Landry. But don't give up on them, okay?"

"Yeah," I reply, waiting for Tenley to walk inside the house before driving across town to my childhood home.

"What are you doing here?" my dad asks when he answers the door.

I sigh. "I screwed up, just like you said I would."

He grunts and moves to let me inside. "Guess I can't blame you. I didn't exactly set the best example for you, did I?"

I blink a few times, his confession taking me off guard. "No, you didn't," I reply after a while.

"Yeah, well, you'd better make the effort to fix it now." He goes back and sinks into his recliner. "Don't wait until it's too late, or one day you'll retire from work just to realize you drove away everyone you love most."

He keeps his gaze locked onto the TV, but I read the sadness in my dad's face for the very first time. And it dawns on me that he's been sitting here alone all day, while half his family celebrated Christmas without him a mere mile down the road.

"You say that like the fixing is easy," I mumble after a while.

He huffs. "Sure it is. You just have to do whatever it takes to make sure they know you care." He looks up at me for a second before he clears his throat. "You staying here all night?"

I nod. "If that's all right with you."

"Last night's leftovers are in the fridge. Help yourself," he says, leaning back in his recliner. But I think I see a faint smile forming on his face.

"Thanks."

"No more of that bread pudding left, though. Think your girl-friend would mind making it again for New Year's?"

I let out a short laugh. "I'm sure she'd be happy to do that, Coach. Especially if you requested it yourself."

His smile grows more pronounced. "Better kiss and make up soon, then."

Landry

"I KNOW you're in there, Landry. Dad told me."

I groan and roll my eyes at the ceiling instead of answering the knock at my bedroom door.

"I'm coming in," Loren warns me.

"You don't want to do that. I'm naked," I lie. Even though I'm already feeling slightly better, between Tenley's pep talk and the borderline heart-to-heart exchange with my dad, I still don't feel like hashing this out with Loren right now.

"Gird your loins, then, because I'm not leaving until you let me in to apologize."

I can't help but laugh. "Suit yourself."

Loren cracks open the door and gropes for the light switch with one hand while covering her eyes with the other. "Is it safe to look?"

I grunt when the bright light makes my head throb, and I'm tempted to hop out of bed and drop my drawers. But I honestly don't have the energy to moon her right now, even if she does deserve it.

"What do you want, Lo?"

She peeks through her fingers hesitantly, then she comes over to sit at the foot of my bed once she sees the coast is clear. "Hmm ... a night nanny, a few Reese's Christmas trees, and the ability to take back most of the horrible crap I said earlier would all be nice."

I huff as I move to sit up. "What, you feel guilty now that your husband set the record straight?"

"No," she pouts. "I felt guilty while I was saying it, too. I was just so angry that I couldn't stop myself, even though I knew most of it wasn't true."

Maybe we're not as different as I thought.

She pauses and stares at me strangely. "Did you trim your chest hair or something?"

I glare back at her as I scratch my bare chest. "What is wrong with you?"

"A lot," she replies with a sigh. "It looks nice, by the way. You know, you're not a bad-looking guy, Landry. You could stand to flaunt your assets a little more."

"What for? I already have a wife, remember?" I reply dryly.

"Aha! I thought this was a marriage of convenience," she points out, narrowing her eyes at me.

"Regardless of my reasons for marrying Daisy, I wouldn't disrespect her by dating around. I'm not that desperate to get laid," I grumble. That last part's not quite as true today as it was yesterday, though.

"Then why'd you suddenly start grooming yourself?" she asks accusingly.

I cross my arms while I think of a reply. "Maybe I thought my wife would like it." I sigh. "Not because I've been trying to sleep with her or anything. But maybe I just can't help doing stuff she'd approve of, all right?"

"Because you accidentally fell for her, even though you didn't want to?"

Now I'm the one pouting. "Maybe."

She smiles and reaches out to pat my leg. "La-*aan*," she drawls. "That's so sweet."

"No, it's not," I retort. "It's like you said before, I'm too old and mean for her. She's probably only into me because I'm the first man she's gotten close to. None of this is right or fair, and—"

"I was wrong. I shouldn't have said any of that. If you have feelings for Daisy, then you deserve the chance to see that through. You're both adults. The age difference shouldn't matter."

I shake my head. "I might have thought for a second that it was okay, but you did the right thing by reminding me I'm not good enough for her."

Her shoulders droop, and her eyes water again. "Tell me you don't really believe that?"

"Of course I do," I say, my voice thick.

"Is it because of what I said, or did you feel that way before?"

"I've never felt good enough for anyone, much less Daisy," I admit, looking down at my hands.

"Is that why you're so anti-commitment, because you're afraid of burdening someone? Because you don't want anyone to feel like they're stuck with you once they realize you're not worth it?"

I swallow hard. No use lying now, since I can't feel any worse. "Yeah. Mostly."

She surprises me by scooting closer and sliding her much smaller hand over mine. "I get it, you know. Boy, do I."

I glance up at her, remembering what Blake had confessed to me before about Loren having trouble with her self-worth. "Is that why you hesitated when he proposed?"

She nods. "The only part of me that didn't want to be with Blake was the part that was convinced he could never really love me or that he'd get tired of me after a while. I couldn't risk ending up like Mom."

"But you're nothing like her. And Blake obviously loves you and the girls too much for that," I find myself telling her.

"Yeah, well, pregnancy hormones don't care about the truth or your feelings. They made me think Blake was only fulfilling an obligation, that it was impossible to believe him when he said he loved me."

I shake my head. "He wasn't just taking care of you because he had to. I mean, even I could see he'd do anything for you. When you love someone that much, you can't help yourself."

She shrugs and smiles. "I know that now, but it was hard to see it a few months ago. Just like it's probably hard for you to recognize what you have with Daisy."

I'm quiet for a while as I think about what she's saying. "Why do you care so much about what happens between Daisy and me?" I ask again.

"Because I love you," she chokes out, her eyes watering again, "despite the way I've done such a shitty job of showing it."

"Because I'm your brother, and you have to love me," I correct her. "And you want to make sure I'm just content enough to stay out of your way."

"No," she says and reaches out to squeeze my hand this time. "I love our parents because I have to. I love Lilley because she's my big sister, and she's fun. But you, Landry, I love you because of who you are—one of the most loyal, selfless, and caring humans I've ever known. You were my very first friend, my ally, and the one person I could always depend on, no matter what. But regardless of the fact that you're my brother, you deserve to feel loved and appreciated, completely apart from everything you've done for me and everything you've overcome to become the man you are today."

I blink away the moisture in my eyes. "Even if I'm still an ass most of the time?" I venture after a while.

"No *buts*, remember?" she says, laughing and bringing her free hand up to swipe at her cheeks. "Although, it has been brought to my attention that I may have antagonized you a time or two, and therefore I might have caused you to develop or even sharpen your *brute* disposition over the years ..."

"I wonder who was brave enough to raise that point," I reply, unable to stop myself from smiling.

"I suppose both of our spouses have had to learn that we Reeds have a tendency to get short-tempered when we're anxious, especially when it comes to our parental responsibilities," she quips.

I sniffle and wipe my own nose. "Parental responsibilities?"

She sighs. "I'm sorry I was too stupid to say this before ... but thank you for taking care of me all this time. I think I've been so wrapped up in my own grief that I never stopped to consider yours. You never got the chance to be sad or angry about us having to raise ourselves; you just did what needed to be done, despite not getting the love, recognition, and acceptance you deserved, especially from Mom, Dad, and me."

My brow furrows. "I didn't do any of that because I wanted you to think you owed me anything. I was only trying to protect you and spare you from the way they made me feel." I pause and exhale before I continue. "And maybe a small part of me thought I could make them proud, you know? Maybe if I kept Mom under control and made sure you were safe and had everything you needed, then Dad would say I was doing a good job at something ... for once."

She reaches up to cover her mouth, and I shake my head again

"I'm sorry, I didn't mean to—"

"No, Landry," she says through her tears. "To hell with Mom and Dad. I mean, sure, they could have been worse, but the nicest thing they've done is teach us exactly what *not* to do as parents. I'm sure I've already started making plenty of my own mistakes, but I'll be damned if I let my kids grow up feeling this way." She exhales and dries her face before she continues. "Okay, maybe not *to hell* with them, but ..."

I huff out a laugh and sniff. "Like you said, we still have to love them, right?"

"Look, I'm no therapist, and I totally recommend getting one, by the way, but I think you need to hear this. Letting go of my expectations for our parents was one of the hardest things I've ever had to do. I'd held on to this ideal for so long, and I thought it was enough to forgive them for making me feel like I wasn't worthy of their attention. But I couldn't learn to love myself until I made the conscious decision to love them for who they are, too. It's like ... I had to mourn the mother I thought I should've had and accept the one I did have for who she is and what she's actually capable of. It wasn't fair of me to keep resenting Mom for falling short, especially once I realized she really was trying, in her own way. And we'll probably never have the mother-daughter relationship I wanted, but I'm grateful for what we do have now."

Her words sound so wise that I have to open and close my mouth a few times before I can form a response. "I guess I could be doing that, too, but with Dad."

"Maybe we're all doing that with one another?" she offers.

"Yeah. Maybe." I look down at our joined hands. "I'm proud of you, though. You're much better at adulting than I've given you credit for, and you're already an amazing mom."

"It took a lot of help, some of it professional, but I think I'm getting there. And you," she reaches up to poke my shoulder, "are going to be an incredible father one day, in spite of all this, all right?"

"I'm never going to be a father," I tell her with a rueful smile. "I can't even stop myself from trying to break up your marriage, much less be bothered to attempt one myself. Well, a real marriage, anyway."

"You could never break up my marriage," she declares with a laugh. "And it's not your fault that Blake and I ended up taking the long road, either. In fact, you're not going to like this, but one of my biggest weaknesses has always been hearing Blake say, 'I'm not afraid of Landry Reed,' in his husky, bedroom voice." She lowers her tone and bounces her eyebrows suggestively, and I grimace as I scoot farther away from her.

"Why do you always have to go and make it so much weirder than it needs to be?"

"Because I'm a weirdo, and it's fun making you squirm," she replies with a grin, and I roll my eyes. "You didn't seriously think what happened back there could cause an actual rift between Blake and me, did you?"

I shrug, embarrassed. "Well, yeah. You seemed pretty upset with all of us."

"Pssht." She waves off my trepidation. "I'm a brat, remember? That's why I married a man who isn't afraid to call me out on my bullshit."

"So, you're not fighting anymore?"

"Technically, I'm still pretending to be mad, but that's only so he'll suck up to me later," she says matter-of-factly. Then she cups her mouth and whispers, "Also, I made Tenley check my chart before I left, and we're not in the clear for makeup sex for another day or two. So I may have to drag this out a little longer if I don't want to end up pregnant again."

I cringe. "Would you stop doing that?"

"Nope." She smiles again. "Not until you admit how badly you wanna do all that mushy, lovey-dovey, spicy stuff with Daisy."

I groan. "I've had enough talking about our love lives for one night, especially while I'm still sitting here in my underwear."

"Ew." She scrunches up her nose and wiggles back to the foot of the bed. "You didn't tell me you weren't wearing pants. And I held your hand and everything."

"Actually, I told you I was naked, and you came in anyway," I retort dryly.

"Because I assumed you were lying," she mutters before she glances back at me. "At least tell me you'll *consider* doing all the mushy, lovey-dovey, spicy stuff with Daisy?"

I exhale loudly, unable to hide my smile now. "Maybe. If I haven't pushed her away yet."

She stares expectantly. "You do realize she's been into you this whole time, right?"

"Even though my chest hair was overgrown?" I pose, reaching up to scratch again.

She scoffs. "You could probably shave a heart between your pecs, and she'd think it was adorable."

"She probably would," I agree with a laugh.

"Daisy's pretty adorable, too, though," Loren adds, nudging my leg again.

"Yeah, she is." I don't even bother disguising the fondness in my voice.

"She's also hot. I mean, I don't blame you for marrying her." Loren purses her lips.

I stifle a smirk. "You know me, I can't resist a damsel in distress."

"Especially when she's marriage-of-convenience-turned-real-thing material."

"Eh, I'm not sure I'm even into that sort of thing," I muse, and her face breaks into a wide grin.

"Oooh, you want to kiss her, love her, and mar-rry her ..." she sings and mimics Sandra Bullock in *Miss Congeniality*.

I shrug. "Maybe. And maybe I've already done all those things."

Loren squeals, and I shush her, not wanting her to wake our dad. "Landry, do you really love her?" she whispers.

"If I do, I'm certainly not going to admit it to you before I get the chance to tell *her*."

She only coos and bats her eyelashes at me. "Come on, promise me you'll declare your undying love for Daisy and ask her to marry you for real and make babies and grow old together? Please? It's the last thing I'll ever ask of you, I swear!" I force a scowl at her, but she adds pleading hands. "Marriage of convenience is my favorite romance trope! You have to live happily ever after now." I grunt, and she continues, "Do it for me. Do it for your nieces, so they'll grow up believing in true love and all that."

"Can't they just look at their parents and godparents for that?" I offer, smiling.

"Then do it for yourself, because you deserve your own little family." My chest tightens again when she says it. "Please, Lando?"

"Go home, Lo-Lo," I reply mockingly before shoving her off my bed with my feet. "Shouldn't you be off tending to your husband and your kids?"

She clicks her tongue as she stumbles and rises to her feet. "Fine. But Blake's probably waiting for me with a sexy apology and that bag of Reese's trees. So if I get knocked up, I'm blaming you."

I shake my head, instinctively readying myself for a lecture about spacing her pregnancies, especially after such a traumatic delivery. But I hear Daisy's voice in the back of my head telling me that Loren's an adult and that she and Blake know better. And that being a medical professional doesn't give me the right to boss my sister around.

Loving and supportive…

"Yeah, yeah. Text me when you get home safely," I say to her instead.

"Don't tell me what to do," she retorts, sticking out her tongue.

I smile and take a fortifying breath. "Thank you, Lo. For this. It means more to me than you think."

Her expression softens. "I needed this, too," she says with a shy shrug. "I love you."

"I love you, too."

"Merry Christmas. Oh, and don't forget to text your wife and tell her you love her as well."

"Merry Christmas. And don't tell me what to do," I say, holding up my middle finger.

She grins and flips me off in return before slipping out the door, and I pick up my phone as soon as she's gone.

LANDRY

Hi. I'm sorry about earlier. I figured you knew by now, but I'm staying at my dad's place for the night.

DAISY

I'm just glad to hear you're safe.

How are you feeling?

LANDRY

Cold. Lonely.

Missing you.

How are you?

DAISY

Same. 👀

LANDRY

I'll be back in the morning, I promise.

DAISY

You gosh darn well better be.

LANDRY

Daisy Colette LaFleur … I'm gonna need you to watch your language, young lady.

DAISY

Why don't you get over here and make me? 

I gulp and shake my head as I stare down at the phone, my heart racing and my stomach burning with desire. Then I toss the blankets aside and allow my feet to hit the ground before I think better of it.

"Dammit, Landry," I mutter to myself before I take a few calming breaths and swing my legs back into the bed.

LANDRY

We'll talk in the morning, Blondie. Have my coffee ready early.

DAISY

I told you I'd make you a morning person. 😉

LANDRY

Double check the locks before you go to bed.

DAISY

What's the point when the Big Bad Wolf has a key?

I tap my fist against the headboard behind me and whimper. I don't know if I've ever felt this way before. Whatever it is that Daisy's been using to get me to do her bidding is even more potent when she uses it to flirt. It's torturous, wanting her this way and having her so close and easily coaxed into satisfying that yearning, yet knowing it's not the right thing to do. And it's only been a couple of days.

DAISY

Landry?

Are you driving home yet?

What if I told you my dress was caught in my hair again? Would you come to my rescue and help me out of it?

I growl and toss the phone down. How am I going to survive going back home after this? I'm not a particularly lustful man, but I am human—a very impulsive one, at that. I've done everything in my power to resist my attraction to Daisy, and it's only grown stronger with time. There's only so much I can take of my hot-to-go wife practically begging me to consummate our marriage before I'm bound to break, especially since I've never actually managed to resist giving her anything she's asked me for before. And this is something I'd *really* like to give her.

Thalassemia, giardiasis, cryptosporidiosis, strongyloidiasis, toxo-cariasis ... I take a deep breath before I work up the courage to text her back.

LANDRY

Sorry, wifey. I think it's best if I stay here tonight.

DAISY

But it's Christmas ... 🙁

LANDRY

I know. But I need a few more hours to clear my head, okay?

Do me a favor and push your dresser over to block your bedroom door.

DAISY

Fine. Merry Christmas, hubby. See you in the morning.

I'll try to untangle my dress before then.

LANDRY

heart react

I'm grinning to myself and reveling in that warm, fuzzy state that only Daisy's attention puts me in when it hits me—this is why people get married. Why wouldn't I want to feel like this for the rest of my life, especially now that I've learned there's less risk involved? After all, didn't Loren and Tenley both just teach me that a little humility and a good apology go a long way and that I actually deserve to experience this degree of love and acceptance?

I stand up and begin pacing my old bedroom while running my fingers through my hair. I need Daisy more than she needs me, and I've got to figure out how to make her my wife for real, even if that means swallowing my pride and admitting that I actually want all the things I've been fighting against for most of my life. I already know I'm in love with her. Hell, I'd figured that out as soon as I'd allowed myself to think about her romantically. And while I haven't been able to admit it out loud yet, I'm pretty sure she understands how I feel, since she can practically read my mind at this point.

Daisy was right about us all along. She's my person. I can't imagine having to spend another day without her, and I have to make sure she knows that.

I've got to tell her right now—I can't afford to waste another second.

She needs to know that I'm crazy in love with her, that I'm willing to do anything to turn this into a real marriage, that I want to dote on her and take care of her forever, and maybe even make a couple of babies together.

I'm about to reach for my pants when I force myself to stop and think this through. If I were to go home right now and declare all this to Daisy, there's a pretty good chance we'd end up making that last part happen sooner than later. And maybe that wouldn't be so bad, except we'd want to check in with her neurologist beforehand to make sure pregnancy and delivery would be safe for both her and our potential children. I also want to make sure Daisy's ready before I allow us to take that risk.

Instead of acting on my impulses and intrusive thoughts, I've managed to pause and fully consider the long-term consequences, both good and bad. And I obviously need to get my dumbass back into bed before I screw this up.

I pick up my phone one more time.

LANDRY

Hey, man. Can I ask you a question?

ROWAN

You just did.

LANDRY

Is already being legally married grounds for fast-tracking a church wedding?

ROWAN

I'm honestly not sure, but I'll take this as a good sign as far as my sister's virtue is concerned.

LANDRY

Don't you have a priest on speed dial or something?

ROWAN

It's Christmas, Landry. I'd rather save my favors for a real emergency.

LANDRY

This could be considered an emergency.

My phone rings, and I laugh to myself before I answer the call. "Where are you?" Rowan demands.

"I'm at my old man's house for the night. It's a long story. Daisy's at our place."

"All right," he says with a sigh. "You—stay put. I'll get an answer by tomorrow."

I smirk harder. "You're my second-to-favorite LaFleur, you know."

He grunts. "Yeah. And you're my second-to-favorite Reed."

"Hey," I protest. "How did I end up ranking below Loren after the way she screwed you over?"

"Oh no, your sister is third on the list. I was talking about your mom," he replies, obviously pleased with himself, and I can't help but laugh.

daisy

I STRETCH and smile to myself before I roll out of bed, giddy with the prospect of seeing my husband again. I go into the bathroom to freshen up before practically skipping to the kitchen to get the coffee started, but I stop abruptly when I find him already standing at the coffee maker.

Landry runs his fingers through his hair and shoots me a shy smile before he steps forward to place a kiss on my cheek, and my face instantly heats up.

"Good morning, beautiful," he murmurs as he backs away.

"Morning. You're here early."

"I didn't really get a lot of sleep last night. I guess I was looking forward to that coffee you promised me."

"Uh-huh." I smirk and step around him to get the coffee brewing, then I turn to the stove and busy myself with the frying pan next. "Eggs?"

"Yeah, sure, thanks," he says, automatically grabbing the carton from the fridge and setting it down beside me before he leans back against the counter.

"So why couldn't you sleep last night?" I pose as I crack an egg. "Loren told me you guys talked everything out, and you sounded okay in your texts."

"Talking to my sister got me thinking … about you, about us. And I felt like I needed to see you right away and tell you about it, even though it seems kind of stupid now," he rambles nervously.

"No, no," I reassure him. "I'm glad you're here. I really did miss you, even if it was only for one night, and I want to hear what's on your mind."

He shakes his head, then he smiles adorably. "There's a lot on my mind this time. It was a long night without you."

I bite my lip and take a step closer, reaching out to brush my fingertips over his shirt. "Well, then, maybe we shouldn't spend the night apart again."

His confidence grows in front of me, and he pulls me in for a short kiss before backing away just enough to graze his nose over mine. Then he goes in to kiss me again, as if he'd planned to stop but couldn't resist coming back for more.

"Daisy," he begins once he finally comes up for air, "I'm moving out."

"What?"

He gazes at me and slides his hands up to cup my cheeks. "I can't live with you anymore," he says softly. "Because I'm in love with you."

The joy I feel after hearing him say that is only slightly overshadowed by the part about him leaving me. "I love you, too," I manage, "but I don't understand."

"Last night brought up some big feelings for me, both good and bad. And as much as it sucked in the moment, I think I was able to resolve some of the stuff with my family that's been holding me back all this time. I know it probably seems like I've been avoiding commitment because I'm afraid of getting hurt, but the truth is that I never trusted myself not to screw it all up. I couldn't bear the thought of hurting someone I loved the same way I seem to hurt my friends and family all the time, so I convinced myself that it was all too reckless."

"I'm sorry you felt that way for so long. And I'm glad you worked through a lot of it," I say, furrowing my brow. "But the only way you can hurt me now is by pulling away from me."

He shakes his head. "I know that. And even though screwing up is inevitable, I also learned about this thing called an apology, which makes relationships seem a little less risky." I laugh softly before he goes on. "Then I thought if there was ever someone I'd want to spend the rest of my life apologizing to, someone I'd give my last breath to make sure she was happy, it's you. Because I love you, Daisy. You're the only person who's ever made me feel so safe and loved, like I can be myself. And I can't stand being apart from you, either." He pauses and gulps before he continues. "I'm pretty sure that means I want to make you my wife for real, because I've finally figured out what I need to be happy, and it all comes back to you."

"Wow," I spit out breathlessly. "I ... I don't know what to say."

He smirks. "That's a first, right?"

I nod. "Mm-hmm."

"That's okay. I know something else we can do for a while until you find your voice again."

This time he slides his right hand up to cup my jaw as he grasps my hip with the left and urges me closer to him. His fingertips curl around and dig into the fabric of my dress as he leans in to kiss me. He surprises me by pushing his tongue into my mouth immediately and pressing his body against mine, warming me from the inside out. It's slow and tender but heated and hungry at the same time. My arms drape around his neck, and he moves his right hand down to my back-side so that he's almost lifting me.

"This is why," he says in between kisses, "I'm moving out, just for now."

"Hmm?" I squeak. I'd all but forgotten that point.

His mouth travels down to my neck as he continues. "I want to be your real husband. I want to give you all the things a husband gives his wife, and I want us to start right now."

"You do?" I ask breathlessly.

"Very, very badly," he growls, his beard scraping my skin. "So much so that I'm willing to do anything for it, even if it means amending our wedding vows."

"Is that so?" I manage to croak out.

"Yes. But I imagine we'd need to make it official, in church this time, with all our friends and family there to witness our first consecrated make out session."

I tilt my head back as he nips at my shoulder. "Let me guess … you're afraid I'm going to let you start collecting on that marital debt now, and you think moving out is going to minimize the opportunity for that to happen?"

"That's part of it, yes. But I also need to prove to you that I've really changed my mind about marriage and that I'm not just conceding for the extracurriculars." He pulls away and smiles as he runs a fingertip down my arm, making me shiver.

I press my lips together, stifling a grin. "You're so smushy," I accidentally say.

"I'm what?" He studies me carefully.

"Smushy," I repeat, my cheeks darkening. "Sexy and mushy at the same time."

He chuckles. "I take it that's a good thing?"

"The best," I whisper.

"Is that what you want when I propose, then?" His eyes search mine, and although he's trying to sound lighthearted, I can tell he's looking for my reassurance.

"*When* you propose?"

His mouth turns up in a wry smile. "Well, yeah. You didn't think I'd tell you all this if I didn't mean to follow through, right? Or try and cheat you out of the full experience?"

My breath catches in my throat, and it takes me a couple of tries to speak. "You don't have to go through any of that. I love you, and I want a real wedding as soon as you're ready."

"You deserve smushy," he replies, running his thumb over my cheek now. I realize after a second that he's tracing my freckles. "If we do this, if you marry me for real, I have to make sure you won't have any regrets. And you can't know that unless we actually date first."

"Date?"

He nods. "Yes. It's the only way to—"

"Landry, we've been living together for *months*. I can't imagine there's anything left to learn about one another, and certainly nothing that could change how I feel about you."

"But you're not exactly getting a choice this way. I don't want you to think back on this later and realize you stayed with me by default because I'm all you've ever known."

"You're all I want to know," I breathe.

"Because you never got to live on your own, and I don't want to take that away from you, either."

I laugh incredulously. "I don't want to live alone. I want *you*."

"Please," he begs. "Let me do this right."

"Hey, if you need more time, just say so," I tell him. "Full transparency."

He shakes his head and offers me a sad smile. "I want you to have more time. I need to know you'd choose me again, even if I hadn't helped you."

"Moving out isn't going to change anything, because there's no part of you that could resist helping someone in need. And no part of me could resist falling for a man as selfless as you, one who finds so much joy in helping others." He blinks down at me, his eyes watering. "But if you feel like this is something you need to do to keep us from falling into sin together, then you should do it. You should also know that it's going to backfire on you, because it's only making me fall deeper in love with you and want you that much more."

His brows draw together, and his throat bobs. "You know, everyone wants to blame the Big Bad Wolf. But I don't think Little Red was all that stupid. She had to have known he was a wolf, right? I mean, wasn't she just messing with him?"

I bite my lip and slide my hand up his chest. "Maybe they were both misunderstood. Maybe she had a thing for wolves."

"Yeah. Maybe the wolf should have been climbing towers instead," he adds with a smile, running his hand over my hair.

A FEW MONTHS LATER

DAISY

"So ..." I begin, waiting for my husband to follow me into the house. Juniper's claws tick against the floor as she leads me on, but I spin around to face Landry. "Whatever shall we do now?"

"Hmm. I suppose we could ..." He pauses and looks up as he kicks off his shoes, then tilts his head from side to side as he pretends to weigh our options. "I don't know, make a baby?"

I grin widely as he lunges forward to scoop me up into his arms, and my service dog yips excitedly and circles his feet. I almost feel guilty telling her to stand down, but she obediently treks to her kennel and drops to her belly, flopping her tongue out and wagging her tail contentedly as she watches us go on down the hallway.

"I hope you don't mind, but it's my first time, so I might need a little more direction than you're used to," I drawl, batting my eyelashes at Landry. "And you *are* the director of first-time experiences, aren't you?"

"Your first time?" he asks, cocking an eyebrow as he walks us toward our shared bedroom. "Last I checked, Mrs. Reed, that ship has sailed. In fact, I, myself, have captained numerous excursions since her maiden voyage. And I must say, she's my favorite ride." I toss my head back as I erupt in a fit of giggles, and Landry smiles down at me, pleased with himself.

"Yes, but I've never tried making a baby before," I say once I settle myself. "Well, at least not on purpose."

"Ah, well, that makes two of us," he admits as he sets me down gently on the bed then lies down beside me. "Are you sure you're ready?" he asks after a while, staring at me with more love and adoration in his eyes than I could have ever hoped for.

I let out a long exhale. We've just returned from my neurologist's office after getting a green light for trying to conceive. I've been seizure-free for the past few months, only having one more minor episode since I first moved to Camellia, and my neurologist agreed that conditions are ideal for a safe and healthy pregnancy. Living with a seizure response dog and a medical doctor while having a maternal-fetal medicine specialist and a midwife in the family all help, too.

Landry's also been going to therapy to learn how to manage his anxiety, something he insisted on doing to prepare for fatherhood, and I can already see the difference it's made for him.

"I'm ready," I reassure him, reaching up to cradle his cheek in my hand. "But ... what if it doesn't happen right away, you know?"

He shakes his head gently. "It's okay if it takes a while, right? There's no rush, and I certainly wouldn't mind putting in overtime."

I smirk at him. "I know, but what if it never happens at all?"

"Hey, you are going to be a mama one way or another, okay? If we don't get pregnant right away, we'll move forward with the adoption plans. And if we're lucky enough to have a baby or two now—"

"Blessed?" I correct him.

"If we're *blessed* with a baby now, we can still adopt later," he finishes.

It's the plan we agreed upon during our marriage prep classes a few months ago, before our second wedding.

We'd told the rest of our family about our arrangement just after Christmas, but it hadn't taken Landry long to decide we were ready to have our legal marriage convalidated in the Church. We'd barely made it through a week of living apart before he surprised me with a smushy proposal, and a day later we were meeting with Father Conrad to plan a ceremony. Luckily, the priest was quite amendable, especially with our NFP instructor putting in a good word for us, and we were able to get our sacramental wedding and move back in together before the start of lent.

By then, Landry had already bought a plot of farmland on the outskirts of town and insisted I trade in my lesson plans for blueprints. In between volunteering at school and the hospital and babysitting the twins as needed, Juniper and I spend our time planning our very own Reed family homestead. It's not going to be as big as the one I grew up on, but it is perfectly situated beside two other large plots, both of which now belong to the Bourgeois clan. Landry and I are still hoping to entice Rowan to take the empty acreage on the opposite side of us, but that's a whole other story.

I nod at Landry, thinking about how much fun it will be to watch our future children run from one house to the next alongside their cousins. "Okay. Let's do it."

He grins and drags a finger over my arm. "And you feel up to getting started right now?"

"I don't see why not," I say casually, though his eyelids get heavy as soon as I reach over and begin unbuttoning his shirt.

He swallows hard, his eyes locked onto mine as I work. "Need help with those buttons, Blondie?"

"Are you worried I'll get one of them caught in your chest hair?" I tease, and the corner of his mouth tilts up in a smirk.

"What chest hair?" he asks, and I pull back his shirt to reveal a patch of smooth skin. I reach out to stroke it and look up at him in confusion, making him laugh.

"What did you do?"

"What does it look like I did? I shaved it. For you."

"For me?"

"Well, yeah. I had a feeling we'd get this opportunity before the end of the day, so I thought I'd do something special to celebrate," he explains shyly.

"So you completely shaved off your chest hair?"

He shrugs. "And a few other places."

I narrow my eyes. "I'm afraid to see what the shower looks like now."

"Why are you worried about the shower when I did all this glorious manscaping for you?" he asks, sitting up to remove his shirt completely. "Don't you see how much I love you?"

I smile and graze my hand over his stomach. "I love you, too. And although I appreciate your efforts, if I'm being honest, I like you hairy and ... wolfy."

He growls. "Do you?"

"Didn't I tell you I had a thing for the Big Bad Wolf?" I continue, moving to kneel in front of him. He hums when I lean in to kiss him.

"Too bad I've always had a crush on Rapunzel and not Little Red Riding Hood," he replies, sliding his hands around my hips and holding me in front of him.

"Rapunzel, you say?"

"You'd probably think it's a hair fetish, and I certainly wouldn't rule it out completely," he begins, tossing my long locks over my back before he slides one of my sleeves down and bares my shoulder. "But those big, green eyes and those sexy freckles ..." He pauses to let out a low groan before planting his lips on my neck while his free hand slips beneath the hem of my dress. "I can't tell you how many of my fantasies start just like this." He nips at another spot on my shoulder, and I know he's kissing the way down his favorite trail.

"And how do the rest of these dreams of yours go?" I ask, my breathing growing more labored by the second, especially with his fingertips tracing another one of his favorite road maps.

"They all have a *very* happy ending," he mumbles against my skin. "But that's probably because I'm such an optimist."

I can't help but chuckle out loud. "Oh, so it's all rainbows and unicorns with you, is it?"

"More like ... sunshine and daisies," he says before he brings his mouth back to mine.

* * *

acknowledgments

This story was written with the intention of bringing glory to God and highlighting His greatest gifts—His infinite love and mercy. Let us remember to ask for His grace and to treasure the sacraments on our own paths to holiness, as well as to invoke the power of prayer and the intercession of the Blessed Mother and all the Saints.

To my husband—I love you. Thank you again for everything, from helping me with my plot and entertaining the kids so I can write, to taking me to author events and spraying book edges. I'm sorry for all the times I go full Lando on you or when I get lost in Camellia with my imaginary friends, but thank you for being the one to bring me back down when I need it the most. And lastly, thank you for believing in me and my silly stories.

To my my daughter, E, who has stepped up in so many ways to make this all possible, and my amazing children, my parents, especially mom, L and my sister, A, who are always willing to help and support me, my aunts and cousins (Candi), and the rest of my (large) extended family—thank you for your patience and your encouragement. You are my greatest blessings, and your support means the world to me. I love you all so much, and I hope this story in particular illustrates how I feel better than I can say it myself.

To my awesome cover designer and best-selling-author bestie, Cindy R—I never could have finished this book without you. I'm so happy Landry is your favorite, because it means you love me, too! Thank you for helping me bring him and Daisy into the world and, more importantly, for the gift of your friendship.

To Kait—Thank you for everything, especially the @big.doc.-lando brainstorming sessions. I know I drove you crazy with this one, but it's finally done. Thanks for always matching my weird and validating my crazy. And most importantly, you know I still love cake.

To Laura N—Well, Well, Well, looks like Daisy and Landry are finally out and about—let that sink in. Thank you for your support and especially for your readiness to help. It means so much to me to know that I can always count on you for ideas and feedback. You know exactly which scenes you inspired, my friend, and I love you for it. This story is as much yours as it is mine.

To Kate L—I hope you can forgive me for the John Denver sacrilege. Per your request, here's the sweet, innocent flower-child who can't cook and loves the color green. Thank you for all of your contributions and your friendship.

To my friends and coworkers—especially RG, Emily C, Rhonda F, ST, KJ, Jahn, Ashley, and the rest of my work family, thank you for your input, your support, and for putting up with "Hoco Me." I am so grateful to you all for your guidance, your friendship, and your prayers.

To my alpha and beta readers—especially Amber, Moni, KL Hester, Logan, Joanna, Abby, Madeline, Krissi, and anyone else I may have missed—I can't tell you how much I appreciate your input. You have all made this story so much better than I could have hoped for!

To my editor, Pauline H—thanks for helping my crazy ideas make more sense.

And to all my readers, especially my ARC readers and those from my hometown, the 'Fettes, and the Bookstagram/BookTok Community—thank you *so very much* for your time and energy. I am truly grateful for your support and reviews. I hope you each get something from this, at least a few laughs or a character crush and at most appreciation for the Catholic faith and the sacraments.

about the author

A former high school literature teacher from South Louisiana, Marie Veillon is still learning to balance her ridiculous accent, Cajun-French—inspired vocabulary, and horrible speaking syntax with writing humorous stories and creating characters and situations relatable enough to make readers forget they aren't real. She enjoys reading books about her Catholic faith and rom coms with guaranteed HEAs, watching football, fangirling, and spending time with her amazing family.

Thank you for reading and reviewing!
marievwrites.com
@marievwrites

instagram.com/marievwrites

threads.com/@marievwrites

marievwrites.substack.com

facebook.com/marievwrites

tiktok.com/@marievwrites

bookbub.com/authors/marie-veillon

goodreads.com/marie_veillon

amazon.com/author/marieveillon

THE CAMELLIA ROM-COM SERIES

Third and Ten
Going for Two
Hail Mary Catch
Walking Green Flag

laqniappe

...A LITTLE SOMETHING EXTRA

Sign up for my newsletter and join the Camellia Crewe Facebook group to receive updates and announcements, including free content and the latest news regarding the next installments in the Camellia Rom-Com Series!

Continue the Camellia Rom-Com series with **Rowan & Claire's Story** and read the first chapter of *Walking Green Flag* for FREE!

Need more Daisy + Landry?
Get a Bonus Epilogue, a Cajun Glossary,
NFP Resources, and more at
marievwrites.com